the SECRET LIFE *of* CEECEE WILKES

Also by DIANE CHAMBERLAIN

THE BAY AT MIDNIGHT
HER MOTHER'S SHADOW
KISS RIVER
KEEPER OF THE LIGHT
CYPRESS POINT
THE COURAGE TREE
SUMMER'S CHILD
BREAKING THE SILENCE

Watch for Diane Chamberlain's upcoming novel

BEFORE THE STORM

Available June 2008

DIANE CHAMBERLAIN

the SECRET LIFE *of* CEECEE WILKES

MIRA

ISBN-13: 978-0-7783-2531-4
ISBN-10:   0-7783-2531-8

THE SECRET LIFE OF CEECEE WILKES

www.MIRABooks.com

Printed in U.S.A.

Acknowledgments

For helping me think outside the box, dig a little deeper and cope with life's adventures this past year, I'm grateful to John Pagliuca, Emilie Richards and Patricia McLinn.

Many people shared their memories of Chapel Hill and Charlottesville with me. Thank you, Caroline and John Marold, Matt Barnett, Sara Mendes, Kerry Cole, Chris Morris and Carole Ramser. You Charlottesville folks made me hungry for a "grillswith!"

My friends at ASA came through with information on everything from infant seats to waitress uniforms.

Adelle D. Stavis, Esq. was my legal eagle.

Brittany Walls and Kate Kaprosy helped me understand CeeCee's trials and tribulations as a new mother. Thanks for the laughs, you two!

Over lunch at the Silver Diner (where we hoped no one was listening in on our grisly conversation), Marti Porter gave me the clinical information and insight necessary to write the harrowing scene in the cabin between CeeCee and Genevieve.

My assistant, Mari Sango Jordan, helped with research and other tasks too numerous to mention, while her daughter, Myya, entertained my dogs so I could get some work done.

And a special thank-you to my editor, Miranda Stecyk, for being so sensible, smart and supportive.

For John

Corinne

Chapter One

Raleigh, North Carolina

SHE COULDN'T CONCENTRATE ON MAKING LOVE. No matter how tenderly or passionately or intimately Ken touched her, her mind was miles away. It was a little after five on Tuesday afternoon, the time they protected from meetings or dinner with friends or anything else that might interfere with their getting together, and usually Corinne relished the lovemaking with her fiancé. Today, though, she wanted to fast-forward to the pillow talk. She had so much to say.

Ken rolled off her with a sigh, and she saw him smile in the late-afternoon light as he rested his hand on her stomach. Did that mean something? Smiling with his hand on her belly? She hoped so but didn't dare ask him. Not yet. Ken loved the afterglow—the slow untangling of their limbs and the gradual return to reality—so she would have to be patient. She stroked her fingers through his thick, ash-blond hair as she waited for his breathing to settle down. Their baby was going to beautiful, no doubt about it.

"Mmm," Ken purred as he nuzzled her shoulder. Thin bands of

light slipped into the room through the blinds, leaving luminous stripes on the sheet over his legs. "I love you, Cor."

"I love you, too." She wrapped her arm around him, trying to sense if he was alert enough to listen to her. "I did something amazing today," she began. "*Two* somethings, actually."

"What did you do?" He sounded interested, if not quite awake.

"First, I took the 540 to work."

His head darted up from his pillow. "You *did?*"

"Uh-huh."

"How was it?"

"Excellent." She'd had sweaty palms the whole time, but she'd managed. For the past few years, she'd taught fourth grade in a school eight miles from their house, and she'd never once had the courage to take the expressway to get there. She'd stuck to the tiny back roads, curling her way through residential neighborhoods, dodging cars as they backed out of driveways. "It took me about ten minutes to get to work," she said. "It usually takes me forty."

"I'm proud of you," he said. "I know how hard that must have been to do."

"And then I did another amazing thing," she said.

"I haven't forgotten. Two things, you said. What other amazing thing did you do?"

"I went on the field trip to the museum with my class, instead of staying at school like I'd planned."

"Now you're scaring me," he teased. "Are you on some new drug or something?"

"Am I remarkable or what?" she asked.

"You are definitely the most remarkable woman I know." He leaned over to kiss her. "You're my brave, beautiful, red-haired girl."

She'd walked inside the museum as though she did it every day of the week, and she bet no one knew that her heart was pounding and her throat felt as though it was tightening around her windpipe. She guarded her phobias carefully. She could never let any of her students' parents—or worse, her fellow teachers—know.

"Maybe you're trying to do too much too fast," Ken said.

She shook her head. "I'm on a roll," she said. "Tomorrow, I plan to step into the elevator at the doctor's office. Just step into it," she added hastily. "I'll take the stairs. But stepping into it will be a first step. So to speak. Then maybe next week, I'll take it up a floor." She shuddered at the thought of the elevator doors closing behind her, locking her in a cubicle not much bigger than a coffin.

"Pretty soon you won't need me anymore."

"I'm always going to need you." She wondered how serious he was with that statement. It was true that she needed Ken in ways most people didn't need a partner. He was the driver anytime they traveled more than a few miles from home. He was her rescuer when she'd have a panic attack in the supermarket, standing in the middle of an aisle with a full cart of groceries. He was the one holding on to her arm as he guided her through the mall or the Concert Hall or wherever they happened to be when her heart started pounding. "I would just like to not need you that way. And I *have* to do this, Ken. I want that job."

She'd been offered a position that would start the following September, training teachers in Wake County to use a reading curriculum in which she'd become expert. That meant driving. A *lot* of driving. There would be six-lane highways to travel and bridges to cross and elevators she would have no choice but to ride. September was nearly a year away, and she was determined to have her fears mastered by then.

"Kenny." She pulled closer to him, nervous about the topic she was about to broach. "There's something else we really need to talk about."

His muscles tightened ever so slightly beneath her hands.

"The pregnancy," he said.

She hated when he called it *the pregnancy*. She guessed she'd misread his smile earlier. "About the baby," she said. "Right."

He let out a sigh. "Cor, I've thought about it and I just don't think it's the right time. Especially with you starting a new job next year. How much stress do you need?"

"It would work out," she said. "The baby's due in late May. I'd take the end of the year off and have the summer to get used to being a mom and find day care and everything." She smoothed her hand over her stomach. Was it her imagination or was there already a slight slope to her belly? "We've been together so long," she continued. "It just doesn't make sense for me to have an abortion when I'm almost twenty-seven and you're thirty-eight and we can afford to have a child." She didn't say what else she was thinking: *Of course, we'd have to get married. Finally.* They'd been engaged and living together for four years, and if her pregnancy forced them to set a date, that was fine with her.

He gave her shoulders a squeeze, then sat up. "Let's talk about it later, okay?" he said.

"When?" she asked. "We can't keep putting this off."

"Later tonight," he promised.

She followed his gaze to the phone on the night table. The message light was blinking. He picked up the receiver and punched in their voice-mail code, then listened. "Three messages," he said, hitting another button on the phone. The light in the room had grown dim, but she was still able to see him roll his eyes as he listened to the first message.

"Your mother," he said. "She says it's urgent."

"I'm sure." Corinne managed a laugh. Now that Dru had spilled the news of her pregnancy to their parents, she'd probably be getting urgent calls every day. Her mother had already e-mailed her to tell her that redheads were more prone to hemorrhaging after delivery. *Thanks a heap, Mom.* She hadn't bothered to reply. She hadn't spoken with her mother more than a few times in the past three years.

"There's one from Dru, too," Ken said. "She says to call her the minute you get the message."

That was more worrisome. An urgent message from her mother was easy to ignore. From her sister, less so. "I hope there's not anything wrong," she said, sitting up.

"They would have called you on your cell if it was so important," he said, still holding the phone to his ear.

"True." She got out of bed and pulled on her short green robe, then picked up her phone from the dresser and turned it on. "Except, I didn't have my cell on today because of the field trip, so—"

"What the—" Ken frowned as he listened to another message. "What the hell are you talking about?" He shouted into the phone. Glancing at his watch, he walked across the room to turn on the television.

"What's going on?" Corinne watched him click through the channels until he reached WIGH, the Raleigh station for which he was a reporter.

"That was a message from Darren," he said, as he punched another phone number into the receiver. "He's kicking me off the Gleason story."

"What?" She was incredulous. "Why?"

"He said it was for obvious reasons, like I should know what the hell he's talking about." He looked at his watch again and she knew he was waiting for the six-o'clock news. "Come on, come *on,*" he said to the television or the phone—or maybe both. "Give me Darren!" he yelled into the receiver. "Well, where is he?" He hung up and started dialing again.

"They can't pull you off that story," she said. "That would be so unfair after all the work you've done on it." The Gleason story was his baby. He'd even attracted national attention for it. People were talking about him being a candidate for the Rosedale Award.

"Darren said, 'Did you know about this?' like I've been keeping something from him." Ken ran his fingers through his hair. "Oh, don't give me your damn voice mail," he said into the phone. "Dammit." She felt his impatience as he waited to leave a message. "What the hell do you mean, I'm off the Gleason story?" he shouted. "Call me!"

He tossed the receiver onto the bed, then pounded the top of the television with his fist as though he could make the news come on sooner through force. "I don't believe this," he said. "When I left the courthouse today, the jury hadn't sentenced him yet and they were supposed to reconvene tomorrow. Maybe I heard it wrong. Maybe I missed the sentencing. Damn!"

Corinne looked down at the cell phone in her hand as she cycled through the list of callers. "I have five messages, all from my parents' house," she said. Something *was* wrong. "I'd better call—"

"Shh," Ken said, turning up the volume as the brassy theme music introduced the news, and anchorman Paul Provost appeared on the screen.

"Good evening, Triangle," Paul said, referring to the Raleigh-Durham-Chapel Hill area. "Just hours before Timothy Gleason was to be sentenced for the 1977 murder of Genevieve Russell and her unborn child, a shocking revelation shed doubt on his guilt."

"What?" Ken stared at the TV.

Footage of a small arts-and-crafts-style bungalow filled the screen. The roof looked wet from a recent rain, and the trees were lush, the leaves just starting to turn.

"Is that...?" Corinne pressed her hand to her mouth. She knew exactly how the air smelled in the small front yard of the house. It would be thick and sweet with the damp arrival of autumn. "Oh, my God."

Through the front door, a middle-aged woman limped onto the porch. She looked small and tired. And she looked scared.

"What the hell is going on?" Ken said.

Corinne stood next to him, clutching his arm, as her mother cleared her throat.

"Timothy Gleason is not guilty of murdering Genevieve Russell," she said. "And I can prove it because I was there."

CeeCee

Chapter Two

Dear CeeCee,

You're sixteen now, the age I was when I got pregnant with you. Whatever you do, don't do that! Seriously, I hope you're much smarter and more careful than I was. No regrets, though. My life would have been so empty without you. You're my everything, darling girl. Don't ever forget that.

Chapel Hill, North Carolina
1977

"GOOD MORNING, TIM." CEECEE POURED COFFEE INTO HIS cup. He liked it black and very strong, and she'd added an extra scoop to the pot that morning that had other customers complaining.

"The morning was pretty good to begin with," he said, "but seeing you puts the icing on the cake." He leaned back in the corner booth, where he always sat, and smiled at her. He had one of those smiles that turned her brain to mush. She'd met him on her first day of work a little more than a month ago, and she'd promptly spilled hot coffee on him. She'd been mortified, but he'd laughed it off and tipped her more than the value of his breakfast. She fell for him right then.

All she knew about him could fit inside a coffee cup. To begin with, he was beautiful. The sunlight poured into the corner booth in the mornings, settling in the curls of his blond hair and turning his green eyes to stained glass. He dressed in jeans and T-shirts, like most Carolina students, but his clothing lacked any University of North Carolina logos even though he was a student there. He smoked Marlboros, and his table was always littered with books and papers. She liked that he was studious. Best of all, he made her feel pretty and smart and desirable, which was something she'd not experienced before. She wanted to bottle the feeling and carry it around with her.

She pulled her order pad and pencil from her jeans pocket. "Do you want your usual?" she asked, but she was thinking, *I love you*.

"Of course." He took a sip of coffee, then pointed toward the front of the coffee shop. "Do you know that every time I walk through that door, I'm afraid you won't be here?" he asked. "As soon as I come in, I look for your hair." He'd told her that he loved her hair. She'd never cut it, and it fell in dark waves to the small of her back.

"I'm always here," she said. "It's like I live here."

"You're off on Saturdays, though," he said. "You weren't here last Saturday."

"And you missed me?" Was she flirting? That would be a first.

He nodded. "Yes, but I was happy to see that you had some time off."

"Well, not time off, really. I tutor on Saturdays."

"You're always working, CeeCee," he said. She loved when he used her name.

"I need the money." She looked down at her order pad as though she'd forgotten why she was holding it. "I'd better put in your order or you won't get out of here in time for your class. Be back soon." She excused herself and walked toward the swinging door to the kitchen.

Inside, the aroma of bacon and burned toast enveloped her, and she found her fellow waitress and roommate, Ronnie, arranging plates of pancakes on a tray.

"You *do* have other tables to wait on, you know," Ronnie teased.

CeeCee clipped Tim's order to the carousel where the cook would see it, then twirled around happily to face her friend. "I'm *useless* when he's here," she said.

Ronnie hoisted her loaded tray to her shoulder. "He does look particularly hot today, I have to admit." She backed up against the swinging door to push it open. "You should say you had a date last night or something," she said as she left the room.

Ronnie, who was far more experienced in dating than CeeCee, was full of bad advice when it came to Tim. "Pretend you have a boyfriend," she'd say. Or "Act indifferent sometimes." Or "Let *me* wait on him so he misses you."

Not on your life, CeeCee'd thought in response to her last suggestion. Ronnie was gorgeous. She looked like Olivia Newton-John. When they walked down the street together, CeeCee felt invisible. She was five-three to Ronnie's five-seven, and although she wasn't heavy, she had a stockier build than her roommate. Except for her hair, her features were forgettable.

She was smarter than Ronnie, though. More ambitious, more responsible, and far, far neater. But when a girl looked like Olivia Newton-John, guys didn't care if she could solve a quadratic equation or diagram a compound sentence. Tim would care, though. She didn't know that for a fact, of course, but the Tim she fantasized about would definitely care.

She checked her other tables, getting extra napkins for a bunch of frat boys who'd made a mess with their cinnamon rolls. The fraternity types were a turnoff. They reeked of stale beer in the mornings, they never tipped, and they treated her like a slave. Then she got tea for the elderly black couple seated in the booth next to Tim's. The husband had very short-cropped gray hair and wore thick glasses. He had some sort of palsy; his hands and head shook uncontrollably. The woman, her own hands gnarled with arthritis, fed him his breakfast with a patience CeeCee admired.

Setting the teapot in front of the woman, she glanced at Tim. His head was lowered over a book and he was taking notes as he read. Maybe she was kidding herself about his interest. Maybe he was just a friendly guy. They probably had zero in common, anyway. She was barely sixteen and he was twenty-two. She'd graduated from high school only four months ago, while he was in his first year of graduate school. And his major was social work, while her only contact with social workers had been as the recipient of their services. This was like having a crush on a rock star.

But when she finally delivered his plate of bacon, eggs and grits, he set down his pen, folded his arms in front of him, and said, "I think it's time we went out. What d'you think?"

"Sure," she said, as though his invitation was no big deal. Inside, she was bursting.

She couldn't wait to tell Ronnie.

"Miss?" The black woman in the next booth waved her over.

"Excuse me," CeeCee said to Tim as she took a couple of steps to her left. "Are you ready for your check?" She pulled out her pad.

"I know we're supposed to pay at the register, miss—" the woman looked at her name tag "—Miss CeeCee. But I was hoping we could pay you. It's so much easier on us that way."

"Oh, sure." CeeCee added the figures in her head, jotting down the total. "It's five seventy-five," she said.

The woman dug through her patent-leather purse with twisted fingers. A gold wedding band, worn smooth, graced the ring finger of her left hand, locked in place forever by a knobby, swollen knuckle.

"Sorry, miss," she said, as she handed CeeCee a ten-dollar bill. "Everything takes me so long these days."

"That's okay," CeeCee said. "I'll be right back with your change."

The couple was standing next to their table by the time she returned. The woman thanked her, then slowly guided her husband down the aisle toward the door.

She watched them for a moment, then looked at Tim. He was cradled by the corner of the booth, coffee cup in his hand and his eyes on her. She started clearing the couple's table, stacking the plates on top of one another.

"So, where were we?" she asked him.

"How about a movie?" he asked.

"Sure," she said, but her eyes were drawn to the seat where the old woman had been sitting. Two crumpled ten-dollar bills rested on the blue vinyl.

"Oh!" She grabbed the money, then looked out the window to try to find the couple, but the sea of students on the sidewalk blocked her view. "I'll be right back," she said. She ran out of the coffee shop and, after searching for a few minutes, found the couple sitting on a bench at the bus stop.

She sat down next to the woman. "You dropped this in your booth," she said, pressing the money into her hand.

"Oh, my word!" The woman drew in her breath. "Bless you, child." She took the bills, then caught CeeCee's hand. "You don't move, Miss CeeCee," she said, reaching for her purse. "Let me give you something for your honesty."

"Oh, no," CeeCee said. "Don't worry about it."

The woman hesitated, then reached out and tugged lightly on her long hair. "God surely knew what he was doing when he gave you hair fit for an angel," she said.

CeeCee was breathless by the time she returned to the coffee shop and began loading a tray with the couple's dishes.

"What was that all about?" Tim asked.

"Two tens must have fallen out of her purse when she was getting money to pay me," CeeCee said.

Tim tapped his pen against his chin. "So let me get this straight," he said. "You need money and twenty dollars just landed in your lap and you gave it back."

"How could I possibly keep it? Who knows how much *they* need it? Maybe a lot more than I do." She eyed him with suspicion. "Would you have kept it?"

Tim grinned at her. "You'd be a great social worker," he said. "You care about the underdog." This wasn't the first time he had suggested she'd make a good social worker, even though he knew she wanted to be a teacher. The world would be a better place if *everyone* became a social worker, he'd said.

He looked at the clock above the kitchen door. "Gotta get to class." He slid across the seat. "How about we meet at the Varsity Theater at six-thirty?"

"Okay." She tried to sound casual. "Later."

He piled his books and papers into a sloppy stack, picked them up and headed for the door. She looked down at his table. For the first time, he'd forgotten to leave her a tip. It wasn't until she lifted his empty plate that she discovered he'd left her one after all: two ten-dollar bills.

Chapter Three

You're probably thinking about college now, CeeCee. You'll need a scholarship, so I hope you've been a good student. I'm sorry I couldn't provide better for you. College is so important. Fight to get there, okay? I always planned to go even if it meant I wouldn't graduate 'til I was fifty and now I'll never have the chance. If you're anything like me at your age, though, you'll be more interested in boys than school. That's okay. You don't need to go right away. Just remember that college men are FAR more interesting than any boys you knew in high school.

If it turns out that you don't go to college, remember you can still get an education from the people you meet. Every single person who comes into your life, from a doctor to a trash collector, can teach you something if you let them.

"IT'S RAINING." TIM RAISED HIS PALM IN THE AIR AS THEY left the movie theater.

CeeCee felt a cool, fine mist on her face. "I like it," she said, as she piled her hair on top of her head and covered it with her floppy black felt hat. She liked the rain; her hair did not.

"Now you look like Annie Hall." Tim grinned at her as they started walking through the throng of students toward the diner two blocks away. They'd just seen *Annie Hall,* a perfect first-date movie. "You're not goofy like she is, though."

"She's goofy in a cute way."

"Yeah," he said, "and you're serious in a cute way."

"Ugh." The thought was deflating. "I don't want to be serious. I want to be fun and…" What was the word she wanted? She raised her arms to the sky and twirled in a circle. *"Madcap."*

"Madcap?" He laughed, grabbing her arm to prevent her from bumping into a group of students. "I actually like that you're serious," he said, letting go of her all too quickly. "You don't take life for granted."

He was right, but how did he know that about her? "You don't really know me yet."

"I'm observant," he said. "Insightful."

"And modest."

"That, too." He stopped briefly to light a cigarette. "So, how come you sound like a Yankee?" he asked as they continued walking.

"Do I? I thought I sounded pretty Southern by now. I was raised in New Jersey until I was eleven."

"What brought you down here?"

She wasn't ready to answer that question. He already thought she was serious enough.

"Family stuff," she said with a shrug.

He didn't press her, but the sudden silence that followed her answer felt awkward. She glanced at him out of the corner of her eye. He seemed older than he did in the mornings, a true grown-up. She wondered if he felt the age gap between them tonight, especially with her spinning on the sidewalk like a ten-year-old. Maybe he wondered what the heck he'd been thinking when he asked her out. He even *looked* different than he did in the coffee shop. Better, if that was possible. She'd never noticed how tall he was. Sitting next to him in the theater, she'd been painfully aware of his long, lean, denim-covered thigh brushing against hers every time he shifted in his seat. *Hold my hand,* she'd thought over and over again. *Put your arm around me.* He did neither, much to her frustration.

"It's unusual for a guy to be a social work major, isn't it?" she asked to break the silence.

"You'd be surprised," he said, letting out a puff of smoke. "There are quite a few in my program. I'm actually more interested in the policy aspect of social work than in working directly with people. I want to be able to influence policy."

"Like what kind of policies?" She saw their reflection in a store-front window as they walked past. She looked like a little munchkin in a big floppy hat.

"Policies that empower people at risk," he said. "Like that couple you waited on today. They're old. One of them is obviously disabled. And they're black. Three strikes against them right there. So, who advocates for people like that? Who makes sure they're taken care of?"

Oh, God. He was so smart and so well educated and he was stuck with a ten-year-old munchkin for the evening.

"That's what you want to do?" she asked. "Advocate for people?"

A group of preppies passed by, and Tim acknowledged one of

the guys with a nod. "Yes," he said, "but the policies I care about most involve prison reform."

"Why?"

"I think we need better prisons," he said. "I don't mean prisoners should be living lives of luxury. That's not what I'm talking about. I think we should *rehabilitate* prisoners, not just incarcerate them. And I think the death penalty is wrong and should be unconstitutional."

"I thought it *was* unconstitutional."

"For a brief period of time, it was. Just this past June, though, it became legal again in North Carolina."

She didn't think that was so terrible. "Well, if someone kills a little kid, for example, I think he—or she—should have to pay the same price."

He stared ahead of him as they walked. She could tell he didn't like her response, but she wasn't going to sell out her own principles just to please him. He turned toward her, a look on his face she hadn't seen before. Was it anger? Disappointment?

"An eye for an eye, huh?" he asked.

"Why not?"

"Well, where do I start?" Tim dropped his cigarette butt to the sidewalk and stepped on it, then dug his hands deep into the pockets of his blue windbreaker. "I believe that some of the people getting executed are actually innocent. Maybe they didn't have a good enough defense because they were too poor to get a decent lawyer. And even if they are guilty, I think it's wrong to take a life. Even the life of someone who murdered someone else. Two wrongs don't make a right."

"So, I guess you think abortion is wrong, too?" Ronnie'd had an abortion two months ago in August. CeeCee went with her to the clinic, and she cried while her friend underwent the procedure, not because she thought it was wrong but because she thought it was sad. Ronnie didn't understand her tears.

"It was only ten weeks old, CeeCee," she said. "Besides. It was going to be an Aquarius. You know I don't get along with Aquarians."

"Sometimes abortion's a necessary evil." Tim looked at her. "Why? Have you had one?"

"Me? I haven't even had *sex* yet." She cringed. Why had she told him that? What an idiot. But Tim laughed and reached for her hand, holding it at his side as they walked.

"You're the coolest girl," he said. "You just tell it like it is."

The diner was packed with students and the whole building seemed to vibrate with their chatter. She and Tim pushed through the crowd toward a booth in the back, Tim stopping to greet people he knew. He had an acquaintance at nearly every table. It didn't matter whether the students were jocks or stoners or preps or the heavy-lidded artsy types. He knew them all. The one thing all his friends had in common was that they were significantly older than she was. He introduced her to a few of them. The guys barely seemed to notice her. The girls smiled at her, but she sensed there was something underlying their cordiality. She hoped it was envy and not disdain.

"I love this atmosphere," she said, once they were seated. This was the world she wanted to be part of. "All the students. It's like I can—" she breathed in the scent of smoke and French fries "—like I can smell textbooks in the air."

He laughed. "I take it back," he said. "You *are* goofy after all."

She took off her hat and watched him smile when her hair spilled over her shoulders.

"You deserve to be one of these students," he said.

"Someday, I will be."

"Is it just the money?" he asked. "I mean, were your grades good enough? Your SAT scores okay?"

She nodded. "I was *this* close to getting a scholarship." She held her thumb and forefinger a quarter of an inch apart.

"I'm sorry." He wore a small frown. "That doesn't seem fair."

"It's okay. Really." She looked down at the menu, uncomfortable with his sympathy.

"When do you think you'll have enough money to go to school?" he asked.

"Another year, if Ronnie will continue to live with me and split our expenses. We just share a room, and I know she really wants us to get an apartment, but she doesn't care about saving money. I'll have to get a better job. In a few months, I should have enough experience to work at a good restaurant and then I'll get better tips."

"I like your ambition," he said.

"Thanks," she said. "So, where do you live? You must live near the coffee shop, since you're there every morning."

"Just a few blocks off Franklin," he said. "I share a house with my brother, Marty. My father owns it, but he lives in California, so he lets us use it."

"Just your father? Are your parents divorced?" She hoped that wasn't too personal a question.

The waitress, a blonde with stick-straight, shoulder-length hair, pouty pink lips and blood-red fingernails set glasses of water in front of them.

"Hi, Tim," she said, but her eyes were on CeeCee. "How're y'all doin' tonight?"

"Good," Tim said. "Bets, this is CeeCee. CeeCee, Bets."

"You watch out for him, CeeCee," Bets said with a wink. "He's a dangerous man."

"Thanks for the warning." CeeCee laughed.

"Y'all ready?" Bets pulled two straws from her apron pocket and laid them on the table.

Tim raised his eyebrows at CeeCee. "Do you know what you'd like?"

She wasn't ready to eat in front of him; she was bound to spill or get something caught in her teeth. "Key lime pie," she said. That seemed safe. Tim ordered a barbecue sandwich.

"What did she mean about you being a dangerous man?" CeeCee asked, once Bets had left their table.

"She's just yanking your chain," Tim said. He took a drink from his water glass. "To get back to your question about my parents, they weren't divorced. My mother died not too long ago."

"Oh, I'm sorry," she said, but it was a half-truth. They now had something in common: they were both motherless. She wondered if his mother had also died of cancer, but didn't ask. She didn't like it when people asked personal questions about her own mother. "Is your brother in school, too?" she asked.

"No, no. Marty's not school material." Tim drummed his fingers on the table as if he could hear music she could not. "He was in Vietnam," he said. "He went there a nice kid of eighteen and came back a bitter old man."

"So, he doesn't work?" She unwrapped her straw and dropped it into her water glass.

"Yeah, he does. He's in construction. Someone was crazy enough to put a hammer and a nail gun in his hands." He laughed.

"What do you mean?"

"Nothing." He shook his head as if clearing it of the topic, then leaned forward, folding his arms on the table. "So back to you, my mysterious CeeCee. You said you're only sixteen. Did you start school early or what?"

"I started early and then skipped fifth grade," she said. "I moved to a new school. Went from a good school to a crummy one and I was way ahead of what the kids were doing, so they skipped me."

"I knew you were smart," he said. "Where's your family?"

She wondered how much to say. "I don't want you to feel sorry for me, okay?" she said.

"Sure, okay."

She played with the wrapper from her straw. "My mother is dead, too," she began.

"Oh, no," he said. "I'm sorry."

"She had breast cancer, even though she was only in her twenties, and we moved down here from New Jersey so she could be in a study at Duke. She died when I was twelve, and then I got kind of shuffled around."

Tim reached across the table and rested his hand on hers. "In her *twenties*." He shook his head. "I didn't think that happened."

His eyelashes were as pale as his hair and very long. She studied them to keep from doing something stupid, like turning her hand over to grasp his. "Neither did she," she said, "so she never looked for a lump or anything." She didn't tell him that she would always have to be vigilant about her own health. She didn't want him to start thinking of her as a woman who would lose both her breasts, the way her mother had.

"What do you mean, you got shuffled around?"

He hadn't moved his hand from hers. As a matter of fact, he tightened it around her fingers, running his thumb over the skin above her knuckles. Her pulse thrummed beneath his fingertips.

"Well," she said, "they put me in this place…I was never sure what it was, exactly…I called it juvenile hall because it was full of kids who were screwed up."

"A residential facility."

She smiled. "Right, Mr. Social Worker."

"Go on."

"I stayed there while they tried to find my father. My parents weren't married and I'd never met him. It turned out he was in prison for molesting kids, so I guess it's just as well that I never did."

"I'd say so." Tim nodded. "It must have been a huge disappoint—"

Bets picked that moment to show up with their orders, and Tim had no choice but to let go of CeeCee's hand while she put his food in front of him.

"Here you go, hon," Bets said to CeeCee as she set down the key lime pie. "You want some extra sauce, Timmy?" she asked.

Timmy? CeeCee squirmed. How well did Bets know him?

"We're good," Tim said.

"Okay," Bets moved on to another table, calling over her shoulder, "Y'all enjoy, now."

Tim pushed his plate an inch or so toward her. "You want a bite?" he asked.

She shook her head. "Looks good, though." She played with her straw wrapper again as he bit into his sandwich.

"So," he said, once he'd swallowed, "after they found your father, then what happened?"

"They put me in foster care."

"Ah," he said. "You've had some experience with social workers."

"Plenty." She drew the tines of her fork across the smooth, pale surface of her pie. "I was in six different foster homes. It wasn't because I was a problem," she added. "Just crazy circumstances."

He nodded. He understood.

"The last one was the best. It was a single woman with some young kids who were really sweet. As soon as I graduated, though, I was on my own."

"You've been through a lot," he said, taking a sip of water.

"It wasn't all bad," she said. "I met a lot of people. You can learn something from everyone you meet."

"That's a very wise statement."

"Hey, Gleason!"

CeeCee turned to see one of the jocks walking toward their table. He was black, clean-cut and handsome, and probably seven feet tall. She'd see him around town from time to time, usually carrying a basketball. Sometimes she could hear him dribbling the ball even before she saw him.

"Hey, Wally, what's up?" Tim set down his glass and slid his palm across Wally's in greeting.

Wally shook his head in disgust. "That chick you saw me with the other night? She laid a bad trip on me, man," he said.

Tim laughed. "Tell me something new."

"You hangin' at the Cave tonight?"

"Not tonight." Tim nodded in her direction. "This is CeeCee," he said.

CeeCee raised her hand in a small wave. "Hi," she said.

"Out to lunch with that hair, girl," Wally said, in what she assumed was a compliment.

"Thanks."

"All right, boss," Wally said to Tim. "Check ya later."

They watched Wally walk away, his hand smacking the air as he bounced an invisible basketball.

"Do you know *everyone* in Chapel Hill?" she asked.

Tim laughed. "I've lived here a long time." He picked up the sandwich from his plate. "You have to talk for a while so I can make a bigger dent in this thing," he said. "Tell me about your mother. Were you close to her?"

He was definitely social-worker material. He wasn't shy about the questions he asked. "Well." She ran the tines of her fork the other way on the pie and admired the checkerboard pattern she'd created. "My mother was an amazing person," she said. "She knew she was going to die and she did her best to prepare me for it, although you can never really be prepared. I guess you know all about that."

He nodded as he chewed, his face solemn.

"At first, she was really angry," she said, remembering how her mother would snap at her for the slightest infraction. "Then she'd sort of...you know, swing between being angry and being down. And then she got very calm."

"DABDA," Tim said.

"Dabda?"

"The five stages of grief. Denial, anger, bargaining, depression and acceptance."

"Wow, yes, that fits," she said. "What's bargaining, though?"

"It's like making a deal with God." He wiped his lips with his napkin. "Dear God, if you let me get better, I'll never do anything bad again."

"I don't know if she did that," CeeCee said. It hurt to imagine her mother trying to bargain her way out of the inevitable. "*I* did, though." She laughed at the realization. "I was always promising God I'd be a good girl if he'd make her better."

"I think you were probably a very good girl." Tim's voice was gentle.

She looked at her uneaten pie. "I'd expected a miracle would save her right up until the end. You know what she did?" She couldn't believe she was going to tell him this. "She wrote me letters before she died," she said. "There are about sixty of them. She put each one in a sealed envelope and wrote on it when I should open it. There was one for the day after her funeral, and then one for each birthday, and then there'd be some that were sort of haphazardly dated, for years when she thought I'd need a lot of advice, I guess. Like for when I turned sixteen, there was an envelope that said 'Sixteen,' then one that said 'Sixteen and five days,' and then 'Sixteen and two months,' and so on."

Tim swallowed the last bite of his sandwich and shook his head in amazement. "How phenomenal," he said. "She was how old?"

"Twenty-nine."

"Man, I don't know if I could be that strong in her shoes."

She was glad she'd told him.

"So you still have dozens of letters from her to open?" he asked.

"Actually, no." She laughed. "I opened every single one of them the day after her funeral." She'd sat alone in the guest bedroom of an ancient great-aunt reading her mother's words, many of which she'd been too young to understand, but not too young to treasure. She'd cried and rocked and hugged herself for comfort as she read them, feeling the loss deep in her bones. There was much in those letters she hadn't understood. She'd skimmed over the advice about sex, too young even to be titillated by it. The words of wisdom on child rearing were meaningless to her. It didn't matter that she didn't understand them; she cherished every stroke of her mother's pen. "I still have them, though." The letters were under her bed in a box that had traveled with her from foster home to foster home. They were all she had left of her mother. "She always told me I could decide whether to be happy or sad," she said. "When she got to the…what did you call that part of the acronym? Acceptance?"

"Right."

"I guess that's when she told me that she realized she could spend her last days being a miserable bitch—her words, not mine—or she could spend them being grateful for the time she and I had together. She made up this song about being thankful for the morning and the trees and the air. She said I should sing that song to myself every morning, and—" She suddenly clamped her mouth shut, embarrassed. She was saying too much, almost giddy with the relief of having an attentive listener.

"Why'd you stop?" he asked.

"I'm talking too much."

"Do you sing the song?"

She nodded. "In my head, I do."

"And it helps?"

"So much. I feel like she's still there with me. So I try to be thankful for everything, including every hard thing that's happened to me." She looked down at her pie. She'd made a mess of it. "Whew," she said. "I never talk this much. About my life, I mean. Sorry."

"Don't apologize," he said. "I like getting to know you better. And I think you were lucky to have that mother of yours as long as you did."

"I haven't given you a chance to talk at all," she said.

"We have time for that, CeeCee." Tim stared at her for a moment, then smiled. "I like you a lot," he said. "I don't think I've ever met anyone as positive as you are."

The compliment meant more to her than anything else he might say. If you were positive, you could do anything.

He offered her a ride home after they left the restaurant. She climbed into his white Ford van, the overhead light giving her a glimpse of the mattress in the back, and her knees nearly gave out from under her. She wanted him to suggest they go into the dark cavern back there. She wanted him to be her first lover. But when he pulled up in front of the Victorian boardinghouse, he got out of the van and walked around to open her door.

"I wish I could ask you in," she said, as he walked her up the porch steps, "but we're not allowed to have male visitors in our room."

"That's okay," he said. He leaned down to kiss her. It was a light kiss and she had to make herself pull away before she asked for more.

"I'll see you tomorrow morning," he said. The porch light was reflected in his eyes, and he gave her hair a little tug, like the black woman had done at the bus stop.

She returned his smile with a wave, then unlocked the door and raced upstairs. She wanted to tell Ronnie about this perfect night, even though her roommate would never understand why she felt such a thrill over being able to talk to someone the way she'd talked to Tim. Look at all she'd told him! He even knew she was a virgin. She could tell him anything about herself and he would receive it all with compassion and understanding.

Next time, she'd give *him* a chance to tell her everything about his life, and she'd listen with the same attentiveness he'd shown her.

She was a completely honest person, though. It would never occur to her that he was not.

Chapter Four

I have no idea what kind of girl you are now, so I don't know what to say to help you and I hate that I can't be there with you. I get so angry sometimes that I won't be able to watch you grow up!

Here are a few things you need to know. First, don't have sex! But if you do, get birth control pills or condoms. You can get them at Planned Parenthood. Second, sex is not all it's cracked up to be. The earth doesn't move, especially not the first time, and any woman who tells you that it does is a liar. Third, don't trust boys! Here are some lies they'll tell you to get you to sleep with them:

1) I never felt this way about anyone before.

2) Of course I'll still respect you in the morning.

3) My balls (testicles) will turn blue and explode if we don't make love.

4) I promise I'll pull out before I come.

I can't believe I'm writing this to you, my little twelve-year-old baby! It's hard to imagine you'll ever be old enough to need this advice, but for what it's worth, there it is.

The room she shared with Ronnie was not much bigger than a closet. Their twin beds were perpendicular to each other, and two narrow dressers lined the wall, leaving barely enough room to walk across the floor. Two nights after her date with Tim, CeeCee came home after working a double shift.

"Any messages?" she asked, her attention darting toward the phone. She'd seen Tim at breakfast that morning, but the coffee shop had been crowded and there'd been no time to talk.

"Uh-uh, sorry." Ronnie looked up from her bed, where she was painting her toenails. "But there's a package for you." She nodded toward CeeCee's bed, where a small, square box wrapped in brown paper rested on her pillow.

"Weird," CeeCee said. It was rare for her to get mail. She picked up the package by the cord tied around it. Light as air. Her name and address were printed in black ink.

"I shook it and it sounds empty to me," Ronnie said. "How'd tonight go? I take it Tim didn't stop in?"

"No." CeeCee sat on her bed and kicked off her tennis shoes. Her feet hurt and she massaged her toes through her kneesocks. "Is he ever going to ask me out again?"

"I hope so." Ronnie sounded genuinely sympathetic.

"Why can't I just ask him?" CeeCee pulled one end of the cord, but it was tightly knotted. "Why do we always have to wait to be asked? Can I borrow your nail clippers?"

Ronnie tossed the clippers to her. "If he doesn't ask you out again, he's a cretin. You don't want him."

Yes, I do. She had constant fantasies about Tim picking her up after her shift, driving to a park, someplace quiet and private, and making love to her on the mattress in the back of the van. "I should never have told him I was a virgin," she said.

"Well, that's a no-brainer," Ronnie agreed. She'd screamed so loudly when CeeCee told her about her "I've never had sex" comment that their landlady rushed in, afraid they were being murdered.

CeeCee clipped the cord and ripped the paper from the package to reveal a flimsy white cardboard box. She lifted the lid and gasped.

"There's money in here!" she said.

"What?" Ronnie set her nail polish on the windowsill and rushed to CeeCee's bed. "Holy crap," she said, peering into the box. "How much?"

CeeCee pulled out the wad of bills and started counting.

"They're all fifties," Ronnie said.

"Six hundred, six-fifty," CeeCee counted, shaking her head in disbelief. "Seven hundred, seven-fifty."

"Oh my God," Ronnie said as the number grew. She grabbed the brown paper the box had been wrapped in. "Was there any name anywhere?"

"Shh," CeeCee said. She was up to twelve hundred and her hands were starting to shake.

Ronnie watched in silence until CeeCee had counted one hundred fifty-dollar bills. Five thousand dollars. They looked at each other.

"I don't get it," CeeCee said.

"Maybe, like, your last foster mother sent it?" Ronnie suggested. "You said she was really nice."

"Really nice and really poor," CeeCee said.

Ronnie picked up one of the fifties, squinting at it as she held it up to the light. "Are there any marks or clues or anything on the bills?"

CeeCee riffled through the bills and shook her head. "I don't think so."

"Well," Ronnie said, "when you were baring your soul to Tim the other night, did you happen to mention that you were penniless?" She was reading CeeCee's mind.

"But why would he do this?" CeeCee asked in a whisper.

"That—" Ronnie gnawed her lip "—is a very scary question."

She poured Tim's coffee the following morning. "I got a package in the mail yesterday," she said.

"A package?" He looked innocent. "What was in it?"

"Money." She set the coffeepot on his table and whipped out her order pad. "Tim, tell me the truth. Did you send it?"

"I don't know what you're talking about." His blond, sun-lit curls gave him a soft, angelic look.

"It was five thousand dollars."

Tim nodded as though impressed. "That would take you through a couple of years of college and then some, wouldn't it?"

She slapped her order pad onto the table. "It's from you?" she asked.

"CeeCee, settle down." Tim laughed. "If it *were* from me, I wouldn't tell you because I wouldn't want you to feel obligated to me. I wouldn't tell you because I'd want you to have it, no strings attached. If you and I broke up tomorrow, I'd still want you to have it. *If* I'd been the one to give it to you, that is."

If they broke up? He considered them a couple? She didn't allow the elation to show in her face.

"I'm getting angry," she said, instead. "Tell me."

"Look, CeeCee." He patted her arm. "Whoever sent it wouldn't have done it if they couldn't afford it, right? So, you need it. Just enjoy it. Buy me supper with it tonight. And put the rest in the bank the first chance you get."

They ate at a Moroccan restaurant, sitting on the floor in a small room all to themselves. Tim ordered a bottle of wine and, away from the eyes of their waiter, she drank from his glass. Soon the money was forgotten, and she felt relaxed and a little loopy. They told every old joke they could remember and sang songs from The Beatles' *White Album,* which she knew because her mother had loved The Beatles. CeeCee told him about the time she saw The Beatles in Atlantic City at the age of five, because her mother's friends had a bunch of tickets and they'd been unable to find a babysitter for her. It had been one of the most traumatic events of her early life. She couldn't hear the music for the screaming of the fans, and everyone had stood on their chairs while she sat on the floor, her hands over her ears. Still, Tim was impressed. He'd never gotten to see them at all.

She tried to pay for their dinners, which had been the deal, but Tim brushed her offer aside. She wanted to tell him, *No more tips, ever,* and that she would pay for everything when they went out, but since he hadn't acknowledged he'd sent the money, she couldn't do that.

After dinner, he drove her to the house he shared with his brother, and she knew for sure that he'd been the one to send the money. The house—a tall, stately brick mansion surrounded by manicured lawns and boxwood hedges—was in the moneyed, historic heart of Chapel Hill. Once inside, CeeCee stifled a gasp. Tim obviously had someone to care for the grounds, but if he also had a housekeeper, she hadn't worked in a very long time. Clothes, dirty plates and pizza boxes were strewn on the small antique tables and chairs in the otherwise elegant foyer. She spotted an overturned chair in the dining room on her left and a broken vase in the living room on her right. The odor of marijuana drifted down the curved staircase, along with the sound of the Eagles singing "Hotel California."

"Maid's day off," Tim joked. "Hope you don't mind a little clutter."

A man, straggly haired and barefoot, walked into the foyer from the living room carrying both a beer and a cigarette. He stopped short when he saw them.

"What's up, bro?" Tim asked.

The man looked at CeeCee, and she took an involuntary step backward toward the door. His eyes were bloodshot and he wore several days' growth of beard. He looked like some of the homeless guys who sometimes hung out on Franklin Street.

"Who's this?" He nodded toward her.

"This is CeeCee." Tim put his arm around her. "And this is my brother, Marty."

Marty's nod was curt. "How old are you?" he asked. "Twelve? Thirteen?"

"Give her a break," Tim said.

"I'm sixteen," she said.

Marty let out a whistle and walked back into the living room. "Tim, get your ass in here," he said over his shoulder.

Tim looked at her apologetically. "Kitchen's in there." He pointed toward one of the arched doorways off the foyer. "Help yourself to something to drink and I'll be there in a second."

The disaster in the kitchen made the foyer look like something out of *Good Housekeeping*. The sink was piled high with dirty dishes. The long blue granite countertops were littered with pizza crusts and beer bottles and dirty ashtrays. Gingerly she opened the refrigerator, expecting to be greeted by the stench of rotting food. It wasn't bad, though. There were bottles of condiments, a few blocks of cheese, a shelf full of beer and a single can of Coke. She took the Coke, popped it open, then tiptoed toward the door, straining to hear Tim and Marty's conversation. Their voices were muffled, but she heard Marty say, "You don't have time for this shit now. You gotta focus."

Was he talking about Tim's schoolwork? It seemed bizarre for someone as clearly out-of-it as Marty to lecture Tim about anything.

"...mess up the plan," Marty said.

"Up yours," Tim responded, and she heard his footsteps approaching the kitchen. She leaned back against the counter and sipped her Coke.

"Sorry about that," Tim said when he came into the kitchen. "Marty can be a little paranoid sometimes."

"That's okay," she said, but she wished Marty would go out and leave them alone. She didn't feel comfortable with him in the house.

Tim took the can from her hand and set it on the counter. Then he put his arms around her, smiled his green-eyed smile and bent down to kiss her. She'd stood like this with a couple of boys before. She'd kissed them and even let them touch her breasts, but that had been it. Tim, though, was not a boy. This kiss was a first for her—a kiss linked by delicate electric threads to her nipples, and that made her instantly wet.

Tim seemed to know the effect he was having on her. "Let's go upstairs to my bedroom," he said.

"I'm not on the pill or anything," she said.

"I've got condoms. Don't worry."

She took his hand and they walked back into the foyer and up the curved staircase, past the room that was the source of the blaring music and the sweet herbal scent of marijuana, and down the hall to Tim's bedroom. It had once been a lovely room, she was sure. The wallpaper was a masculine blue stripe. The double bed and dresser and desk were all made from the same dark red cherry. But it was hard to notice the details with clothes and books strewn on every surface, and she didn't let herself think about how long it had been since he'd changed his sheets. She didn't care. He closed his door and locked it, then drew her down next to him on the bed, and she let the electricity in her body take over.

They cuddled together afterward. He'd left his closet light on, and she was just able to make out his features on the pillow next to her. He ran his fingers down her cheek and wound them in her hair.

"Are you okay?" he asked. "Are you sore?"

"I'm better than okay," she said. As her mother had warned her, the earth hadn't moved. At least not when he was inside her. He'd already made her come three times by then with his expert fingers and amazing mouth, but once he was inside her, she didn't feel much at all. Maybe it was the condom. If she hadn't loved being so close to him in whatever way she could, she would have been disappointed.

There was a knock at the door and she tightened the sheet to her chest.

"Going out," Marty said.

"Hold on." Tim got up, the closet light catching the long line of his body. He unlocked the door and walked naked into the hallway, pulling the door shut behind him. "Did you take your meds?" she heard him ask Marty.

"You know, if you need to get laid, you've got the van to do it in," Marty said. "You don't need to..." The rest of his sentence was muffled. CeeCee thought of getting out of the bed and dressing quickly, but her body felt frozen beneath the sheet. Could that be all she meant to him? An easy lay?

After a few minutes, Tim came back into the room, lying down next to her with a sigh that told her the mood was broken and unrecoverable.

"He thinks I just want you for your body," he said. "And I want you to know that's not it. I like you. I liked you the first day I met you in the restaurant when you spilled coffee on me. I think you're...adorable and I love being around you because you have such a great attitude. You're a little naive when it comes to what's happening in the world, and maybe that's why you're so upbeat most of the time. Ignorance is bliss and all that. I don't care."

She listened until she thought he was finished, relishing the compliments and embarrassed by the allusions to her naiveté.

"You're right," she said. "I hardly know anything about Vietnam, for example, except that there were a lot of protests about being there. And it messed up some guys. Like, what happened to Marty. What kind of medication is he on?"

Tim lay on his back, staring at the ceiling. "You heard our conversation?" he asked.

"Part of it."

"He's paranoid. He thinks every sound is something coming to get him. And he doesn't trust people much. If you could've known him before, you would have liked him. You'd understand why I care about him. I'm just glad he came back alive. So many people didn't. And he's still smart. Smarter than my sister and me."

"You have a sister? Does she live here, too?"

"Nope," he said in a way that told her the subject was off-limits.

She sat up, hugging her knees through the blanket, and surveyed the dimly lit trash heap that was his room. She had to face it: she was in love with a slob. An idea popped into her head. A way to put a smile back on his face.

"I'd like to clean up your house for you," she said. "I'm a fantastic organizer."

"No way," he said.

"I want to do it. Please let me." It was the least she could do for someone who'd, in all likelihood, given her five thousand dollars.

He stroked her bare back with his fingers. "Are you going to apply to go to school in the spring?" he asked.

"Absolutely."

"Then the house is yours," he said. "Do what you like with it. Just…stay out of Marty's room."

"I plan to stay out of Marty's *way*," she said.

"Good thinking."

"Do you have some studying to do?"

"I need to do some typing," he said. "But I don't need to—"

"I'll start right here, right now," she interrupted him. "You don't mind me doing things in your closet and your drawers?"

He laughed, reaching beneath the sheet to stroke the side of her breast. "You've already done some pretty good things in my drawers," he said, and it took her a minute to get it.

She gave him a little shove. "You study and I'll straighten up," she said.

He got out of bed and pulled on his jeans. She followed close behind him, feeling his eyes on her body as she got dressed. When she looked up he was smiling at her. "I don't know if I'll be able to just sit here while you're slaving around in my room looking cute as a button."

"You won't be just sitting there, you'll be working." She flipped on the overhead light, took his arm and guided him to his desk. "And I *love* doing this kind of thing. Honestly. When I left one of the homes I was in, my foster mother told the social worker she'd miss how I always straightened up after everyone."

"I'd miss a lot more than that," Tim said, taking a seat at his desk.

She bent over to kiss the top of his head. It was hard to believe that twenty-four hours ago she'd thought this relationship was over. Now she felt at ease, as though they'd been together for years. She hoped that's what was ahead of them: years of being together.

She started with his clothes, tossing the ones that were obviously soiled into the overstuffed hamper and hanging and folding the others. Then she worked on his bookshelf, where papers and notebooks were piled helter-skelter. Tim typed at his desk. He was a good typist, and she worked to the clacking sound of his fingers flying over the keys.

After an hour or so, he pushed back from his desk and looked down at her. She sat cross-legged on the floor, surrounded by piles of books and papers. She rested her hand on one of the stacks.

"These are things I don't know what to do with," she said. "And what's this?" She held up a packet of papers she'd found stapled together. On the cover sheet was a line drawing of a man with his head over a block, an executioner standing next to him, ax raised and ready to fall. The picture gave her the creeps. Across the top of the paper, in large handwritten letters, was the word *SCAPE*. "What's SCAPE?" she asked.

Tim looked at the sheaf of papers in her hand. He stared at it a long time as if trying to remember where he'd seen it before. Then his eyes met hers. "If I tell you something, can you keep it between us?"

"Tim," she said, as if she couldn't believe he'd ask such a question. "Of course," she said. "Look at everything I've told you."

He still looked dubious. Then he stood up and held out his hand for her. She got to her feet and walked with him from his room, down the hall and into a huge bedroom that she guessed had belonged to his parents. It was a relief to be in a room the brothers had yet to trash. The queen-size bed was a four-poster and the floor was covered by a red-and-beige Persian rug that stretched nearly wall to wall.

Tim sat down on the edge of the bed and picked up one of the framed photographs from the marble-topped night table. She sat next to him, and he put his arm around her as he held the picture on her knees. It was of three teenagers, two boys and a girl, grinning at the camera in a moment of simple joy. The boy on the left was Tim. His blond curls were longer and wilder, and his smile was different than it was now. More open. Less jaded by time and experience.

"That's you," CeeCee said.

"Right." Tim pointed to the boy on the right. "And that's Marty."

The grinning young Marty bore the clean-cut, steel-jawed good looks of a soldier. "Wow, I wouldn't have recognized him."

"He'd just turned eighteen here," Tim said. "Shipped out the next week. Andie——" Tim pointed to the girl standing between them "——and I were fifteen."

"She's your...this is your sister?" CeeCee asked.

For the first time since she'd asked him about SCAPE, Tim smiled. "My twin," he said, his fingertips lightly touching the glass over Andie's picture. His voice sounded swollen with love for his sister. "And that's where SCAPE comes in."

"I don't get it," she said.

Tim let out a long sigh. "A couple of years ago, Andie was arrested for murder."

CeeCee caught her breath. "Murder?" she asked. "Did she do it?"

Tim didn't answer the question. "When she finally got her day in court last summer, the jury came to the conclusion that she did."

CeeCee suddenly understood Tim's concerns about prison reform. "Why did they think she did it?"

"Because they didn't really know her. Andie couldn't hurt anyone. And the thing is... Marty screwed things up for her. I don't blame him for what he did, but he still feels like crap about it."

"What did he do?"

Tim stared at the picture. "See, what happened was, this photographer was supposed to come take pictures of our house to do a spread for *Southern Living Classics*. You know, the magazine?"

She nodded, although she didn't know the magazine at all.

"My parents were in Europe," Tim continued, "so the guy was just going to photograph the exterior and do the rest when they got back. Andie was home, but she was studying in her room. We were both finishing up our sophomore year at Carolina. She'd——

we'd—just turned nineteen. Anyhow, she said she didn't even know the guy was here taking pictures, and the next day, one of our neighbors saw him dead in the backyard. He'd been stabbed about a dozen times with a kitchen knife. The neighbor said she saw Andie outside talking to him the day before." Tim set the photograph back on the night table and stood up, running his fingers through his hair. "So, then things got all screwed up," he said.

CeeCee tried to mask her horror. A man had been murdered in the yard behind the house she was sitting in. Stabbed a dozen times. She shuddered at the thought.

"The cops interviewed Andie and Marty and me separately." Tim idly touched objects on the long dresser. Another photograph. A hand mirror. A silver cigarette lighter. "And we all said different things. I told the truth. I said I was on campus around the time they figured the guy was murdered, which I was, and that I'd met Marty for lunch. He'd just gotten back from Vietnam and was kind of a mess."

Tim opened one of the top dresser drawers and pulled out an unopened pack of Winstons. CeeCee sat quietly as he lit a cigarette and let out a stream of smoke. He held the pack toward her and she shook her head.

"Marty lied, though," Tim said. "He said he was home with Andie all afternoon, that she never went outside. He said it to protect her, of course." He laughed mirthlessly. "This is so screwed up," he said.

"And what did Andie say?" she asked.

"That she was home alone and never saw the guy. Her prints were on the knife, and she said that was because it was from our kitchen and she used it all the time. So, Marty got a slap on the wrist for lying and Andie got put in jail for a year and a half while she waited for a trial. My parents came home right away and got her a decent lawyer, but Andie's story was screwy and the jury knew it. The prosecution made the case that it was premeditated. That Andie killed him for his camera equipment, even though they could never prove anything was missing. The thing is, Andie never believed she'd be convicted, so she never told anyone what really happened. She lied during the trial and lied to her lawyer because—" he took a long drag on the cigarette and looked squarely at CeeCee "—because she really *did* kill him, but thought things would go worse for her if she admitted it."

"She did it?" The scene in the yard grew more vivid in her eyes. She saw the pretty blonde in the photograph plunging a knife into a stranger's heart. Twelve times.

"She told the truth *after* she got convicted. It was…devastating. We were all in the courtroom when the verdict was announced. My mother started sobbing, and Andie stood up and shouted, 'I want to tell the truth! I want to tell the truth!' It was a little late for that."

"What *was* the truth?"

"The guy *raped* her." Tim raised the cigarette to his lips, his hand trembling. "He got her to let him inside to shoot some of the interior and then he—" Tim stopped himself. "Let's just say he was a brutal son of a bitch. She went a little crazy after he left the house and she grabbed the knife and went out in the yard and let him have it. Got him back for what he did to her. I believed her. We all did. But her attorney didn't and it was just too little too late. If she perjured herself once, she'd do it again. That's what they figured." Tim leaned against the dresser, his arms folded across his chest, and looked directly at CeeCee. "She got the death penalty," he said.

Everything fell into place. "Oh," she said.

"And our mother couldn't take it. Mom always had problems with depression and she felt guilty that she and my father traveled so much and she hadn't been there for Andie. Even though we were all old enough to take care of ourselves. So," Tim said, and raised his hands in a helpless gesture, "I came home a few days after the trial to find my mother dead of an overdose." He looked at the bed where CeeCee still sat, and she knew that's where he'd found his mother. She stood up.

"I'm so sorry," she said, overwhelmed. His family, apparently once prosperous and happy, had quickly turned to dust. A daughter sentenced to death. A brother gone crazy in Vietnam. A mother's suicide. She wrapped her arms around Tim, pressing her cheek to his bare chest. "It's all so horrible," she said.

He returned the embrace and she felt his chin rest on the top of her head. "You still want to be here with me?" he asked.

"More than ever," she said. She could comfort him. They could comfort each other. "Is Andie...is she still alive?" she asked.

"On death row," he said. "And I still haven't told you about SCAPE," he said.

She leaned back to look up at him. "What is it?"

He put out his cigarette and drew her back to the bed again. "We—Marty and I and some lawyers—have been trying to get her sentence reduced. SCAPE is an organization of people who are against the death penalty. It stands for Stop Capital Punishment Everywhere. But it's kind of an underground group."

"What does that mean?"

"Did you ever hear of the Weather Underground?"

CeeCee shrugged. The name was familiar, but she didn't know why.

"It was a group of people who believed things needed to be different and who gave up on conventional channels. So, in the case of SCAPE, we try to find ways to get rid of the death penalty. We protest and…that sort of thing."

"Have you tried writing to President Carter?" she asked.

"It's really not up to Carter," Tim said. "The only person who could stay her execution is Governor Russell. We've written to him and tried to get in to see him. He doesn't give a shit. He's a hard-liner who's glad to see the death penalty back. He's an asshole. I think he sees Andie as someone he can use as an example. 'See? Even women will pay if they disobey the laws of the land.'"

"There's got to be *something* you can do," she said.

He looked at her and for the first time since he'd started talking about Andie, there was a smile on his face. "I love your optimism," he said. "And I think I'm falling in love with you."

They were the words she was waiting for. "I *know* I love you," she said.

Tim wound a lock of her hair around his index finger. "I can honestly say I've never felt this way about a girl before," he said. "You're young, and I thought that might be a problem at first, but you have such a way about you. You're so positive and you make me feel more positive. Thank you."

She nodded.

"And *please* keep this…this stuff about SCAPE between you and me."

He looked worried and her heart filled with love for him. "I would do anything for you," she said, and she meant it.

Chapter Five

Dear CeeCee,

It's hard for me to give you more advice about boys and men without scaring you. How do I balance preparing you without frightening you? I guess I can only tell you about my own experiences.

When I was fifteen, I was raped. (This was not your father, so don't worry about that!) I worked after school at this nursery (the plant kind) and he was a regular customer there, so when he offered me a ride home one evening, I took it. It was dark when we got to my house and I stupidly told him my parents weren't home. He walked me to the door and the next thing I knew I was on the porch, flat on my back, his hand over my mouth. I couldn't do a thing. He just stood up with a smile afterward and drove away. That was the angriest I've ever been in my life. If I'd had a gun, I would have killed him.

I never told anyone about this except you, CeeCee, because I was so ashamed of how stupid I was.

So I guess there are some good ones out there, but I

never had the pleasure of meeting one of them. Just be
careful and don't do anything as stupid and trusting as I
did, okay?

EVERY MOMENT SHE SPENT WITH TIM, HER LOVE FOR HIM
deepened. In the coffee shop in the morning, she felt the sweet secret
of their relationship in the air between them. Oh, Ronnie knew how
much she loved him, but she didn't know—and she could never
understand—the bond that was growing between them. Ronnie
was still into playing games with guys. She told CeeCee to flirt with
other customers in the coffee shop to make Tim jealous. She told her
to fake orgasms in order to boost his ego. The orgasm problem *did*
worry her, but for the most part, she laughed off her friend's advice.

She'd not been loved this way since she was twelve. Everything
she did was appreciated, even applauded. They were lovers and
best friends. He was helping her with her application for Carolina.
The deadline was mid-January, but he said the sooner she applied,
the better. She had to get her high-school transcripts and write an
essay, among other things, and she felt him holding her hand every
step of the way. She thought her acceptance would mean as much
to him as it would to her.

She'd moved from organizing Tim's room and closet to straightening the rest of the house. The once-filthy kitchen was now
spotless, every pot and pan in its place. She'd polished the living-
room furniture with lemon oil and scrubbed mildew from the tile
in the bathroom. Tim told her she didn't need to do any of it, but
it gave her a sense of satisfaction. He did so much for her; she loved
being able to give back, and she began to feel some ownership in
the beautiful mansion.

Pictures of Andie were everywhere. She'd pick them up and study the girl's eager smile, thinking, *You had no idea what fate had in store for you.* She would imagine Andie being raped by the photographer, and even though she knew the rape had occurred inside the house, in her mind it took place at night on the front porch—a front porch that didn't even exist at the mansion. Tim told her childhood stories about his sister, how she brought home stray kittens and how, at age seven, she tried to sneak into his hospital room when he'd had his appendix out because no one would let her visit him. How she'd tried to climb into the coffin at their grandmother's funeral. The love CeeCee felt for Tim began to expand to encompass his sister.

"Can I meet her?" she asked one night when he was telling her Andie stories in bed.

"I'll look into it," he said. "She's in Raleigh and they limit who can visit, but I think you *should* meet her. Y'all would really love each other."

Funny how love could double and then triple. She even felt some of it toward Marty. Marty began to see her as friend rather than foe, and the night he said that her fried chicken was the best he'd ever tasted, she knew she was winning him over. That same night, he'd brought his guitar into the living room and played a lot of Creedence Clearwater Revival songs that he knew all the words to, while she and Tim stumbled through the lyrics. He'd had a guitar in 'Nam, Marty explained to her, and music got him through some rough times.

The day before Halloween, she bought three pumpkins and she, Tim and Marty sat in the kitchen, carving jack-o'-lanterns and nibbling roasted pumpkin seeds. At first she'd wondered if it had been a mistake to put a knife in Marty's hands, but he was careful with his carving, and his design turned out to be the most intricate, if also the most frightening, of the three.

Her mother had liked to dress up to open the door to trick-or-treaters, so CeeCee made a Jolly Green Giant costume out of green tights, a green turtle neck and an abundance of green felt. She had the feeling that Tim thought she was going a bit overboard, but he still told her she looked adorable in her outfit.

On Halloween night, she put on her costume, lit candles in the jack-o'-lanterns, and set them out on the front stoop. When the first trick-or-treater arrived, though, Marty panicked.

"Don't open the door!" He'd been sitting in the living room with Tim, but now he headed for the stairs.

"It's all right, Marty," Tim said. "It's just a kid looking for a handout."

"Don't open it!" Marty stood at the top of the stairs, and CeeCee, cradling a bowl of chocolate kisses, saw real terror in his eyes.

"It's okay, Marty," she said. "I won't open it."

Tim looked at her with gratitude. "Sorry," he said.

She went outside and blew out the candles inside the jack-o'-lanterns, then Tim turned out the front lights. Standing in the middle of the foyer in her Jolly Green Giant outfit, she looked up at Marty, who was now sitting on the top step like a little kid, elbows on his knees and his chin resting on his hands.

"Get your guitar, Marty, and come downstairs," she said. "We've got some chocolate to eat."

Four weeks after their first date, Tim called her when he got out of his evening class. It was nearly ten-thirty, and CeeCee and Ronnie were lying in their beds reading, but when he asked if he could come pick her up, that he had something important he wanted to ask her, she didn't hesitate.

"I'll wait for you out front." She hung up the phone and hopped off her bed. "He said he has something important to ask me," she said to Ronnie as she stripped off her pajamas.

"Oh my God!" Ronnie put down her magazine. "Do you think he's going to propose? Today is, like, your one-month anniversary and everything, right?"

That had been CeeCee's first thought as well, though she and Tim had never even mentioned marriage. The tone of his voice, though, told her that whatever he wanted to ask her was serious business.

"I don't know." She pulled a T-shirt over her head, not bothering with a bra. "I just can't see him asking me to marry him right now." Did she want him to? She wasn't sure.

"You're practically his wife already," Ronnie said. "You do his *laundry,* for Pete's sake. Maybe he figures he should make it legal."

CeeCee ran a brush through her hair, bending low to see her reflection in the mirror above the dresser. "It's probably nothing like that."

"I bet it is." Ronnie sat up on her bed, hugging her knees. "What will you say if he asks you?"

She gave her hair one final swipe with the brush as she thought about the question. "I'd say no," she said finally. "I mean, I know he's the right one, but I want to be out of college and supporting myself before I get married. I don't want to be dependent on him."

Ronnie held up the issue of *Cosmopolitan* she'd been reading.

"You need to take a look at this article," she said. "He's *rich*. Let him support you."

CeeCee opened the door, then turned back to her friend with a smile. "One day," she said. "But not today."

Chapter Six

*Today you rubbed my back after I got sick. It felt so good.
It's like you're the mother now and I'm the child. You're a
natural-born caretaker, CeeCee. How did I get so lucky to
have you as a daughter?*

SHE CLIMBED INTO TIM'S VAN AND LEANED OVER TO KISS
him, and she knew right away that he was nervous. His smile was
brief and false and he didn't hold her gaze the way he usually did.
Instead, he started driving.

"What's wrong?" she asked.

"Nothing. I just don't want to talk in front of your house."

He probably thought Ronnie would be watching from the window.

"Should we go to your house?"

He shook his head and turned the corner into the parking lot
of an old Baptist church. "Marty's there," he said, "and I want to
talk to you alone."

Oh, God. He *was* going to propose.

He turned off the ignition. "It's getting kind of chilly out. Will
you be okay if we just sit here for a while?"

"I'm fine," she said.

The parking-lot lights filled the car and he looked pale, almost sick, in their glow. "I've got something heavy to talk to you about," he said.

She couldn't stop her smile. "Okay." She would have to be very kind when she turned him down, very loving. She'd make sure he knew it was the timing that was wrong, not the proposal itself.

Tim rubbed his palms together as if trying to warm himself up. "There's a way you can help Andie," he said.

Surprised, she swallowed the words she'd been ready to say. He was not going to ask her to marry him. She wasn't sure if she was relieved or disappointed.

"How?" she asked.

He looked at her squarely for the first time since she got in the car. "I'm not sure how to tell you," he said, pressing his hands together. "I guess what I need to say first is that Marty and I have been working on a plan. But it's illegal." He watched her face for a reaction. "And it's dangerous," he added.

She clutched his arm. "What are you talking about?" She remembered the waitress, Bets, who told her Tim was a dangerous man, and she felt a quick, sharp fear that she could lose him. He could get arrested and locked away, the way Andie was.

"You don't have to say you'll do what I ask. Okay?" He covered her hand with his. "I mean, I love you, babe. I'm going to go on loving you whether you help me with this or not. Is that clear?"

"Yes," she said, "but—"

"Do you want me to tell you the plan or would you rather not know?"

"Well, I have to know what I'm saying yes or no to, don't I?"

"If I tell you, you have to swear that you won't breathe a word to anyone. Not Ronnie or anyone. So, if you might have a hard time doing that, please let me know now so I don't—"

"I won't tell anyone," she said. "I promise." They were planning to break Andie out of prison. What else could make him this jumpy and anxious? Maybe they'd ask her to drive the getaway car or something. If that was the only way to save Andie's life, could she do it? "Dangerous" was an understatement. "If she's on death row," she said, "won't it be nearly impossible to get her out?"

"What?" Tim looked confused. "Oh. No, that's not it, CeeCee." He let go of her and ran both hands through his hair. "You know we've tried every legal way to get her sentence reduced, right?" he asked.

"Yes," she said.

"Now, we have to play hardball. Listen to me." He took both her hands in his. "Marty and I are going to kidnap Governor Russell's wife."

"What?" She giggled. "Are you kidding?"

He looked away from her, not a hint of a smile on his face, and she knew he was not kidding at all. "I'm very serious," he said.

"Tim." She let go of his hand, reached up and turned his face toward hers. "This is crazy," she said. "This is like something Marty would come up with. Is this his idea?"

"Mine, actually," he said. "And it's not crazy. We've got it all worked out."

"I can't believe you'd even *think* of doing something like this."

"I won't tell you anything more about it, then," he said. "Just don't say anything to anyone."

"I told you I wouldn't. But I'm not following you at all. How will kidnapping the governor's wife help Andie?"

"We'll let her go when he commutes her sentence."

"Then you could end up in prison, too," she said.

"I won't."

"What if he won't do it?"

"I believe he will."

"But you—"

"*Look.*" He raised his hands sharply in the air, suddenly angry. "It's going to work, okay? I *need* it to work. So please, cool it with the 'but this' and 'but that.' It doesn't help."

It was the first time he'd ever raised his voice to her and she had to struggle to keep from crying. "I'm sorry," she whispered.

He pressed his palms against his eyes, his breathing harsh. "Shooting holes in a plan you know nothing about…it doesn't make it any easier on me, CeeCee."

She bit her lip, unsure what to say. When he dropped his hands from his face, his eyes were red and wet.

"It's my *sister,* damn it!" He pounded his fist on the steering wheel. "I have to help her."

"I know," she said, "and I know how much you love her." She leaned forward to embrace him, wanting to absorb some of his pain. "What exactly did you want me to do?" she asked.

"Don't worry about it. We can get somebody else to do it." He pulled a pack of cigarettes from the pocket of his jacket and lit one, drawing the smoke deep into his lungs. "There's this girl in SCAPE who'd probably—"

"Tell me what you wanted me to do," she repeated.

He sighed, rolling his head back and forth as though the conversation was making his neck ache. "It's like this," he said. "Some relatives of ours have a cabin on the Neuse River near New Bern. Do you know where that is?"

"Sort of," she said. "It's a couple of hours from here?"

"Right. They don't ever use it this time of year, so that's where we'll take the wife. Then Marty and I will stay in this other house in Jacksonville and communicate with Russell—the governor—from there. Once Russell says he'll do it, we'll go get the wife and return her to him. Unharmed," he added.

"You'll just leave the wife alone in the cabin? Won't she—" She caught herself. She was shooting holes again.

"That's where you'd come in," he said. "You…or the girl from SCAPE or whoever…you'd stay with her."

She tried to imagine herself, sixteen years old, trying to keep a grown woman under lock and key. "I don't think I could do it," she said.

"I know you don't think you could." He touched her cheek, and she was relieved that his anger had passed. "You don't want to do it, and that's cool. You're just someone Marty and I knew we could trust. We need someone who'd make sure the wife stays safe and who'd take care of her. You're really good at that kind of thing. I don't know the girl from SCAPE all that well, but maybe she'll be good at it, too. You care about Andie and Marty and me, so it just made sense to ask you."

Guilt rested on her shoulders like a lead weight. He'd done so much for her. The girl from SCAPE, sure of her values and ready to fight for them, would be willing to help them when she didn't even know them.

"Tim." She leaned across the space between their seats to put her arms around him, careful to avoid the cigarette. "I wish you wouldn't do this. It's too dangerous."

He let out a long sigh and she heard both frustration and disappointment in the sound. "It's the only choice we've got, CeeCee," he said, turning the key in the ignition. "And we're going to do it. With you or without you."

Chapter Seven

The hospice counselor asked why I never cut your hair. I said it was your decision when to cut it. You've made good decisions from the time you were little. (With the exception of the time you flushed Teddy-Doodle down the toilet, remember that?) I think the important thing about making a decision is just to make it. Otherwise you can go nuts thinking about the pros and cons. It's like when I decided to come to Duke for the breast cancer study. It was a big decision, uprooting you from your friends and trying a new drug and everything. My mind was saying, "Don't do it!" but my heart said, "You've got to give it a try." Was it the right decision? I don't know. I'm dying, so I guess you could say it was the wrong one, but if I never did it I would probably be dying in New Jersey, wondering if I should have taken the risk. So, when it comes to making a decision, look at both sides, listen to your heart, then pick one and dive in.

IN THE COFFEE SHOP THE FOLLOWING MORNING, SHE SET Tim's plate of eggs and grits in front of him, then leaned over to whisper. "I'd like to talk to you and Marty about—" she shrugged "—you know."

Tim's eyebrows shot up. "Are you considering it?" he asked.

"I have a lot of questions."

"Sure you do." Tim touched her hand briefly. "Come over tonight. We'll get pizza and talk."

"With Marty," she said. "I need to know we all agree on the plan before I make a decision."

"I'll make sure he's there," Tim said. "And I'm sorry if I was hard on you last night."

Ronnie had been awake when CeeCee got home the night before. She wanted to know if Tim had proposed. CeeCee shook her head with a smile, having planned on the question. "I can't believe we thought that," she said, making light of it. "He wanted my advice on getting a gift for an aunt."

"Ew." Ronnie winced. "Are you disappointed?"

"Relieved," she said. "It's not time yet." But she was hardly relieved by Tim's actual proposal. It was a lamebrain idea, wasn't it? Or could it actually work? She stayed up much of the night thinking about his outrageous plan, making a list of her concerns and questions. She had to remember that Tim was one of the smartest people she'd ever known. He knew so much more than she did about how the world operated, especially when it came to politics and that sort of thing. He wouldn't do something so risky unless he was certain of the outcome.

Two pizzas were being delivered as she arrived at the mansion, but she doubted she'd be able to eat a single slice. She watched Tim pay with a twenty, telling the delivery boy to keep the change.

Marty was already seated at the head of the massive dining-room table by the time she and Tim carried the pizzas into the room. Marty's straggly brown hair looked like it needed washing, but he'd shaved for the occasion. His hands were folded on the table in front of him as if he were chairman of the board. "So," he said. "I hear you might help us out."

CeeCee sat down across the table from Tim. It was an incongruous scene, she thought. Formal dining room, crystal chandelier, heavy gold jacquard draperies that must have cost a fortune, eating pizza on paper plates, planning a kidnapping.

"I don't know," she said. "I still think it's a crazy idea."

Marty smiled his lunatic smile. "Sometimes you gotta bend the rules to get any action," he said.

"You said you had questions," Tim prompted her as he put a slice of pizza on her plate.

She reached into her jeans pocket and pulled out the list she'd made the night before, flattening the paper on the table.

"Won't the governor know it's the two of you doing this, since you've been working to help Andie all along?" she asked.

"Unless he's a complete asshole, which is certainly possible, yes." Marty took a bite of pizza.

"So…then won't you get locked up after you let his wife go?"

"Only if they find us," Marty said, his mouth full.

She looked at Tim. "What does he mean?"

"We'll go underground," Tim said.

"You mean like…into hiding?"

"Yes," Tim said. He was watching her for a reaction. "We'll change our names. Change our looks a bit."

"*Tim.*" She was incredulous. "Then how would I see you?"

Tim set down his pizza and reached across the broad table to take her hand. "Saving my sister's life is the most important thing in the world to me right now," he said, "but I don't plan to lose you in the process." His eyes could melt her. "You'll know where I am. Just no one else will."

"Do you promise?"

He nodded.

"You'll know where we are if you can keep your mouth shut about it, that is," Marty added. There was a threatening quality to his voice that reminded CeeCee of her initial discomfort around him.

"Of course she will."

"But…" CeeCee was trying to see into the future. *Her* future. "Does that mean I'd always have to see you on the sly?" she asked.

"Not necessarily," Tim said. "If you come to wherever I end up, we can have a relationship out in the open. I just won't be Tim Gleason anymore."

"But I'm applying to *Carolina,*" she said. "I have to stay here."

"We should have you apply to a couple other schools, too, then," he said.

"You two lovebirds can talk about this later," Marty said. "Let go of each other so I can reach the pizza, okay?"

Tim let go of her hand and leaned back in his chair as Marty helped himself to another slice.

"There's one thing, though," Tim said. "A lot of people know that you and I are seeing each other. They'll ask you questions after I so-called *disappear.*"

She hadn't thought of that.

"So whether you agree to help out or not, you and I have to fake a breakup, okay?"

"*No.*" She felt like crying.

"It's for your own protection, CeeCee," he said. "We don't want anyone to think you're in on it. And it will all be an act."

This was so complicated. She loved things the way they were. She loved seeing him in the coffee shop in the morning and spending her leisure time in the beautiful mansion. Whatever she decided, things would never be the same. Andie's fate hung like a shroud over the brothers and she knew Tim would never rest until he'd done everything he could to save her.

"Okay?" Tim asked, when she didn't respond.

"When do we have to act like we're breaking up?"

"Soon," he said. "This week sometime. Even Ronnie has to think we did."

She nodded. She looked down at the piece of paper on the table. "If I helped out," she said, "the governor's wife would be able to identify me."

"We'll work up a real good disguise for you," Marty said. "Get a blond wig. Or maybe a redhead." He looked at her long wavy mane of dark hair. "Will that hair fit under a wig? Maybe you need to cut it."

"No, man," Tim interjected. "She's not cutting her hair."

"I can pin it tight to my head," she said, though it would be a challenge.

"I think you'd be a fine-looking blonde." Marty tipped his head to assess her. "And you'd wear a mask. Tell the wife a name other than CeeCee. She'll never know who you really are."

"Is there a phone at the cabin?" she asked. "How would I know what's going on between y'all and the governor?"

"There's no phone," Tim said. "Which is why we can't stay there for our negotiations."

"So, how will I know—"

"You won't, at least not right away. We're going to give him, like, three days. My guess is it'll only take a few hours."

Marty laughed. "Who knows, though? The dude might like having some time away from his old lady."

Tim didn't smile. He glanced at her list. "What else do you need to know?" he asked.

"Would I have to keep her tied up or something?"

"No," Tim said. "I mean, we might have to cuff her in order to transport her if she doesn't…cooperate. Once she's in the cabin, there are dead-bolt locks and you'd have the keys, so you wouldn't have to worry."

"She could scream, though. Neighbors could hear her."

"It's a very isolated area," Tim said.

"Ain't nobody for miles." Marty took a swallow of beer. "Might be bears, though. How d'you feel about bears?"

"Shut up, Marty," Tim said. "You're not helping."

"What if I fall asleep?" She couldn't believe she was asking questions as though she might actually agree to help them. "If it turns out to be two or three days, I'll have to sleep sometime."

"Well, yeah, you'll need to sleep," Tim said. "She might have to be handcuffed to something then. To her bed or something. You're smart enough to be the judge of what you need to do."

"She'd fight me, though, wouldn't she?" She could just see herself getting into a fistfight with the wife of the governor of North Carolina.

"You'll have a gun," Marty said.

Tim shot his brother a look. Marty had crossed some kind of line.

"I don't want a *gun,*" she said.

"We'll give you an empty one," Tim said. "Just to use as a threat."

The fact that Tim had a gun bothered her more than anything. She didn't want to lose sight of who he was: the man she was sure had given her five thousand dollars and who treated her like a gem and who loved her more than anyone had since her mother was alive. The serious graduate student who wanted to advocate for people who had no power of their own. Suddenly she gasped.

"Your degree!" she said. "If you do this…underground thing, how will you finish your degree?"

"Some things are more important."

"But you've worked so hard."

He smiled at her as if she were too young or too naive to understand. "It really doesn't matter all that much, CeeCee," he said. "It's a piece of paper versus my sister's life."

Marty leaned toward her. "The government kills innocent people all the time," he said. "Andie got fucking railroaded, and we're not going to let her be one of them."

"We won't be in this alone, CeeCee," Tim said. "Some other SCAPE people know what we're planning and are behind us one hundred percent and are ready to help. They live underground, so I'm not going to tell you much about them yet. Not that you'd tell anyone," he added quickly. "I know you wouldn't."

She shook her head.

"They live near this cabin we're talking about, so we can stay with them 'til we're ready to move on the whole thing," Tim continued. "We'll make sure the cabin has food and everything you'll need. They have an old car you can use, so the day of the…" He seemed suddenly hesitant to use the word *kidnapping.* "The day we do it, you'll drive to the cabin and we'll drive to Jacksonville where the house with the phone is and then meet you back at the cabin. Make sense?"

"How will you do it?" she asked. "How will you be able to get to her?"

"We know her schedule," Marty said. "She teaches an evening Spanish class at Carolina. It's dark when she gets out, so we'll nab her in the parking lot."

She pictured the scene: a woman walking alone to her car at night, two men jumping out of the darkness, muffling her screams with a hand over her mouth as they drag her into the rear of a van. "You'll *terrify* her," she said.

"Well, yeah." Marty laughed. "Brilliant deduction."

"We'll make it as easy on her as we can, babe," Tim said. "We won't hurt her. Our whole objective is to *prevent* people from being hurt."

She looked down at her plate, translucent with grease around her uneaten slice of pizza. Both men were quiet, as though they knew she needed a minute to absorb what they'd told her.

"When would you do it?" she asked finally.

"A few days before Thanksgiving," Tim said.

"And what if the governor says he'll commute Andie's sentence and then goes back on his word once his wife is home?" she asked.

"He'd damn well better not," Marty said in a threatening voice. "Or then we go to plan B and I don't think you want to know about that."

Alarmed, she looked at Tim. "What's plan B?"

"He's jiving you," Tim said. "We're not going to need a plan B. Plan A is foolproof." He pushed his plate away and lit a cigarette. "Don't decide right now, CeeCee," he said. "We'll finish up here, then have a nice relaxing night. In the morning, you can see how you feel about it."

After dinner, she and Tim went upstairs to his bedroom. They made love without uttering a word about the kidnapping, and she put it out of her mind as best she could, pretending that things would always be this easy between them. She lay awake after he'd drifted off, though, thinking. Other people were ready and willing to support Tim and Marty in their scheme. She found that reassuring; it made the plan seem less crazy. She thought of the photographs of Andie displayed around the house. Her beautiful smile. The brutal rape that had driven her to murder her attacker. She imagined how frightened Andie must have been during her trial as she concocted alibis to try to save herself. She'd failed miserably. Now it was up to her brothers to do whatever they could to save her. No one would be hurt. The objective was to *prevent* people from being hurt, Tim had said. And Andie's life would be saved.

Listen to your heart, her mother had written. Make a decision and dive in.

And that was exactly what she planned to do.

Chapter Eight

I want you to know what happened between your father and me. I met him at a high-school dance my sophomore year and he swept me off my feet. He didn't go to my school. I didn't find out 'til much later, but he was a dropout. He was a good liar and very handsome and charming. He had hair just like yours. Dark and wavy and kind of out of control and beautiful. As a matter of fact, he was kind of out of control and beautiful himself, and I think that's why I fell for him. He was just so different.

When I got pregnant with you, I was afraid to tell him. I was almost three months along before I got up the nerve. I had this fantasy that when I told him, he'd ask me to marry him and then he'd take care of me. I went over to his house—he lived with his parents—and we were hanging around in the rec room playing Ping-Pong while I tried to figure out what to say. He was in the bathroom when the phone rang. No one else was home, so I answered it. It was a girl asking to speak with him. Her name was Willa, and I knew she was pretty just by her voice. When he came out of the bathroom, I told him about the call and his face lit up. He didn't even try to hide it. We started playing Ping-Pong again, but I knew his mind was on Willa, because he was hitting the ball any old way. We finished the game and he said he didn't feel well so maybe I'd better go home. I left, and I knew I'd never hear from him again. I was right.

ONCE SHE TOLD TIM AND MARTY THAT SHE WOULD HELP them, she felt as if she were on a roller coaster. The ride started out nice and easy, as the brothers perfected their plan with little involvement from her, but she knew it was going to speed up quickly and she would have no way to get off.

Her role now was to set the stage for her breakup with Tim, so she began fabricating problems to discuss with Ronnie.

"He got a phone call from another girl while I was there last night," she confided to Ronnie as they dressed for work one morning. It was very early. Still dark outside.

"How do you know?" Ronnie pulled on her jeans, then peered over her shoulder to check them in the mirror, making sure they were flattering to her backside.

"I answered the phone," CeeCee said. She tugged a wide-toothed comb through her hair. "There was this pause. Then a girl's voice asked for Tim. He sounded happy to hear from her and went in another room to talk."

Ronnie turned to look at her, hands on her hips. "Did you ask him who it was?"

"No." CeeCee set down her comb. "I don't want to be clingy."

"You have a right to know." Ronnie was indignant. "You're in a serious relationship, not some fling. You should know everything."

CeeCee flopped down on her bed. "He seems...kind of distant all of a sudden," she said.

"CeeCee." Ronnie sat next to her. "You've given him the idea you're his, no matter what. It's really time you act like other guys are interested in you. And that you're interested in them. You've got to let him know he can't take you for granted."

"I don't want to pretend I'm interested in someone else," she said. "I just want Tim."

She was surprised when tears filled her eyes. It was easy to imagine how she would feel if she lost him, because that was currently her biggest worry. How were they going to continue their relationship with him in hiding? She'd raised the issue a few times since their meeting with Marty, and each time he would hold her close, reassuring her that they would work it out.

"It's too good between us to just throw it away," he'd say. If she pressured him for details, he'd get annoyed. "I don't *know* the specifics, CeeCee. I don't even know where I'm going to end up yet. You'll just have to trust me on this." She *did* trust him, but she'd never been comfortable with uncertainty.

He told her that the breakup had to be public. "Did you take drama in high school?" he asked one night as he drove her home after a movie.

She shook her head. "Did you?"

"Yes," he said. "So I figure, I'll pretend I'm really pissed at you for something." He glanced at her with his full-lipped smile. "I can't imagine what you could do to piss me off, though."

"I told Ronnie I thought you were interested in someone else."

"Brilliant!" He nodded appreciatively. "Except it makes me look like a shithead. I want the breakup to be your fault."

"Uh-uh," she said with a smile. "It's got to be yours."

"Okay," he said. "I've already asked enough of you, so I'll take the heat. We'll make it my fault. An old girlfriend's come back into my life and being a typical male asshole, I'm leaving you for her."

"What's she like?"

"She looks kind of like Telly Savalas, but she has some kind of hold on me," he said.

"*What?*" CeeCee laughed.

"She can be moody, too," Tim continued. "And she's hard to get, so I've always been intrigued with her. So, now that she wants me, I just can't help myself."

He seemed so absorbed with the fantasy that CeeCee felt uncomfortable. "This is all made up, right?"

"Oh, babe, do you think I could ever leave you?" Was there a trace of annoyance in the question? She was afraid she was starting to sound as insecure as she felt. "No other woman compares to you," he said. "You've got the world's most amazing hair and you're smart and you've organized my entire house and won my brother over. Plus, you're dynamite in bed."

She blushed at that. She was not dynamite in bed; she'd still not had an orgasm with him inside her. Maybe she didn't move enough or something. His fictional girlfriend was probably multiorgasmic. No wonder he wanted to go back to her. In her imagination, she named her Willa.

As planned, Tim came to the coffee shop two weeks before Thanksgiving. Instead of sitting in his booth, he asked CeeCee to walk outside with him. He looked appropriately troubled.

Ronnie was headed for the kitchen, and CeeCee caught her

arm. "Tim wants to talk to me in private," she whispered. "Could you cover my tables for a few minutes?"

Ronnie glanced at Tim. "What's going on?" she asked.

"I don't know." CeeCee shrugged. "Nothing, I hope."

"Go ahead," Ronnie said. "I'll cover."

She and Tim walked outside and stood on the sidewalk by the coffee-shop windows. Students walked past them in either direction, crowding them, brushing up against them, but they held their ground. This was to be a show, primarily for Ronnie's sake.

"Just remember I love you," he began.

She nodded. The sunlight gave him a halo of golden curls. She wanted to touch him but kept her arms folded rigidly across her chest.

"My old girlfriend's come back," he said. "And she made me realize that I was never really in love with you. I'm sorry. I need to break up with you."

"I *knew* it!" She stomped her foot on the sidewalk. "I knew there was someone else."

Tim started to smile at her false anger, but caught himself. "It only just happened," he said. "It's not like I've been with her all along or anything."

"How can you do this to me?" she shouted, louder than she'd intended to. A guy walking past her told her to "settle down."

"I never wanted to hurt you," Tim said. He hadn't shaved that morning; she could see the pale stubble on his cheeks.

"Well, you're doing a good job of it," she said. "What does she have that I don't have?"

"It's not you, CeeCee. It's me," he said. "You're wonderful and I just…it's completely my fault."

"Damn straight," she said.

"I'm really, really sorry." He put his hands on her shoulders, but she raised her arms quickly to cast him off. "Can you cry?" he asked.

She put her hands to her face and let her shoulders heave.

"That's better," Tim said. "I'd like to think that losing me would tear you apart. Like losing you would do to me." He pulled her toward him. "Okay, now I'll comfort you tenderly for one last time."

She buried her head on his shoulder. "Oh, Tim, I don't like this," she said.

"I know, babe." He patted her back in the halfhearted manner of a lover who's already moved on. "Me, neither. But you and I know what's really still between us. Come over tomorrow night, okay? Just be sure to show up after dark so no one sees you. And come around to the back door."

"Okay," she said.

He pulled away from her. "Now look pissed off before you go back in," he said.

"Pissed off isn't good enough." She wiped her dry eyes with the back of her hand. "I'm going for complete devastation."

"Don't forget who loves you." He winked at her.

"Ditto," she said, and without thinking, she drew back her hand and let it fly, her palm connecting with his stubbled cheek in a slap that turned every head on the street.

He looked at her, wide-eyed with shock as he raised his own hand to his crimson cheek.

"Oh, my God, Tim, I'm sorry." She tried to reach for him, but he backed away.

"That's it," he said. "I'll put your things out on the curb for you."

She watched him walk up Franklin Street, losing him quickly in the crowd of students. She looked down at her palm. What had gotten into her? And why had hitting him felt so good?

She was stoic once inside the restaurant, as she pretended to tamp down the raw emotions of a woman scorned. Ronnie was solicitous and comforting, and CeeCee knew that she and their manager, George, were talking about her behind her back. She hated being the object of their pity and she hated that they now viewed Tim as a selfish womanizer. But she knew this was only the beginning of her necessary lies.

Chapter Nine

I wish I could see you now, at sixteen. You're an amazing twelve-year-old, so I can only imagine you'll get more amazing as you get older. Yesterday, when the nurse tried to keep you out of my room because I was so sick, I could hear you talking to her through the closed door. You told her, "That's MY mother, not yours. I'll take care of her." Even though I had my head over the basin, it made me laugh. And it let me know how strong you are and that you're going to be just fine without me.

How did you ever get so brave?

EVEN THOUGH THEY WERE ONLY A FEW MILES OUTSIDE OF Chapel Hill, the tension in Tim's van was already so thick CeeCee could feel it on her skin. They still had a good hour and a half before they reached New Bern. The bucket seat felt lumpy to her, pressing against her back in the wrong places. Marty sat on a beach chair turned sideways behind Tim's seat. He held a hand-drawn map on one knee and a beer bottle on the other, and he and Tim had been arguing about which roads to take since pulling out of their driveway. She wanted to tell them to shut up; if they couldn't agree on something as simple as how to get to New Bern, how were they going to make the more critical decisions that lay ahead of them in the next couple of days? But she said nothing, afraid of making Tim any more agitated than he already was. They were on edge, all of them. These were their last few hours as law-abiding citizens.

The mattress in the back of the van was covered with suitcases, duffel bags and backpacks. It had taken Tim a full day to pack and she'd felt sorry for him as she watched him weigh what to take and what to leave behind. He and Marty would never be returning to the mansion. She, on the other hand, brought only a couple of changes of clothes and her toothbrush. That was all she expected to need. Three days, max, Tim had told her. Then Andie would be safe, the governor's wife returned to hearth and home, and CeeCee could go back to Chapel Hill.

She was in charge of the cassette tapes on this trip. The Eagles, of course. Creedence and Queen and Chicago and old Stones. None of it very soothing.

"Turn that crap off," Marty snapped at her when Queen started singing "We are the Champions."

"Don't talk to her that way," Tim said.

"It's all right," she said, pressing the eject button. "What do you want to hear, Marty?"

"I don't know." He sounded desolate all of a sudden. "Stones, I guess."

She put in the cassette, and "Under my Thumb" filled the van.

"Turn it down," Tim said.

She did. She would do whatever she was told to keep peace in the van.

Tim turned onto a highway, and Marty grabbed his shoulder from behind. "I told you not to go this way!" he shouted.

"Let go of me." Tim's knuckles were white on the steering wheel. "It's a straight shot from here, Marty."

"Stop it, you two!" she said. "We have to pull together, okay? Y'all told me this would be easy and now you're at each other's throats."

The two men shut up, probably stunned into silence by the fact that she'd confronted them more than by her request to stop fighting. No one said a word for nearly an hour. She put on the Eagles when the Stones tape was finished, then tried to get comfortable as she watched the terrain grow flatter, broken up by miles and miles of tall pines. The small houses were acres apart from one another. Some of them were well maintained, with white wrought-iron railings on the front steps and gazing globes in their yards. Others had sheet plastic over the windows, sloppily patched roofs and weedy, knee-high lawns.

"We're in the boonies, boys and girls." Marty finally broke the silence.

"The boonier, the better," Tim said.

Marty leaned forward between the bucket seats and pointed to an opening in a grove of pines. "Turn here," he said. She could smell tobacco and beer on his breath.

Tim turned onto a narrow one-lane road.

"Now, watch for a road off to the right," Marty said. "It's about a mile down, I think."

He knew the couple who would put them up for the night, and he'd been to their house once before.

"Is that it?" Marty leaned even farther between the seats to peer out the front window.

CeeCee spotted a road veering off to the right.

"Yeah," Marty answered his own question. "Turn here."

Tim did as he was told. They were on a rutted dirt road, so tightly surrounded by pines and shrubs that the sun was stolen from them and branches scraped the side of the van. It was three in the afternoon, but it might as well have been evening for all the light on the road.

They grew quiet as they bounced along. The cassette tape ended, but CeeCee didn't even notice. In the silence, she could almost hear her heart beating. In a few minutes, everything would change and their journey would begin in earnest. Guiltily she hoped something would interfere with their plan. The kidnapping was to occur the following night. Maybe the woman would be ill and unable to teach her class. Maybe the people they were going to stay with would talk Tim and Marty out of the whole crazy idea.

She'd told Ronnie and George that she was taking Thanksgiving week off to visit a high-school friend who now lived in Pennsylvania. George was annoyed, but Ronnie was so supportive that CeeCee felt guilty.

"You need to get away," Ronnie said. "You've been so down since the breakup with Tim."

She wasn't depressed, but she'd apparently done a good job of acting as though she were. She saw Tim nearly as much as before the so-called breakup. She'd lie to Ronnie about meeting a friend for dinner, then go to Tim's house for lovemaking and reassurance that everything would turn out all right.

"You sure this is it?" Tim asked now, after they'd driven through the dark tunnel of trees for several minutes.

"Yes, I'm sure," Marty said. A house suddenly appeared in a small clearing on the right. "That's it," he said.

The house was tiny, the white paint peeling. Smoke rose from the crumbling top of the brick chimney. A rusting swing set stood near the woods, and a little girl swung on it, leaning back so far that her long blond hair dusted the ground. Three cars, ancient and rusting, sat in the weeds on the other side of the house, and a truck and an old VW bus were parked next to them.

"Looks like Forrest has a leak," Marty said, and CeeCee noticed a man on the roof spreading a piece of blue sheet plastic over the shingles. He stood up as they pulled in behind the old cars, and he hesitated a moment before heading for the ladder that rested against the eaves.

Two mangy dogs, barking and baring teeth, ran up to the van as CeeCee and the men started to get out. She was afraid of the dogs, but she didn't want Tim to think she was a chicken. If she couldn't handle two dogs, how was she going to handle the task she'd agreed to?

"Hi, fellas," she said, holding her arms close to her sides. The dogs sniffed her legs, tails rising into uncertain wags.

The man climbed down the ladder from the roof and approached them. He was tall, bearded and big-boned but not overweight. He looked like someone accustomed to physical work. He wiped his hand on the rag hanging from his belt, then reached out to shake Marty's.

"What's the buzz, bro?" he asked.

"Not much," Marty answered. "This is my brother, Tim, and his girlfriend, CeeCee. And this is Forrest."

The little girl ran from the swing set and grabbed on to Forrest's leg. "Is this the company?" she asked.

Forrest rested one big hand on the child's head. "Yes, honey," he said, then to the three of them, "And this is Dahlia."

"I'm five," Dahlia said.

CeeCee laughed nervously, charmed by the little girl's blue-eyed beauty. "Wow, five," she said. "Are you in kindergarten?"

"Mommy teaches me," Dahlia said. "Where does your hair end?" She let go of her father to walk behind CeeCee. "It's all the way to your bottom!" she said, delighted. "I'm going to grow *my* hair that long."

"Leave her alone, Dahlia," Forrest said. His voice was gruff, all business. "You guys have any trouble finding us?"

"No problem," Tim said. "We'll just have to figure out how to get from here to the cabin."

It was the first time the cabin had been mentioned on this trip, but as much as she would have liked to, CeeCee had not forgotten about it. That was where she would create the prison for the governor's wife.

"I've got a map you can take a look at," Forrest said.

"Great." Tim nodded.

They followed Forrest through the front door. The inside of the house was an unexpected contrast to the ramshackle exterior. There was a fire in the small fireplace and the living room smelled of smoke and something else, something savory. The furniture was old and threadbare, but the room was neat and cozy. They walked through the living room into a kitchen, where a woman, dressed in a long pale yellow skirt and blue-trimmed peasant blouse, pulled a loaf of bread from the oven.

"Smells good in here," Tim said.

The woman set the bread next to two other loaves on the counter and shut the oven door. She did not look pleased to see them.

"Naomi," Forrest said, as he lifted Dahlia onto his shoulders. "You remember Marty?"

"You shouldn't have come here, Marty," the woman said. Her shoulder-length hair was light brown, part of it caught in a barrette on the back of her head.

Marty ignored her comment. "This is Tim and his girlfriend, CeeCee," he said.

A small cry came from the corner of the room, and CeeCee noticed a cradle near the doorway. Naomi walked over to it and lifted a baby into her arms. She walked out of the room, jostling the baby, cooing to him.

"She's upset you're here," Forrest said, looking toward the door through which Naomi had disappeared. "You have to understand, it's been years for us. We've got a good life here and she's afraid you'll screw it up."

"That ain't gonna happen," Marty said.

"I know." Forrest reached over his head to tickle his daughter, who giggled and covered his eyes with her hands. "Don't get me wrong," Forrest said, prying Dahlia's hands from his face. "Naomi's got a good heart. She knows what you're doing and supports you in it, but she doesn't want us to be part of it. So I'm telling you boys—" he looked from Marty to Tim "—forget you were ever here. You, too, CeeCee. You can stay with us tonight and we'll give you a car, like I said, but once you're out of here, you just forget you ever saw the place."

"A car?" CeeCee asked. Why did they need a car?

"You'll need one when this is over," Tim said. "You know, when

Marty and I take off. You'll have to go back to—" He suddenly slapped his forehead with his palm. "Damn!" he said. "You probably don't even have your license yet, do you?"

"I do. I'm supposed to have an adult with me, but I know how to drive." She cringed. She'd said *adult* as though she were not one herself, but Tim didn't seem to notice.

"Good," he said. "That's great. So you can use one of Forrest's."

"Not just *use* it," Forrest corrected. "*Keep* it. We've got more than we need, and like I said, we don't want any of you coming back here leaving a trail behind you for the pigs to follow."

"What pigs, Daddy?" Dahlia asked.

Forrest lifted Dahlia off his shoulders and set her on the floor. He leaned down. "The little pig that went to market," he said.

Dahlia ran out of the room, squealing with laughter as her father chased after her.

Tim turned to Marty. "You said they'd be happy to help us," he said. "Overjoyed. Isn't that the word you used?"

"Fuck off," Marty said. "It's gonna be fine."

They ate beef stew and honey-wheat bread for supper, and no one said a word about the plans for the following day. It took CeeCee a while to realize that was for Dahlia's sake: they wouldn't talk about it with a child in the room. Dahlia talked to CeeCee throughout the meal, telling her about the latest geography lesson she'd had from her mother, in which she learned the names of the states in alphabetical order. She rattled them off with only a few mistakes. When supper was over, Forrest handed the baby to Naomi, who sat back in her chair, tucked the infant beneath her peasant blouse, and began to nurse him.

"Dahlia," Naomi said, "would you go into the other room now and play? We need to have some grown-up time."

Dahlia grabbed CeeCee's hand. "Let me show you my toys," she said, as though she knew CeeCee would be more comfortable playing with her than she would staying with the "grownups."

"Go ahead," Tim said. "We'll fill you in on anything you need to know later."

Letting Dahlia drag her into the living room, she felt relieved. The conversation in the kitchen wasn't going to be pretty. *Please talk them out of it,* she thought to herself. *Please.*

"This is my Barbie." Dahlia sat down on the braided rug and pulled a brunette Barbie doll from her toy box. It seemed laughable that this child of hippies owned a Barbie doll.

"She's pretty." CeeCee sat down next to her.

"She's from a garage sale," Dahlia said, running a finger over the doll's miniature denim jeans. "So I'm happy I could give her a good home."

CeeCee smiled. The little girl touched her heart. She heard Tim say something in the kitchen but couldn't make out the words. Forrest's voice, deep and resonant, responded. Then Naomi said something unintelligible. She should be in there, taking part in their discussion.

What's wrong with you? she asked herself. She felt very young, as though she truly belonged here with Dahlia instead of in the kitchen. She was sixteen and looked more like fifteen and felt more like thirteen. Did everyone know it? Were they whispering about her in there? Wondering if it had been a mistake to involve her and if she was up to the task?

"We're not dragging you into anything!" Marty suddenly shouted. Someone else said, "Shh!"

Dahlia looked at CeeCee, alarmed. "Why is that man yelling?" she asked.

"Oh, it's nothing," she said. "He yells a lot. That's the way he is."

Dahlia looked toward the kitchen for a moment, then returned her attention to the toy box. "And this is my wedding doll," she said, pulling out a naked baby doll.

"A wedding doll?" CeeCee asked, confused.

"Wet-ting!" Dahlia said. She lifted the doll so CeeCee could see the hole between its legs. "She *pees*."

"Oh!" She laughed. "I get it."

There was an innocence in Dahlia that she envied. The little girl had no idea what her parents were discussing with Tim and Marty. She had no idea that her parents had once done something illegal and had at one time been known by other names. They'd had other lives. Was this how Tim would end up? Would she have to drive miles into the woods to be able to see him?

"You have pretty eyes." Dahlia stared at her.

"Thank you." CeeCee stroked her hand over the girl's hair. "And you have the prettiest hair I've ever seen in my life."

"It's gossamer," the girl said.

"It is." CeeCee smiled. She wanted a child like this someday. She looked toward the kitchen. She couldn't see Tim, but she could picture his green eyes and blond curls and full lips. They could have beautiful children together. She wanted to raise children the right way, with both a mother and a father. She would write letters to them every year, in case she died. She teared up at the thought.

Dahlia reached out to gently touch CeeCee's cheek. "Why are you crying?" she asked.

"Oh, I think my eyes are a little burny today." CeeCee used her fingertips to wipe away the tears. "I'm allergic to something, maybe."

"Agnes?" Dahlia pointed to the cat asleep on the back of the couch. "Mom's friend is allergic to her."

"Maybe," she said. "It's not too bad."

Naomi came into the room, the baby, whose name was Emmanuel, in a sling tied over her shoulder. She squatted down next to Dahlia, her skirt flowing over her knees and touching the floor.

"Hope she's not wearing you out," she said to CeeCee. Her smile looked forced.

"Not at all," CeeCee said.

Naomi smoothed a hand over her daughter's head. "Time for you to get ready for bed," she said.

"No, Mom," Dahlia said. "I can stay up 'cause of company."

"This company has a lot to do tomorrow, so we can't tire them out." Naomi stood up, her hands under the sling and her baby's little body. "Come on," she said. "Hop to it."

The little girl got to her feet. She leaned over and kissed CeeCee's cheek. "Good night. I love you," she said, then turned and ran toward the hall.

CeeCee watched her go. "She's the nicest girl," she said.

"Thank you." Naomi watched her daughter disappear into a room at the end of the hall. "She's an angel most of the time." She turned to CeeCee. "You come with me," she said.

CeeCee followed her down the hallway. They walked past a bedroom just big enough for a double mattress on the floor.

"You and Tim can sleep in there." Naomi nodded toward the room. "Marty can have the sofa." She poked her head into another bedroom, this one with bunk beds. Dahlia was sitting on the bottom bunk, a Golden Book open on her lap.

"You can skip your bath tonight," Naomi said to her.

"Yippee!" Dahlia bounced on the bed.

"Daddy and I will come in later to tuck you in."

"Okay," she said, returning her attention to her book.

"She loves when we have company," Naomi said as she turned the corner into the bedroom at the end of the hall. "Partly because she can't tie up the bathroom."

This had to be Naomi and Forrest's room. The double mattress rested on a frame off the floor and there were two old mismatched dressers. The room was poorly lit and smelled stuffy.

"Sit here in front of the mirror," Naomi said.

Obediently, CeeCee sat on the edge of the mattress. She felt young and shy with Naomi, who had to be at least fifteen years her senior. In the dim light, she could barely see herself in the mirror above the dresser. She looked a little like a nun—pale-faced, with a habit made of long brown hair.

Emmanuel let out a whimper as Naomi lifted him from the sling.

"Can you hold him for a minute?" she asked. "I have to get something out of the closet."

"I'd love to." She took the baby from Naomi's arms and cradled him on her shoulder. Emmanuel mewed a little, then let his head fall against her as he sucked his fingers. His feathery blond hair brushed her cheek, and she pressed her lips to his temple. "How old is he?" she asked.

"Four months." Naomi opened a closet that was so neatly organized CeeCee felt a kinship with her. The outside of the house and its yard were a mess, but inside, it was clear that Naomi was in control.

"You really have a nice house," she said, as Naomi climbed onto a step stool inside the closet.

"Thanks." Naomi reached for a cardboard box on the shelf above the clothes. "We've been in it eight years, which is hard for me to believe. Time flies." Grunting a little, she lowered the box to her chest and stepped off the stool. "Eight years, CeeCee." Blowing away the thin layer of dust on the top of the box, she set it on the bed. "We've worked so hard to build a new life for ourselves here," she said. "I know I've been…I've been an ungracious hostess tonight. Forrest thinks that helping you is no big deal. And I think what the three of you are doing is magnificent. I don't disapprove at all, don't get me wrong. That girl—Andie—she's a victim of the system and you're doing what needs to be done."

It meant something to her, hearing Naomi say that. She trusted this capable woman, and if Naomi thought what they were doing was magnificent, then maybe it was.

"But involving us…" Naomi's voice trailed off as she looked at Emmanuel, asleep on CeeCee's shoulder. "We have too much to lose now."

"I'm sorry." She felt terrible. "I just went along with what they told me. They said SCAPE members would help us and I—"

"And we *will* help you. Just please…please forget you ever met us."

CeeCee nodded. "I will," she said. "We will."

"Now let me take him back so we can give you an alter ego." Naomi lifted Emmanuel from CeeCee's arms and settled him once again in the sling. She opened the top of the box. "You've never done anything like this before, I take it," she said.

"Like what?" CeeCee asked.

"Something you need a disguise for." Naomi began pulling out wigs and masks.

"Oh," CeeCee said. She was amazed that anyone would have a box of disguises in her closet. "No, I haven't."

Naomi put her fist into a short brunette wig and fluffed up the curls. "I hope it's not only your first time, but also your last," she said.

"Me, too," CeeCee said.

Naomi set down the dark wig, then pulled out one with fluffy blond hair. She turned it upside down and gave it a shake. "It's brave and loving, what you're doing," she said. "I'd like to think that if my kids were ever in the position Andie is, someone like you would help them out of it. But we have to make sure you can't be identified. Not just for your sake, but for ours. So if you ever wake up in the middle of the night with a guilty conscience, kindly don't turn yourself in. They'll pick your brain until you can't see straight, and the next thing you know, you'll lead them right to our door."

"I won't," CeeCee reassured her again. "Tim said it's really impossible for me to get caught. That there's no way they can figure out where we'll be holding the wife."

"You'll be spending a lot of time with her, though. And once she's free, they'll be looking for the person who held her hostage. That's why this disguise has to be foolproof." She held up four wigs, two in each hand. "So, which color do you like?" she asked.

CeeCee was still stuck on her words: *They'll be looking for the person who held her hostage.* God, that was a frightening sentence!

She studied the fake-looking hair with a new intensity. "This one." She pointed to the blond wig. "It's as different from mine as it can be."

Naomi dropped the other wigs to the bed. "Put your hair up and we'll pin it." She stood up, one hand under Emmanuel, and pulled a box of bobby pins from a dresser drawer. CeeCee wrapped her hair around and around her head, flattening it in place with the pins. Then she pulled on the wig.

"A perfect fit," Naomi said. "How does it feel?"

"Okay," she said. She looked in the mirror. It was clown hair, thick and curly and silly looking. She touched it with her hands, then closed her eyes, suddenly weary. "Naomi, can I ask you a question?"

"You can always ask," Naomi said. "Whether I answer is another matter."

"I'm..." She wasn't sure how to express her thought.

Naomi had her hands in the box again. "You're what?" she asked.

"I'm worried about how Tim and I will get to see each other after this is over, with him having to go underground and everything."

"It won't be easy." Naomi pulled out a black eye patch, glanced at it, then tossed it on the bed. "Forrest and I managed to find a way, though."

"But you're *both* in hiding, right?"

"We met in SCAPE many years ago," she said, "but more than that, it's better you don't know."

"Okay," she said. She was catching on that no one wanted to know too much about anyone else in this business.

"You have very distinctive features." Naomi studied her face. "You'll really need a full-face kind of mask." She rummaged through the box and pulled out a plastic mask, the face of a princess topped by a gold crown. "I think this is supposed to be Sleeping Beauty or something," she said. "It might be a little small." She stretched the elastic over CeeCee's head and set the mask in place. "No, it's perfect," she said. "Can you breathe okay?"

"I can breathe," she said, although she wondered how long she could wear the mask without going crazy.

"Good. Don't take it off while you're with the wife. If you have to eat, do it where she can't see you. And try to disguise your voice when you talk to her," Naomi said. "And the final thing is, you don't want to leave fingerprints anywhere in the house or cabin or whatever it is. So." She pulled out a plastic bag filled with gloves. Yellow rubber gloves. Clear latex gloves like a doctor would wear. Heavy wool men's gloves. "Let's go with these light white ones." Naomi handed her a pair of lacy white gloves. They looked as though they'd never been worn. "Try them on."

CeeCee pulled on the gloves. The fabric was stretchy and felt warm on her hands. "Good thing it's not summer or I'd die in this getup," she said.

Naomi nodded, adjusting the mask a little. "It *was* summer when I had to wear a disguise," she said. "I threw away that mask. I never wanted to see it again."

"What were you?"

"What do you mean?"

"Like, I'm sort of Sleeping Beauty..."

"Oh. I was some kind of space alien or something. It was weird."

"Can you tell me what you did?" she asked. *Was it as bad as what I'm going to do?*

"That's one question you don't ask someone who's gone underground," Naomi said. "It would put both you and me in jeopardy. I don't like that we know as much as we do about what you guys are plotting." She put the other wigs back in the box. "I'll tell you though, people died because of what Forrest and I did. That part was an accident. We never meant that to happen, but we'd end up on death row alongside Andie if we got caught. And our kids…" Naomi's voice trailed off. She peered into the sling at her son, then closed her eyes for a moment as though imagining the worst.

CeeCee shivered. She could feel the dread that hung over Naomi's world. "You won't get caught," she said, as if she knew that for a fact. She looked at herself in the mirror. A blond Sleeping Beauty stared back at her. "I can't believe I'm really going to do this."

"You're scared?" Naomi asked.

CeeCee nodded.

Naomi closed the box and moved it to the floor. "Think of a time you were courageous," she said.

CeeCee thought. She'd never done anything that qualified as courageous. "I can't think of anything."

"I don't mean mountain climbing," Naomi said. "I mean something courageous you did in your everyday life."

She suddenly remembered being with her mother when she died. She'd been terrified, unable to imagine what it would be like to be with her when life left her body, yet she knew her mother needed her there, and so she stayed. She held her mother's bruised hand as she left the world. It had taken all the courage she had.

"Did you think of something?" Naomi asked.

"I stayed with my mother while she died," she said.

"Oh, CeeCee." Naomi touched her shoulder. "How old were you?"

"Twelve."

"Damn, you *were* courageous," Naomi said. "I couldn't have done that when I was twelve. When you start getting nervous, remember the courage you had that day and you'll start feeling it again. Okay?"

She doubted it would be that simple. "All right. I'll try." CeeCee lifted the mask from her head. "Thanks, Naomi," she said. "For everything."

She and Tim made love on the mattress in the small bedroom that night. Her body felt even more numb than usual when he entered her, and she was angry at it. She thought of Ronnie telling her to fake it. Who knew when she and Tim would get to make love again? How long would they be apart? It would be a gift for him. A gift that would keep her in his mind until they were together again.

She began to pant, to writhe a little beneath him. Not wanting to overdo it, she only let a small moan escape her lips, but she felt his excitement mount and she grew more vocal. It was pretty easy once she got into it. She arched her back, biting the corner of the pillow as she shuddered with her counterfeit orgasm.

Tim came an instant after her performance. "Oh, babe," he said, his breath hot against her ear. "That was the best ever. The best *ever*."

"It was," she agreed.

He rolled onto his side, pulling the covers over her shoulder as he held her close.

"I love you so much."

"I love you, too," he said. "I want you to know how much I appreciate what you're doing for me. For Andie. It's so generous."

"Thank you." She liked the acknowledgment.

"And that was phenomenal sex."

"It was," she said again. She felt guilty for misleading him.

"You weren't faking that, were you?"

Damn. Why did he have to ask her straight out like that? How could she lie to the man she loved? It would make a mockery of their relationship.

"Of course not," she said, her heart sinking a little with the words.

Tim let out a long sigh. "Tomorrow's going to be hard, babe," he said. "And I realized when I saw you in that Sleeping Beauty getup that you have the hardest job of the three of us. Do you regret saying you'd help us?"

She hesitated. Did she? She was doing something magnificent, Naomi had said. "I don't think I'll know the answer to that until it's over," she said. "I...you know what I'll regret, Tim. I've told you so many times, you're sick of hearing it."

"What?" He sounded puzzled. How could he possibly not know?

"I'm worried about how we'll ever get to see each other again," she said.

He hugged her. "That, my little Sleeping Beauty, should be the least of your worries."

What did he mean? Why couldn't he, for once, tell her exactly how they would work it out? She was tired of his vague responses to the question. She needed to know more. She needed details. And this was her last chance to ask for them.

"Tim," she whispered, gathering her courage, "I need to know what you mean when you say it will work out. At least tell me what might happen. How will you be able to let me know where you are? How can you do that without putting yourself…putting both of us, at risk?"

He didn't respond, and she turned to look at him. His eyes were closed, his breathing soft and even, and she knew she would get no answers from him tonight.

Chapter Ten

It just occurred to me that you might have your driver's license by now. All I can say about that is "Watch out, world!"

THERE WAS SOMETHING NO ONE HAD ANTICIPATED: Although CeeCee knew how to drive—barely—she'd never driven a stick shift. She'd had her provisional license less than a year, and her foster mother had let her drive their car to run close-to-home errands, but the clutch and stick shift were alien to her. So alien that she hadn't even thought to mention it the night before, when they'd told her she could have one of Naomi and Forrest's cars.

"All we've got is manual." Forrest blew out a stream of smoke and looked from one rusted car to another. The dented vehicles appeared no better in the morning light than they had the afternoon before. Their paint was worn so thin it was hard to tell what colors they'd once been.

She shivered inside her jacket. "I'm sorry," she said to Tim.

"Why didn't you tell us you couldn't drive?" Marty asked.

"I *can* drive," she insisted. "Just not a stick."

"Okay." Tim put his hand on her neck and gave it a squeeze. There was so much strength in his fingers that she wasn't sure if the gesture was affectionate or threatening in nature. "It's no big deal," he said. "She's smart. I'll teach her in ten minutes."

Thank God, Naomi and Forrest lived in the middle of nowhere so that she and Tim had the dirt road to themselves. The car bucked and stalled as she tried to find the balance between the gas pedal and the clutch. She felt nervous laughter bubbling up inside of her, but she stifled it, knowing that Tim was in no mood to make light of the situation. He'd awakened in his own head that morning. Any warm words from the night before were forgotten. He was a man on a mission to save his sister and that was it.

"Well," Tim said, as they parked the car in the yard after her lesson. "The good news is that there's not much damage you can do out here in this thing. You'd better take your time getting back to Chapel Hill, though. You're not ready for the highway."

Inside the kitchen later that evening, CeeCee hung back, rocking Emmanuel in her arms, while the three men studied the map spread out on the kitchen table. Naomi was baking trays of granola in the oven and the smell was tantalizing.

Tim looked over his shoulder at CeeCee. "You should take a look at this, babe," he said.

"Here, let me take him from you so you can see." Naomi slipped the baby from CeeCee's arms and into the ever-present sling she wore over her shoulder.

CeeCee stepped between Tim and Forrest and leaned over the table.

"We're here right now." Tim pointed to a spot on the map. "And the cabin is here." He ran his finger over barely visible lines on the map until he reached a long narrow strip of blue. "That's the Neuse River. The cabin's right next to the river, on a road that's not on the map," he said, "but I'll remember it when I see it."

"Where do we get groceries?" CeeCee asked.

"Closest store is ten miles from here," Forrest said. "Over here." He pointed to a spot on the map.

When they'd figured out their route, CeeCee and Tim took the van to the grocery store. At Tim's insistence, she wore her gloves as they perused the aisles so that any groceries she touched would not bear her prints. They bought canned tuna, soup and vegetables, a loaf of bread, toilet paper, paper towels, tissues, eggs, pasta, peanut butter, cookies, tomato sauce and two pounds of ground beef.

"All this?" CeeCee asked worriedly as Tim put the ground beef in the cart. "How long do you really think this will take?"

"I'm still hoping for a few hours," he said. "Overnight at the most. But you should have enough food in case it's longer."

They drove back to Naomi and Forrest's house, where CeeCee transferred the groceries to the old car that she could now, for what it was worth, call her own. Marty decided to ride with her, in case she had any problems with the clutch, and they would follow Tim to the cabin. They said goodbye to their hosts, who couldn't mask their looks of relief at seeing them leave.

She stayed close behind Tim in the old car. Twice she stalled, once at a turn and once on a hill when she stepped on the brake instead of the clutch. To his credit, Marty didn't utter a word. He was too wound up to chide her, she thought. All three of them were so focused on what lay ahead that they barely noticed what was happening around them.

Ahead of her, Tim turned onto a road that was even more rutted than the one Naomi and Forrest lived on. She felt every jarring dip of the road in her spine, and Marty put his hand on the dashboard for balance. They were in the middle of nowhere. There was nothing except acres of tall pines and the narrow ribbon of dirt on which she was driving.

Finally they came to a fork in the road. Ahead of her, Tim stopped his van and although she couldn't see him, she imagined he was looking in one direction, then the other.

"I think we go right," Marty said. He had started to open the car door when Tim apparently came to the same conclusion, driving onto the right tine of the fork. CeeCee followed him, her hands gripping the steering wheel as potholes threatened to wrench it from her grasp.

"Man," Marty said, looking from left to right and back again. "Not sure how we're going to find this place. It's so overgrown out here."

Just then, Tim turned right onto a gravel road. She followed him and, after about a hundred yards, spotted the corner of a building.

"All *right!*" Marty gave the dashboard a celebratory slap with his palm. "Eureka!"

The minuscule cabin was sided with bleached-looking cedar. It had white shutters, a cutout of a pine tree on the bottom of each one, and a steeply sloping roof. It appeared to be in good shape. Better than Naomi and Forrest's house, at any rate. She parked behind the van, and as soon as she opened the car door, she heard the roar of rushing water.

"Come see the river!" Tim shouted to them over the din.

They climbed over rocks and tree roots to the rear of the cabin, where the yard fell away to the bank of the river. The water swirled over a cluster of smooth boulders, striking them with such force that thousands of small puffs of foam shot into the air. She could feel the spray on her cheeks.

"Isn't this a cool place?" Tim came to stand beside her.

"It's nice," she agreed. She wished she were looking forward to a romantic week in the cabin with Tim instead of a few hours with a woman she didn't know. Being here made it all so real. She held her jacket closed against the chill air and stepped away from the river. What was she doing? What had she gotten herself into?

"Do you have your gloves?" Tim asked.

She pulled them out of her pocket.

"Put them on now," he said. "And don't take them off until you're miles away from here, okay?"

She helped the men carry the groceries and her small suitcase into the cabin. It was cold inside and Tim turned the knob on the thermostat. The electric baseboard heat clicked on, and the smell of burning dust quickly filled the air.

The cabin was a small square box, divided into three main rooms—a living room and two bedrooms—as well as a tiny kitchen and tinier bathroom. She and Tim put away the groceries in silence. The empty pantry had mouse droppings on every shelf. She turned on the faucet, which did nothing, and Tim searched for the shutoff, finally locating it in a cupboard. The water poured from the tap in a rusty-brown stream.

"It'll clear," Tim said. "Just let it run a while."

She dampened the paper towel with the brown water and wiped

away the mouse droppings, then lined the open trash can in the corner with one of the grocery bags.

"Let's check out the place," Tim said, taking her gloved hand.

One bedroom had a double bed with an iron headboard. The other had two sets of bunk beds.

"This is the room Marty and Andie and I would stay in when we visited our cousins," Tim said, a look of nostalgia in his eyes. "We brought sleeping bags, because there were too many of us." He lifted the bedspread from the corner of the upper bunk. "Maybe you should have the governor's wife sleep up here," he said. "That way she can't do anything fast and fake you out. You can cuff her to the headboard if you end up being here overnight."

"Okay," she said, but she was thinking, *This isn't really going to happen.* "Where are the…the handcuffs?" she asked.

Tim gave a quick nod as though he'd only now remembered them. "I've got them in the van in case we need them when we pick her up," he said. "I'll give them to you when we bring her tonight."

"Tim…" She was still wearing her jacket and folded her arms across herself in an anxious hug. "I'm nervous," she said. "You're going to just drop her off here with me and then leave, and I'm somehow supposed to keep her from escaping during the night. Couldn't you at least stay here for a while after you bring her?"

"Squ-a-awk! Squ-a-awk!" Marty walked into the room making barnyard noises. "Do I detect a chicken in here?" he asked.

CeeCee ignored him. "Please?" she asked Tim.

"Can't, babe," Tim said. "We've got to start on the negotiations right away and we can't do that from here. You know that. We have to strike while the iron is hot." He tugged a strand of her hair and gave her a distracted smile. "It's going to be fine." Reaching into his jacket pocket, he pulled out two keys held together by a rubber band. "These are to the dead bolts," he said, handing them to her. "We've got to take off now."

"Already?" she asked, startled. "You've got to leave *now?*"

He nodded. "We have to be in the parking lot when her class gets out." He kissed her cheek. "You're gonna do great."

She wasn't so sure. Through the bedroom window, she watched the brothers leave the cabin. Daylight was fading, highlighting Tim in its red sunset glow, and he looked slim and young and vulnerable. What if the police caught him during the kidnapping? What if they killed him? Her heart twisted at the thought. How would she ever know? She had no way to communicate with the outside world.

She locked the dead bolts on the front and back doors and pocketed the keys. Then she checked the windows. All but one were swollen too tight to raise, although she supposed her captive could break the glass. Even with the windows closed, the sound of the rushing river filled the cabin.

The bunk beds were neatly covered with bedspreads, but unmade. She found musty-smelling sheets and pillowcases in the closet of the larger bedroom and made the bottom bunk of one set and the top bunk of the other. She wandered through the rooms, peering into closets stuffed with sleeping bags, blankets and games. The medicine cabinet contained a bottle of aspirin, a packet of razor blades and some dental floss. She found cleaning supplies under the kitchen sink, so she scrubbed the counters and then cleaned the sink and tub in the little bathroom. There were a few books on a shelf in the living room, and she sat down on the ragged living-room sofa and tried to read, but concentration was impossible.

Giving up, she lifted her legs onto the couch, wrapped her arms around them, and tried to push away the dark and troubled thoughts that filled her mind.

Chapter Eleven

You don't get scared very often, but you shake like a leaf when you do. You came into my room this afternoon, trembling all over, and I knew Dr. Watts must have told you I don't have much longer. You were trying hard to hide your fear. You handed me a glass of juice and spilled it all over the blanket and when you tried to clean it up, your hands and arms were shaking so hard, you couldn't. I felt so bad for you. I wanted to fix it, like I do your scraped knees and bee stings. But there was nothing I could do except hold you. I held you until you finally stopped shaking. Do you remember?

NIGHT FELL EARLY OUTSIDE THE CABIN. SHE ATE TUNA FROM the can for supper, barely tasting it. There were no shades at the windows, and she felt exposed to whatever or whoever might be lurking in the woods. A strong breeze came up and the world outside crackled with the sound of swaying branches. She jumped at a thud on the small front porch and unlocked the dead bolt to peer into the darkness, but the chilly wind made her shiver and she quickly shut the door and bolted it again.

Should she sleep? Who knew when she'd next get the chance? She turned off all the lights in the house and lay down on the bottom bunk bed she'd made, but she was trembling all over. She got under the covers, but the blankets didn't help; it was not the cold that was making her shiver. How was she going to control a grown woman? She'd felt so young these past few days, so aware of the age difference between her and Tim and Marty and Naomi and Forrest. She wondered again if Tim regretted asking a mere kid to be responsible for an important part of his plan. He should have asked the girl from SCAPE.

She curled into a ball. Maybe they wouldn't be able to get the governor's wife. *Please don't let them get her.* Tim would be sorely disappointed and she felt bad about that, but self-preservation was kicking into gear.

The slamming of a car door jolted her awake. She sat up in the darkness, still shivering, although the cabin had grown quite warm. She heard voices outside. Jumping from the bed, she ran into the living room to peer through the window into the darkness. She couldn't see anything at first, and she felt dizzy, as though she might pass out or throw up. Her heart pounded in her ears, and she grabbed the back of a chair to steady herself.

Moving to another window, she spotted the light inside the van. She watched Marty reach into the passenger seat and pull a woman to her feet. CeeCee caught a glimpse of a white blindfold tied around her eyes.

Her mask! She raced back to the bedroom and quickly wrapped her hair around her head, dropping some of the bobby pins on the floor with her trembling, gloved hands. One of the brothers pounded on the front door as she pulled on the blond wig and slipped the mask over her face.

"Coming!" she called. "Oh God, oh God, oh God," she whispered to herself as she ran into the living room and unlocked the dead bolt.

It took both Marty and Tim to pull the blindfolded woman through the doorway. She was nearly as tall as they were.

"Stop it!" the woman yelled, her cuffed hands batting the air. "Let go of me!" Her short red hair was mussed, her cheeks crimson, from the cold or from crying. She wore a fur coat. *Real* fur, CeeCee thought. Dark and rich and shimmery. And she was very fat.

"She's an obstinate bitch," Marty said to CeeCee as he pushed the woman past her, but even with her eyes covered, the woman's expression looked more anxious than obstinate.

"Don't be afraid," CeeCee said to her.

The woman stopped fighting. "Who's that?" she asked.

She hadn't thought of a name for herself. "Sleeping Beauty," she said. "What's your name?"

"Her name's Genevieve," Tim said, as though the word tasted bad in his mouth. He reached up and untied the woman's blindfold. She blinked against the light, blue eyes red and puffy from crying, and her gaze fell on CeeCee. "Who are you?" she asked. "Why are you wearing a mask? What's going on?"

"Does she have to have the handcuffs on?" CeeCee asked Tim.

"You going to behave now?" Tim asked the woman.

Genevieve didn't respond. She stared at CeeCee, trying to peer into her eyes behind the mask and CeeCee felt an unexpected connection with her: They were both trapped in this situation.

Tim pulled a small key from his pocket and unlocked the cuffs. The moment Genevieve's hands were free, she slapped him hard across the face, much the way CeeCee had during their breakup performance on Franklin Street.

"You bitch!" Marty grabbed the woman's wrist, but Tim merely smiled. He looked unsure of himself, though, as if he'd gotten in over his head. It scared CeeCee to see him that way. She needed him to be certain that what they were doing was right. Certain enough for both of them.

"Let go of me!" Genevieve tried to twist her wrist out of Marty's grasp.

"Let go of her," CeeCee agreed. She was not trying to protect the woman as much as ease her own discomfort. She didn't like physical conflict, always fearing it might escalate into something worse. The woman was a massive and imposing figure in the fur coat. She could do some damage if she chose to. "She's okay," she said. "She can't go anywhere."

Marty let go, and the woman rubbed her wrist.

"Take off this animal you're wearing," Tim said. He helped her as though he was helping his girlfriend in a restaurant. When the coat slipped from Genevieve's shoulders, it was clear she was not fat after all.

"She's *pregnant*," CeeCee said.

"Well, at least *one* of you can face reality," the woman said. She was wearing a long, navy-blue sweater and pale blue slacks. "I've been telling these jerks that the whole way here. I'm thirty-seven weeks and this is a high-risk pregnancy." Her voice broke as she rested one hand on her belly. "*Please* take me back," she said to Tim.

"Did you know she was pregnant?" CeeCee asked Tim, but Marty answered.

"It's no big deal," he said.

It *was* a big deal, CeeCee thought. This was a human being they were dealing with. *Two* human beings.

"If your husband does what he's told," Tim said, his eyes were on the woman's huge belly, "you'll be home before you know it."

"Thirty-seven weeks," Genevieve repeated to him. "That's more than eight months. Do you understand?"

"I've got it," Tim said. "That's all the more reason the gov should want you back safe, and soon."

"If anything happens to this baby," Genevieve said, "you two will be in worse trouble than you are now, I can tell you that." She leveled her eyes at CeeCee. "You *three,*" she said. "My husband will never give in to blackmail."

"This ain't blackmail, bitch," Marty said to her. "It's a kidnapping. Much more elegant than blackmail."

Genevieve reached behind her to rub the small of her back. "If you take me home now," she said to Tim, obviously guessing he was the softer of the two men, "I can make sure they go easy on you."

"No way," Tim said. "I'm not crapping out on Andie."

"You're a fool," Genevieve said.

"Look." Tim touched her arm, and she snapped it away from him. "You sit here with Marty and I'll get you some tea and something to eat." He looked at CeeCee, nodding toward the kitchen.

"Sit down," Marty ordered her. CeeCee felt a little afraid to leave her in his care. The woman lowered herself to the old couch, looking defeated and suddenly very tired.

In the kitchen, CeeCee lifted her mask. "Oh, God, Tim, please don't leave me alone with her!"

"Put the mask down," he snapped, and she dropped it over her face again. Tim filled a pot with water and set it on the stove. "She's going to be fine," he said. "She's really a pussycat." The red mark on his cheek suggested otherwise. "Don't get too close to her, though. She might try to grab your mask or something."

"I just...I..." CeeCee stammered. "She's so much taller than me."

"Babe." He held on to her shoulders. His smile was meant to reassure her, but it was tight and uncertain. "I'm sure this isn't going to last long. It's actually good that she's pregnant. It makes her less able to cause you any problems, right?" He waited for her to answer and she offered a reluctant nod.

"You're doing a wonderful thing for me," he said. "For my family. Whatever you need, anytime, I'll be there for you. I owe you."

Be there for me *how,* she wanted to ask? How could he be there if he was going underground? But she knew better than to bring up that subject again.

"Now look." He reached inside his jacket and pulled out a gun, and she backed away.

"It's not loaded, right?" she asked.

"Actually, it is," he said.

She took another step backward until she was up against the pantry. "You said it wouldn't be. Take out the bullets."

"I think it's better if it's loaded. Just in case. I don't mean you would shoot her." He looked suddenly worried. "Whatever you do, don't shoot her. She's all we've got to trade with. But you might need to shoot the ceiling or something to keep her in line. She's feistier than I anticipated."

"Oh, Tim, I don't want a gun!"

"The safety is on," he said. "Let me show you how this thing works."

She watched carefully as he toggled the safety back and forth.

She supposed he was right. It would give her more confidence if she had a weapon. It didn't matter that Genevieve was taller or bigger or stronger if she was the one with the gun.

She took the gun from him, her gloved hands trembling.

"Man, you haven't stopped shaking since we got here," he said.

"Not since you *left* me here, actually," she admitted. "I can't stop."

"It's all going to work out, I promise," he said as he took a tea bag from the box in the pantry. "That asshole governor will want to keep this quiet and get her back before anyone's the wiser. He's that way. Very private. So I want you to stop worrying, okay?" He lifted her mask a couple of inches and planted a kiss on her cheek.

She poured boiling water into a mug, spilling some of it onto the worn wooden counter.

"You get the cookies," he said, taking the mug from her. "And try to calm down. Don't let her see how rattled you are."

She was worrying him, she thought, as she put a few sugar cookies onto a plate. Disappointing him.

Genevieve was still sitting on the old sofa when they walked back into the room, and Marty stood at the window, looking less confident than he had a few minutes earlier.

"I heard something out there," he said. "A thud or something."

"It's nothing." Tim set the mug on the coffee table.

"I heard it a lot while you were gone," CeeCee said. "I think it's just a branch brushing against the porch." How was someone as paranoid as Marty going to survive on the run? She placed the plate of cookies next to the mug, taking one of them for herself, although she was hardly hungry. She needed something to do with her hands.

Genevieve suddenly picked up all four of the cookies and threw them at the men. Then she threw the plate at CeeCee, catching her on the side of her face. Of Sleeping Beauty's face.

"You bitch!" Marty was on the woman in a flash, pinning her arms to the sofa, and CeeCee saw a sharp flicker of fear in her eyes.

"Leave her alone," she said, surprised as the words left her mouth. "You can't blame her." It suddenly occurred to her that befriending the woman might be the right approach. Her sympathy for her was genuine. As Marty backed away, CeeCee could tell that Genevieve was struggling to keep from crying. Her lower lip quivered and her eyes blinked back tears. She sat down next to her. "It's going to be okay," she said.

Genevieve stared at her. "What have you let these guys talk you into?" she asked.

CeeCee quickly stood again as she felt the upper hand slip away from her. "I think for myself, bitch," she said, but Genevieve's eyes bored hard into CeeCee's until she had to look away.

Tim pointed to the governor's wife. "Do what Sleeping Beauty says, or there'll be trouble," he said. "Marty and I are leaving."

"I don't feel well," Genevieve said, her hand rubbing her back again. "I could be going into labor."

"Right," Tim said with disdain. He looked at Marty. "You ready?"

"You bet," Marty said, but he opened the door slowly and peered outside before walking onto the porch.

CeeCee stood next to the coffee table, watching the men leave. She listened to the van doors slam shut and the engine cough to life, and she thought, *What now?* She felt Genevieve's eyes on her. The woman hadn't touched her tea. "Do you want more cookies?" she asked.

Genevieve ignored the question. "So, what happens now?" she asked. "Will they tell my husband where I am and he can come get me?"

A horrible thought. Surely they wouldn't send the husband here. She'd be a sitting duck if he showed up.

"They'll come get you and take you back," she said, as if she knew that for a fact.

"Where are they going now?"

"Someplace where they can call your husband."

"Why didn't they call him from here? Then I could talk to him and let him know I'm alive. That would make more sense."

"There's no phone here."

Genevieve rolled her eyes. "Then why didn't they take me someplace where there *is* a phone?"

It was a good question and CeeCee didn't have the answer. "Look," she said, "this is the way it is, so we'll just have to make the best of it."

Genevieve suddenly got to her feet and CeeCee panicked. "You sit down!" she said.

She thought Genevieve was going to ignore her, and she suddenly realized she'd left the gun in the kitchen. Her voice must have carried power, though, because the woman dropped onto the sofa again.

"I wasn't kidding that I don't feel well," she said. "My back aches."

"You probably pulled something when they nabbed you," CeeCee said.

"It ached before that. It's ached all day."

"When is your baby due?"

"Three weeks from now."

"Then it's not the baby," CeeCee said as if she knew about these things. Babies did come early, but a backache had nothing to do with labor. At least she hoped it didn't. She walked over to the bookshelf. "You want a book to read?" she asked.

"I don't want a book," Genevieve said. "If you think I can concentrate on reading, you're as crazy as your friends."

CeeCee sat down in the chair by the window and folded her hands on her lap.

"What color's your real hair?" Genevieve asked.

"None of your business." She realized that she'd completely forgotten about disguising her voice. Too late now.

"I don't think you're as tough as you pretend." Genevieve almost smiled. "You really should have gotten a tougher mask than that."

CeeCee touched the thin plastic mask.

"Do you go to Carolina?" Genevieve asked. "You're not one of my students, are you? You sound like one of them."

"I wouldn't tell you if I were," CeeCee said.

Genevieve looked annoyed. "I have to go to the bathroom," she said.

Damn. She'd hoped they could get through this entire fiasco without either of them needing to use the bathroom.

"I have to go with you," CeeCee said.

"Are those your orders?" Genevieve moved forward on the couch as though preparing to stand up. "Don't let her out of your sight?" She was talking to her like she might a child. It was irksome enough to be annoying, and CeeCee was glad. It made Genevieve less sympathetic.

"I think for myself," CeeCee said.

"Fine," Genevieve said. "I need to go to the bathroom. *Now.*"

"Stay here one minute." CeeCee darted into the kitchen and grabbed the gun. Just touching it started her hands shaking again. She checked to be sure the safety was on, then carried it into the living room.

"Whoa!" Genevieve said. "You don't need that!"

"You can get up now, and I'll walk with you," CeeCee said.

Genevieve struggled to her feet, giving CeeCee a wide berth as she walked toward the hallway. She held one arm out as if she could block a bullet with her hand. The other hand she held protectively over her belly.

"It's that door on the left," CeeCee said.

Genevieve walked into the bathroom and started to shut the door behind her, but CeeCee stuck out her foot to keep it open.

"Oh, come on," Genevieve said. "What do you think I'm going to do in here?" She pointed to the small, square window above the toilet. "I'm hardly going to be able to get through that window."

That was true. CeeCee didn't want to watch her while she went to the bathroom, anyway.

"Okay." She removed her foot from in front of the door. "You have to leave it open a crack, though."

"Fine," Genevieve said again.

CeeCee leaned against the wall, waiting, listening to the rustle of clothing on the other side of the door. Genevieve urinated for a long time, then flushed the toilet. CeeCee straightened, gun held in front of her, as she waited for her captive to walk into the hallway. Then suddenly, so quickly CeeCee had no time to react, the bathroom door slammed shut and the key clicked into place in the lock.

Chapter Twelve

Oh, CeeCee, I get so scared sometimes! I'm not afraid of dying anymore, but I'm afraid of what will happen to you and that's what keeps me awake at night. During the day, when I'm thinking rationally, I know you'll be okay. At night, though, the worst thoughts fill my head. I have to remind myself that you have loads of gumption! I think you may need it, darling girl.

"OPEN UP!" CEECEE POUNDED ON THE BATHROOM DOOR.

"I just want to be by myself," Genevieve said. "I told you. I can't get out through the window, so just give me some space, all right?"

"No, it's not all right." CeeCee was frantic. She kicked at the door and rattled the knob. "Open it!" She heard the medicine-cabinet door squeak open and remembered the razor blades. The cookie she'd eaten rushed into her throat. Hands trembling, she aimed the gun at the doorjamb near the lock, released the safety and pulled the trigger.

The explosion nearly knocked her off her feet, and Genevieve screamed. The door and jamb were splintered and CeeCee reached for the knob. The damn thing was still locked. "Open the door!" Behind the mask, tears burned her eyes.

"All right, all right!" Genevieve pulled the door open and raised her hands in the air. "Are you out of your mind?" she asked. "Don't shoot!"

Holding the gun on the woman, CeeCee checked the medicine cabinet and was relieved to see that the packet of razor blades was still there. "Get into the living room," she said.

"Fine," Genevieve said. "Just stop pointing that thing at me."

CeeCee flipped the safety back on and lowered the gun to her side as they walked into the living room. Genevieve sat down on the sofa again, leaning forward and rubbing her back. "You're a loose cannon, aren't you?" she asked.

"Keep quiet," CeeCee said. She was glad now of the mask. The plastic features would remain frozen no matter what emotions she felt behind them. Her trembling hands in their white gloves, though, were a giveaway.

"Put that gun away. Please," Genevieve said.

She sat down in the chair by the window again and rested the gun in her lap, wondering what they would do now. Would they sit there facing each other for the entire night? Maybe all day tomorrow as well? Exactly how far was it to Jacksonville? She looked at her watch. Quarter past midnight! She'd had no idea it was that late. Were Tim and Marty in Jacksonville yet?

"Please take off that mask," Genevieve said.

CeeCee shook her head. Her scalp was perspiring beneath the wig. It felt like worms crawling through her hair and she wondered who else might have worn the wig before her. She longed to rip it off and scratch her head.

"Why are you doing this, Sleeping Beauty?" Genevieve's voice had softened, and with it, her features. She was very pretty. Maybe beautiful under other circumstances. Right now, her skin was a little too pale. Wan, even. Her blue eyes looked clouded and troubled in the overhead light, and there were two small, vertical lines between her eyebrows.

"I'm doing it because Tim's sister is a victim of the system," she said, parroting Naomi's words. They sounded as inauthentic as they felt coming from her mouth.

"What's that supposed to mean?" Genevieve asked. "'A victim of the system'?"

"I don't want to talk about it." CeeCee felt the tremor in her hands again. She clutched the handle of the gun between her hands to stop their shaking.

"Do you know her? The sister?"

"No, but I know Tim and I know he loves her and I love him so I want to help him." The words spilled out before she could stop them.

Genevieve cocked her head, looking at her differently. "You're in love with Tim?" she asked.

"Yes, but that's not the only reason I'm—"

"There's something you should know about your…boyfriend," Genevieve said. "I taught him in my Spanish class, Sleeping Beauty. He's a…a womanizer."

"You taught him?" She remembered Tim saying that Genevieve was a Spanish professor, but not that he'd had her.

"He's a lady-killer." Genevieve sat as far forward on the couch as her belly would allow. "He played around with every woman in that class. He even had an affair with one who was married."

CeeCee raised the gun and pointed it at her. "Shut up," she said.

"I don't want to hear your lies. You may have taught him, although I'm not sure I believe that, but you don't know him."

"Please put the gun down."

"You promise to shut up?" CeeCee asked.

"Not another word about your darling Casanova."

"I said *shut up.*" CeeCee lifted the gun higher, the barrel jerking through the air in her uncertain hands. She had to be careful. The cotton fabric of her gloves was slippery.

"I'm sorry." Genevieve leaned back on the sofa, clearly afraid of the gun. "Put it down, okay?"

CeeCee lowered the gun to her lap again.

Genevieve sighed and rubbed her forehead. "How long is this going to take?" she asked.

"That depends on your husband," CeeCee said. "What's he like? How do you think he'll react?"

Genevieve shot her an angry look. "He's a man of integrity," she said. "He loves me tremendously, but he won't do anything that would compromise his integrity."

CeeCee squirmed. She loved Tim tremendously. Was she compromising her integrity for him? Holding a gun on a pregnant woman didn't feel all that magnificent at the moment. It felt wrong.

Suddenly Genevieve started to cry, pressing a hand to her mouth. "I want to go *home.*" She looked at CeeCee. "I have a five-year-old daughter," she said. "I was supposed to pick her up at the sitter's after my class. She's probably so scared."

Was this her new tack, CeeCee wondered? She'd failed in her character assassination of Tim, so now she was trying to win sympathy for her daughter. At least that would give them something safe to talk about.

"What's her name?" CeeCee asked.

"I truly don't feel well." Genevieve adjusted her girth on the sofa.

"It's just nerves," CeeCee said. She didn't feel well either. "What's your daughter's name?" she repeated.

"Vivian. I dropped my purse when they grabbed me or I could show you her picture."

"What does she look like?"

Genevieve closed her eyes and leaned her head against the back of the sofa. "Strawberry-blond hair," she said. "I'm glad she's not a redhead, like me. I'm glad she was spared that."

"Why?" CeeCee asked. "Your hair's a beautiful color." She felt her true personality slipping out and knew she'd better keep her guard up.

"Thanks, but I don't like it." Eyes still shut, Genevieve patted her hand on her belly. "I hope this one is a blonde or a brunette," she said, her voice tired, as though she knew they were simply filling dead air with their conversation. "Anything but a redhead."

CeeCee remembered being five or six, waiting for her mother to pick her up from school. She'd waited by the wide double doors for a long time, watching for her always-prompt mother, but she hadn't been afraid at all. She'd played hopscotch with imaginary lines on the sidewalk, looking up only when a neighbor called to her from a car, saying that her mother had to work late and she would take her home. She hoped Vivian was similarly resilient and unafraid when her mother didn't show up. She hoped that fervently.

"I guess we should try to sleep," CeeCee suggested. "I made up a bed for you." She glanced at the handcuffs Tim had put on the end table. With Genevieve's pregnancy, the cuff-her-to-the-top-bunk plan wasn't going to work, that much was clear.

"Oh." Genevieve screwed up her face, both hands on her belly.

"Are you okay?" CeeCee asked.

It was a moment before Genevieve seemed able to speak. "I don't know," she said. "I've had some Braxton Hicks…some false labor contractions…the past few weeks. That's probably what this is. But maybe I'd better lie down."

CeeCee didn't trust her. "You walk ahead of me," she said, getting to her feet.

It took Genevieve a moment to push herself up from the sofa. CeeCee thought of helping her but didn't dare. In a heartbeat, Genevieve could tear off her mask or punch her in the face and grab the gun. She couldn't get that close.

They reached the bedroom with the bunk beds. "Oh, no," Genevieve said when she saw the beds. "I can't fit on one of those. Is there a real bed I can lie down on?"

What the hell, CeeCee thought. "There's a double bed in the other room. I haven't made it, though."

"I don't care." Genevieve left the room, her face still tight with pain, either real or affected, and crossed the hallway into the larger bedroom. CeeCee followed, the gun at her side, and watched Genevieve kick off her navy-blue pumps and slowly lower herself to the bed. She stretched out on her back, then winced with discomfort and rolled onto her side, one arm over her eyes. "Can you turn the light out?" she asked.

"No," CeeCee said. There was a small, upholstered chair in the corner of the room and she sat down on it. "Not unless I cuff you to the headboard."

"What?" Genevieve's arm flew from her face. "Oh, give me a break, Sleeping Beauty. I'm eight months' pregnant and feel like

death warmed over. If you think I'm going to run off, you're…"
She shook her head. "Just turn it off. Please."

CeeCee walked out of the room and turned on the hall light.
Then she switched off the light above Genevieve's bed and took
her seat again. The room was bathed in shadow, but she could still
see Genevieve clearly enough.

Now all she had to do was stay awake.

Chapter Thirteen

You've wanted to be a teacher ever since kindergarten when you had Mrs. Weiss. Is that still what you want to do? I see you watching all the nurses I've had and I know you admire them. I know how surprised you were, too, when you realized Dr. Watts was a woman. I wonder if you might end up being a nurse or a doctor? You're sure smart enough. I think you'd be good at it.

CEECEE SNAPPED AWAKE WITH A START. SOMEONE—OR *something*—was moaning, and it took her a moment to remember where she was. In the dim light, she saw Genevieve on the bed, propped up on her elbows.

"Oh, no," Genevieve said. "Oh, God, help me."

CeeCee got to her feet. "What are you doing?" She walked across the room to turn on the light.

Genevieve was panting, gulping air. "I think these are real contractions," she said. "I really do. This is how it felt with Vivvie."

"People don't go into labor that fast," CeeCee said. She hadn't been asleep all that long; it was still dark out. Genevieve *had* to be faking.

"You think you're a doctor all of a sudden?" Genevieve flopped back on the bed, blinking at the overhead light. "Oh, my God," she said, both hands covering her face. "You've got to get me to a hospital."

"I don't believe you."

"*Please.*" Genevieve looked at her. "You've *got* to believe me. I'm having contractions."

"It's too early. You said—"

"Don't you think I know it's too early?" Genevieve snapped. "Babies can come early, you stupid girl. And it's not good when they do. They need to be someplace where they can get special care. And I almost bled to death after Vivian was born."

"Why?" CeeCee asked. *She's faking this,* she told herself. *Stay calm.*

"They just said that redheads can bleed more. They can hemorrhage."

"That's crazy," CeeCee said.

"Look!" Genevieve snapped as she struggled to sit up. "I don't care if you believe me or not, but you've got to get me to a hospital. If anything happens to this baby…" She shook her head. "Do you want that on your conscience?"

"How do I know you're telling the truth?" CeeCee asked. Even if Genevieve *was* telling the truth, what could she do? Where was a hospital? She had no idea. Nor could she imagine driving the car on the dark, rutted roads. She was once again glad that the mask hid her fear.

"Oh, no." Genevieve spread her legs a little and looked down at the rapidly darkening crotch of her blue slacks.

"Are you…?" Was she urinating on herself?

"My water broke." Genevieve locked eyes with hers. "Oh, my

God," she said. "I'm scared." If the wet splotch on her pants wasn't enough, there was something in her voice that told CeeCee she wasn't faking. "Where's the nearest hospital?"

"I don't know." CeeCee stood still, holding the gun at her side. She felt a tiny finger of panic run up her spine. How could she take her to a hospital? What about the plan? What about Andie? They'd all end up in jail.

"Is there a phone book here?" Genevieve asked.

"There's no phone."

"I mean for the address."

"I'll see." CeeCee ran out of the room, knowing that she'd looked through every cupboard and closet before Genevieve's arrival and she did not recall seeing a phone book. Maybe, though, she'd missed it.

In the kitchen, she lay the gun on the counter and pulled out drawer after drawer. She opened cupboards she knew were empty, all the time wondering what she should do. On the refrigerator, there was a magnet advertising a restaurant in New Bern. It had a phone number and an address, and she realized that even if she had the address of a hospital in New Bern, she would have no idea how to get there. Could she possibly find her way back to Naomi and Forrest's? She doubted it, and they would kill her if she showed up there, with or without the governor's wife. She heard Genevieve scream and put her hands over her ears. *What do I do?*

"Sleeping Beauty!" Genevieve called.

CeeCee ran back to the bedroom. Genevieve was propped up on two pillows, one tremulous hand at her throat. "Listen," she said. "This is happening too fast. You might have to deliver the baby."

"Oh, no!" CeeCee said. "Maybe we should just start driving. Try to get to New Bern."

"Is that where we are? New Bern?"

"Near it." She grimaced. Tim had gone to the trouble of blind-folding Genevieve so she wouldn't know where she was being taken, and she'd just told her.

"There's a hospital in New Bern," Genevieve said.

"But I don't know where it is. I don't even know what direction to go. We're way out in the woods."

"Damn it." Genevieve choked back a sob. "You are worse than useless!"

"We have to try," CeeCee said. "We can't stay here. I might be able to get us to…a friend's house. They have a phone there. But I'm not sure I—"

"Why didn't you say that before?" Genevieve sat up and tried to get to her feet, but she doubled over, leaning hard against the night table and howling with pain. It was the sort of sound a wounded animal might make. CeeCee grabbed her arm to help her onto the bed, but let go suddenly, worried that she was being duped after all. Maybe Genevieve *had* urinated on herself to make it look as though her water had broken. She took a step backward and let the woman struggle, panting and perspiring, onto the bed alone.

"It's too late to go anywhere," Genevieve gasped. "The baby's coming. It's coming."

To CeeCee's horror, Genevieve started to pull off her slacks.

"You're going to have to—" Genevieve stopped tugging at her slacks and held still on the bed, eyes closed, panting, concentrating hard on something CeeCee could only imagine.

"I don't know what to do," CeeCee admitted, more to herself than to Genevieve. She'd seen a film on childbirth in her senior health class, but that was hardly enough to prepare her to deliver a baby.

"Get these off me," Genevieve said, nodding in the direction of her slacks. Her hair was pasted to her forehead with sweat.

CeeCee stood by the door, paralyzed.

"Listen to me!" Genevieve said sharply. "You need to help me. You chose to be part of this fiasco, now you have to see it through. I'll tell you what to do. Help me get my pants off, damn it!"

CeeCee moved forward and tugged off Genevieve's pants, dropping them behind her on the floor. Then, feeling squeamish, she pulled off her underpants, which were soaked with a pink-tinged liquid.

Genevieve's eyes were closed, her head pressed into her pillow. "My poor baby," she said. "My poor baby."

"What do I do now?" CeeCee asked.

"Boil water." Genevieve spoke without opening her eyes. "Get clean towels. It's cold in here. We'll have to keep the baby warm after it comes. Boil scissors and something to tie... *Oh.*" She screamed, then started panting again. "Go!" she shouted between breaths. "Do it!"

CeeCee ran back into the kitchen and pulled the huge spaghetti pot from one of the lower cabinets. She put it under the tap and started the water running. "Tim," she said out loud. "Please come. Please come now. Please please please."

She went through the utensils drawer, hunting for scissors, and found none. She foraged through the other drawers. Nothing. But there was a knife block on the counter and she pulled out the chef's knife and examined the sleek blade. It looked sharp enough. *Something to tie...* Genevieve had said. CeeCee knew she meant the cord that ran from inside the mother to the baby's navel. What part did you tie? What could she use? *My poor baby,* Genevieve had said. CeeCee choked back a sob. How would she get through this? And how would she keep a premature baby alive?

The pot was full of water and so heavy she could barely lift it onto one of the ancient electric burners. It would take forever to boil. She ran back to the bedroom.

Genevieve was propped up on the pillows, panting again, her knees bent and her legs spread wide open. CeeCee didn't know where to look. "Are you okay?" she asked.

The woman didn't answer. Her body relaxed momentarily and she shut her eyes. Tears streamed down her cheeks and her entire face was crimson. CeeCee went into the bathroom and wet a washcloth with warm water. She sat on the edge of the bed and smoothed the cloth over Genevieve's face, the way she used to do with her mother. "The water's heating up," she said.

"Boil scissors," Genevieve said.

"I can't find scissors, but I have a knife."

"And string. Is there string?"

"I couldn't find any, but maybe I can—"

"Your shoelaces."

CeeCee looked down at her tennis shoes. "Okay," she said.

"Both of them. You need two."

"Okay," she repeated, trying to sound calm. Genevieve's sweater was pulled up nearly to her breasts, and the huge perfect orb of her belly was exposed. CeeCee felt nauseous at the thought of the baby trying to push its way out of that snug enclosure.

"Put a clean towel under me," Genevieve said. "There's going to be some blood. Listen, Sleeping Beauty. If I hemorrhage, and we'd better pray that I don't, you're supposed to massage my uterus. That's what the nurses did the last time."

"How do I do that?" Was Genevieve telling her to reach inside her to find her uterus?

"On my belly. Here." Genevieve rested her hand on her massive belly. "Massage here to make the uterus contract after the baby is born."

"All right," she said, hoping it wouldn't come to that. She got a stack of clean towels from the hallway closet. Slipping one of them under Genevieve's bottom, she got an idea. "I'll be back in a minute," she said. In the bathroom, she pulled down the plastic shower curtain and carried it back into the bedroom. Genevieve was screaming again. Writhing. CeeCee vowed she would never have a baby. She wouldn't have the strength to go through this. She managed to get the shower curtain under the towel, then went back to see if the water was boiling.

It was. She dropped the knife into the pot, then sat down on the floor and unlaced her shoes, slowly, taking her time, because she was afraid to go back in the bedroom. Standing up, she dropped her laces into the boiling water.

"Help!" Genevieve cried.

CeeCee had no choice but to return to the bedroom.

"You've got to catch it," Genevieve said as soon as CeeCee entered the room. "I need to push. I don't know if I'm supposed to yet, though. I don't know when. I don't know *when*."

"Let me get the knife and laces," CeeCee said, anxious to leave the room again. In the kitchen, she poured most of the water into the sink, then carried the pot into the bedroom, where she set it on the rug near the bed.

"Can you see it?" Genevieve asked.

CeeCee looked between her legs. "Oh, my *God*," she said, both awed and horrified by the sight of the baby's scalp stretching Genevieve's taut pink skin. "*Yes.* Doesn't it hurt?"

Genevieve panted. "What…do…you…think?" she asked. "I've got to *push!* Hold your hand under its head."

CeeCee rested her gloved hand on the bed between Genevieve's legs. The circle of bloodstained hair grew larger with each push. "It's coming!" CeeCee said, ripping off her mask so she could see better.

Genevieve tightened her face up as she pushed again. CeeCee felt the light weight of the baby's head in her hands. She saw the crown of its head, then its small ears, but its face was pointed toward the mattress. How would its shoulders get out? Then, as if reading her thoughts, the baby turned its head in her hands, the tiny nose resting in profile on her palm. Its neck felt strange, as if something was bulging out of it, pressing against her fingers. She leaned over for a better look and it took her a moment to realize that the umbilical cord was wrapped twice around the baby's neck. She started to tell Genevieve but didn't want to alarm her any more than she already was. She pulled off her right glove, then hooked her finger beneath the cord and slipped the loops around the baby's head. Suddenly, one shoulder, then another, popped into her hands and the baby slid out onto the towel and into the world.

"It's a girl!" CeeCee announced. So tiny, she thought. *Too* tiny. And too quiet. "I'm supposed to hold it upside down now, aren't I?"

"Rub her." Genevieve could barely get the words out. "Clean out her mouth."

Before CeeCee could do either, the baby let out a mewing sound like a kitten, followed by a loud and forceful cry.

Genevieve laughed with relief and held her arms out for the baby.

"Should I clean her first or do something with the cord?"

"Give her to me," Genevieve demanded.

The baby was so slippery. CeeCee wiped her off as best she could with one of the towels, then carefully lifted her into Genevieve's arms. The baby's cry was lusty and rhythmic, and Genevieve began sobbing.

"I want Russ here!" she said. "I need Russ."

"Who?" CeeCee asked.

"Cut the cord so I can hold her closer," Genevieve said.

CeeCee pulled one of the shoelaces out of the water. "Where do I tie it?" she asked.

"Tie one close…a couple inches from the baby. And one farther up. Then cut in between them."

CeeCee tied the laces around the cream-colored cord and pulled them as tight as she could. Then she sliced through the cord with the knife, and Genevieve drew the baby up to her lips to kiss her.

"The afterbirth has to come out, right?" CeeCee looked at the long cord coming from inside Genevieve.

"It'll come out on its own," Genevieve said. Her voice was slow, almost slurred. She had to be exhausted. "Get me a blanket…cover her," she said. "I need…try to nurse. Never could with Vivvie." She shut her eyes, pressing her head into the pillows. "The room is spinning," she said.

"Do you want water?" CeeCee asked as she opened the closet door and pulled a blanket from the top shelf. "Food?"

Genevieve didn't answer. She was staring at the ceiling, a vacant look in her eyes.

"Genevieve? Are you okay?"

"Freezing," Genevieve said. She was shivering all over.

CeeCee wrapped the blanket around and around the screaming baby, then got a second blanket and put it over Genevieve. Her skin felt cold and damp and she looked even paler than she had before.

"Can you hold her?" CeeCee asked. "I'll get you some tea."

"Mmm," Genevieve said.

"It'll be light out in a couple of hours. Then I'll get you to a hospital somehow. I promise." She thought her voice sounded calm, but she was panicky inside. She would have to drop Genevieve and the baby at the hospital without being caught herself. Genevieve would have seen the car by then. And she'd already seen her face, although she hadn't seemed to notice, or at least to care, that CeeCee was no longer wearing the mask. She had the presence of mind, though, to pull her glove back on over her hand, sticky with blood.

In the kitchen, she once again put water on to boil and took a tea bag and a mug from the cabinet. She'd just delivered a baby! She would never be able to tell a soul other than Tim about it, but she knew what she'd done. Now she needed to be sure the tiny infant survived.

She longed for Tim and Marty to return, imagining their shock when they realized what had happened in their absence. Tim would be proud of her for handling it as she did. He would know the way to New Bern and they could put Genevieve and the baby on the mattress in the rear of the van. Still, how could they drop her off without being caught? Maybe they could leave her in the cabin and go somewhere to call an ambulance, telling them where to find her. That might be the best plan.

From the bedroom, the baby started her rapid, rhythmic crying again. CeeCee poured boiling water over the tea bag, dunking the bag up and down a few times to hurry the steeping. As long as the baby was crying, she was alive and okay and that was all that mattered.

She carried the mug down the hallway, but stopped short at the doorway to the bedroom. The blanket was above Genevieve's wide-apart knees. Between her legs was a pool of blood. Was that the afterbirth? Should there be so much of it? The blood had completely saturated the towel she'd placed under her and was spilling onto the plastic shower curtain.

Oh, God. There'd been nothing like this in the film she saw at school. The screaming baby had fallen from Genevieve's arms to the bed and the woman's eyes were closed. Something was terribly wrong.

"Genevieve!" CeeCee dropped the full mug on the floor and picked up the bundled baby who continued to wail in her ear. Was this the hemorrhaging she'd talked about? She bent over to shake the woman by the shoulder. "Genevieve! Wake up!"

Genevieve rolled her head toward her. She opened her eyes, but didn't appear to be looking at CeeCee. She didn't appear to be looking at anything at all.

"There's a lot of blood!" CeeCee said. "Is that the afterbirth or are you hemorrhaging?" *Please say afterbirth.*

Genevieve's eyes fixed on hers. "My baby," she slurred. "Don't let die."

"She's fine," CeeCee said. "Listen to her. She's fine. But—" she looked at the widening pool of blood. "I think you're hemorrhaging. How do I stop it?"

Genevieve's eyelids closed.

"Genevieve!" CeeCee shook her shoulder again. "Stay awake! Please, Genevieve!"

She climbed onto the other side of the bed, laying the baby down next to her, and put her hands on Genevieve's belly. She rubbed it lightly, afraid of hurting more than helping. Everything felt loose and flabby beneath her hands. Where was the uterus? She moved her hands around. "Genevieve!" she yelled. "Am I massaging the right spot?"

Genevieve's chin rested against her chest. Her skin was white. Waxen. She was so still. CeeCee had seen that stillness only once before—the day her mother died.

Abruptly she lifted her hands from Genevieve's belly. "Genevieve?" she whispered. She couldn't hear her own voice over the baby's wails. "Oh, God, Genevieve?" She ripped off her glove and lowered her fingers to Genevieve's wrist, knowing exactly where to touch. There was no pulse beneath her fingertips. "No!" she cried. "No, no, please!" She leaned forward to touch Genevieve's throat, searching for the artery, but she touched only cool, lifeless skin.

Paralyzed with terror, she stared at Genevieve's body. Then she shifted her gaze from the woman to the baby who lay wailing and helpless at her mother's side. She had to do something fast, and there was only one option she could think of.

Grabbing the screaming baby, she ran into the living room. She lay the bundled infant on the sofa, then retrieved her jacket from the coat rack by the door and put it on. She was sobbing by the time she slipped the baby inside the jacket against her flannel shirt. She ran outside into the darkness and got into the driver's seat of the car. Turning the key in the ignition, she reminded herself about the clutch. She found the knob for the headlights, and they illuminated the bleached cedar of the cabin. She managed to get the car into Reverse and backed it out onto the road. It stalled when she shifted to Drive, but she got it going again. The lights cut a path through the eerie trunks of the loblolly pines, and she drove slowly, crying and battling nausea as she searched the darkness for the roads that would lead her to Naomi and Forrest's house.

Chapter Fourteen

We've had to rely on welfare and food stamps and the kindness of others. I want so much better for you than that.

THE NIGHT WAS MOONLESS. CEECEE WAS STILL SOBBING when she reached the fork in the road, but she remembered to stay to the left. She drove slowly, afraid to take the potholes at anything more than a crawl. The baby grew so still and quiet inside her jacket that she stopped the car to make sure she was breathing. Slipping her hand beneath the blanket, she rested it on the newborn until she felt the rise and fall of the tiny chest.

"Baby, *live*," she pleaded. "Please live."

She came to another intersection. Tears blurred her vision and she couldn't clear them away long enough to get her bearing. Sitting there in the dark, she began to wonder if Genevieve was truly dead. What if CeeCee had simply been unable to find her pulse?

She was making herself crazy. Finally, she turned right, and the trees tightened around her, dark walls on either side of the car. It seemed as though she would come to a dead end at any moment with no room to turn the car around. Then suddenly, like magic, she came to a clearing. The moon slid out from beneath the clouds and illuminated the decrepit house and rusted cars. CeeCee cried harder, this time with relief.

She barely remembered to turn off the ignition before jumping out of the car, her precious cargo cradled inside her jacket. The dogs started barking from somewhere behind the house, and she braced herself for their approach as she ran up the two front steps and pounded on the door.

"Naomi!" she shouted. "Naomi!" She couldn't hear her own voice over the din from the dogs. She guessed they were chained in the backyard, since they were nowhere to be seen. The house was dark, and she was about to go around to one of the windows when a light came on inside. She pounded again. "Hurry!" she called.

Forrest opened the door a few inches. Naomi was close behind him, pulling a sweater on over her flannel pajama top.

"CeeCee?" she said, stepping next to Forrest. "What are you doing here?"

CeeCee pushed past them without waiting for an invitation.

"She died!" she screamed as she raced into the living room. "She had a baby."

"What are you talking about?" Forrest asked.

"Genevieve! The governor's wife."

"She *died?*" Naomi said. "You mean while she was with you?"

CeeCee opened her coat and held out the bundled newborn, whose face could barely be seen beneath the layers of blanket.

"Holy shit!" Naomi's hand flew to her mouth. Quickly she grabbed the baby from CeeCee's arms. "Is it alive?" she asked, tugging the blanket away from the infant's face.

Forrest ran his hands through his hair. "Why the hell did you bring it here?" he asked.

"Shut up, Forrest," Naomi snapped. "Where else was she supposed to bring it?"

"It's alive," CeeCee said. "It's a girl. But Genevieve's dead."

"Oh, Lord." Naomi closed her eyes. She looked as though she might keel over as the realization of what CeeCee was telling her sank in. "This is a disaster," she said.

"You should have dropped her off at a hospital," Forrest said.

"I would have if I knew where one was." CeeCee wiped the tears from her face with her hands.

The baby opened her petal-like lips and let out a howl.

"Thank God," Naomi said. "She was too quiet." She whisked the infant down the hallway and CeeCee followed her.

Naomi and Forrest's bedroom smelled of incense. Naomi laid the baby girl on the bed and carefully unwrapped her. "Get some towels out of that closet," she said. "And get me a bowl—a big bowl—of warm water from the kitchen."

CeeCee quickly moved to the closet. She felt dizzy and disoriented, as if in a dream. Or a nightmare.

Forrest must have heard Naomi's request for water, because he appeared in the doorway with a green mixing bowl full to the brim. CeeCee took the water from him and rested it on her lap as she sat down next to the infant. She watched as Naomi gently cleaned the baby, who was now crying hard, barely stopping to take in a breath between each wail. Her pink arms were screwed up at her sides, hands in tight little fists. She looked furious.

"We need to get both of them out of here," Forrest said.

"I know, I know." Naomi brushed her husband's words away with a wave of her hand. She looked from the infant to CeeCee. "How did she die?" she asked.

"It was right after the baby was born," CeeCee said. "There was tons and tons of blood. It was so awful."

"She *bled* to death?" Naomi frowned.

She doesn't believe me, CeeCee thought.

"She said she had some kind of condition," CeeCee said. "I didn't believe her at first that the baby was coming or…" She started to cry again, or maybe she hadn't yet stopped. "If I'd believed her, maybe I could have gotten her to a hospital somehow."

"You really screwed up." Forrest pulled a cigarette from the pack on the dresser and lit it. "Just what we need is the governor's dead wife's kid here."

His words cut into her. He was right. Her presence was a danger to them. But what else could she have done?

"Look at her," Naomi said, moving the washcloth over the baby's head. Her voice was calm, but her trembling hands gave her away. "She's absolutely perfect."

CeeCee looked at the baby's features, really seeing them for the first time. Her head was round, not like the elongated or misshapened heads of some babies she'd seen. Her mouth was a perfect 0 when she cried, and now that Naomi had washed her head, it was clear she had inherited Genevieve's red hair.

"She should go to the hospital, shouldn't she?" CeeCee asked. "She's three weeks early. Will she live?"

"No way we're taking her to a hospital." Forrest blew a stream of smoke into the air.

"Listen to her." Naomi nodded toward the wailing baby. "Does she sound like she's dying to you? She's not all that small, actually.

Bigger than Dahlia was." Naomi held the end of the umbilical cord between her thumb and forefinger. "Did you do this?" she asked.

CeeCee nodded. "I used a knife. Boiled. Did I do it okay?"

"Yeah, you did great," Naomi said. "You're a tough cookie, CeeCee. There's some alcohol and Q-tips in the bathroom under the sink. Get them, please."

She found the supplies and brought them back to the bedroom, where Naomi showed her how to clean the umbilical cord. "It'll fall off naturally in a couple of weeks," she said.

CeeCee sat down on the bed again, her legs too shaky to keep her upright. "Do you think there was something I could have done to keep her from dying?" she asked. "She said to massage her uterus, and I tried, but I wasn't sure what I was doing."

"They might not have been able to save her even if she'd been in a hospital," Naomi reassured her.

"How do we get them out of here?" Forrest asked.

"Forrest." Naomi sat back on her heels, annoyed. "It was your big idea to help them in the first place," she said. "Now we have to deal with the fallout. Get some of Emmanuel's newborn clothes from the bag in the hall closet, please. And then start a fire. The baby's freezing."

Forrest shook his head, mumbling to himself as he walked out of the room.

"I'm sorry," CeeCee said, after he left the room.

"As soon as we get her dressed and warmed up, we'll feed her," Naomi said. "I have formula I use to supplement my breast milk." She patted the baby dry with one of the towels CeeCee had handed her, then wrapped her tightly in another and lifted her up. "Hush, little one," she said, rocking her back and forth. "Shh." She looked at CeeCee. "Do you know what's happening with Tim and Marty?" she asked.

CeeCee shook her head. "There was no phone in the cabin and I don't know where they are, except someplace in Jacksonville. I don't know what's going on with them and the governor or even if they're still there or on their way back or..." Her voice trailed off as she imagined Tim and Marty walking in on the horrific scene in the cabin. "How do I let them know what happened?"

"I think I know how to reach them, if they're still there," Naomi said. She pressed her lips to the baby's temple. "Shh, Sweet Pea."

"You know where they are?"

"I'm guessing," Naomi said. "I don't know for sure, but there are some SCAPE people in Jacksonville. They might be there. I don't like using our phone, but I guess I'll have to. I'll call after we get the baby taken care of."

CeeCee let her breath out in relief. She needed to talk to Tim. She needed him to tell her that none of this was her fault and that he still loved her.

"What about Genevieve?" CeeCee said. "I just left her lying there on the bed. Blood was everywhere."

Naomi squeezed her eyes shut with a sigh. "Did you touch anything?" she asked.

"I wore gloves the whole time except when the baby was born and when I took Genevieve's pulse. I left one of them on the bed and the other is in the car. And the mask, too. The mask is at the cabin. I...I guess I touched the door knob getting out of the house."

"Did you touch anything else without the gloves?" Naomi asked.

"The knife," she said. "And maybe the closet door." She couldn't remember if she'd opened the closet door before or after she'd removed the glove. "The gun!" she said. "I didn't touch it, but I left it there, too."

"Okay." Naomi seemed exhausted by the list. "I'll ask Forrest to take care of all of it."

"Take care of it? What will he do?"

"It won't be the first grave he's dug," she said.

CeeCee stood up. "Oh no!" she said, horrified.

"Do you have another suggestion?"

"Her family needs to…" Her voice trailed off. Needs to what? Know what happened? Pick up her body? What? She closed her eyes. "This is terrible," she said.

"It's a mess, all right," Naomi said.

"Are you sure Forrest will do it? He's so mad at me."

"He'll do it," she said. "He'll do it to protect us as well as you. You get caught, we all get caught. Can you tell him how to get there?"

"I…maybe. I'll try."

"You're a mess." Naomi eyed her clothes. "You need to clean up."

CeeCee looked down at her flannel shirt, growing stiff with blood. Her jeans were cold and wet against her thighs, and her laceless shoes were splattered with red. She sat down on the bed again. Seeing Genevieve's blood on her made her dizzy.

"Take a shower," Naomi said. "Put your clothes and that wig in a bag and we'll burn them along with Forrest's when he gets back."

CeeCee touched her head. She still had on the blond wig.

"Then help yourself to some of my clothes." Naomi sounded as though she'd done this many times before. "Go ahead." She nudged her with an elbow when CeeCee didn't move. "I'll take care of the baby."

* * *

She took a bath instead of a shower because she didn't trust her legs to support her. She leaned back to wet her hair, washing it with Naomi's shampoo. Then she scrubbed herself hard with soap that smelled like lemons, and she cried the whole time. Images of Genevieve ran through her mind. Genevieve reaching for the baby. Asking CeeCee to keep her alive. Genevieve had known how much trouble she was in, CeeCee thought. She'd known.

She got out of the tub and pressed a towel to her eyes, picturing Genevieve's five-year-old daughter, Vivian, left motherless. *Don't think,* she told herself. Dropping the towel, she shook away the image. The time for crying was over. Now she needed to figure out how to get the baby to the governor. And she needed to talk to Tim. As much as she'd wanted him to rush back to the cabin when she was there, now she hoped he had not yet left Jacksonville. She didn't want him to discover Genevieve as she'd left her.

She dressed in a pair of Naomi's jeans that were too long for her, a red-and-white checked flannel shirt, and moccasins that fit perfectly, and by the time she walked out of Naomi and Forrest's bedroom, two babies were crying. She found Naomi in the kitchen, heating a bottle of formula in a pan on the stove. Emmanuel's sling was over her shoulder, and CeeCee could tell from the size of the infant that she had placed Genevieve's crying baby in it. Emmanuel cried from his cradle in the corner, as if he knew he'd been displaced.

"Can she breathe in there?" CeeCee tried to peer inside the sling.

"Does it sound like she's breathing?" Naomi lifted the baby out of the sling and handed her to CeeCee.

When CeeCee'd held her before, the baby had been a bulky little package wrapped in a blanket made for a double bed. Now she felt so light. So tiny. She was dressed in a blue terry-cloth sleeper and wrapped in a green baby blanket and she smelled powdery clean. CeeCee rocked her back and forth the way Naomi had done earlier, trying unsuccessfully to still her wailing. The baby had been crying for so long. Could she be injuring herself? She sounded as if she were in terrible pain, a little catch in the intake of breath between each cry.

"Is she hurting herself with all this crying?" CeeCee asked.

"She's fine. Just hungry, and we'll take care of that soon enough."

"Can we try to call Tim while we're feeding her?" she asked.

"Sit in the rocking chair by the fireplace," Naomi said. "I'll bring you the bottle and you can feed her while I'm nursing Emmanuel. Forrest's gone to the cabin. He said he thinks he knows how to get there from looking at the map with Tim and Marty." She peered out the window. The sky was beginning to grow light. "He wanted to do it before it got too light out," she added wearily.

CeeCee had turned this family's world upside down. "I'm sorry, Naomi," she said.

"It will all work out okay," Naomi said. "Go on. Go in the living room."

CeeCee sat down in the rocker by the fireplace. Naomi came into the room carrying both Emmanuel and the bottle, which she handed to CeeCee. "Do you know how to feed a baby?" she asked.

CeeCee nodded, taking the bottle from her. "I did a lot of baby-sitting, although not with a baby this little. This *new*." She touched the nipple to the baby's lips and within seconds, the infant latched on and began to suck.

Naomi nodded approvingly. "She's going to be an easy baby," she said, as she sat down on the other side of the hearth. She lifted her sweater, did something CeeCee couldn't see with the front of her bra, then raised Emmanuel to her breast. "Ah," she said, as all crying ceased. "Peace." She nearly smiled as she looked at CeeCee. "I trimmed one of Emmanuel's diapers for her. We can cut some more later."

"Okay." CeeCee wished Naomi shared her sense of urgency about calling Tim. "I think we need to try to reach Tim before he and Marty—"

Naomi held up her hand to stop her. "I've already spoken to Tim," she said.

"You *did*? I wanted to talk to him!"

"I know you did, but it's better this way. There was really no time for that."

"He's still in Jacksonville?"

Naomi nodded.

"What did he say? Is he furious with me?"

"One thing at a time," Naomi said. "He's still in Jacksonville and he's had several conversations with Governor Russell, but nothing firm yet. He's not mad at you. He gets that this was a situation out of your control. He's going to up the ante and ask that Andie be set free."

CeeCee was astonished. "He's going through with this even though Genevieve is dead?" she asked.

"Of course he is," Naomi said. "But now he has to get Andie's freedom. If Russell agreed to commute her sentence and then Tim couldn't produce the goods, Andie'd be in worse trouble than before. So he has to get her out of there."

"But…" This had gotten so out of hand. "It's wrong," she said. "This whole thing is so wrong."

"You're finding religion a little late." The tone of Naomi's voice was kinder than her words. "He said for you to go underground right away."

"Underground?" CeeCee was stunned to hear the word applied to herself. "I can't do that," she said. "I mean, I don't know how—"

"We'll help you."

"I don't want to have to—" She stopped herself. She was going to say that she didn't want to be on the run, but she suddenly realized this could work to her advantage. "If Tim and I are both underground," she said, "then he and I could be together like you and Forrest."

Naomi shook her head. "Forrest and I had a completely different situation," she said. "Yours is too dangerous. You should never see him again."

"But I want to be *with* him." Once more, she felt the threat of tears. "We planned to—"

"Grow up, CeeCee." It was the first truly harsh thing Naomi had said to her. "You're playing in the big league now. You have to forget about him. You won't be CeeCee anymore, and he won't be Tim. You have to start over."

"What if I…I could just go back to my old life." Oh, she would give anything to have her old life back! "My roommate thinks I'm visiting a friend. That I broke up with Tim. I could just go—"

"The pigs are going to find out who your boyfriend is. Or was," Naomi said. "It doesn't matter which. Then they're going to find you and interrogate you. First, you're so green that you're going to crack, but even if you were…streetwise, how are you going to prove you were with this friend? Who's the friend who'll vouch that you were visiting her? Do you get it? You're up to your eyeballs in this mess and you can't get out."

"Where will I go?" CeeCee asked. The baby must have sensed her panic, because she lost the nipple for a moment and started to cry. CeeCee slipped it between her pink lips again. "What will I do?" she asked.

"You can stay here for a couple of days until we can get you some documentation," Naomi said. "But you have to stay inside. No one can know you're here."

"What do you mean, documentation?"

"A new name. A new identity for you and the baby."

"The *baby*? She needs to go to the governor."

"CeeCee." Naomi sighed. "How do you propose to do that?"

"I don't know, but we have to."

"No, we don't. She's going with you."

"I can't take care of a baby!"

"Well, you'd better learn how in the next few days."

"Can I leave her at a police station?"

"How? Will you walk into a police station, drop her off and skip out, no questions asked? You have to avoid leaving any kind of a trail behind you, CeeCee. You wouldn't be putting just yourself in jeopardy, but Tim and his brother and sister and Forrest and me and our children. No one knows this baby exists, okay? That's the one lucky thing you've got going for you. No one's going to be looking for a baby. Just a pregnant woman."

"But it's completely wrong for me—"

"Everything you've done for the last few days has been completely wrong, even though you did it with the best of intentions. This is the risk you agreed to take. There are always consequences."

"Can I leave the baby with you?" she asked. "You're so good with children."

"How will we explain a new baby to our friends and neighbors?"

"I'm only *sixteen*." Panic rose inside her.

"Plenty of sixteen-year-old girls have babies."

CeeCee looked down at the infant in her arms. The baby's face was peaceful as she sucked, vacant eyes a dark blue-gray, blinking open and closed. How had her own mother felt, holding her, feeding her for the first time? Had she ever considered getting rid of her?

"My mother had me at sixteen," CeeCee admitted.

"Well," Naomi said, "there you go."

Chapter Fifteen

Promise me you'll hold on to these letters. I know you might not appreciate them when you're young. Maybe you even think they're silly. But when you get older, I think you'll be very glad to have a little piece of me. At least, I hope you will.

THERE WAS SOMETHING SEDUCTIVE ABOUT SLEEPING WITH a baby.

At first, CeeCee thought it was a terrible idea. "I could roll over and crush her," she said when Naomi suggested it. "I could suffocate her."

"You won't," Naomi said. "It'll be good for both of you."

By the second night, CeeCee wondered if sleeping with the baby was Naomi's plot to create a bond between her and the infant. If so, it was working. She wasn't getting much sleep; the baby was hungry more often than not and going through an unbelievable number of Emmanuel's altered diapers. But as she cuddled the infant while she fed her, brushing her lips over the downy red hair, as she held her floppy little head while she burped her, she felt intoxicated by the soft, delicious baby smell that filled the air around her.

Dahlia was thrilled to find that CeeCee was back, and even more excited that she'd brought a baby with her.

"What's her name?" Dahlia leaned on the arm of the rocker as CeeCee fed the baby.

"Um…" CeeCee looked at Naomi, who was sitting on the floor with Emmanuel in her lap, trying to get him interested in a ring of large, plastic keys.

"Sweet Pea," Naomi said.

Dahlia laughed. "That's a silly name."

"Not really," Naomi said. "A sweet pea is a flower, just like a Dahlia is a flower."

"It is? Which is prettier?"

"Totally different," Naomi said. "A Dahlia is big and round and explosive, like fireworks. And a sweet pea is delicate and ruffly."

"Wow." Dahlia giggled. She gently touched the baby's back, then looked at CeeCee. "Was she in your tummy?" she asked.

CeeCee looked helplessly at Naomi again.

"Yes, she was," Naomi said.

Dahlia rested her head on CeeCee's shoulder so she could get a better look at the baby.

"Now you've got your very own wetting doll," she said.

She had no idea what was happening between Tim and Marty and the governor. Naomi and Forrest had no television, just a small transistor radio that received a Christian music station and that was it. Not one of their vehicles had a working radio.

She pleaded with Naomi to let her talk to Tim on the phone. Was he still in Jacksonville? Had he already gone underground?

"It's too dangerous to call him from our phone," Naomi said as she loaded diapers into the old avocado-colored washing machine in the kitchen. "I only called him that one time because I had no choice."

CeeCee pulled a towel out of the dryer, folded it and set it in the laundry basket. "Give me the number and I can drive to a pay phone somewhere," she suggested.

"You can't leave the house," Naomi reminded her. She set the dial on the washing machine and it chugged to life. "Get over him, CeeCee," she said. "Let him go. He has enough to deal with, and even though you may not know it yet, so do you."

"I know it." CeeCee sobered.

"Then act like it." Naomi grabbed a bunch of diapers from the dryer and began folding them. "Focus on your future, not your past."

"*What* future?" CeeCee said. "I don't feel like I have one. Where am I going to go? To live?"

"Now you sound like a real sixteen-year-old drama queen," Naomi said. "We're working on your future, so relax."

"What does that mean?"

"There are a couple of options and we're figuring out which is best." Naomi added a folded diaper to the stack on the dryer. "I'm not going to tell you about them 'til I've got one firmed up for you."

"What do you mean by options?"

"Places to live. A new life for you. A *future*. Don't worry. You'll have one."

Fighting with Naomi was fruitless. It was almost impossible to get her to bend, so she continued folding the laundry in silence.

Once before, she'd had this feeling of entering a new phase in her life with no choice in the matter. It was a time filled with loss, with a future that stretched ahead of her like unknown territory. It had taken her years after her mother's death to recapture her sense of well-being and optimism—the optimism Tim had so admired. It was slipping away again, flowing through her hands like water when she tried to grasp it. Her simple life—working at the restaurant with Ronnie, being with Tim, her dream of college nearly a reality—was once again being replaced by something frightening and unknown. The only difference was that her mother's death had been thrust on her. This she had done to herself.

On Thanksgiving, three days after her arrival at Naomi and Forrest's, CeeCee fell in love with the baby. She knew the exact moment her feelings shifted from "like" to "love." Naomi, Forrest and their children were at a friend's house all afternoon and evening, and she was alone with the infant for the first time since her arrival. She lay on the bed with her, having just fed her, and she studied her face, scrutinizing her features for hints of Genevieve. She stroked her finger over the little arm and wrist, and the baby suddenly circled CeeCee's finger with her tiny, perfect hand. Her blue-gray eyes looked into CeeCee's as though she could truly see her and they held her gaze. Held it for a minute. Two minutes. Maybe longer. Long enough for CeeCee's heart to crack in two.

"Oh, Sweet Pea," she whispered, lowering her head to kiss the tiny hand wrapped around her finger. Were maternal feelings so innate that a sixteen-year-old who had never even been pregnant could feel them?

Both of them were motherless. Motherless, alone, just trying to survive.

But unlike CeeCee, the baby wasn't fatherless.

In between nighttime feedings, when CeeCee was both too tired and too troubled to sleep, she tried to come up with ways to get the baby to the governor, something she didn't dare discuss with Naomi or Forrest. She had a vague idea where the governor's mansion was in the heart of Raleigh. She'd once been there on a school trip. She could go in the dead of night, leave the baby on the doorstep, ring the bell and leave. Or maybe not ring the bell, because it would take her a while to get back to the car. It was too cold, though, to leave the baby outside for someone to find in the morning. Maybe she could figure out a way to call the mansion to tell them to look on the front step. Her mind reeled with ideas. She might not know until she saw the mansion what would work and what wouldn't, but one way or another, she was getting this baby to her father.

Then she would think about Tim and Marty and Andie. If she left the baby at the mansion, how would that affect what they were doing? Maybe Andie was free by now. But if Tim was still in the middle of negotiations with the governor, perhaps close to a resolution, would she be creating more problems than she was solving?

Saturday morning, while both babies napped and Naomi gave Dahlia a reading lesson in the living room, CeeCee spoke to Forrest over the dirty breakfast dishes at the kitchen table.

"I'm supposed to come home tomorrow from my trip to Phila-delphia," she said. "I have to let my roommate know I'm not coming back."

Forrest looked at her over the rim of his coffee mug. "You can't use our phone," he said.

"If I don't let her know, though, she'll call the police. She'll report me as a missing person and they'll be looking for me."

Forrest tipped his head back and looked at the ceiling, consid-ering her argument. "All right," he said finally. "I'll drive you to a pay phone tonight in New Bern. You can call her from there. But you'd better think through what you're going to tell her. Be very careful."

The drive to New Bern took a little more than a half hour, and as they drove over the extremely long, two-lane trestle bridge—a truly frightening experience in the dark—the lights of the small town came into view on the other side of the river. CeeCee ached with the realization that help for Genevieve had not been that far away. She must have looked upset, because Forrest suddenly asked her, "What are you thinking?"

"How close help was for the baby's mother, and I didn't know it. And I didn't believe her when she said she was in labor. And I wouldn't have known how to get here. And—"

"What's done is done." Forrest turned into a gas station, pulling up close to the phone booth, and handed her a fistful of change. "Don't be long," he said.

She got out of the car and closed herself inside the phone booth, which smelled like urine, and it took her a moment to remember her own phone number. It seemed like months since she'd left Chapel Hill.

"Hello?" Ronnie picked up on the second ring. Thank God she was home.

"Ronnie, it's CeeCee," she said.

"Oh, my God, CeeCee! I've been dying to talk to you. Isn't this absolutely unbelievable?"

She was caught off guard. "Isn't what unbelievable?" She was afraid she knew the answer.

"You haven't heard?"

"Heard what?"

"You must not be watching the news. It's—God, you are going to freak out."

"What?"

"It's about Tim. He *kidnapped* Governor Russell's wife."

"*What?* You've got to be kidding."

"You are so lucky he broke up with you," Ronnie said.

"Oh, my God, that's…why? I can't believe he'd do something like that. Are you sure you're talking about Tim Gleason?"

"And his brother Marty. You said Marty was crazy. I think Tim is, too. They have a sister who's in jail for murder. Did you know about her? They kidnapped Russell's wife to get him to set their sister free. Isn't that *insane?*"

It *was* insane. Why hadn't she realized that before it was too late?

"So…" CeeCee said. "What happened? Did the governor set her free or what?"

"The last I heard on the news this morning was that he wasn't giving in to them and that a search was on for them and his wife. And CeeCee! A cop came to the restaurant this morning asking to talk to you. Somehow they found out you'd been his girlfriend. I told them you'd broken up with him and you were in Philadelphia visiting a friend. They want to talk to you. They'll call when you get back."

Her heart skipped a beat, and she leaned against the glass of the phone booth, her head spinning. They were looking for her, as Naomi had predicted. It was happening already. "Listen, Ronnie, I'm calling to tell you I've decided to stay in Philadelphia."

Ronnie hesitated. "Because of this?" she asked.

"No, no. I decided a couple of days ago. I really like it here and I—"

"You're staying…you mean like permanently?"

"Well, I don't know if it's for the rest of my life, but my friend found me a job here at a really good restaurant and…I needed to get away from the memories of Tim and everything."

Ronnie said nothing, and CeeCee wondered if she believed her.

"I can't afford the room on my own, CeeCee," she said finally.

CeeCee had not even thought of that. "I know, and I'm going to send you money from my first few paychecks until you can find someone to take my place." She winced at the lie. She hated leaving Ronnie in the lurch. She *would* send her money if she ever got any. Her bank account had five thousand dollars in it, but she would have to kiss that money goodbye if the cops were looking for her. If only she could simply hand it over to Ronnie.

Ronnie was thinking the same thing. "You've got that money in the bank," she said. "Couldn't you at least send me enough for next month's rent?"

"Oh, right!" CeeCee said as if she'd forgotten. "Of course. The money's in a savings account so I don't have checks or anything, but as soon as I get an account there…I mean here, in Philadelphia, I'll send you some. And you can just keep all my stuff," she added.

Ronnie hesitated again. "You're not even coming back to get your clothes and things?" she asked.

God, this had to sound suspicious! She hoped the police didn't question Ronnie again.

"I just…I'm going to start fresh here. I'd have to take the bus and everything, and lug my stuff back and it would just be a hassle."

"What about your mother's letters?"

It was CeeCee's turn to fall silent. *The letters.* She didn't care about her clothes or her records or her two beaded necklaces. But the letters! Her heart felt empty at the thought of leaving them behind.

"I don't have my friend's address right now, but I'll send it to you and then you could mail the letters to me, okay?"

"Okay. What's your friend's name?"

She'd been prepared for that question. "Susan," she lied.

"How come I never heard of her?"

"She wasn't like a close friend or anything, but her invitation to visit came at the perfect time. And we're really getting along. She's cool. Not as cool as you, of course."

"You have to turn on the news, CeeCee," Ronnie said. "It's all over the place about Tim. And you should call the police. Maybe you know something that would help them find Tim and Governor Russell's wife."

"I can't imagine what I'd know that could help."

"Did they have a secret hideaway kind of place or anything?"

"Not that they ever told me about."

"What should I tell the police if they come around again?"

"Just the truth. I called you from Philadelphia and wasn't able to give you an address or phone number yet."

"But you're going to send me an address for the letters, right?"

"Sure," CeeCee said, but she knew she would never be able to let Ronnie know where she was. The cops might talk to her again. When Ronnie told them about her abrupt move to Philadelphia, they'd put two and two together and realize CeeCee was part of the Gleason brothers' diabolical scheme.

For the first time, she realized how essential it was that CeeCee Wilkes disappear.

Chapter Sixteen

You never asked me why I named you CeeCee. I spent a lot of time with one of those little baby name books they sell at the grocery store, checking the meaning behind all the names. A lot of girls' names mean "pure" and "soft" and "womanly," when I wanted you to be tough as nails. The two I liked best were Carol, which means "strong," and Constance, which means "unyielding." I was still undecided when you were born, and both names seemed so grown-up for my little baby. Pam suggested CeeCee to better suit a strong little girl. I think it's perfect for you.

"WELL, IF YOU DON'T HAVE THE LOOK OF A NEW MOM," Naomi said with a laugh when CeeCee walked into the kitchen Sunday morning. "Completely exhausted."

CeeCee lowered herself into a chair at the table. Naomi had made her a sling like the one she used with Emmanuel, and she was carrying Sweet Pea in it. The sling had magical powers, she was convinced. After a night of changing wet diapers, cleaning spit up, stumbling to the kitchen to heat formula, and listening to that rhythmic crying that tore at CeeCee's heart, she'd put the baby into the sling and was rewarded with utter silence and calm.

"There's oatmeal on the stove," Naomi said.

CeeCee got to her feet again and scooped some of the oatmeal into a bowl, leaning over so she wouldn't spill any of the hot cereal into the sling.

"Before you sit, there's something for you on the counter." Naomi nodded toward the counter by the stove. CeeCee picked up the manila folder and carried it back to the table.

"What is it?" she asked, taking her seat again.

"Open it and see."

She opened the folder and pulled out two birth certificates, a social security card and an Oregon driver's license.

"The top birth certificate is yours," Naomi said. "That's your new name."

CeeCee stared at the typewritten name. Eve Bailey, born in Portland, Oregon, on March 7, 1960. Her parents were Marjorie and Lester Bailey. She stared at those names, picturing the imaginary people to whom they belonged. Marjorie and Lester. They sounded so solid, the names of caring, attentive parents. She already loved them. Maybe she'd grown up in a middle-class neighborhood in a house with a swimming pool. Did people have swimming pools in Oregon? She doubted it, but the image was sharp in her mind.

"My name's Eve?" She looked at Naomi.

"Now and forever more," Naomi said. "What do you think?"

"Eve." She repeated the name out loud. It made her feel older. Older, wiser, more sophisticated. "I don't think it fits me."

Naomi smiled. "That's how I felt about Naomi at first."

"I keep forgetting you've been through all of this yourself," CeeCee said.

"Oh, yes. And I remember how hard it was to give up my old name and take on a name as oddball as Naomi. But you'll be amazed how quickly you'll adjust. I'll start calling you Eve right now."

CeeCee smiled slowly. There was safety in a new identity. She had to remember that. "There is no Eve Bailey, right?" She wanted to be sure she understood. "This is a made-up name?"

"That's right."

She looked at the birth certificate again. "She's a year older than me."

"That's good. It won't seem quite so weird that you've had a baby." She leaned forward. "So remember now. You're seventeen."

CeeCee peeked inside the sling to make sure the baby was breathing, then picked up the social security card and driver's license. The social security number was very different from hers and the card was made out, of course, to Eve Bailey. The license had no picture on it. The address was in Portland.

"I've never even been west of Chapel Hill," she said. "Why Oregon? Because it's as far from here as possible?"

"Oregon doesn't have pictures on their drivers' licenses, that's why," Naomi said. "When you get to Virginia, go to the Department of Motor Vehicles and get a Virginia license."

"Virginia? Why am I going to Virginia?"

"I'll tell you in a minute. First, check out Sweet Pea's birth certificate."

She pulled the final document from the envelope. The certificate showed that Corinne Bailey had been born a week ago in

Charleston, South Carolina. Eve Bailey was her mother. Her father's name was blank.

"Who's her father supposed to be?" CeeCee asked.

"You don't know. That's best in a situation like this. Just pretend you slept around and weren't sure. Otherwise, you can have all sorts of problems later."

"Like what kind of problems?"

Naomi shrugged. "Like, if you ever needed the father's permission to do something, now you don't. And if she finds her birth certificate when she gets older, she won't go looking for some mythical man."

"But she'll think her mother was a tramp." CeeCee almost laughed.

"Better a tramp than a felon," Naomi said.

Felon. The word was sobering. CeeCee Wilkes was a felon. Eve Bailey was a pure blank slate.

"So, why Virginia?" she asked again.

"There's a woman in Charlottesville named Marian Kazan. You can stay with her while you get your feet on the ground. I've never met her, but I've heard she's really nice and she runs a day-care center, so she can take care of the baby—of Corinne—while you find a job. That's got to be the first thing you do when you get up there. Look for work."

"How do I...I mean I can't tell them where I worked before."

"That's right, you sure can't. What kind of work were you doing?"

"Waitressing."

"Perfect. Start at a dive, something low-level where you can tell them you have experience but where they won't care enough to check your references. If they ask where you worked, make up the name of a place and say it was in Charleston, since that's where the baby was born. Get experience in your new name, then you can build up a work record and you'll be home free."

Naomi made it sound so simple, but CeeCee's head spun.

"You'd better say your parents were from South Carolina or something, too, because I don't think people from Oregon sound like you."

CeeCee nodded.

"And we want you to leave tonight," Naomi added.

"*Tonight?*" CeeCee asked. "How am I going to find my way to Charlottesville at night? How far is it, anyway?"

"About four hours," Naomi said.

"Don't make me leave tonight," CeeCee said. "Please. With the baby and everything." How would she manage the baby on her own, without Naomi to turn to with every question and insecurity? She suddenly remembered, though, that her plan to leave the baby at the governor's mansion required darkness. She could pass through Raleigh on her way to Charlottesville and leave the baby on his doorstep. "What about the formula?" she asked. "How will I heat it?"

"We'll give you a big jug of water to mix the formula with. Put it inside the car instead of the trunk so it stays at room temperature. That car still has heat, doesn't it?" Naomi looked momentarily worried, until CeeCee nodded. "Okay, then you'll just give her room-temperature formula. It'll be fine. Forrest is in town right now buying diapers and formula."

"What if...what if she chokes or something? Do you know baby CPR?"

Naomi's smile was patient. "I'll give you a quick first-aid lesson before you take off," she said. "You're really good with her, Eve. You're a natural mom. You just need to stop worrying so much about everything."

"Let's face it," CeeCee said dryly. "I've got a lot to worry about."

"Pretend you don't. You'll attract attention if you seem too paranoid."

"This lady…Marian?"

"Kazan."

"She knows I'm coming?"

"She's expecting you and Sweet Pea late tonight or early tomorrow morning. Stop if you need to sleep, but do it in a parking lot somewhere with a lot of cars so you don't attract attention. If a pig stops you, you're on your way to stay with a friend in Charlottesville. You can give them Marian's name and phone number."

Marian Kazan would be expecting a girl and a baby. CeeCee would have some explaining to do when she showed up alone.

"The license plate on the car isn't from South Carolina," she said.

"We're taking care of that this afternoon."

"Man," CeeCee said. "How do you do all this?" She lifted the birth certificates.

"There's a good network," Naomi said. "We haven't had to use it in a long time and it frankly scares me to get involved with them again, but we have to. Everyone's pitching in to help you, CeeCee. I mean, *Eve.* And by helping you, they're helping us and Tim and themselves. We all protect each other."

"Is Marian part of SCAPE?" CeeCee asked, and knew as soon as the words left her mouth that she shouldn't have asked. Naomi raised her eyebrows, waiting for her to take the question back.

"Don't ask, I know." She was beginning to think half the people in the country were part of SCAPE.

Forrest arrived at two that afternoon, laden with supplies for CeeCee and a South Carolina plate for the car. He'd bought diapers, formula and a pacifier for the baby, who already had a complete wardrobe, thanks to Emmanuel's hand-me-downs.

"This is your baby shower," he joked. She'd never met a man more unpredictable than Forrest. Nice one minute, curt the next. He was anxious to have her leave, so he'd probably enjoyed buying her the things that would help her do that.

He'd also bought a flashlight, a laundry basket to serve as a car bed for the baby, and some clothing for CeeCee—jeans and two sweaters that were too large.

"It's good they're too big," Naomi said, looking at the tags on the sweaters. "You'll look like you recently had a baby."

Forrest once again spread a map, this one of North Carolina and Virginia, on the kitchen table. He wrote directions for CeeCee and handed them to her. "Don't forget you're driving a stick," he said. "Last thing you need is to screw up and get stopped by the fuzz."

"Okay," she said, glancing at the directions. "Would it be okay if I took that map with me, in case I take a wrong turn or something?" She'd need it for the side trip to Raleigh.

He looked at the map for a moment as though considering his answer. "Yeah, you can take it," he said, folding it up.

"Y'all have been great to me," she said.

"Like we had a friggin' choice." Forrest actually smiled at her. He reached into his shirt pocket and handed her five twenty-dollar bills. "For the road," he said. "Just remember, you were never here. And you're never coming back. This time for real, okay? I don't want to see you on my doorstep again."

"I know," she said. She understood the rules now.

Since it was still light out, Forrest carried her things to the car for her. Then she fed the baby in the rocker in front of the fireplace. Naomi sat across from her, nursing Emmanuel. CeeCee was quiet, her fear mounting. Once she walked out the door of this safe haven, she could never come back.

She looked up to see Naomi smiling at her.

"That's your baby." Naomi nodded at the infant. "Look at her in your arms. Tell me she doesn't feel like yours."

"She doesn't," CeeCee said. "She feels like something I stole."

"No," Naomi said. "She's something you saved."

Chapter Seventeen

I'm mad at Pam. She told me that leaving letters for you to open after I die is selfish. She said I'm dragging out my goodbye in a maudlin way, trying to stay a part of your life instead of letting you get over losing me. She doesn't understand what it's like to be dying at twenty-nine years old. She gets to be part of her son's life for many years to come. All I want is to be able to touch your life as you get older.

Is writing letters a way to console you or myself? I could spend a few months pondering that question, but I don't have a few months. So I'll keep writing, doing what feels right to me and what I think is best for you. If it turns out to be a selfish thing, please forgive me.

SHE SAT AT THE INTERSECTION OF A COUNTRY LANE AND Route 70, trying to get the courage to pull onto the wider road. For the past hour, she'd been creeping along the back roads from Naomi and Forrest's house, wishing she could get to better, less rutted, less isolated streets. Now here she was, paralyzed at the Route 70 entrance. There were not many cars, but those that zipped by did so at a frightening speed. When Tim was teaching her to drive this car, she'd never made it out of third gear.

At least the baby was cooperating. Naomi had suggested keeping her in the sling as she drove, since the infant was sleeping so soundly by the time she left, but that seemed too dangerous. What if she crashed into a tree? So the baby—she refused to call her Corinne, since it wasn't her place to give her a name—slept in the laundry basket on the floor in front of the passenger seat. Still not the best place in an accident, but she was near the heater and that seemed important.

A car pulled up behind her, honking impatiently. She stepped on the gas and let out the clutch, lurching forward, grinding gears, and her entire body tensed as she pulled onto the road and worked her way up to fourth gear. Then, suddenly, she was flying.

The baby woke up with a wail at seven o'clock. CeeCee pulled onto a quiet, tree-lined country road, and she left the engine running so the car would stay warm as she mixed the formula and fed the infant.

"This is the last time I'll feed you, Sweet Pea," she said, lowering her head to kiss the baby's downy hair. "I'm going to miss you so much. You've been my little buddy the past few days." She blinked back the tears welling in her eyes. How much loss could one person bear? Her mother. Tim. This beautiful baby. She refused to believe that Tim was lost to her, though. Once things settled down, he would find her. And she could read about the governor and his family in the news from time to time. She could follow this little baby as she grew up, watching her blossom, knowing she'd helped her come into the world. She'd feel proud, then, that she'd made the decision to get the baby to her father where she belonged. She felt proud already.

Traffic increased only slightly as she neared Raleigh. It was eight o'clock, and she was relieved when she spotted a sign for Garner. Finally, a place she'd heard of! She pulled off the road and, as quietly as she could, opened the map to study the small diagram of Raleigh in the upper right corner. She used the flashlight Forrest had given her, and the circle of light shivered on the paper: She was getting nervous.

It looked like 70 would turn into Wilmington Street and lead her to downtown Raleigh, but then what? How would she find the governor's mansion? She decided she would turn right on Western—that looked like a major street. Then maybe she would recognize something.

With her itinerary firmly in mind, she got back on 70. She missed Western altogether, but turned right at the next corner. Suddenly, she saw the sign for Blount Street. That was it, wasn't it? It sounded so familiar. She started to turn left onto Blount, but it was one-way. She made the next left, her stomach twisting with anxiety. Leaning forward and peering into the darkness, she clutched the steering wheel as she made a few more turns, trying to get to her destination. The moon lit the houses on either side of her as she hunted for the mansion. All she remembered from her middle-school tour of the building was that it had been big and imposing and, she thought, made of dark brick. She and her girlfriends had been more interested in the cute high-school senior who was acting as their chaperone than in anything having to do with the mansion.

There were not many cars on the street, which was good, because she was driving very slowly. A car pulled up behind her, though, nearly touching her fender. Cautiously she pulled over to the curb to let it pass, then decided to write the note she would leave with the baby. She propped the flashlight between her chin and shoulder and set a notepad on her leg. She ripped off the top sheet of the pad to get rid of her fingerprints, then slipped a diaper beneath her hand as she thought about what to write. In spite of her rehearsal of this moment, she still was not sure what to say.

Dear Governor, she printed in broad letters that looked nothing like her usual handwriting. This is your baby girl. I am sorry, but

But what? Genevieve died? She wasn't even sure how to spell Genevieve. And what if the governor were deep in negotiations with Tim and Marty when he received this news of his wife's death? She tore the page from the pad and started over.

Dear Governor. This is your baby girl. Period. Bending over, she fastened the note to the baby's blanket with a diaper pin. What if he didn't believe the note? What if he rejected this baby as not being his and she grew up in foster homes? He'd get a doctor to do a blood test or something, wouldn't he? She held the beam of the flashlight on the note, using her hand to protect the baby's eyes from the light. *This is your baby girl.* Shutting her own eyes, she rested her palm on the sleeping infant. "She really is yours," she said out loud. "Please don't reject her."

Starting the car, she drove past huge Victorians, their windows filled with buttery light behind leaded glass. The houses with their enormous pillars, curly gingerbread and towering turrets were a little spooky. Suddenly the mansion came into view on the left, il-luminated by spotlights on the ground.

"Oh, no," she said to herself, as she realized the building was surrounded by a massive brick-and-wrought-iron fence. Why hadn't she remembered that? She drove very slowly in order to peer through the slim black iron posts. The mansion was an eerie, bulky monster rising up from the broad lawn and greenery. Only a downstairs light burned inside, and she pictured the governor sitting at a desk, talking with Tim on the phone as he desperately plead for the return of his wife.

Someone was in the wide, circular driveway and she was so surprised at seeing a person outside the mansion that she stalled the car. She fought with the clutch and got back in gear, then quickly turned the corner, pulled over and shut off her lights.

Her heart pounded as though she had run a mile. She could see now that there were several people in the driveway, and with a sinking heart, she realized that they were police officers. Even if she could find a way inside that intimidating fence, there were cops everywhere. Of course. The governor's wife had been kidnapped. What had she expected?

She slumped low in the driver's seat, afraid to attract attention as she tried to figure out what to do. Ahead of her on the left was a police car parked in the darkness. If it was unlocked, maybe she could put the baby inside it and let the policeman find her when he got in. What if he didn't return to the car for hours, though? The baby would wake up alone and cold and hungry. Maybe the cop had the night shift and wouldn't return to the car until morning.

She couldn't think of anything else to do, though. The street was dark, the police car protected from the streetlights by the trees and shrubs at the edge of the mansion property. If the car was unlocked, she would put the baby on the seat. Then, when she got about an hour away, she'd call the Raleigh police from a pay phone and tell them to look in the police cars near the mansion.

Naomi would be furious if she knew what CeeCee was contemplating. How, though, could this implicate Naomi? She lifted the laundry basket to the passenger seat, then carefully unsnapped the legs of the baby's sleeper and wiped off any fingerprints that might have been on the plastic, duck-shaped heads of the diaper pins. She didn't dare leave the basket in the police car, though; it was covered with fingerprints from all of them.

She gave her car enough gas to roll along the curb in the direction of the police car, stopping across the street from it. The car looked empty. Better yet, it was out of sight from the front of the mansion. She lifted the baby from the seat and held her against her chest, breathing in her scent for the last time. The baby whimpered but didn't cry. "I'll miss you," CeeCee whispered. "I'll check on you somehow. I'll make sure you're doing all right."

She visualized what she had to do. She'd leave her car idling, quickly cross the street and put the baby on the seat of the police car. What if the officer returned before she had a chance to call, though, and sat on her in the dark? The thought made her shudder. She'd put her on the back seat, then, closing the car door very quietly. Then she'd get the hell out of Raleigh.

Drawing in a deep breath, she held the baby close and slowly opened her car door. She walked quickly across the street and, without giving herself a chance to change her mind, grasped the handle of the rear door and pulled it toward her.

An alarm cut through the air. Gasping, she let go of the door handle, but the alarm didn't stop. She heard a shout from the front of the mansion. CeeCee raced across the street and dove into her own car, the baby wailing in her ear. She nearly tossed her into the laundry basket, then put the car in gear and took off. She was blocks away before she heard the sirens above the baby's crying. She made a few turns, driving as fast as she dared, relieved by the lack of traffic on the roads. The sirens faded behind her as she came to a major intersection. She turned left and immediately saw a sign for the Beltline. *Thank God!* She'd never driven on the Beltline and had always felt a little terrified of it, but now she welcomed the anonymity the highway would offer her. She merged into the safety of the traffic and began to cry, her own sobs joining the baby's. The muscles in her arms and legs quivered so hard they hurt, and she could feel her heart bouncing around in her chest like a water-filled balloon. If something happened to her right now—did sixteen-year-olds have heart attacks?—what would become of the baby?

She reached over, resting her hand on top of the infant in the basket. "Hang on, Sweet Pea," she said. "I'm so sorry about this. I'll make it up to you, I promise."

When she felt safe, she pulled off the highway and into a parking lot. She changed the screaming infant, then mixed the formula and fed her. Even then, it took the baby a while to calm down, and CeeCee worried that the trauma she'd just put her through— sirens blaring in her ears, being tossed into a basket, the crazy drive through dark streets—might scar her forever. There would be no more police cars tonight. No more thoughts of dropping the baby off at a police station. Maybe she would try again once she was in Charlottesville and had a chance to catch her breath and think clearly. But not tonight.

When she finished feeding the baby, she held her on her shoulder, rubbing her back, nuzzling the silky skin of her neck. *She's something you saved,* Naomi had said. CeeCee pressed her cheek against the sleeping infant's temple. She cried a little, guilty that she'd failed to leave her with the governor, but she would be crying much harder if she'd succeeded. She was deeply in love with the baby in her arms. It was different from the love she felt for Tim. More like the love she'd had for her mother—pure and bottomless and open as the sea.

Eve

Chapter Eighteen

IT WAS NEARLY ELEVEN BY THE TIME SHE REACHED Charlottesville. She drove through the downtown area and felt almost as if she'd been there before. Even though it was late, young people—students?—walked along the sidewalks, carrying books, talking and laughing with one another.

"Look at this, Sweet Pea," she said to the sleeping baby. "It's like Chapel Hill."

At a stoplight, she checked the directions Forrest had given her, then drove another half mile until she came upon an old, white two-story house. She checked the house number illuminated by the gas lantern near the front steps. One seventy-six. This was it. She parked directly in front of the building.

The house had a slightly lopsided look to it, but the light from the lantern bounced off clean white siding and black shutters, and above the railing of the wraparound porch, she could see the tops of four ladder-back rockers. Lights burned in all the downstairs windows.

She lifted the baby into her arms and got out of the car, inhaling the scent of burning wood. Heading up the sidewalk to the house, she suddenly stopped short, wondering if the police might be waiting inside for her. She searched the quiet street for police cars, but she was too tired to feed her paranoia anymore than that, and she started walking again.

Three pumpkins rested on the top step of the porch, and the front door was adorned with a wreath made from greenery and gold-painted gourds.

The baby stirred against her shoulder as she climbed the steps, and she rubbed her tiny back.

"We're here, Sweet Pea," she said. "I'm not exactly sure where 'here' is, but we're going to find out."

A bell hung from the center of the wreath and she pulled the short chain to ring it, the sound clanging in the still air. The door flew open almost instantly, and a woman stood in front of her wearing a welcoming smile.

"Eve?" she asked. She was sixtyish, give or take a few years, and she wore a denim jumper over a cream-colored jersey. Her nearly white pageboy haircut was unfussy, just shy of being severe, and her black wire-rimmed glasses reflected the light from the gas lamp.

"Yes," CeeCee said. "I'm Eve Bailey."

"And I'm Marian. Come in, come in." She took CeeCee's arm and drew her gently inside. "You must be so tired, driving with a baby all the way from Charleston! Do you believe how cold it is already?"

Momentarily confused, CeeCee started to tell her that she'd come from New Bern before realizing that Naomi had set a cover in place for her. She stepped into the warm foyer. On her right was the living room, awash with light from table lamps and a crackling fire. A sofa and chairs, all overstuffed and soft looking, filled the room, and she longed to sink into one of them.

"Let me hold the little one while you take off your coat, honey." Marian took the baby from her arms with a confident sort of force, while CeeCee removed her jacket and hung it in the foyer closet.

"Oh, your hair is divine!" Marian shook her head in amazement, reminding CeeCee of the way Tim reacted to her hair. He would look at it as if it were too wonderful to be believed.

"Thank you," she said.

"Sit by the fire." Marian nodded toward the living room.

CeeCee headed for the sofa and sat down, the cushions as soft and cradling as she'd imagined. There was a bassinet in the corner, made of white wicker and trimmed with pink ribbon. After a very difficult journey, she felt suddenly, unexpectedly, safe.

"Are you hungry?" Marian held the baby close to her chest, and CeeCee noticed that she was wearing black tights and red sneakers. "I have chicken soup I can heat up. Or if you're a vege-tarian, I have some canned lentil soup."

She hadn't thought about food since leaving New Bern, but at the mention of it, she felt famished.

"I don't want to put you to any trouble," she said. She sounded like an adult, the words strange to her own ears.

"I've been waiting for you, honey," Marian said. "They told me you were coming sometime overnight, so I made plenty of soup. It's no trouble at all."

"I'd love some chicken soup, then," CeeCee said.

"First, though, I have to take a good look at this little dumpling." Marian sat down on the couch and rested the baby on her knees.

Don't wake her, CeeCee wanted to say. She'd only gotten the baby to sleep shortly before reaching Charlottesville.

"Why she's brand-new, isn't she?" Marian gently pulled the

blanket away from the infant's face. "And she's a beauty. When did you have her? Are you nursing her?"

Startled, CeeCee tried to think of a response. Marian thought the baby was hers! Along with surprise, she felt an undeserved rush of pride.

"She was born——" she tried to remember the date on the birth certificate "——about a week ago, I think. The time's all run together. And I'm not nursing," she added quickly. "I have formula with me. It's in the car though. And diapers. I brought everything I need for a couple of days."

Marian's frown was full of sympathy. "You poor sweet girl," she said. "I can tell you've been through something rougher than words can say, haven't you?"

CeeCee felt tears burn her eyes and she blinked hard to hold them back.

"You can't even remember what day you had this little one," Marian said. "What's her name?"

"Corinne." CeeCee's voice came out as a whisper. She cleared her throat. "Corinne," she said with more confidence.

"Cory," Marian said. "Is it okay if I call her Cory?"

CeeCee nodded. She liked that better, actually. Corinne was too elaborate a name for a baby.

"She's going to be a redhead, I think." Marian ran a slightly crooked index finger over Cory's pink cheek. "Is her father a redhead?"

How was she supposed to answer that question? she wondered. She opened her mouth, but nothing came out.

"I'm sorry," Marian said. "None of my business." She handed the baby back to her. "I'll go out to your car and get your formula and whatever else there is and——"

"No, I'll do it." She felt guilty for putting her out.

"Stay. That's an order. I'll put the soup on to heat, then go out and get your things. You had a baby a week ago and just drove for who knows how many hours. You sit."

"Okay," CeeCee said, relieved. It would feel good to be taken care of, if only for a few minutes.

She'd almost fallen asleep by the time Marian called her into the kitchen to eat. She lay the baby in the bassinet, then walked into the kitchen and sat down at the table.

"Here you go." Marian put a bowl of soup in front of her, and CeeCee's mouth watered at the sight and smell of it. There were corn muffins, too, and a little tub of butter.

"It's honey butter," Marian said. "And would you like juice or soda or—"

"Just water, please," CeeCee said. "You're not eating?"

Marian laughed. "I had my dinner about five hours ago," she said, setting a glass of water on the table.

Of course. It was nearing midnight. "I'm sorry to keep you up so late," she said.

"I'm a night owl." Marian sat down across from her with a cup of tea. "Also, a mourning dove. I'm one of those people who can get by on a few hours' sleep."

"This is so good," CeeCee said, swallowing a mouthful of the soup. "Thank you for getting a bassinet for me. For Cory."

Marian looked surprised, then laughed. "Oh, honey," she said. "Wait till you see upstairs. I have a little day-care center, so I not only have a bassinet down here, but one upstairs as well. Plus a crib and a changing table and toys galore. And another crib out in my garage, which I converted to a playroom." Marian's accent was impossible to place, but she was not Southern by birth, of that CeeCee was certain. She couldn't figure her out. She was not quite the grandmother type. Not even the kindly old aunt. She was maternal and soothing, yet there was a little bit of drill sergeant lurking beneath her calm blue eyes and denim jumper. "I don't do as much of it as I used to, though," Marian continued. "Right now, I take care of two-year-old twin boys. They're a handful, let me tell you. And I have a four-year-old girl who is my little helper. I've had them all since they were babies, so I always have baby stuff around."

"I guess I came to the right place." CeeCee tried to smile. "But the truth is…I don't really know what I'm doing here. I mean…I guess that sounds stupid. They…I was told to come here and that I could stay with you a little while, but I really don't know if that's okay with you or—"

"It's certainly okay." Marian folded her hands on the table and leaned forward as if sharing a confidence. "You're not the first person I've taken in, honey, believe me. Here's what would work out great, if it suits you. You stay here as long as you need to, and at least in the beginning, you can help me with the day-care kids."

"Yes," CeeCee said quickly, pleased to have a plan. "I…that would be great."

"Now." Marian sat back in her chair. "First things first. Has a doctor looked Cory over?" she asked. "Was she born in a hospital?"

"No, she…I had her…" She stammered and Marian held up her hand.

"It doesn't matter. Anything you think you'd better keep to yourself, you do that. I understand. Listen to me." She leaned forward again. "I understand your name is probably not really Eve. I understand the police or someone who'd like to do you harm is probably looking for you. This is a given, okay? I understand all that, but we don't talk about it. We move forward from today. You're Eve Bailey. I'm Marian Kazan. The baby in the living room is Cory...Bailey?"

CeeCee nodded.

"She has a birth certificate?"

She nodded again.

"Excellent. There's a clinic near here. You'll take her and get her a checkup, just to make sure everything's okay with her. You prepare some answers to that 'where was she born' question. Then we get an OB appointment for you."

"OB?" CeeCee asked.

"Obstetrician." Marian tipped her head to study her. "Honey, just tell me this, did a doctor deliver your baby?"

"No." She thought she was sounding very stupid. Marian probably thought she'd invited a half-wit into her home.

"Okay, we should get you checked out then. Make sure you're healing just fine. Are you having any problems?"

"No. None," CeeCee said. "I don't think I need to go to the doctor."

"You didn't tear or anything?"

CeeCee shook her head, more to clear away a sudden image of Genevieve than to answer the question.

Marian tipped her head again. "How old are you, honey?" she asked.

"Seventeen."

"Oh. Well, that's a bit of a relief. Not that seventeen is old enough to be a mommy, but I thought at first you were only about fifteen."

"Everyone thinks that," CeeCee said.

"Cory's tiny, so I guess it wasn't too bad for you," Marian said. "I'll leave that up to you, then. If you change your mind, there's a wonderful woman OB in town you can go to. She's at a clinic, too, so it costs a pittance. Could even be free, if you don't have any money, and I'm guessing you don't."

"I have a hundred dollars," she said. "I could help buy food or—"

"No, you hold on to your money, okay? I have all the money I need. I do day care because I love children, not because I need the money. Speaking of which, I don't want you to help me with my day-care kids right away, either. I think you need to take care of *you* first. You seem a little shell-shocked right now."

"I'm just…" She smiled weakly. "I guess that's a good description."

She wanted to tell Marian the truth. Marian would understand, and she would know a way to get the baby to the governor. But she didn't have the energy to go into it all and Marian had made it clear she didn't want to know. CeeCee felt as if she were being swept along by a current she no longer had the will to stop.

Marian put her in a bedroom wallpapered with huge pink cabbage roses that reminded CeeCee of one of the foster homes she'd lived in. One of the *good* foster homes, where her stay had been cut all too short by the sudden illness of the foster mother. The room had a double bed, a mauve-colored contemporary upholstered chair that seemed out of place in the house, and a six-drawer dresser. Marian moved a second bassinet into the room from somewhere else on the second floor.

"She's been sleeping in bed with me," CeeCee said.

Marian looked as though she might want to say something about that, but bit her lip. "We'll put the bassinet right next to your bed, then," she said. "Keep her close and safe at the same time."

Marian ran a bubble bath for her in a deep claw-foot tub, and CeeCee pinned her hair on top of her head and sank into the lavender-scented water with relief. She'd fed and changed Cory, and Marian was rocking her to sleep in the living room. For the first time in days, she felt calm, and she leaned her head back against the tub and closed her eyes.

She was soaping herself when she heard the jangle of Marian's doorbell. She froze, holding the washcloth against her neck. Listening hard, she heard voices. A man's. A woman's. The police?

She scrambled out of the tub, barely drying herself before pulling on her jeans and sweater. By the time she ran down the stairs, she was certain Cory had been taken away by the police. That was what she'd wanted a few hours ago; now the thought was unbearable.

Marian sat reading on the living-room sofa, and she looked surprised when CeeCee raced into the room in her bare feet.

"What on earth's the matter, honey?" Marian asked.

"Where's Cory?"

"Sound asleep." Marian nodded toward the bassinet in the corner.

CeeCee peered into the bassinet and saw the baby, asleep beneath a soft, pink blanket. She grabbed the edge of the bassinet to keep from toppling over, light-headed from the hot bath and fear. She felt Marian's hand on her back.

"What is it, Eve?" Marian asked.

"I heard someone at the door. A man's voice. Who was it?"

"A neighbor," Marian said. "He saw my lights on and wanted to be sure I was all right."

"It wasn't..." She didn't dare mention the police. "It wasn't someone looking for me?" She examined Marian's face for the truth.

"No, honey." Marian nearly chuckled. "You're safe with me. I've lived here forever. People think I'm the guardian angel of the neighborhood. The widow lady they can turn to with any problem. I'm not." Marian laughed. "But they think I am, and that's what counts. You'll come to trust me in time. You just need to relax."

"I do trust you." She glanced at the window, where the shades were wide-open, exposing her to the world. "I was just afraid they might have followed me. That maybe they'd take Cory away."

"You have that protective instinct new mothers get," Marian said. "Isn't it wonderful? It's a hormonal thing."

I doubt that, CeeCee thought to herself. "It's just that I love her so much," she said honestly.

"Of course you do." Marian nodded.

"I'll..." CeeCee lowered herself to the straight-backed chair next to the bassinet. "I'll just sit with her for a while, okay?"

Marian nodded. "Sure," she said, and she walked into the kitchen as though she knew CeeCee needed some time alone with the baby.

CeeCee's heart still pumped against her rib cage as she held on to the edge of the bassinet. What if the police *had* taken her away? Wouldn't that be the best thing for her? It didn't matter if she loved her; the baby's welfare had to come first.

"What should I do, Sweet Pea?" she whispered.

She looked into the bassinet, where Cory moved her lips and wrinkled her nose, lost in the peace of a baby dream.

Chapter Nineteen

WITHIN DAYS, SHE BECAME EVE BAILEY. MARIAN introduced her as Eve to the parents of her day-care charges and to a couple of neighbors who stopped by to meet the new houseguest. She felt very young, meeting the adults in Marian's world, much as she had on her first visit to Naomi and Forrest's house, when she'd been more comfortable with Dahlia than with the grown-ups.

She was grateful that Marian didn't want her help with the day-care children right away, since she was more tired than she'd expected, the events of the previous couple of weeks catching up with her. Cory needed her attention every few hours, even during the night, and Eve's scattered, nightmare-filled sleep left her dazed and forgetful. She now understood how a mother could get to the end of her rope and wind up hurting a child, and yet she knew she would never be that sort of mother. Even in the middle of the night, she could see straight through Cory's crying to the distress behind it, and all she wanted was to ease the baby's discomfort.

There was one other thing she wanted—she *needed*—and that was to know where things stood with Tim and Marty and the governor. Marian had a small television set in the living room, which she rarely watched, and Eve felt too new in the house to ask if she could turn it on.

On the fourth morning after her arrival, though, she was eating breakfast in the kitchen, Cory asleep in her sling, when Marian walked into the room and set a folded newspaper, the *Richmond Times-Dispatch,* on the other side of the table. Eve stared at the paper, her fingers itching to open it. Would the story be covered in a Virginia paper? It had been nearly a week since Naomi had spoken to Tim. She had to know what was going on.

Marian bustled around the kitchen as she waited for her day-care children to arrive. She talked about the hassle she'd had getting a permit to convert her garage to a playroom. She talked about the neighborhood—she'd lived there for forty years—and she described the nearby park where parents took their children in the afternoon. "When Cory's a little older, we can take her over there," she said. Eve tried to sprinkle appropriate comments throughout Marian's chatter, but all she could think about was opening the paper.

The doorbell jangled.

Marian grabbed a bottle of juice from the counter and a stack of small, plastic cups. "Take it easy today," she said. "I'll herd the kids right out to the playroom, so if you need anything, that's where I'll be."

"Thanks," Eve said. She heard Marian greet one of the parents at the front door. Small feet thundered in the foyer. A child spoke in a soft voice, while another growled like an animal. Then the front door closed and all was quiet. She reached for the newspaper.

The article was on the front page, topped by the headline Russell Still Optimistic. Eve read it through twice, barely breathing. There seemed no doubt in anyone's mind that Timothy and

Martin Gleason were responsible for the disappearance of Gene-vieve Russell. The brothers' last contact with the governor had been on Thursday morning, four days ago. Authorities had so far been unsuccessful at finding the men. There was a quote from Peter Gleason, Tim's father. "I'm in shock," he said. "My sons were destroyed by Andie's imprisonment, but I still can't believe they would do something like this. I'm hoping it's a mistake, and I'm praying for the safe return of Mrs. Russell." The article described Marty's psychological problems since his tour of duty in Vietnam and stated that Tim was a graduate student in the Social Work De-partment at the University of North Carolina. A professor at UNC was quoted as saying that, while Tim was intelligent and studious, "he was consumed by a passionate obsession with our penal system, to the extent that he was not completing assign-ments in unrelated courses and probably would not have received his Master's in Social Work in the spring."

Oh, Tim. She thought of how hard he'd worked, the books spread out on the table in the coffee shop. She'd never realized that his focus had been entirely on his sister. She wished she'd known. Maybe she could have talked to him about it. If he'd opened up to her, maybe she could have found a way to prevent this tragedy from happening. Her heart ached for him all over again.

The governor had refused to release Andrea Gleason, of course. *He has integrity,* Genevieve had said. He said he was still hoping for a "good outcome" and that he felt hopeful his wife and unborn child were alive and safe. There was a picture of him, and Eve carefully avoided looking at it as she read the article. She held her breath, ex-pecting to see the name CeeCee Wilkes at any moment, but it was not there. The authorities seemed to think the brothers acted alone.

Or maybe they *did* know about her and were playing their cards close to their vests, hoping she would begin to feel safe enough to come out of hiding. Maybe they even knew where she was. She imagined the police following her tire tracks from the cabin to Naomi and Forrest's house, breaking down their door in the middle of the night and questioning them under bare lightbulbs until they cracked and told them they'd sent her to live with Marian Kazan.

The governor's eyes drew her to his picture before she had a chance to think. She'd seen his face in the papers and on TV, but she'd never paid much attention to him before. He looked young for a politician, with a slender build and a full head of dark blond hair, and he stood alone in front of five or six microphones. There were deep hollows in his cheeks and bags beneath his eyes. She touched his picture with her fingertips.

"I'm so sorry," she whispered.

She lowered her gaze to the sling and Cory. The baby sucked two of her tiny fingers. Her eyes were closed but she raised her eyebrows every once in a while, as if an idea had just come to her.

"I need to get you to your daddy," Eve said, but even as the words left her mouth, she knew she didn't mean them. She wouldn't try again. She could rationalize her inaction out of concern for Tim, Marty, Naomi and Forrest, but it was more than that. Every day, the bond between her and the baby was growing more complex and unbreakable. Everyone—Marian, her day-care parents, the neighbors—thought Cory was hers, and she was coming to believe the lie herself.

She still cried every single day. She had not really cried, not this way, since the months after her mother's death. She'd developed a strength that had gotten her through the years in foster care. She needed to find a new kind of toughness now and wasn't sure how to do it. "Your bladder's near your eyes," Marian said to her one day, and it took her a few minutes to understand her meaning.

She felt dumb, too. Not like the girl who had performed well in school and whose intelligence Tim had admired. She was someone who'd gotten involved in a terrible crime and had allowed—maybe even *caused*—a woman to die. Someone who'd failed to get an infant to her father and had set off a police car alarm. What had she been thinking? Of *course* that car would have an alarm. She was someone who couldn't think straight to save her life.

Plus, she felt like an incompetent mother. *I'm only sixteen,* she kept saying to herself as she struggled to take care of the baby. If she were older, she thought, the skills she needed would come naturally to her. She couldn't master the disposable diapers Marian gave her. Cory hated being changed and screamed the entire time, making Eve so anxious that she'd get the tape tabs stuck to the baby's knees and shoulders and hands. One terrible night, she was so tired when she heated Cory's bottle that she must not have screwed the lid on tightly. She brought the baby into her bed to feed, and when she turned the bottle upside down, the formula spilled all over Cory's face. Eve grabbed the baby and ran to Marian's room, terrified that Cory would inhale the formula or be blinded by having it in her eyes.

She woke Marian up in tears.

"I can't do anything right!" she said. "I'm afraid she's going to die because I'm such a stupid mother!"

She knew that the older woman was trying not to laugh as she helped her clean up the mess. Marian didn't know how deep Eve's fears went, though, how she lay awake at night, going over the steps Naomi had taught her for baby CPR and peering into the bassinet to listen for Cory's breathing.

The next day, Eve taped the lid on every bottle she fed the baby.

"You know," Marian said as she watched Eve feeding Cory with a bottle half-covered in masking tape, "why don't you switch to the bottles with the disposable liners? I have some that I use for the baby I take care of sometimes." She went to the kitchen, returning with a hollow plastic bottle and a nearly empty roll of liners. "It's so easy to use, and better for the baby, because she won't swallow as much air. You know how she gets those air bubble pains sometimes?"

Eve nodded.

Marian pulled the last liner from the roll, showing her how to open it and fit it into the bottle. Eve transferred the formula to the new bottle and screwed the lid ring on tightly. She tipped the bottle up and Cory latched on easily, even though the nipple was a very different design.

"I swear," Marian said, "that baby is the best eater I've ever seen."

"She's wonderful," Eve said. She looked at the empty roll of liners. "I'll buy some of these today."

"I've got another whole box of them in the cupboard next to the fridge," Marian said. "You're welcome to them."

Marian was at the grocery store when Cory next needed to be fed. Eve found the box of liners, but couldn't get the first one open. She tried to remember how Marian did it; it had seemed so simple. She tried a second liner, then a third, as Cory screamed from the bassinet in the living room. By the time Marian returned from the store, the counter was littered with dozens of unopened liners and Eve had tears pouring down her cheeks as she once again taped the lid to the glass bottle she'd brought with her.

"What's going on?" Marian set the grocery bags down on the counter.

"I can't even get these stupid liners to work!" Eve said. "And Cory's starving to death."

Marian picked up one of the liners, frowning as she tried to open it. "There's something wrong with this one," she said. She picked up another. "These are…they're fused together. This must be a defective roll."

Eve stared at her. "You mean it's not just me?"

Marian reached into one of the grocery bags and pulled out another box of liners. "Try these, honey," she said.

Eve opened the box, pulled out a liner, opened it and fit it into the bottle. She looked at the masterpiece she'd created. "I thought I was just screwing up again," she said, wiping her cheeks with the back of her hand.

Marian put an arm around her shoulders. "You're doing a wonderful job with her, Eve," she said softly.

She felt the warmth of Marian's body against hers and wished she could lay her head on the older woman's shoulder, close her eyes and stay like that for the rest of the day.

The next couple of weeks at Marian's house were a whirlwind of activity and emotions. Marian swept her into helping with the children, and while she was playing with them, she felt moments of actual joy. She could forget Genevieve during her busy days and stop thinking about how deeply she missed Tim. At night, though, she was consumed by them both. In the few hours of sleep she was able to get between feedings, she dreamed of Genevieve. The woman's face, smeared with blood, stared up at her from the bed in the cabin. *You stole my baby,* she'd say. *You killed me and then you stole my baby.*

When she'd try to fall back to sleep, she longed for Tim. She missed talking to him and being close to him. She hated that her memory of their last night together was tarnished by her stupid fake orgasm. Why had she done that? She worried, too, that he blamed her for what happened with Genevieve, which in turn had hurt his chance to get his sister off death row.

She fantasized that Naomi would tell him where she was living now and he would come for her. Sometimes, when she was outside, she'd spot a white Ford van and her heart would race as she tried to see the driver. The likelihood that he would still be driving that van was slim, but she couldn't stop herself from looking for it each time she stepped out the door of Marian's house.

She missed her quiet, easy, goal-centered life in Chapel Hill; her job at the coffee shop, where she'd see the same faces of the same students day in and day out; the little room she'd shared with Ronnie; the big box stuffed with her mother's letters.

Yet if she were still in Chapel Hill, if none of this had happened, she wouldn't have Cory.

The temperature warmed up considerably in the afternoons, and on sunny days she'd help Marian bundle the two-year-old boys into a double stroller, while she swaddled Cory in blankets and placed her in a carriage Marian provided. Then, along with the quiet and serious little four-year-old girl, they'd walk to a park where five mothers gathered with their young children, pushing them on swings and exchanging information about diapers and rashes and first words and sleep problems. Three of the mothers were the wives of graduate students; the remaining two were students themselves. They all seemed to know and like Marian, and while they were courteous to Eve, she had the feeling they talked about her behind her back. She was years younger than any of them, and she both looked and felt it. They probably wondered who Cory's father was and why Eve hadn't had an abortion and, of course, why she lived with Marian.

"That beautiful hair," one of the women said to her the first day she met them. "It's a shame you'll have to cut it."

Eve sat on a bench near the swings, gently moving the carriage back and forth. "Why will I have to cut it?" she asked.

The other women chuckled over whatever motherhood secret they shared. "It'll get in your way, you'll see," one of them said. "It gets pulled and tangled and you just won't have time for it anymore."

Eve looked from one woman to another. They all had short hair. "Did y'all have long hair before you had babies?" she asked.

"I did," one said.

"Me, too," said the blondest of the bunch.

"Oh, you had gorgeous hair!" another said to the blonde.

The blonde shrugged. "Your priorities change when you have a baby," she said.

"Well, I think Eve can keep her hair if she wants," Marian said. She was pushing the twins on the swings and keeping one eye on the four-year-old, who was playing on the slide with another little girl.

She *had* to keep it. If Tim were able to track her down, she wanted him to find her with the hair he loved.

At three o'clock the following morning, though, she was

walking around the dark bedroom with Cory on her shoulder, bleary-eyed. The baby was having a fitful night, a rarity for her, and Eve was upset that she couldn't find the cause. Cory strained against her shoulder, arching her back and tangling her hand in a hank of Eve's hair. Suddenly she let out a wail so loud it hurt Eve's ears.

"What's wrong, Sweet Pea?" Eve asked. "You pulled *my* hair. I'm the one who should be crying." Maybe her diaper was wet again? She carried the baby into the nursery, laid her down on the changing table, then turned on the lamp in the corner. Cory's diaper was dry, but in the lamplight, Eve saw a small cut, like the fine red line of a paper cut, in the delicate skin between her thumb and index finger. "You cut yourself on my hair!" she said. "Poor baby." She lifted her up and cuddled her, holding Cory's little hand to her lips to kiss it better.

Once she'd gotten Cory back to sleep, she went into the hallway bathroom and studied herself in the mirror. All she could find in the drawers beneath the sink were cuticle scissors, but she didn't hesitate, and it took her only fifteen minutes to turn herself from Tim's girlfriend to Cory's mother.

Chapter Twenty

"WHAT DID YOU DO?" MARIAN WAS SITTING IN THE living room watching the *Today Show* the following morning, and her mouth dropped open when Eve carried the baby into the room.

Eve glanced at the TV, where Jane Pauley was interviewing Barry Manilow. She smiled as she sank into the sofa. "The women at the park were right," she said.

Marian was speechless, her hand over her mouth.

"Does it look that bad?" Eve asked as she slipped the nipple of the bottle into Cory's mouth.

"Oh…well, oh my," Marian stammered. "It's just such a shock."

It had been a shock to Eve that morning as well. She'd forgotten her middle-of-the-night haircut until she walked into the bathroom and saw the pile of dark hair on the counter near the sink. It took courage to look in the mirror. Her hair, once a long, wavy, wild, dark mane, was now a short, wavy, wild, dark mess. Cuticle scissors had clearly been a poor choice for the job. She stared at herself, waiting to cry, but she didn't. Nothing she could do about it now.

"Cory cut her hand on my hair last night, so I chopped it off," Eve said.

Marian laughed. "She cut her hand on your *hair?*"

Eve held the baby's little hand in her fingers. The cut was now barely visible. "Like a paper cut," she said.

Marian shook her head. "You are something else. Do you want..." She laughed. "Don't take this the wrong way, okay? But let's get an appointment with the woman who does my hair. Just to—" Marian touched her own neat white pageboy "—you know. Smooth it out a bit?"

"I used cuticle scissors." Eve grinned, and it felt strange, as though her grinning muscles had atrophied during the past few weeks. She would like to have someone cut her hair properly, but she also wanted to buy a little car seat for Cory. Two of the women at the park told her it was dangerous to keep a baby in the laundry basket in the car and that they sold these new padded, plastic baby seats at Kmart for twenty dollars. She'd bought gas and formula and more disposable diapers, and her hundred dollars was fast disappearing. If it was a choice between one of those car seats and a new haircut, there was no contest.

"Well, you let me know if you want an appointment," Marian said. "My treat."

"Thanks," Eve said. She looked down at Cory, who was staring up at her. "She does this all the time now," she said to Marian. "Stares at me. I love when she—" She stopped talking and looked at the TV. Someone had said the words "Gleason" and "break in the case."

"She's starting to recognize you now," Marian said, but Eve barely heard her as she leaned toward the TV.

A policeman was on camera, speaking into a bank of microphones. "Yes," he said in response to a question Eve had missed.

"We spoke with Timothy Gleason's girlfriend, who had initially been hesitant to come forward."

"What?" Eve asked out loud.

"She's a reluctant witness, but she did lead us to a house in Jacksonville, where the Gleason brothers made their calls to Governor Russell. We found evidence that they'd been there, but they're not there now. And there's no sign at all of Mrs. Russell having been there."

"Does the girlfriend know where Mrs. Russell is?" The voice came from somewhere off-camera.

"She denies knowing where Mrs. Russell was held and where she might be now."

Without warning, Tim and Marty's pictures were flashed on the screen. "Timothy and Martin Gleason are probably traveling under assumed names and may have altered their appearances," the newscaster said. He gave a phone number viewers could call with more information.

Eve forgot to breathe. She stared at the TV. The picture of Tim was one she'd seen in the mansion. He was smiling, shirtless, and a little younger than he was now. Although you couldn't tell from the close-up on the television screen, he was sitting on a beach. His curly hair was washed almost to white by the sun. And those clear green eyes! She'd almost forgotten them.

She started to cry, doing her best to keep her tears silent. She felt Marian's gaze on her as the older woman stood up to turn off the television. Marian sat down again, hands locked around her knees.

"I don't want to know your connection to what we just saw," she said quietly. "But I can tell you something about me."

Eve looked at her, waiting.

"My husband went to jail in 1960 for a murder he didn't commit," Marian said. Her voice was tight. "There were witnesses who swore he was at the scene and that they even saw him do it, but I am completely certain it was a case of mistaken identity. Yet no one could verify his alibi because he was asleep in a hotel at the time, so he was convicted. And he was executed in 1966."

"I'm sorry," Eve whispered.

"I joined SCAPE after that," Marian said, and Eve looked up sharply. "No one around here knows that. My friends and neighbors always believed Jim was innocent, but they didn't know I became an activist. SCAPE was instrumental in getting rid of the death penalty several years ago. Of course, it's back now." Marian shrugged. "Anyway, that's my story. I try to help out when I can."

Eve didn't know what to say. She was still lost in Tim's face and confused by the officer's allusions to his "girlfriend."

"Just tell me this," Marian said gently. "Was one of them….one of the Gleason brothers…Cory's father?"

Eve looked down at the infant in her arms. She nodded as if she really believed it.

"I'm sorry, honey."

"I keep thinking he'll find me somehow. I keep thinking I see his van on the street. When it's not him, I…" She shook her head. "And they said they talked to his *girlfriend*. *I'm* his girlfriend."

Marian held up a hand. "First, they'll say anything to get what they want. They're probably just trying to flush you out of wherever you're hiding. Second, and more important," Marian said, wearing a serious expression behind her glasses, "we're having a conversation we shouldn't be having. You need to be more careful. It was obvious to me you had some connection to that situation, but you can't be so obvious with other people, all right?"

Eve nodded.

"You jump every time my front doorbell rings, and now I understand why. You *should* be a little paranoid. You'll never know who to trust, so don't trust anyone. A friend can become a foe, and it's not just you who's at risk."

"I know," she said. "It's Tim and Marty and their sister. And Na—" She caught herself. "The people who helped me get to you."

"And you've got me to protect, too, now," Marian said. "I'm aiding and abetting. So never a word to anyone, for as long as you live. Promise?"

Eve nodded again, then looked at the dark television screen. "Do you think I'll ever see him again?" she asked.

"I know your heart must be broken, Eve, but it would be a mistake for him to try to find you or vice versa. He can only put you and your baby in danger, and I'm sure he knows that. So, no matter how much he loves you, he shouldn't try to find you. For your sake and Cory's."

She had not thought about it that way, that he would stay away to protect her. She bubbled up with love for him all over again.

"I just wish I could help him somehow," she said. Cory grew fussy on her lap and she lifted her to her shoulder, patting her back.

"The best way you can help is to raise his child well," Marian said. "Which brings me to our next topic."

"What?" Eve asked.

"You need to get a job."

"But…you need me here."

Marian smiled. "I've done this work for over ten years without you, honey. You're a huge help, but I don't need you. What's important for your future is that you start *becoming* Eve Bailey. You need to build a work record under that name."

That was exactly what Naomi had told her.

"I know it's only been four weeks since you gave birth," Marian said, "but you seem to be in good shape, so I think you're ready for a little part-time work. I've talked to a friend, Steffi Green, who manages the University Diner on the Corner. That's where the UVA students hang out. They can use a waitress for their evening shift. It'd be from six to ten. Just four hours, at least in the beginning. Do you think you could handle that?"

"But…what about Cory?"

"Hi, there!" Marian waved her hand as if in greeting. "Remember me? I'll take care of her. My day-care kids'll be gone and it will just be Cory and me."

Eve rested her cheek against the baby's head. "I don't think I can leave her," she said. "Even with you."

"I insist, Eve," Marian said firmly, the drill sergeant in her voice. "Not just because you can use the money, but because you need to get out. You need to make friends and have something to think about besides Cory and this—" she waved toward the television "—her father. You need to start a life, honey. All right?"

She nodded. "I should pay you rent if I have a job," she said, then immediately wondered if Marian wanted her to get a job so she'd be able to leave. Maybe her revelation that she knew Tim Gleason had frightened her. "If I can still stay here, I mean," she added.

"You can stay here as long as you want," Marian said. "And you can pay me one fourth of the utilities, if that will make you more comfortable. How's that?"

Eve's eyes filled again. "It's good," she said.

Marian got to her feet. "And now," she said, heading for the telephone, "we're going to make an appointment for a haircut."

Chapter Twenty-One

THREE DAYS AFTER CHRISTMAS, EVE DROVE THROUGH A snow flurry to the University Diner for her first evening at work. Holiday decorations hung from the lamp posts along Main Street and the town was dark and quiet. She was glad she was starting back to work during winter break. The diner would be less crowded, letting her ease into the transition from warming bottles to making milkshakes.

Cars lined the curb in front of the diner and she groaned. Parallel parking. The one driving skill that nearly destroyed her chance for a North Carolina driver's license. There was a single tiny opening between the parked cars, about a block from the diner. She struggled with the gear shift, rolling the car backward and forward until her palms grew sweaty on the steering wheel and she finally gave up. Already five minutes late, she drove several blocks away to find a spot she could pull into nose first, then ran through the blustery snow toward the diner. This was not a good start.

She was breathless by the time she reached the diner. As she opened the front door, a gust of wind tore it from her hands and sent it crashing against the exterior wall with a bang. Customers, some seated at tables, others at the counter, looked up at the sound, and a tall, young waitress stopped pouring coffee to gawk at her.

"Damn," the waitress said. "Make an entrance, why don't you."

Eve felt herself blush at the sudden attention. The customers, most of them students, smiled and went back to their conversations as the waitress set down the coffeepot and walked toward her.

"Are you Eve?" she asked. "Please tell me you're Eve." She had very short blond hair and enormous brown eyes, and she wore a white bib apron over a red jersey and jeans.

"I am," Eve said.

"Hooray and hallelujah!" The woman grabbed her arm and walked with her through the diner at a quick pace. "We're so short today," she said, her accent almost Tar Heel thick. "There's five of us in the evenings, but one has a bug and another's on vacation and even though we're not as busy as we could be, I swear I'm about to quit. I'm Lorraine, by the way. I'm, like, your supervisor, but don't sweat it, 'cause as long as you work your butt off, I don't care what else you do."

Eve smiled. "I can do that." She liked Lorraine already.

"You have experience?" From beneath the counter, Lorraine grabbed an apron like the one she was wearing and handed it to her.

"Uh-huh." Eve pulled the apron over her head. "In Chapel—" Damn! "In Charleston," she said.

"Anywhere near a college?"

"Right near one," she said, wondering if there were any colleges in Charleston.

"Cool. Then you know waiting on students is the least rewarding, most degrading and best possible job there is."

Eve laughed. "Right," she said. She glanced toward the far corner of the diner as if expecting to see Tim there, waiting for her to pour his coffee, but the corner booth was empty.

Lorraine followed her gaze. "It's winter break, now, so don't start thinking it's always this leisurely in here."

"Are we close to the campus?"

"Very," Lorraine said. "But don't call it the 'campus.' No one does. It's the grounds."

"Oh. Okay."

"You and I have the counter tonight," she said, "so let's get to it."

Working felt good. Once she learned what a "grillswith" was—a doughnut cooked on the grill, then topped with ice cream—she had the job down. She was quick and efficient behind the counter, and it had been over a month since she'd felt that sort of confidence. The students were friendly to her, and she had the same feeling she'd had in Chapel Hill—a longing to be one of them.

Except for the times she imagined Tim coming to find her, she was glad she'd cut her hair. Marian's hairdresser had created a soft, chin-length bob with deep bangs that were a challenge to keep straight, but she felt freer and lighter as she moved around the diner, and she knew the shorter hair made her look at least a year or two older.

The only hard part of the evening was being away from Cory. If she hadn't realized how attached she'd become to the baby, she certainly knew it now. Halfway through her shift, she used the phone in the diner's kitchen to call Marian to check on her.

"Everything's fine," Marian said. "Now go back to work."

Lorraine chatted with her as they set plates on the counter and scooped ice cream onto fried doughnuts. She was a third-year student at the university, a twenty-year-old journalism major from Galax, wherever that was, and she'd worked at the diner for two years. She was irreverent, straightforward and unpretentious, all qualities Eve appreciated in her.

"Steffi said you have a baby," Lorraine said as they stood side by side, cutting whole pies into wedges.

"Uh-huh," Eve said. "Cory."

"Did your boyfriend give you that crap about withdrawal working or what?"

Eve laughed. "Exactly," she said.

"My girlfriend got that line, too." Lorraine licked a bit of cherry-pie filling off her thumb. "Her little girl's four now. I live with them."

"How old was your friend when she had the baby?"

"Nineteen," Lorraine said. "And you're…?"

"Seventeen."

"Ouch. Marian's taking care of her while you work, huh?"

"Yes. You know Marian?"

"Everyone knows Marian. She's saved my butt once or twice."

Eve wanted to know how Marian had helped her, but it felt like prying.

"As a matter of fact," Lorraine continued, "Shan—my girlfriend Bobbie's little girl—is one of her day-care kids."

"Oh!" Eve held the knife in midair, thinking of the well-behaved four-year-old who came to the house every day. "She's adorable," she said.

"Yeah, she is." Lorraine smiled as though picturing the little girl. "So, is your boyfriend still around?"

She had to come up with answers to questions about Cory's father, and she had to learn to keep her story straight. "No, we broke up when I was about six months' pregnant."

"Bastard," Lorraine said. "What was his name?"

"Patrick." She pulled the name out of the air, but it was a good one. Patrick sounded like a redhead.

Lorraine stopped cutting to look at her. "You're seventeen, working as a waitress, and raising a baby on your own." She shook her head. "Girl, you have my admiration," she said. "I knew I was going to like you the moment you crashed into the restaurant."

"I felt the same way when I saw you," Eve said shyly.

"I'm taken, though, so don't get any ideas."

"What?"

Lorraine laughed. "Teasing you, Eve." Under her breath, she said, "Bobbie—Shan's mother—is my *girl*friend."

It still took Eve a moment to understand. Then her eyes flew open. "Oh!" she said. She'd known a couple of lesbians in North Carolina, but only as acquaintances. And she'd even met Bobbie, a conservative-looking accountant with a thick New England accent. She never would have guessed.

"I'm not gay," she said. She thought she should make that clear.

"Like I couldn't tell." Lorraine laughed again, then grew serious. "I hope we can still be friends," she said. "That it doesn't make a difference."

For the first time all evening, Eve saw something other than cocky abandon in Lorraine's demeanor. There was a line between her eyebrows, too deep for someone only twenty. What was it like to realize you were different, that you liked girls better than boys? Did everyone have some burden they had to carry?

"Of course we can still be friends," she said. She wanted that very much.

Cory was asleep when she got home, and Marian wanted to hear everything about her first night at work.

"You've got pink in your cheeks," Marian said when Eve sat down on the sofa. "I think you had fun."

"I did." Eve smiled. "It's not hard work. And one of the other evening waitresses, Lorraine, is a lot of fun. You know her, I guess."

Marian set down the book she'd been reading. "Oh, sure. And Shan is Bobbie's—her partner's—daughter, did you know that?"

"She told me," Eve said. She liked how easygoing Marian was about everything and everybody. "She said you saved her butt once."

"Well, I don't know about that," Marian said. "She came out of the closet while she was in high school, and her parents made her life a living hell, so I let her live here."

"That was nice of you," she said, although she felt an unexpected twinge of sibling rivalry that Lorraine had also enjoyed Marian's care and attention.

"So, it's not hard, huh?" Marian asked. "Are the students a pain?"

"It was on the quiet side since it's winter break, but I actually like being around students. I was planning to go to Caro…to college when everything happened."

"Really? Majoring in what?"

"Social work."

"You'd be a good social worker," Marian said.

"Maybe someday." She couldn't see how she'd ever get to college now.

"You could go to school while you're living here," Marian said.

"I want to spend my nonworking time with Cory, though."

"I understand. But you could get started. Take a class here, a class there. That's pretty much the way Lorraine started out."

Marian made it sound like a real possibility. Just one class. She could almost envision it. Except…how did you apply to college without a high-school transcript?

Two in the morning found Eve downstairs, heating water to warm Cory's formula. Cory lay just below her breasts in the sling, making her "I'm going to cry any minute" whimpering sounds. Eve opened the cabinet beneath the sink to throw away a paper towel and noticed a newspaper in the garbage can. She'd gotten into the habit of reading the paper over breakfast, hunting for updates about the kidnapping, but Marian had told her the paperboy missed them that morning. Eve read the headline as she pulled the paper from the can, and knew she'd caught her landlady in a lie.

Gleason's Girlfriend Commits Suicide

She read the article in confusion.

Timothy Gleason's girlfriend, twenty-two-year-old Elizabeth Jones, who led investigators to the Gleason brothers' hideout in Jacksonville, North Carolina, was found dead of an overdose in her Chapel Hill apartment yesterday.

Elizabeth Jones? Who was that?

Jones's roommate, Jeannie Parker, said that Jones had been distraught lately. "The cops were hounding her and she couldn't take it anymore," Parker said. "She didn't want to be involved in that whole mess, anyway, and now she was getting dragged into it. Plus she missed Tim and was afraid she'd never see him again." According to Parker, Jones had been stockpiling sedatives from several different doctors over the last week.

Eve suddenly realized that the photograph of a young woman on the right side of the page accompanied the article. She stared at the stick-straight blond hair and pouty lips, while the water boiled over on the stove.

Chapter Twenty-Two

EVE LEFT CORY IN THE BASSINET, THEN WALKED UPSTAIRS and knocked on Marian's bedroom door, the *Richmond Times-Dispatch* clutched in her hand. She heard a catch of breath, then the rustling of blankets. In a moment, Marian pulled open the door, wearing a robe, her glasses askew.

Eve waved the paper in front of her. "How could you keep this from me?" she asked.

"Oh," Marian said, as she realized the reason for the intrusion. "I'm sorry, Eve." She sounded tired. "I...I just wanted to spare you from it. But maybe it's better that you found it after all."

"Do you know something about this...situation?" Eve asked. "Are you keeping things from me? You're in SCAPE. Do you know what—"

"Shh." Marian touched her arm.

"What do you *know*?" Eve asked. Downstairs, Cory started to cry.

"I don't know a thing, Eve. Honest, I don't. I've told you. We all keep each other in the dark."

Eve lowered the newspaper to her side, suddenly deflated. "I can't handle the dark anymore," she said. "I have to...I need someone to help me figure out what's going on." She pressed a hand to her temple and closed her eyes. "I feel like I'm going crazy."

"Okay," Marian said. "Let me get my slippers and I'll meet you downstairs."

They were both silent as Marian brewed tea and Eve fed Cory. She knew she had to wait for Marian to begin this conversation. Anything she said would come out in a jumble of emotion, and that was not going to help.

Marian poured tea for both of them, then took a seat across the table from her.

"You can talk to me about this," she said, as if laying ground rules, "but I'm only allowing it because I want you to get it out of your system so you don't talk to anyone else. All right?"

Eve nodded.

"I'm a little concerned, Eve," she continued. "You've got to have a better handle on yourself than this. You can't be so impulsive, coming upstairs and pounding on my door like that. I understand you're upset and my door happens to be a safe one. Others won't be."

Eve felt chastened. How many times had she been told not to utter a word about what had happened? "I know," she said. "But I—"

"Here's what I know," Marian said. "I received a call from a woman who didn't give me her name. They never do. She knew some... some facts that let me know she was part of SCAPE. She told me a young girl and her new baby were living in Charleston—which I recognized was probably a lie, but that was immaterial—and they'd gotten caught up in a SCAPE activity they didn't belong in and needed a place to go underground. Could I help. I said yes. I didn't ask questions. You don't ask questions in this business."

"You don't know anything about Tim or this girl in the paper?" Eve nodded toward the newspaper on the table.

Marian shook her head. "I didn't know anything at all about it until you reacted to that television piece the other day. If I'd been listening to that story about kidnapping the governor's wife in order to get freedom for a death-row inmate...well, I would have thought SCAPE was involved in some way. Supporting the effort at the very least. But that was all."

Cory had fallen asleep, and Eve sat her up on her lap to burp. "I'm so confused," she said. "I *know* this girl. I mean, I know who she is. And nothing makes any sense."

Marian hesitated. "Who is she?" she asked finally.

"Her name is Bets," Eve said. "She waited on Tim and me in a restaurant once in...where we were living. It was obvious she knew him, but...not like *that*." She shook her head, still trying to make sense of the article. "She didn't act jealous of me or anything. Tim and I were even holding hands in the restaurant."

Marian sipped her tea, listening in silence.

"I just don't *understand,*" Eve said. "Was he seeing both of us at the same time? I mean, if *she* was his girlfriend when he disappeared and *I* was his girlfriend when he disappeared...I guess that's the only explanation."

"Maybe." Marian's tone gave away her doubt.

"Maybe she *thought* of herself as his girlfriend, but he didn't," Eve suggested. "Maybe it was all her big fantasy."

Marian set her tea cup on the saucer. "How old was he, honey?" she asked.

"Twenty-two." She winced at the realization that he was the same age as Bets.

"I think...he may have been using you," Marian said. Eve could tell she was carefully picking her words. Just not carefully enough.

"I don't want to hear it," she said. Until that moment, she'd forgotten Genevieve's warning about Tim being a "womanizer."

"You're only seventeen," Marian said. "You're a little...compared to a twenty-two-year old, anyway, you're a little naive."

"Only sixteen," Eve said.

"You were sixteen when you met him?"

"I'm *still* sixteen." Eve was suddenly angry, though whether it was at Marian or Tim or the world, she couldn't be sure. "The *real me* is sixteen. Eve Bailey is seventeen."

Marian sat back in her chair. "Oh, my God," she said. "Did he know your age?"

Eve nodded.

"Well, Eve." Marian let out a heavy sigh. "I realize that he's Cory's father and that he was someone special to you, but I have to say, I don't like this man at all."

"He was really good to me, though," Eve argued. "He appreciated me. He loved me. One day I got five thousand dollars in the mail, and I'm sure he sent it."

Marian's eyes were wide behind her glasses. "Cash?" she asked.

Eve nodded. "He wanted me to be able to go to school."

"Where's the money now?"

"I had to leave it when...everything happened."

"Why are you so sure he's the person who sent it?"

"'Cause he was rich."

Marian made a sound of disgust. "He bought you in every way possible, then," she said.

Eve lifted Cory to her shoulder and stood up to slip her into the sling. "I just can't believe that," she said. She reached for her untouched cup and saucer to carry them to the sink.

"Sixteen," Marian said to herself. "You're not even a high-school graduate, then?"

"*Yes,* I'm a high-school graduate!" Eve washed the cup and placed it on the dish drainer. "I'm a high-school graduate with a B-plus average and thirteen-sixty on my SATs." It was definitely the world she was angry at. She felt the fury boiling inside her as she turned around. "This doesn't make sense!" she said. "Why would he go to so much trouble to use *me* for sex if he had—" she pointed to the newspaper "—*her?*"

"Sex isn't the only thing people use each other for," Marian said. "Maybe he could get you to do what he couldn't get her to do when it came to the kidnapping."

Eve glared at her. The words *I hate you* rose in her throat and were ready to explode, but she forced herself to swallow them. She didn't hate Marian. She only hated what she was saying.

"I just don't understand," she said again. "I can't believe he didn't love me."

"You deserve so much better than this, Eve," Marian said. "I want you to start believing that for yourself."

From inside the sling, Cory let out a cry.

"I think my voice is upsetting her," Eve said, lifting the baby from the sling. She rocked Cory in her arms, "shhing" her as she kissed the top of her ear and stroked her back. She looked down at the tiny face, and Cory stared back with eyes that touched her soul. Eve bent her head to nuzzle the cheek of the baby she loved. The baby she'd stolen.

She wasn't sure anymore what she deserved.

Chapter Twenty-Three

Summer 1978

EVE PUT ON DENIM CUTOFFS AND A WHITE TANK TOP, THEN checked her reflection in the bathroom mirror. Her hair almost reached her shoulders now, and the humidity was making a dark frizzy mess out of it. She pulled it back, securing it with a long barrette at the nape of her neck.

She was only taking one class—Psychology 101—during the summer, but her financial-aid application had been approved and she would be able to take several more in the fall, with an eye to becoming a full-time psych major the following year. As it turned out, there was no school of social work at UVA, but she was not as devastated by that news as she would have predicted. Her confused feelings about Tim marred her desire to follow in his footsteps.

Marian had provided her with not only a transcript from a high school in Oregon, but SAT scores that rivaled those earned by CeeCee Wilkes. The documents appeared as if by magic one morning, much the way her birth certificate and driver's license had appeared at Naomi's. Eve asked no questions. She simply made copies of them and filled out her application for school.

She loved her class, reading far beyond what was required, devouring books on Freud and Jung and Erikson, and she'd completed the main textbook by the end of the second week. She read over breakfast in the morning and during her break at the diner and while she rocked Cory to sleep. She'd intended to be invisible in the classroom—she had no desire to stand out anywhere in her life—but she quickly became the professor's clear favorite. Her classmates didn't seem resentful in the least. Instead, they turned to her as a leader, asking her, "What was yesterday's assignment?" or "What's the difference between the sensorimotor stage and the pre-operational stage?"

She knew all about the sensorimotor stage, since she was witnessing it at home every day. Cory would try to grab the mobile hanging above the crib, and she delighted in turning the switch for the overhead light on and off, on and off. She could play a game of peekaboo for hours. On the down side, she was starting to show signs of separation anxiety, crying whenever Eve left for school or work. It was a normal stage of development, Eve knew from her studies, but she was awed by the knowledge that she'd become that huge and irreplaceable person in Cory's life: her mother.

Downstairs, she found Marian in the kitchen making tuna salad, while the twins colored and Cory supervised everyone from her bouncy chair. Bobbie's little girl, Shan, was in day camp for much of the summer, and Eve knew Marian was happy to have one less child to care for. The week before, she'd announced that she was retiring from the day-care business, although, she was quick to assure Eve, she would still watch Cory while Eve was in school.

"I want to take painting lessons," Marian had said. "Maybe cello lessons. I've always had a yearning to play the cello, if these gnarled old fingers will let me."

Eve lifted Cory out of the bouncy chair and spun her around, and the little girl squealed and giggled, the sound as light and tinkling as wind chimes.

"Do you want your lunch?" Eve asked her. She lowered Cory into her high chair. "What would you like? Peas? Carrots? Chicken?"

Cory grinned her toothless grin. She was a skinny little thing, though very long: ninetieth percentile, according to the pediatrician. "She's a natural ectomorph," he said when Eve asked if her low weight was a problem. "We should all be that lucky."

Marian spread the tuna salad on white bread for the boys. "There's mail for you on the table," she said.

Eve picked up the small envelope. The only mail she ever received at Marian's was from the university, but this looked more like a wedding invitation, the envelope thick and cream-colored. Her name and address were typewritten, but there was no return address, only an Oklahoma City postmark. A little unnerved, she opened the envelope and gasped.

Inside were three folded hundred-dollar bills and a small typed note. *For the baby,* it read.

She dropped the money as if it burned her, then looked at Marian. "Is this from you?" she asked.

Marian bent over to pick up the bills and set them on the table. "Of course not." She looked at the note. "I'd just give you money. I wouldn't mail it."

Eve thought of the customers she'd met at the diner who

knew she had a child, and of Lorraine, with whom she'd become good friends but who couldn't possibly spare three hundred dollars. She thought of her psychology professor, who admired and encouraged her and who knew she had a baby to care for. But Oklahoma City?

And then she thought of the last time she'd received unexpected money in the mail.

Marian read her mind. "Cory's father?" she asked.

"I don't know." Eve sank into a chair, touching the money she'd imagined Tim had held in his own hands. She still looked for Tim in every white van she saw. When she was being honest with herself, she knew she was still waiting for him as well. She wanted to see him, to have him explain away the idea that Bets had been his girlfriend. She still talked to him in her mind as she waited for sleep, telling him what she was learning, knowing he'd be happy for her that she was finally in school. Sometimes she dreamed about him. They were good dreams—not like the nightmares about Genevieve that continued to jolt her awake in the middle of the night. Some days she could barely remember what he looked like. Other days, she found him in the face of every man she saw.

She felt happy these days, yet there was always an undercurrent of sadness just below the surface. Sometimes she would feel it there and not even know its source. Then she would remember: A dead woman. A kidnapped baby. She couldn't even list the charges that would be brought against her if she were ever caught. There had to be fifteen or twenty of them now.

"Spend the money on Cory," Marian said, touching the bills where they rested on the table. "It doesn't matter where it came from. It's hers now."

* * *

At work that evening, two police officers came into the diner. It wasn't unusual to see cops there, and Eve's heart no longer skipped a beat when she spotted a few of them seated among the customers. The first time she saw a policeman walk through the front door, though, she'd dropped the coffeepot she was carrying, sending coffee and shards of glass all over the floor. Nothing like attracting attention. But the officer was only there for coffee and pie, and if he wondered why her hands shook when she served him, he didn't say anything about it.

This evening, though, the police officers looked like they meant business. Eve watched as they approached an older woman sitting at the counter. She listened in as they arrested her for buying beer for minors, slapping handcuffs on her and hustling her out the door. The woman reminded her a little of Marian, and watching the cops lead her away made her feel fiercely protective of the woman who was doing so much for her by risking her own neck. She would never, ever, do anything to put Marian in harm's way.

One hot morning in August, Eve was upstairs getting a hat for Cory, so that she and Marian could take the baby and the twin boys to the park. When she walked back into the kitchen, Cory was in the high chair, Marian cleaning the little girl's hands with a washcloth. Cory saw Eve and pulled her hand from Marian's to reach toward her.

"Mama!" she said.

Eve caught her breath. For weeks now, Cory had been babbling to herself, saying "mamamamama" among other things, but this was the first time she seemed to equate the two syllables with her.

Marian laughed. "You look like you've seen a ghost," she said to Eve.

She had. *Genevieve.*

"That's right, Cory," she said, moving forward to lift the little girl out of the high chair. "You're so smart."

"Mama, Mama, Mama," Cory repeated as Eve tugged the hat over her red curls.

"Okay, let's go," Eve said, and she held Cory's hands as they walked outside. It wouldn't be long before she was walking on her own. Eve pulled the stroller from the shed at the side of the house and Cory tried to climb into it herself.

"She's going to be into everything soon," Marian said, taking a hand of each of the boys.

"I know," Eve said. "And I noticed there's an outlet in the bathroom that isn't covered with a safety plug."

"Where?" Marian frowned.

"You know. There's only one outlet."

"Above the sink?"

"Uh-huh."

Marian laughed. "She's a smart little girl, but I think it's going to be a couple of years before she can climb up on the bathroom counter."

"I guess." Eve laughed at herself. She was growing into an overprotective mother. She saw danger everywhere.

Alison and Vicki, two of the young mothers who frequented the park, were already pushing their toddlers on the swings when Eve and Marian arrived with the children. Alison's husband was a medical student, and Vicki was working on a teaching degree. Alison had a new baby and she wore the sling Eve had made her as a baby gift.

"The sling is fantastic!" she said as Eve slipped Cory into one of the bucket swings.

"I'm glad you like it." Eve leaned over to peer at Alison's infant. "How's he doing?" She could talk diapers and formula with the best of them now. Alison reported on the baby's sleeping and eating habits, and Marian joined in the discussion from a nearby bench.

"Did you hear they finally executed that girl?" Vicki asked, during a lull in the conversation.

"Oh, I know," Alison said. "I saw it in the paper this morning. Good riddance."

Eve's muscles went tight. *What girl?* she wanted to ask but didn't dare.

"What girl?" Marian did it for her.

"The sister of those guys who kidnapped that governor's wife last year."

Eve kept her eyes on Cory's hair, curling out from beneath the hat, startling red in the summer sun. She pictured Tim counting out the three hundred-dollar bills, licking the envelope sealed. She thought of him getting the news that his sister was dead.

"Why would you say good riddance?" Marian asked, an edge to her voice.

"Marian, you're such a liberal diehard." Vicki laughed, and Eve felt like smacking her. These women knew nothing of how Marian had lost her husband.

"She was a murderer," Alison said.

"A junkie," Vicki added.

"A junkie?" Eve repeated.

"Uh-huh," Vicki said. "She broke into this lady's house and killed her and her daughter, then stole her jewelry to pay for drugs."

"That's completely wrong," Eve said.

The three women looked at her. Marian's face was the only one that held a warning.

"I mean," Eve said, "that's not what I'd heard. I heard she killed a photographer after he raped her."

Alison frowned. "I don't know where you got that," she said. "Maybe you're thinking of someone else."

"The woman she killed was a photographer," Vicki acknowledged.

"That's true," Alison said.

"Could you have misunderstood what you read?" Eve couldn't stop herself. "Could the photographer have been at——"

"No," Alison interrupted her. "I read it less than an hour ago."

"I didn't read it," Vicki said, "but Charlie read it to me while I was getting dressed and it said she robbed a woman—a photographer—in Chapel Hill."

"To get money for drugs," Alison piped in.

"Cory said 'mama' this morning." Marian made a lame attempt to hijack the conversation.

"Cory, is that right?" Alison leaned over to speak to Cory when the little girl swung toward them. "Did you say 'mama,' sweetie?"

Eve rarely read the paper anymore. The kidnapping had faded from the news, and her psychology books took precedence. Now, though, she wanted to race home and find the story.

"Oh!" Marian suddenly got to her feet. "I just remembered this is the morning I was supposed to wait for the plumber."

Eve stared at her, perplexed, before she realized that Marian was rescuing her.

"Oh, right," she said. "I'll go back with you."

"You just barely got here," Alison said.

"The plumber said he'd come between eight and noon," Marian said, "and you know how it is. If I don't go back now, it'll be the one time he comes at eight." She chuckled. "You don't need to come with me, Eve."

"I think I should." Eve lifted a protesting Cory out of the bucket and set her down in the stroller. "I don't want Cory to get burned."

Vicki laughed. "It's eight in the morning," she said. "And that hat's wide enough to protect an elephant."

Eve barely heard her as she and Marian collected the twins, and they bade goodbye to the women and started home.

"Did you read the paper this morning?" Eve asked Marian, as soon as they were out of earshot.

Marian shook her head.

"Let's go to the minimart." Eve turned the corner toward the little market. "I can't wait two more blocks to read it."

She bought the paper while Marian remained outside with the children. Back on the street, she found the article at the bottom of the front page.

"Andrea Gleason," Eve read, "the sister of Timothy and Martin Gleason, who are allegedly responsible for kidnapping North Carolina Governor Irving Russell's wife last year, was executed yesterday at the North Carolina Correctional Institution for Women. Gleason was convicted in the 1975 murder of photographer Gloria Wilder of Chapel Hill and her thirteen-year-old daughter. She broke into the Wilder home, killed the mother and daughter, then stole fifty thousand dollars' worth of jewelry. Wilder, who was found in her bedroom, had been shot four times; her daughter, shot once in the head, was found in the hallway."

Eve looked up. "Oh, my God," she said.

"Go on," Marian nodded toward the paper. "What else does it say?"

Eve began reading again. "On November 24 last year, Gene-vieve Russell, the governor's wife, was kidnapped after teaching a class at UNC. The Gleason brothers negotiated unsuccessfully for their sister's release. They have not been found, nor has Mrs. Russell, who was pregnant at the time of her kidnapping. Governor Russell had no comment today on Andrea Gleason's execution, although sources close to the governor's mansion speculated that he was instrumental in getting Andrea Gleason's execution moved to an earlier date."

Eve looked up from the paper. "He lied to me about everything," she said.

Marian nodded. "It sure looks that way."

They started walking again, this time in silence, and for the first time, Eve felt real anger building inside her at Tim. She'd been an inexperienced sixteen-year-old, an easy mark. Bets had been in on it, no doubt, the reason for her easy acceptance of CeeCee when she waited on them at the restaurant. Maybe Tim had taken CeeCee there to show Bets how little a threat she was—a young girl still wearing Alice in Wonderland hair down to her butt. She imagined Tim saying to Bets, *We'll get her to babysit the governor's old lady so you don't have to get involved.* He'd probably kissed her then. *She's dis-pensable, babe,* he would have added. *You're not.* Son of a *bitch.*

"I don't think I've ever been this furious," Eve said, her hands tight around the handle of the stroller.

She felt Marian's arm slip around her shoulders. "Good," Marian said. "It's about time."

The fury clawed at her for the rest of the day. She punched the pillows on her bed and stormed around the house as she vacuumed, cursing under her breath and stomping on the floor. By the time she went to bed, though, she felt different. She would no longer be held captive by every white van she saw. She could stop waiting. Stop hoping. A sort of peace came over her as she drifted off to sleep: Tim had finally set her free.

Chapter Twenty-Four

1981

ON MARCH SEVENTH, EVE TURNED TWENTY-ONE. IT WAS the fourth time she'd celebrated that date as her birthday, and she'd written it on dozens of forms over the years. It felt like her birthday now, as surely as she felt like Eve Bailey.

Marian took her to dinner and then to a play at the Helms Theater on the grounds.

"I know one of the actors in the play," Marian said as they pulled into a space in the parking lot. "His name's Jack Elliott. He's the nephew of one my oldest friends."

Eve barely heard a word Marian said. "Maybe I should call Bobbie and Lorraine before the play starts," she said. They were watching Cory this evening. Cory could be a handful, not because she was a rambunctious or disobedient three-and-a-half-year-old, but because she was always a little afraid when Eve was away. She was fine with Marian, and she knew Lorraine and Bobbie well and adored Shan, who was now eight, but the last time Eve had left Cory with a sitter, the little girl had cried the entire time and wouldn't eat or go to bed.

"She'll be fine," Marian said now. "She needs to know she can survive without you."

And I need to know I can survive without her, Eve thought.

They had excellent seats in the theater. The play was *See How They Run,* and the actor Marian knew, Jack Elliott, played Clive, a soldier who disguised himself as a priest. He was tall and reedy, with a slightly awkward handsomeness that reminded Eve of a young Cary Grant. The play was hilarious, and Eve laughed harder than she had in a very long time.

"Let's go backstage," Marian said when the play was over. "I want to say hello to Jack."

Eve looked at her watch. It was only ten. "Okay," she said.

Marian had obviously done this before. She knew the way to the area backstage where some of the actors were gathered. Jack Elliott was standing on a chair, makeup still outlining his eyes and sharpening his cheekbones. He was reciting lines from *Hamlet,* hamming it up for an audience of two young guys and a girl. They were laughing.

"Do I have to stand on a chair when I do it?" the guy asked.

Jack spotted Marian and stopped speaking midsentence.

"Auntie Marian!" He hopped from the chair and swept across the room to wrap Marian in a hug. He was not as tall as he'd appeared on stage, but he was even better looking. "Excuse my chair-standing," he said to Marian. "I was coaching a friend who's going to play Hamlet. Did you like the play?"

"We loved it," Marian said. "You were hysterical. Has your mother been able to see you in it?"

"Next weekend," he said. "She'll call you when she gets here, I'm sure. And who's this?" Jack turned his attention to Eve, curiosity in his brown-eyed gaze. Guys at school never treated her as a potential date: she was too serious, too involved in her studies, and far too vocal about her daughter. This man, though, looked at her with clear interest.

"This is my housemate, Eve Bailey," Marian said. "Eve, this is Jack."

Eve shook the hand he offered. "You really were good," she said. "Excellent timing," she added, as though she knew something about drama.

He didn't take his hand away. "Oh, Eve, are you taken? Will you go out with me?"

Eve laughed at his brazenness, unsure if he was serious.

"Lord, Jack, you haven't changed a bit," Marian said. "Jack has always been a little, shall we say, 'out there,'" she said to Eve. "You never have to guess what he's thinking. One time when he was little, his mother and I were in a restaurant and he said to the waitress, 'You've got the longest nose I've ever seen.'"

Jack groaned. "Ignore her, Eve. Are you taken?"

"Only by a three-and-a-half-year-old daughter," she said.

"A bonus?" His face lit up, but she reminded herself that he was an actor. "As long as her father isn't the type to come after me with a gun, I'd still like to take you out. What do you say?"

"Sure," she said, surprising herself. She hadn't gone out with anyone since Tim. Her social life consisted of meeting Lorraine for coffee on the grounds, where her old friend was now working on a graduate degree in telecommunications, and participating in a playgroup with some other mothers and kids in the neighborhood. She didn't have time for anything else. But it was as though Jack had slipped a noose around the "yes" in her throat and pulled it out into the air. "I'm very busy, but—"

"But she'll make time," Marian said.

"I'll call you at Marian's," he said. He hadn't taken his eyes off hers, and she didn't mind the steady gaze. There was no threat in it. She returned his gaze with a confidence she hadn't known she possessed. She was not the girl who had been smitten and seduced by Tim Gleason. She was a woman who could take or leave the attention of a man, and right now, she chose to take it.

As she and Marian returned to the lobby, though, she grew quiet and pensive. It wasn't until they reached Marian's car that she spoke.

"Can I trust him?" she asked.

"Like the sunrise," Marian replied.

He called her the next day. Marian answered the phone and covered the receiver with her hand as she turned it over to Eve.

"I'll babysit, no matter when it is," she whispered, clearly enjoying her role as matchmaker.

"Hi," Eve said.

"I've nabbed two tickets to the Springsteen concert tomorrow night," he said. "Want to join me?"

"Let me check with the babysitter," she said, turning to Marian. "Tomorrow night?"

Marian nodded.

"I'd love to," she said into the phone.

He told her what time he'd pick her up and that was that. Less than two minutes from start to finish. She hung up the phone, looked at Marian and bit her lip.

"What did I just do?" she asked.

"Something a normal, healthy, twenty-one-year-old woman has every right to do," Marian said. "You accepted a date."

"I don't want him to meet Cory when he comes to pick me up, though," she said.

"Heavens, no!" Marian's tone mocked her overprotectiveness. "Don't worry. Cory and I will hide out upstairs."

She was sitting in the living room the following evening, watching through the window for Jack's arrival, when a car pulled up to the curb in front of the house. It was a sedan, painted Kelly-green with yellow doors and a blue roof.

"Oh, no," she said to herself, but couldn't help laughing.

Jack got out of the car, dressed in khakis, sandals and a short-sleeved blue shirt over a white T-shirt. She liked the way he walked, the way he tossed his car keys into the air and caught them, as if he didn't have a care in the world.

She expected to feel shy when she got into his car, but he started talking the minute she sat down, and she felt the tension slip from her muscles.

"I was hoping I could meet your little girl," he said.

"Marian's reading her a story upstairs."

"Marian read me stories when I was a kid," he said. "She'd act out the parts. You know, change her voice for each of them."

"Yes, she does it really well."

"Might even be the reason I got into acting. She'd get me to act out the parts, too."

"She said your mother is one of her oldest friends."

"We lived next door to Marian and her husband when I was a kid. Bill and my father were good friends, too."

"I forget about him sometimes," Eve said. "Marian doesn't talk about him much."

"She—— *Hey!*" he shouted as a car pulled in front of them, forcing him to step hard on the brake. "Jeez," he said. "What a goofy Gus."

"A goofy Gus?" She laughed.

"So." Jack started driving again. "What I was about to say was that Bill, Marian's husband, is a sore subject for her. How much do you know?"

"That he was executed," she said. "And Marian thought he was innocent."

"Yeah, and I think she's probably right, but who knows?" he said. "You never really know what a person's capable of. Someone can be a really nice guy and still, you know, have two sides to him."

No kidding, she thought. "So you think he did it?"

"I don't know. The important thing to me is the impact it had on Marian." He glanced at her and smiled. "So, how'd we get on such a serious topic already?" he asked.

She shrugged, worried it was her fault. Did she know how to have a light and casual conversation with anyone anymore?

"Do you like Springsteen?" he asked.

"I have to admit I'm not all that familiar with him," she said.

He smiled. His teeth looked as though he'd never had a cavity in his life. "You'll be familiar with him after tonight," he said. "What music do you like?"

She had to think. She used to like Fleetwood Mac and Rod Stewart and Crosby, Stills and Nash, but she hadn't listened to much music in years. "I'm into lullabies and 'Inky Dinky Spider,' I'm afraid."

Jack laughed. "You were what…seventeen when you had her?"

Here we go, she thought.

"Yes."

"What's her name?"

"Cory. Corinne."

"Must've been hard," he said.

"It was," she admitted. "I don't know what I would've done if I hadn't met Marian." She studied Jack's hands as he turned the steering wheel. His fingers were long and tanned.

"How'd you meet her?" he asked.

"A friend put me in touch with her. She said Marian might have a room I could live in. I didn't know I'd be getting so much more than a landlady."

"You lucked out," he agreed. "So, where are you from? Where did you grow up?"

He certainly asked a lot of questions. "Oregon," she said.

"No kidding!" He turned to look at her. "I lived there for a couple of years when I was a teenager. Where were you?"

This was the reaction she'd been dreading for the past three-and-a-half years. She'd told any number of people she was originally from Oregon, but he was the first who'd ever set foot in the state. She, of course, had not.

"Portland." She held her breath, waiting for the "Me, too!"

"Oh, I was in Klamath Falls. My father was transferred there for a few years." He looked at her, a cute grin on his face. "That's cool, huh? We both lived in Oregon. Gorgeous state."

"Yes." She smiled her relief.

He had a perfect profile. Absolutely perfect. His nose was straight, not too large, not too small. His nostrils had the tiniest flare to them. His chin was strong without overwhelming the rest of his face, and his eyebrows were jet-black and thick above his dark eyes. His hair was curly, but not the least bit frizzy like hers.

Still, those curls probably gave him fits as he tried to control them. Or maybe he'd given up at the attempt. He frankly didn't seem like the type of guy who'd get too worked up over anything.

"You have great hair," she said now.

He looked surprised. "Why, thank you, ma'am. I was admiring yours the other night, too."

He *was?* "It used to be really long," she said. "I chopped it off when Cory was a baby because she cut her hand on it." She now wore her hair in layers that left it feeling light against her neck.

"What?" He reached over and touched her hair, his fingers brushing her shoulder as he did so. "It's very soft," he said. "Did it used to be like razor wire or something?"

Eve laughed. "It was a little paper-cut kind of thing. Right here." She touched the web of skin between her index finger and thumb.

"So you cut it off."

"Uh-huh. In the middle of the night. With cuticle scissors."

Jack laughed, and hit the steering wheel with his palm. "I think you're as impulsive as I am," he said.

"I doubt it," she said. "I have the feeling you're an extremely spontaneous sort of guy."

"You might be right. My car used to be this ugly brown color. I painted it on a whim."

"Any regrets?"

"Hell, no. I love Peggy Sue." He ran his hand over Peggy Sue's dashboard as he drove into the parking lot. "We have arrived!" he said.

She wondered if he always spoke in exclamations. She liked it. In the past few years, her joy had come from watching Cory change from day to day and from her classes, when she'd learn something new and feel the possibilities wrapped up in it. She had that feeling now, a thrill that raced through every cell of her body.

Jack maneuvered Peggy Sue into a parking space, then got out and opened her door for her. He took her hand as though they'd done this many times before, and they started walking toward the stadium.

"'Peggy Sue, Peggy Sue,'" he sang, "'pretty pretty pretty pretty Peggy Sue.'"

She barely stopped to think before joining in. "'Oh, Peggy, my Peggy Su-ue-ue.'"

Jack laughed, letting go of her hand to give her shoulders a squeeze.

"'Oh, I love you gal,'" they sang together. "'Yes, I love you. Peggy Sue-ue-ue.'"

He harmonized on the last line, and she grinned when the little song was over. She suddenly felt high, as if there were a drug in the air around Jack, something she was inhaling that lifted worry from her shoulders and left joy in its place. And she'd been with him all of twenty-five minutes.

The concert was wild and the crowd wilder. People passed cups of cheap wine, from which she and Jack sipped freely. She turned down the rare joint that came her way, as did Jack, and she wondered if he would smoke if she did, if he was passing up the chance out of deference to her. She couldn't afford to be arrested for anything, ever. She couldn't afford to be fingerprinted, either. She'd been careful at the cabin on the Neuse River, but she could never be certain she'd been careful enough.

After intermission, things got even wilder. Jack grabbed her hand and pulled her to her feet, and they joined other people dancing on the stairs. She'd never danced in her life, but it didn't matter. She raised her arms above her head, singing along with "Rosalita," even though she was making up two-thirds of the words, dancing with a strange and welcome abandon.

They sang "Born to Run" as they walked back to the car, Eve stumbling over the words and not caring. "This was so much *fun*," she said. "I mean, really. I haven't had this kind of fun in...well, a very long time."

"You're good at it," Jack said.

"I think I was at one time," she said, remembering the person she'd been before Cory. Before Tim. Before everything had turned so deadly serious in her life.

"You mean before you had to become a responsible parent?" Jack asked.

She nodded.

"You rose to the challenge, Eve," he said, his face sober for the first time all night. "I admire you for that, but I think you still have some fun left in you. What do you think?"

She nodded. "I think I do," she said.

"And you know what we need now? Desperately?"

"What?"

"Ice cream!"

She laughed. "Wow, yes!" she said, the suggestion of ice cream creating an instant need in her. His enthusiasm was infectious. If he'd said they needed toothpaste, she might have responded the same way.

It was late and they drove to the one place that was always open: the University Diner.

"I used to work here," she said as they settled into a booth.

"You did? Was it fun?"

She thought about his question, remembering the hours she and

Lorraine had spent serving up grillswiths together. "Yeah, it was, actually," she said.

A waitress took their order—two hot-fudge sundaes—and then Jack reached across the table and held both her hands in his.

"So," he said. "Brothers? Sisters?"

"Neither."

"Are your parents still in Oregon?"

Back to reality. "My mother died when I was twelve," she said, "and my father is a question mark. I spent ages twelve to six...seventeen in foster homes."

He looked stunned by the answer, and she quickly added, "It wasn't that awful. I mean, losing my mother was awful, of course, but the foster homes weren't that terrible."

For the first time that evening, Jack seemed at a loss for words. Eve held her breath as he stared at her.

"I just dumped a lot on you." She tried to smile. "Sorry."

"No, don't be sorry," he said quickly. "I was just trying to imagine what it would be like to go through what you've gone through. Maybe that's why you seem so strong."

"I do?"

"Hell, yes. You have a...quality about you."

"I do?" she repeated.

"It's like you're made of steel." He let go of her hand to touch her hair. "And I don't just mean your razor-wire hair." He smiled. "I don't mean that you're cold, either. You're anything but cold. But you're tough. I knew it the minute I saw you the other night with Marian. You can't be kicked around."

She lowered her gaze to their hands. She *had* been kicked around, but he was right: she would never be kicked around again.

"I'm glad I seem that way," she said. "I had no idea."

For a moment, neither of them spoke.

"I don't even know your major," he said finally. "What are you studying?"

"Psychology," she said. "I love it. I'm working on a paper about foster care right now."

"Good," he said fervently. "You can use your past to fuel your future."

I like you, she thought.

"My family—my parents and brother—all live in Richmond," he said. "I took time off between high school and college to travel, so that's why I'm only now, at the ripe old age of twenty-seven, in my fourth year."

Tim's age, she thought. But that was the only thing the two men had in common.

"You've been lucky."

"I don't take it for granted," he said, and she nodded. "Can I meet Miss Cory?" he asked.

"Yeah."

"I like you," he said.

She stood up and leaned over the table, intending to kiss him softly, quickly on the lips, but he grabbed her shoulders to keep her from sitting down again, and the kiss turned into something she would not soon forget.

She called Lorraine when she got home, waking her up and not bothering to apologize.

"I met a guy I really like," she said.

"Well, damn, Eve." Lorraine sounded sleepy. "For a while there, I thought you were going to come over to our side. Do I know him?"

"He's in the drama department. His name's Jack Elliott."

"You went out with Jack?"

"You know him?" She tensed, afraid Lorraine might say something that would ruin the precious sense of joy she felt.

"If you've got to be with a guy, he's a good one to be with," she said. "I mean, he's not bad-looking."

"He's gorgeous, really," Eve said.

"If you say so." Lorraine laughed. "And he's not a jock. Not the macho type."

"That's true," Eve said, "but he's still very..." She wrinkled her nose, searching for the right word.

"*Manly*," Lorraine supplied with a chuckle.

"Yeah, that's it," she said. It was a silly word, but the image of Jack's masculine hands and perfect teeth stayed with her for the rest of the conversation, and by the time she hung up the phone, her belly felt tight with desire.

Chapter Twenty-Five

Jack arrived at one o'clock the following day carrying a canvas bag he called the "Cory-Dory bag." Cory was not an easy child to win over, however. Especially not by a man. She'd had so little experience with them. She was generally clingy with Eve, even when she met a new woman at the park or in a store, but when Jack arrived, she leaned against Eve and buried her head against her hip.

"Ah," Jack said. "*S-h-y.*"

"*Y-e-s,*" Eve replied. "Let's go in the living room."

She walked with difficulty, Cory clinging to her leg.

"So, what do you have in the Cory-Dory bag?" Eve asked.

"We have to sit on the floor to find out," Jack said.

"Let's sit, Cory." She pried her daughter's hands from her leg and sat down on the carpet across from Jack. Cory sat next to her, leaning against her as she eyed the stranger with suspicion.

Jack peered inside the bag. "Hmm," he said. "Cory, what do you think? Would you like to see the B-thing first? Or the G-thing? Or the P-thing?"

"Wow, Cory," Eve said. "You've got a lot to choose from. Which do you want to see first?"

Cory pressed against her, lowering her gaze to the floor.

"Well, I want to see the B-thing," Eve said to Jack.

"Oh, a very good choice," Jack said. He pulled a long green balloon from the canvas bag and began to blow it into a slender tube. "Would you rather see a giraffe or a doggie?" Jack asked.

"Giraffe." Cory's voice was so soft it was barely audible. Eve started to repeat the word, but Jack had heard it.

"A giraffe it is," he said. He gave the balloon a few twists, pulled another couple of balloons out of the bag, blew them up and incorporated them into the sculpture until he had a reasonable facsimile of a giraffe.

Cory giggled, her blue eyes crinkling up the way they did when she was amused. "Do the doggie now," she said.

"Please," Eve reminded her.

"Please," Cory said.

"We need hats first," Jack said. "I never do the doggie before everyone is wearing a hat."

He made three hats out of balloons and placed them on their heads, then began working on the dog. By that time, Cory was completely captivated.

Marian came home from the grocery store and laughed at the sight of them sitting on the floor, wearing their hats, surrounded by a menagerie of balloon animals.

"Make a hat for Marian!" Cory glanced at Eve. "Please," she added. She was on her feet by then, moving between Eve and Jack, her small, fair-skinned hand resting at times on his shoulder as he worked. Eve studied him with gratitude. From where she sat, his dark eyelashes lay long and thick against his cheeks, his intent concentration a sham for Cory's sake, as he created a green-and-purple hat for Marian.

"Can you make a cat?" Cory asked.

"A big cat," Jack said. "A lion." He roared at her, shaking his curly head against her midriff and she giggled wildly.

"A lion, a lion!" She jumped up and down.

Eve looked at Marian, who stood in the doorway, arms folded across her chest, a smile on her face. She caught Eve's gaze, her eyes telling her, *This is it, Eve. This is the man for you and Cory.*

The G-thing turned out to be water pistols. Guns. Before Jack reached into his bag for them, he insisted they go into Marian's small backyard. When he first pulled out the gun, Eve gasped. Suddenly she didn't know him. He was a stranger, capable of hurting them.

"Cory!" she shouted at her daughter, who stopped her wild running and looked up at the alarm in her voice.

By then, Jack had produced a yellow gun and a red gun, and she realized they were all made of cheap plastic. Still, her heart thudded in her chest.

"They're already filled." Jack didn't seem to notice her reaction. He handed her the red pistol, and Cory the yellow.

"What am I 'upposed to do?" Cory looked in bewilderment at the water pistol in her hand.

"Should I show her, Eve?" Jack pointed his pistol at Cory.

"No, don't shoot her!" Eve said. "You'll scare her."

"I had no intention of shooting her," Jack said. He pointed the gun at Eve and pulled the trigger. Eve screamed, then laughed as the cold stream of water caught her on the neck. She aimed her gun at Jack and shot him squarely in the face.

"How do you do it?" Cory was still studying her gun.

Jack walked over and helped her aim the gun. She was not a good shot, but she loved the game anyhow, and within minutes all three of them were soaked and cold and laughing.

"Somebody needs to change her clothes and have her nap." Eve ran a hand over Cory's damp red hair once they were back inside.

"No," Cory said.

"Yes." Eve took her hand. "Let's go. I'll be back in a minute, Jack."

Cory wouldn't budge. "What's the other thing?" she asked.

"What other thing?" Eve was puzzled.

"The other thing in the Cory-Dory bag," Cory said, her focus on the canvas bag on the sofa.

"You have a good memory, Cory," Jack said. "The P-thing. We'll save it for another day, okay?"

Cory looked reluctantly at the bag. "Okay," she said.

Eve took her upstairs and into the nursery, where they'd replaced the crib with a twin bed. "Do you like Jack?" she asked her as she helped Cory out of her jersey.

"Yes," Cory said. "He's silly."

"I guess he is." She tucked Cory under the covers and pulled the shade.

"Leave the door open," Cory said, although Eve had never once closed it.

"She's beautiful," Jack said, when Eve came downstairs again.

"You were amazing with her." She sat on the other end of the sofa from him, curling her feet under her. "She's usually so shy with men."

"Her father must be a redhead, huh?"

She nodded without hesitation, used to the deceit. In her mind, Cory's father looked exactly like Tim with red hair.

"Is he very involved with her?" he asked.

She shook her head. "He was killed in a motorcycle accident when Cory was a baby." This was the lie she'd told Lorraine and the women at the park and anyone else who inquired. It was the lie she would one day tell Cory. She'd decided it was best to get Cory's mythical father completely out of the picture.

"Oh, I'm sorry," Jack said.

"I didn't even put his name on the birth certificate because I didn't want him to be involved with her. He wasn't the sort of guy I thought he was." She ran her hand over the floral fabric on the sofa. "He turned out to be a criminal."

"Drugs?" he asked.

"Among other things," she offered vaguely.

"It's hard for me to imagine you with a guy like that," Jack said.

She thought of Tim and how he'd used her. "It's hard for me to imagine it, too," she said.

For the next week, they met twice on the grounds for a bite to eat and they spoke every night on the phone. On Saturday, Jack arrived with a twelve-inch, red, Radio Flyer bicycle with training wheels. He called Eve outside to see it before showing it to Cory.

"I wanted to make sure you're okay with this before I give it to her," he said.

"Oh, my God, Jack!" Eve said when she spotted the bike. She was both astonished and a little unsettled by his generosity. "This is too much." She meant it. Generous gifts came with obligations.

"I know," Jack admitted. "And I promise not to be Santa Claus every time I see her. But indulge me right now, okay? I'm having fun." His kidlike grin was hard to resist.

"Okay," she said.

They called Cory outside and watched her eyes light up at the sight of the bicycle.

"Wowie!" she said, running over to it. She looked at the bike from front to rear, then up at Jack. "You got the same color as my hair!" she said.

Jack laughed. "You're right, Cory-Dory. And I had to look high and low for it, too. Why don't you hop on?"

Eve helped Cory onto the bike, but she stayed on only three seconds before getting off again. "It's scary," she said.

"Scary?" Jack looked surprised. "I asked the guy in the bicycle store to sell me the unscary one."

Cory looked at him, and Eve knew she didn't quite follow what he was saying.

"Maybe in a few days you'll feel brave enough to get on it," Eve said.

"I think she's brave enough now, aren't you, Cory?"

Cory put her skinny leg over the bike again, and Eve had an image of her riding down the slightly sloped driveway and into the path of a car. "The first thing we'll teach you is how to brake," she said.

Cory sat down on the bicycle seat and gripped the handlebars.

"Great job!" Jack said.

"You look like a big girl," Eve added.

Cory bit her lower lip. "Will I tip over?" she asked.

"Impossible," Jack said. "You have these cool training wheels in the back to keep you from tipping over."

Cory peered around her shoulder to look at the training wheels. "So, how do I make it go?" she asked.

They gave her a lesson in the driveway, and soon she was riding on her own, but as if she could read Eve's mind, she back-pedaled to brake every few feet.

"Excellent!" Jack said once she'd managed the length of the driveway without braking. "You're ready for the sidewalk." He helped her turn onto the sidewalk, and Eve walked next to her as she rode.

"There's a big bump!" Cory cried. The sidewalk up ahead was cracked over a tree root.

"It's not that big," Eve said. "You can go over it."

Cory shut her eyes and let out a yelp as she rode over the bump.

"All right, Cory!" Jack called from behind them. "Cory-Dory rose to the challenge, boys and girls. She went over the bump like a pro."

Cory didn't seem to hear him, her forehead furrowed in concentration. She brought the bike to a standstill and put her feet on the ground.

"I want to get off now," she announced.

"Let's just ride it back to where Jack is," Eve said quietly as she turned the bike around. "And you didn't thank him. This is an extremely nice gift."

"I don't want to go over that bump again," Cory said.

"You're not going to tip over."

Cory eyed the bump as if it were the Grand Canyon, but she climbed aboard.

"You hold on, Mommy," she said.

"I'm holding on." Eve put her hand lightly on the back of the seat and they negotiated the sidewalk with relative ease.

"Well, we all survived," Jack said, rolling his eyes at Eve with a smile.

"What do you say to Jack?"

"Thank you for the bike," Cory said. "Did you bring the Cory-Dory bag?"

Jack laughed. "Greedy little Gus, aren't you?"

"What does that mean?" Cory asked.

"It means you want everything handed to you on a silver platter," Eve said.

"What's a silver platter?"

"It just means you're a normal three-year-old girl," Jack said. "And Marian's going to stay with you this afternoon while I steal your mom away for a while."

Cory looked truly alarmed. "You're going to steal her?"

"She's in her literal phase," Eve said to Jack.

"Your Mom and I are going to a bookstore for a while. Okay?"

"Can I come, too?"

"No, honey," Eve said. "You'll stay here with Marian. But I'll buy you a book, okay?"

"Okay." Cory ran into the house. "Marian! I'm staying with you for a while!" she yelled.

Eve turned to smile at Jack. "This was really wonderful of you," she said, her hand on the seat of the bike. "She's going to love it."

The used bookstore was near the university. She'd not been in it before and the ceiling-high stacks crammed with old books took her breath away. She found an ancient book on psychology, some of the theories and approaches in opposition to those she was learning, and she found a copy of *Charlotte's Web* to read to Cory, but then remembered about Charlotte dying at the end and decided against it.

"I have to be so careful with Cory," she said to Jack. "She's afraid of so much. I don't want to make it worse."

"Maybe you're too careful," Jack suggested gently.

"I don't think I can be," she said. "What makes you say that?"

He pulled a dusty book from the stacks and studied the cover. "I shouldn't have said anything," he said. "What do I know about raising kids?"

"Come on," she said. "What made you say I'm too careful?"

"I've only seen you with her for a few hours, so I really have no right to—"

"Jack! Tell me."

"Maybe you coddle her a little too much," he said. "When she's afraid, like on the bike or when she was shy about meeting me, you sort of...I don't know, comforted her. I think she liked that comfort."

Eve was quiet. Marian had said similar things to her and the criticism worried her. She was so afraid of failing her daughter.

"I'm sorry," Jack said. "It really isn't my place to—"

"No, I..." Eve let out a sigh. "You might be right. I'm not sure how else to be. I worry about her so much."

"What are you afraid of?" he asked.

Where to start? "Of losing her somehow," she said. "Of having her get hurt. Of having her suffer in any way."

"Part of life, Evie," he said. "Although I understand that you've had more than your share of the bad stuff."

"I know."

"You're a good mom," he said. In the privacy of the stacks, he put his arms around her and kissed her. "And a beautiful mom."

She wasn't beautiful. She was a plain Jane, but she believed that he meant it, that he saw something in her another man might not see. He pressed gently against her, his erection connecting with her belly. It had been so long since her body had reacted to a man. So long! Lowering her hand between them, she let the back of her fingers brush over him. He sucked in his breath.

"Jeez, girl," he said. "You are brazen."

"I'm sorry."

"I'm not complaining." He laughed.

"I'm not usually…brazen," she said, then laughed herself. "I don't even know what I am usually. It's been so long since I liked anyone."

"My fault," he said. "Coming on to you in a bookstore. You know, usually I—this is going to sound bad, but I want to be straight with you. Usually, if a girl—a woman—wanted it and I liked her and found her attractive, I'd take her to bed right away. As soon as I could. But I don't want that with you. I mean, I defi-nitely *want* you. I just don't want to move too fast and spoil what could turn out to be a really good thing."

"Of course," she said, drawing away from him.

"So," he said, "show me what you found in the old psych book."

They sat on the floor and leaned against the wall, flipping through the pages of the musty old book.

Afterward, he gave her a tour of the inner workings of the Helms Theater, where she'd seen his play. He talked about wanting to teach drama to high-school kids. She told him how she planned to work for a while after graduating, then go back for her master's in counseling. Soon, they knew nearly everything there was to know about their lives in the here and now. That was how she planned to keep it. She had no past. The here and now was where they would begin.

Chapter Twenty-Six

WHEN THE SCHOOL YEAR ENDED, THEY FELL INTO A pattern. Eve took a class four mornings a week and worked at an adolescent halfway house on the weekends. Jack's summer job with the Virginia Theater Company was primarily on the weekends as well, so they had only a few weekday evenings together, most of them spent with Cory in tow. Jack was an amazing man, willing to share the little bit of time he and Eve had together visiting amusement parks or roller-skating rinks or working on Cory's bicycling skills. She'd gotten much braver on the bike, which gave Eve both hope and trepidation.

On the Fourth of July, Cory helped Marian prepare a picnic dinner, while Eve and Jack had some time alone. They spent a lazy afternoon in the bookstore, ending up back at the house Jack shared with two other guys, both of whom were out of town for the holiday. In the four months they'd known each other, this was the first time they'd been alone together in one of their houses. Eve had started taking the pill two months ago in preparation for this day when she would have him to herself, undisturbed. She'd fallen in love with him, although she had not yet told him that. She loved his energy and playfulness, his patience and generosity with Cory. Occasionally, though, she wondered if he had the ability to be serious about anything. That concern was what kept her from saying those solemn words, weighted with expectations, to him.

As soon as they walked into his house, he shut the door behind them and drew her into his arms. "Ah," he said, kissing her. "Alone at last. Would you like to see my etchings?"

"Yes," she said. "I've been waiting a long time to see your etchings."

"You go upstairs and I'll meet you in a minute. Can I get you anything to drink?"

"No, thanks." Refreshments were the last thing on her mind. She was twenty-one and felt like a virgin. CeeCee had made love; Eve had not. CeeCee had been so stupid, so gullible, so naive. She'd needed Tim to guide her, to teach her. Eve did not.

Upstairs, she pulled the shade in his bedroom, and the room filled with a pale mellow light. She took off her clothes, folding them and setting them on his dresser. His double bed, which took up nearly all the space in the room, was neatly made, and when she climbed between the sheets, she smelled the sunshine-and-soap scent of freshly laundered linen. He'd prepared for this, too, she though happily.

She stretched out beneath the covers, the touch of the sheets exciting against her bare skin. Folding her arms behind her head, she waited.

"I'm coming, don't give up on me," he called. She heard his foot-steps on the stairs and in a moment he appeared in the doorway. He grinned when he saw her.

"My woman's hot to trot." He laughed. He had something in his hand which he set on the floor by his side of the bed.

He lay down next to her, rolling onto his side. "You look beautiful," he said, running his fingertips over her cheek. "There's a stripe of sunlight on your hair and face."

She touched her cheek as though she might be able to feel the sunlight there, then smoothed her hand over his arm.

"You're precious to me, do you know that?" he asked. He *could* be serious. She was wrong to think otherwise.

"I feel the same way," she said. Her voice felt thick.

He bent over to kiss her and she pulled his T-shirt over his head as he drew away. He stood up and unbuckled his khakis and let them fall. He pulled off his shorts, and she rolled to the edge of the bed to touch his erection, to press it against her cheek. He groaned, then lay her back on the bed. The next thing she knew, she felt something cold on her neck and heard a hissing sound.

"What...?"

He licked her neck. "Mmm," he said.

She pulled back laughing, spotting the red-and-white can in his hand. *"Whipped cream?"* Well, he could be serious for a few seconds, anyway.

"Hold still." He drew the sheet from her breast. "Oh, stunning," he said. Then he slowly covered her nipples with whipped cream before lowering his mouth to them, and she knew their lovemaking would be long, passionate—and very, very messy.

Chapter Twenty-Seven

1982

EVE SAT ON CORY'S BED AND TURNED THE LAST PAGE OF the book they were reading together. Cory already recognized many words. Puppy, for example. Elephant. Run. Boy and girl. And for some reason, asparagus.

Eve tucked the covers beneath Cory's chin and leaned over to kiss her forehead. Her own mother used to read to her at night, then sit and talk with her about everything under the sun. She'd loved that tender time with her mother, and she loved recreating it with Cory.

She brushed a lock of red hair from Cory's cheek and slipped it behind her ear. "Marian said you saw a dachshund at the park today," she said.

Cory nodded. "And I wasn't afraid of it because it was little," she said.

She *had* been afraid of it, Marian had told Eve, but she didn't correct her. She'd let Cory have her fantasy of bravery.

"Mommy," Cory said suddenly, "is Marian my daddy?"

Eve had been waiting a long time for Cory to ask about her father, but she'd never expected the question to come in this form.

"No, honey," she said. "Daddies have to be men." She wondered if Cory was thinking about Lorraine, Bobbie and Shan. Clearly, there was no man in that triad, and she wasn't sure how to explain those family dynamics. "Marian's just a very special friend," she said. "She's not related to us."

"Then is Jack my daddy?"

"No. Jack's a very special friend, too."

She waited, and for a moment thought that was the end of it. "What makes you ask about your daddy, honey?"

Cory pressed her lips together until they nearly disappeared. "Kelsey's daddy brings her to the park every morning," she said, referring to the only man who took part in the morning get-together of moms-and-kids at the park. "And Hank has a daddy. And Calvin. I think everybody at the park has a daddy except me. I said I had one, too. I said Marian was my daddy, and Hank laughed at me."

Eve's heart broke a little. She wished she could remember having this conversation with her own mother. How had her father's absence been explained to her? She didn't recall, but she did remember the pain of being fatherless when it seemed that all the other children had two parents active in their lives, even if they were not living together.

This would be the first outright lie she'd told her daughter.

"You had a daddy, Cory," she said. "But he died."

"Like Dino?" Cory asked, referring to a dog who used to play with the children—the *other* children—at the park.

"Yes. Like Dino."

"My daddy's in heaven?"

"Yes."

"Was he really sick like Dino?"

"No. He had an accident."

"Oh."

"I grew up without a daddy, too," she said. She wasn't sure if this was too much information to give her, but it seemed important to say.

"Your daddy died, too?"

She could make it easy on herself and say yes, but she didn't want to tell any more lies than she had to.

"He just wasn't a very good daddy. I never even knew him."

"Will I ever get to meet my daddy?"

She didn't get it. She was still a little mixed up about the concept of death.

"No, honey. I'm sorry. He can't come back. Just like Dino can't come back."

She saw the tears welling in her daughter's eyes and felt her own eyes burn.

"Come here, Cory." She drew the covers back and pulled her daughter into her arms. Rocking her, she felt Cory sniffling against her chest, grieving for the father she could never know.

"I had a painful conversation with Cory tonight," she said to Jack when he phoned her that evening. "She suddenly realized she doesn't have a daddy. I guess the other kids at the park talk about their fathers. She asked me if Marian was her daddy."

"Oh," Jack said. "Poor baby."

"Then she asked me if you were her daddy."

Jack was quiet. "What did you tell her?" he asked after a moment.

"I told her no, of course. I explained that her daddy died in an accident."

"Do you think she understood what that means?"

"I don't know. She asked if he could come back. I think she finally got it, though. She cried, and so did I."

"I'm coming over," he said.

"Now?"

"I just want to hold you. I know this must have been really hard."

Her eyes burned again. "It's late," she said, although she suddenly realized how much she needed him to be with her.

"I'll be there in a few minutes," he said.

She hung up the phone, grateful that this compassionate man was a part of her life.

Sitting on the sofa with him later that night, she let him hold her. His arms had become her favorite place to be.

"Evie," he said after they'd sat in silence for a while.

"Hmm?"

"I'd wanted to do this in some well-planned-out, dramatic sort of way, but I don't think I can wait."

"What are you talking about?"

"I want to be Cory's daddy," he said. "And I want to be Eve's husband." He leaned away to look into her eyes. "Will you marry me?"

A thousand responses ran through her mind. *Are you sure you want to take on a woman with a little girl?* And, *You don't know the truth about me and you never can.* But she thought of all he'd come to mean to her. He was her dearest friend, her playmate, her lover—one who had taught her that she was, indeed, capable of having orgasms with him inside her.

She smiled, leaning forward to kiss him.

"Yes," she said. "Absolutely, yes."

Chapter Twenty-Eight

1983

IN MAY, EVE GRADUATED WITH HONORS AND A BACHELOR'S degree in psychology, and in June, she and Jack were married in the wedding chapel on the grounds. Jack's family was there, along with Marian, of course. Lorraine, who was now a production assistant at television station Channel 29, was Eve's maid of honor, even agreeing to wear a dress for the occasion, and Jack's brother, Rob, was his best man. Cory was supposed to be the flower girl, but she had an attack of nerves at the last minute and wound up sitting next to Marian in the pew instead.

Jack taught high-school drama now, and a few of his students attended the ceremony, along with several of Eve's classmates. It was a quiet, simple wedding, with Jack as serious as Eve had ever seen him. There were tears in his eyes when he spoke the vows he'd written. He promised to be faithful, devoted and honest. She said nothing about honesty in her own vows and hoped no one noticed.

They moved into a small rental house a half mile from the university and within walking distance of Marian's. Although Eve felt a huge loss in leaving her safe haven at Marian's house, she was more concerned about leaving the older woman alone. Marian was sixty-seven now and starting to show her age. Eve noticed it for the first time when everyone gathered outside the chapel after the wedding. The sun illuminated every wrinkle on Marian's face and left shadows under her eyes. She wanted to let Marian know she would always be there for her. She and Cory would not have survived the past six years without her help. Maybe the time was coming for her to return the favor.

That summer was one of the most stable and comfortable periods Eve could remember enjoying in her life. She, Jack and Cory were a true family. Jack taught summer school, while Eve looked for a job she could start in September. She planned to work part-time, while Jack began a graduate program in drama so he could teach at the university level. Eve understood. He missed being part of UVA. She already felt the same way.

Eve and Cory puttered around in the mornings, going to the park or visiting Marian, who would play "Twinkle, Twinkle Little Star" on her cello while Cory sang along. But the day really began for them when Jack came home. They would go to a museum or a movie or have a barbecue with friends. At night, they'd crowd into Cory's bed and read a book together.

In early August, Eve and Cory spent a week at a cottage in the Outer Banks of North Carolina, right on the beach. The cottage cost them nothing; it belonged to one of Marian's friends, who encouraged them to use it. Eve missed Jack, but she loved having the quiet, bittersweet time alone with her daughter. In a few weeks, Cory would start kindergarten and everything would change.

A few days before Cory started school, Jack legally adopted her. Cory quickly took to calling him "Daddy," and her occasional questions about who and where her father was came to a halt.

Kindergarten, though, marked the end of their idyllic, celebration-filled summer.

Cory's elementary school was two blocks from their house, and Eve walked her there on the first day. Cory was quiet at her side, holding tightly to Eve's hand, ignoring the other children who raced past them on the sidewalk.

"Your new shoes look adorable," Eve said to her. Marian had bought Cory a first-day-of-school outfit: blue pants, a blue floral T-shirt and navy-and-white sneakers that looked like little saddle shoes. Cory had put the outfit on very slowly, a somber expression on her face as though she were dressing for a funeral.

Inside the school, Eve saw that Cory was not the only child in distress. A mother tried to calm her weeping son in the hallway, and the teacher, an extremely tall black woman, coaxed a little girl into the classroom. The teacher, Mrs. Rice, looked scary even to Eve. She was fortyish, with blue-black skin and teeth as white and smooth as porcelain. She wore her thick, straight hair in a bowl cut that framed her face. Cory took one look at her and started to whimper, her arms wrapping around Eve's legs like a vise.

"Oh, my, now," Mrs. Rice said, walking toward them where they stood just inside the classroom door. "What's going on here? Oh, you're a lovely girl. Isn't she?" She looked at Eve as if for confirmation.

Eve nodded. "Yes, but a bit nervous about the first day." She whispered the word "nervous."

"Well, we're going to have so much fun today," Mrs. Rice said.

"We're going to play some games to help us get to know one another."

"Cory, did you hear what Mrs. Rice said? You and the other children are going to play games this morning. And I'll be back in just a few hours to pick you up."

"No, Mommy!" Cory hugged her legs, looking up at her with her pleading blue eyes. "I don't want to stay here!"

Eve's armpits suddenly felt damp. "Maybe she's not ready for kindergarten," she whispered to Mrs. Rice.

"Oh, I bet she is," the woman said. "Maybe her mama's not ready, though." She smiled at Eve with her porcelain teeth, and the look in her eyes said, *Gotcha!*

Mrs. Rice excused herself to talk with another parent, and Eve knelt down in front of Cory, putting her hands on her arms. "See all the other boys and girls in here?" she asked. "Most of them are already having fun together."

Cory sniffed, her lower lip trembling as she looked around the room. There were a few kids seated on the edge of an indoor sandbox. Others worked with clay or played with blocks. The weeping boy trudged past them, rubbing his eyes with the backs of his hands as he walked toward the sandbox. His mother rolled her eyes at Eve with a smile as she left the room. "He's my third child to have Mrs. Rice," she said. "And my third to scream the first time he laid eyes on her. In a week, the kids'll think the sun rises and sets on her. You wait."

"Thank you." Eve appreciated the reassurance.

She stood up as Mrs. Rice returned to her and Cory.

"Okay, Cory." Mrs. Rice had a singsong, upbeat voice now. "It's time to come into the classroom and for your mama to go home.

You loosen up now, Mrs. Elliott. Come on. You're holding her tighter by the minute."

Was she? She looked down to see the white of her knuckles where her fingers clasped Cory's shoulders. Opening her hands, she took a step back, leaving Cory in Mrs. Rice's grasp.

"Perfect!" the teacher said. "You go now. Go." Eve took another step backward, this time into the hallway, and Mrs. Rice closed the door between her and Cory.

"Mom!" Cory wailed. "Mommy, don't leave me!"

Eve put her hand on the doorknob, let it sit there for a moment. If she opened the door, she had the feeling Mrs. Rice would throw something at her. She let go of the knob and walked quickly from the building and into the sunlight, and she swore she could still hear Cory screaming as she crossed the street to walk home alone.

Chapter Twenty-Nine

THE ONLY JOB EVE COULD FIND WITH HER BACHELOR'S degree was at the Cartwright House, the same residential halfway house where she'd worked while in school. Her new job had a different title and more hours, but she was discouraged that she barely made enough to pay their rent. If it were not for Jack's family, they wouldn't be able to get by. Still, she liked working with the teenagers. She saw her younger self in so many of them. They operated on emotion and impulse as they pushed toward adulthood with bodies ready for the challenge but brains lagging far behind. Watching and listening to them, she knew how far she'd come in six years. Thank God for second chances.

Cory, though, was her everyday reminder of her own impulsive decisions. She tried hard to be a good mother. People said she was; they complimented her all the time on how she put her own needs second to those of her daughter. Still, Cory was so clingy and insecure. Somehow, Eve was failing her. When Mrs. Rice called to ask her and Jack to come in for a meeting, she knew she was going to come face-to-face with that failure.

"She's the prettiest little string bean, isn't she?" Mrs. Rice said, once Eve and Jack were seated across the desk from her in the kindergarten classroom.

Eve nodded. "Thank you." She clutched Jack's hand on her knee.

"And she's smart. She's doing very well in all our lessons. She's well behaved and never makes an ounce of trouble. She's the kind of student it would be easy to ignore since she doesn't make waves, but I don't want to ignore her, because she deserves better."

"What are you getting at?" Jack asked.

"She's not doing well socially," Mrs. Rice said. "The little boys all treat her like a princess. They're gaga over her. About five of them consider her their girlfriend." She chuckled. "Even at five, they're into good looks. But she's made no real friends among the girls because she's so shy. She's afraid to do things the other children do, like climbing on the jungle gym, for instance. One of the other girls will try to persuade her to climb with them, but Cory stands on the ground and shakes her head. Eventually, the girls give up on her."

Eve licked her lips. "She's afraid of a lot of things right now, but I think she'll outgrow it."

"You might be right," Mrs. Rice said. "I just wanted to let you know what I'm observing, because often a child will be just fine at home and you'd never know this is going on."

"What can we do?" Jack asked.

"Build her self-confidence," Mrs. Rice said. "Give her things to do that she can excel at. She is going to be a phenomenal reader. I can tell you've done a great deal of reading with her."

"Yes," Eve said, relieved that she'd done something right. "I've read to her since she was tiny."

"And it shows. So that's something I make sure to reward her for. I've put her in charge of handing out the little books we use."

Eve smiled at the thought of Cory being in charge of anything at all. "I don't think I've done that with her enough," she said to Jack. "You know. Had her take responsibility for things."

He nodded. "We can let her decide what we do on Saturdays. Give her some choices and let her pick."

"That's the idea," Mrs. Rice said.

"Yikes," Jack said when they'd left the school and started walking home in the crisp darkness. "That's the tallest woman I've ever seen. I felt like a shrimp next to her. She must tower over her students."

"She does. I told you how scared Cory was of her at first, but she seems to like her now."

"You know, though, she has a point," Jack said. "You don't like her to ride her bike because you're nervous about the traffic— even though she's riding on the sidewalk. You're afraid she'll fall. The other day when she was afraid of the dinosaur skeleton at the museum, you took her out of the room, like you were verifying for her that she was right to be afraid of it."

Cory had been screaming and cowering and creating a scene. "I didn't think it was fair to everyone else in the museum to be subjected to her screams." Eve felt defensive.

Jack hesitated before speaking again. "I worry, though, that she picks up on your fears about her."

Eve felt a flash of anger. She'd been parenting Cory for six years. Jack had known her for only two. She bit her tongue, though, because she knew he was right.

"You know what I think would help Cory a lot?" Jack asked.

"What?"

"Having a brother or sister to boss around."

Eve laughed, and she wondered if he heard the anxiety in the sound. She longed to have a baby with him. She longed to see how his features would blend with hers. She loved the way he lit up around Cory and wanted to see that joy doubled in him. But having a baby could only force her to tell more lies. Any doctor would know she'd never been pregnant before. How would she keep that fact from Jack?

"We're poor people, Jack," she said. "We're way below the poverty line. It would be irresponsible for us to have a baby right now."

"Cory's nearly six years old," he said. "If we wait 'til we're rich, she'll be old enough to raise the kid on her own." He stopped walking and turned her toward him. "You know my parents aren't going to let us starve," he said. "They'll help us out as long as I'm in school." He kissed her. "So, let's go home and throw away your pills."

Chapter Thirty

THE DAY AFTER HER TWENTY-FOURTH BIRTHDAY, EVE FELT woozy as she drove to work. Two blocks from the halfway house, she pulled her car to the side of the road, opened the door and threw up into the street.

She leaned back in the seat and closed her eyes. *Oh, God, Jack,* she thought. *I'm sorry.* There would always be dishonesty in their marriage no matter how much she wished otherwise. Jack was so forthright, so sincere, and she wanted to open her heart to him in return, but she couldn't. So, although she had news that would thrill him, she wouldn't tell him right away. She needed to keep her pregnancy to herself for a while first, as she figured out how to deal with all that lay ahead.

By that weekend, though, he'd guessed. Although she got out of bed quietly on Saturday morning and turned on the bathroom fan to mask any sound she might make, he knew.

"Are you all right?" he asked when she came back to bed.

"Just feel a little off this morning," she said.

He stroked her cheek. "You haven't been yourself in the morning lately," he said. "Any chance you're…?"

She bit her lip, then smiled weakly at him. "I think I might be," she said. "I didn't want to say anything to you until I knew for sure."

"Yippee!" Jack jumped to his feet on the mattress and did a little dance. She couldn't help but laugh at him. He was perfect daddy material. "I'm with child!" he shouted.

"Shh! You'll wake Cory."

He flopped down again next to her. "Oh, Evie." He kissed her shoulder and rested his hand on her flat stomach. "This is wonderful. I'm sorry you feel bad, but I'm...I'm exquisitely overjoyed."

She kissed the tip of his nose. "Me, too," she said, and she meant it.

"Let's call my parents," he said.

She shook her head. "I want to wait until we know everything's okay," she said. "Can you suppress your enthusiasm for a couple of months?"

"I guess. What should we name him?" He caught himself. "Or her?"

"I was thinking we might name him after your father if he's a boy."

"Alexander," Jack said. "I love that name and Dad would be proud as punch. And if it's a girl, how about after your mother?"

She'd actually been thinking of that, and it touched her that Jack had the same idea. "Would that upset your mother, though?" she asked. She got along well with Jack's parents, but was careful never to ruffle their feathers. She and Jack owed them too much.

"She'd understand," he said. "And I really like the name Dru. Was it short for something? Drucilla?"

"Nope. Just Dru." Her eyes welled up at the thought of

bringing another Dru into the world. If only her mother could be with her. If only she could hold her hand through the next eight months.

"Did you have a lot of morning sickness when you were pregnant with Cory?" Jack asked.

Here we go, she thought. "It was just like this," she said. "That's how I knew I was pregnant this time. It feels the same."

"This time you won't be alone, though," Jack said. "I want to go to every doctor's appointment with you and be there when you have him. Or her. When do we tell Cory? Do we have to wait to tell her, too?"

She nodded. "Yes, definitely," she said. "For now, it's going to be our little secret. Okay?"

Eve was cleaning up after lunch that afternoon when Jack walked into the kitchen with the mail.

"Anything important?" she asked, drying her hands on the dish towel.

Jack shuffled through the mail. "A couple of bills and a fat envelope for you with no return address." He handed the envelope to her. She knew without looking at it that her name and address would be typewritten, and she knew what she would find inside. Since leaving Marian's house, she'd received two of the envelopes filled with money. Both had been forwarded to her from Marian's address; this one had her new address on it.

"Oh, thanks," she said. "You can just put it on the counter."

"Don't you want to see what's in it?" Jack patted the envelope between his thumb and fingers. "Feels like an invitation or something. Do you know anyone who's getting married?"

Eve drew in a breath and leaned back against the counter. She didn't need to lie about this to him.

"I think I know what it is," she said. "Open it up."

"It's addressed to you, though."

"Go ahead. Open it."

He slid a finger beneath the flap and slit the envelope open, then peered inside.

"Holy crap," he said, drawing out the bills. "They're fifties!"

"How many?" she asked.

He counted them onto the counter. "Twenty of them! A thousand dollars in cash." He frowned at her. "Who would send you a thousand dollars in cash?"

"Well," she said, "I don't really know. I've gotten several of those envelopes since Cory was born. The first one came to me at Marian's house and there was a note inside. Just a scrap of paper. It said 'for your baby.' It was a few hundred dollars then. Now I get one a couple of times a year, and though there's no note with them anymore, I assume it's money meant for Cory."

Jack hadn't lost his frown. "What have you been doing with it?" he asked. He sounded not suspicious exactly, but more than curious. She didn't blame him. They were hard up for money, and here she was getting cash she hadn't told him about.

"I've put it in a bank account for her," she said. "In the beginning, I bought things she needed. Baby supplies. That sort of thing. But for the past couple of years, I just socked it away." She looked at the money on the counter. "This will make it close to four thousand dollars," she said.

"Why didn't you ever tell me this was happening?" Jack asked.

She couldn't look him in the eye. "I felt kind of weird about it," she said. "I wasn't trying to hide money from you, Jack. I hope you don't think that."

"Of course not," he said, "but I do wish you'd told me. Why do you feel weird about it?"

"Because I can't explain where it's come from. There's always a different postmark on the envelope. Oklahoma. Ohio. Where's this one from?"

He turned the envelope over and looked at it. "El Paso, Texas," he said.

"See what I mean?"

"Could it be someone in Cory's father's family?" he asked.

"That's what I figure," she said. "But who knows? Are you upset? Do you think we should use the money to pay our bills or get a better place to live or—?"

"No," he said. "Whoever sent it wants it to go to Cory, so that's who it should go to." He pouted, jutting out his lower lip like a little kid. "Our new baby's not going to have a crazy benefactor, though," he said. "He's going to be a poor little Gus."

She smiled. "We'll make it up to him—or her—somehow," she said.

She managed to go alone to her first appointment with the obstetrician. She scheduled it for a day when she knew Jack would be at a Dramatic Arts Conference in Washington, and she drove to the appointment with a heavy heart. She was hurting herself as well as him; she longed to have him at her side throughout her entire pregnancy. They should be sharing the experience together, just as he wanted, but she could think of no way to make that possible.

The doctor's name was Cheryl Russo. She had a thick New York accent that was out of place in Charlottesville, but her manner was soft and slow and Southern. She was so lovely, in fact, so easy to talk with, that for one brief insane moment, Eve considered telling her the semi-truth about Cory. *My husband thinks she's mine, but she's really adopted, so please don't let on that this is my first pregnancy.* But then Dr. Russo would think she was a terrible woman and terrible wife. She would ask questions Eve would be unable to answer. She'd wonder how a twenty-four-year-old woman happened to have an adopted six-year-old. Once Eve started down the path of telling half-truths to the doctor, she'd be dodging land mines right and left. So she opted for the simplest deception she could come up with: she would have to keep Jack away from her appointments, one way or another. That was all there was to it.

The deception, though, tore her apart. It was so unlike her to be manipulative with Jack. When he returned from the conference and was unpacking his suitcase in their bedroom, she told him that she'd seen the doctor, and he stared at her in disbelief.

"Please don't be upset," she said quickly. "When I made the appointment, I didn't realize it was when you'd be out of town, and I didn't tell you because I knew you'd feel terrible."

"I *do* feel terrible." He stood with a pair of jeans in one hand, a shoe in the other, and he looked crushed. "Why didn't you change it?"

"It took me so long to get," she said. "I'm really sorry."

"Well, what did the doctor say?" he asked.

"It was all very unexciting," she said.

"That's because you've been through this before." Jack dropped the jeans back into the suitcase, not only hurt but angry. "It's new for *me*. I think you forgot that."

"I'm sorry. I wasn't thinking." She had the feeling she would be saying "I'm sorry" throughout the course of her pregnancy.

In June, they decided it was time to tell Cory.

Cory had, as that other mother had predicted on the first day of school, come to love Mrs. Rice, who had capitalized on the little girl's reading skills to help her feel important and self-confident in the classroom. She was still shy with the other children, still afraid to join in their rough-and-tumble activities on the playground. Looking at her, it was almost understandable. Even at six, she possessed a fragile beauty. She was tall and long-limbed, with pale blue eyes, delicate fair skin and small, feminine features, and she looked as though she might shatter into a thousand pieces if she fell from the jungle gym.

"We have some exciting news for you," Jack said, as he and Eve tucked Cory into bed.

Outside the window next to Cory's bed, fireflies twinkled in the trees, and Cory had to tear her attention from them to her father.

"What?" she asked.

"You're going to have a little brother or sister," Eve said.

The night-light on the wall illuminated Cory's look of surprise. Her eyes were wide, her mouth open. Then she grinned.

"*When?*" she asked.

"Sometime in November," Eve said.

"It'll be like a special birthday present for you," Jack said. Cory would turn seven November twenty-second.

Cory's gaze dropped to Eve's belly. "Is the baby in your tummy now?" she asked. "It doesn't look like it."

Eve laughed, resting her hand on her stomach. "Uh-huh," she

said. "She or he is very tiny now, but in a few months, you'll see a big difference."

"I can't wait!" Cory clapped her hands together. "This is the best news since I was four," she said.

Eve laughed again. "What happened when you were four, honey?" she asked.

Cory looked up at Jack, admiration in her face. "That's when I got my daddy," she said.

Somehow, Eve was able to go alone to her prenatal appointments. Although she and Jack never talked about it, he seemed to guess that she was uncomfortable about having him at the appointments with her, and he stopped badgering her about them. She did bring him to her sonogram appointment, hoping there would be no reason for the technician to mention the fact that this was her first pregnancy. She told Jack that she'd had no sonogram when she was pregnant with Cory, so he had no reason to be surprised by her tears of amazement when the technician pointed to the baby's beating heart on the monitor.

He took her to a romantic restaurant for dinner afterward. They held hands across the table, then went home and made love, and Eve wept as she told him how much she loved him. She told him that regularly, worried that he might interpret her need for privacy as something more than not wanting him around when her feet were up in stirrups.

After the first few months of her pregnancy, she felt very well. But then, suddenly, the nightmares started. In them, she gave birth to a baby girl and then started to hemorrhage, blood flowing out of her while she lay in a hospital bed trying to scream for help but unable to make a sound. Several times a week, she'd awaken in the middle of the night gasping for breath, scrambling out of bed and throwing back the covers as she turned on the light to check the sheets for blood. Jack would hold her, sing to her, and whisper words of comfort in her ear. Still, nothing could erase the image in her mind of Genevieve Russell lying pale and cold on the bed in the cabin, the life ebbing out of her body.

She knew she'd never be able to keep Jack away from her labor and delivery, nor did she want to. She needed him by her side. He went through the childbirth classes with her, and when people asked if this was her first pregnancy she would always answer that it felt like it, because she'd been so young and naive the first time around.

"It must have been so hard for you when Cory was born," he said as they drove home after one of the classes. "You had no support at all."

"I barely remember it," she said. "I mean, I remember pain, of course, but they must have knocked me out, because all I really remember is holding Cory in my arms."

"Well, I hope it's that easy for you this time." Jack reached over to squeeze her hand.

She hoped he wouldn't say anything about her "first pregnancy" during her labor and delivery, when the medical staff would be there to hear him. As jittery as she was growing about delivering a baby, she was even more afraid that her lies might come crashing down around her.

Chapter Thirty-One

IN EARLY OCTOBER, EVE WAS WORKING AT THE CARTWRIGHT House when one of the other counselors knocked on the door of her small office. She was in the middle of a session with a boy whose tough facade and pink Mohawk disguised a tender soul, and she was surprised anyone would interrupt her.

"Eve?" the counselor said through the door. "I'm sorry to disturb you, but your daughter's school is on the phone. They said it's urgent."

Eve managed to say "excuse me" to the boy before racing out of the room as quickly as her huge belly would allow. She ran down the hall to the main office and the telephone. In the space of thirty seconds, she pictured broken bones. Blood. Worse. The last couple of months had been so easy with Cory, her transition to the first grade seamless compared to the early days of kindergarten. Cory liked her teacher, Mrs. Judd, a short, dark-haired woman who resembled Eve, which seemed to give the little girl comfort. Her grades were good, and she now had her own library card. It was hard to keep her supplied with books, she zipped through them so quickly.

In the office, she grabbed the receiver from the desk.

"This is Eve Elliott," she said, winded. "Is something wrong?"

"This is Mrs. Judd, Mrs. Elliott," Cory's teacher said. "I don't know how concerned we should be, but I needed to let you know that Cory didn't return to the classroom after recess. I thought maybe you or your husband came to pick her up?"

Eve ran a hand through her hair, trying to think. Had she forgotten an appointment? Might Jack have gone to the school to get her for some reason? She looked at her watch. "I didn't pick her up, and her father's in class right now," she said. "Are you sure she's not in the restroom?" Cory occasionally got stomach cramps when she was nervous about something.

"We've checked everywhere," Mrs. Judd said. "None of the other children noticed her leaving the playground, but…she tends not to hang around with them, anyhow, so they might not have been paying attention. Usually she just sits on the grass and reads during—"

"I'll be right there," Eve said. She slammed the phone down, asked her co-worker to apologize to the boy she'd been counseling, then took off for the school.

Please, God, let her be there, she prayed as she drove through Charlottesville. It was so unlike Cory to wander off on her own. She was not that courageous.

Eve was trembling by the time she reached the office of the elementary school.

"Did you find her?" she asked as she burst into the room.

A police officer stood near the secretary's desk, and he looked up from the notepad in his hand. "Mrs. Elliott?"

"Yes. Have you found her?"

"No," he said. "We need to know how to reach your husband. Is there a chance she could be with him?"

Eve shook her head. "He's in class."

"Is there anyone else who might have picked her up from school?"

She shook her head. "I've got to find her," she said. "She's only six years old!"

"Her teacher said she was wearing green pants and a white cardigan sweater today, is that right?"

"Yes." Her hand shook violently as she brushed her hair away from her face. "She—"

"You sit down, ma'am." He interrupted her, his eyes on her stomach. "I don't want you to have that baby right here."

She sank into the seat and pictured Cory as she'd looked that morning when she walked her to school. "She had on sneakers and was wearing a green backpack. Unless that's still in the classroom. You said she's—"

"They found her!" The secretary suddenly ran into the room. "One of the police officers has her. He's bringing her here."

"Oh, thank God." Eve stood up again. "Is she okay? Where was she?"

"I don't know any of that, Mrs. Elliott," the secretary said. "Can I get you some water?"

Eve shook her head.

The officer closed his notebook. "Sounds like a happy ending." He smiled at her. "Sit down again, Mrs. Elliott. Are you all right?"

"I'm okay," she said, but she clutched the edge of the counter.

Cory walked into the room, holding the hand of a police officer. The moment she spotted Eve, though, she let go of the officer and sprang toward her mother.

"Mommy, Mommy!" she cried, grabbing Eve's hand.

Eve wrapped her arms around her. "I'm so glad to see you," she said, bending down to kiss the top of her head. "Oh, baby, I'm so glad."

"We found her three blocks away, by the Piggly Wiggly," the officer said.

Eve lowered herself onto the chair again to be eye level with her daughter. "Who took you there, Cory?" she asked.

"I walked there."

Eve shook her head at the officer. "She wouldn't do that," she said. "She'd be afraid to go off on her own like that."

"I was going to the Carter house," Cory said.

"The Carter House? You mean the Cartwright House? Where I work?"

Cory nodded. "I needed to find you."

"Oh, sweetie, you can't do that. I work too far from here." She was filled with terror over what might have happened. "You never would have found me. You must never, ever walk off on your own again."

She leaned over to whisper in her ear. "But I needed to tell you something," she said.

"What?"

"Caitlin said her aunt *died* when she had a baby," Cory said. "The baby was born too soon and she *died*. And you said to Daddy last night that you were ready for the baby to come *right now* and I was afraid you'd go have the baby be born now and you'd die. And I had to find you to tell you not to do that so you wouldn't die, Mommy."

"Oh, the poor little thing," the secretary said.

There was such sincerity in Cory's face. Such love and concern. How terrified she must have been to do something as brave and out of character as leaving the school, unsure where she was going, to try to find her and keep her safe!

Eve pressed her hands lightly on the side of her head and leaned forward to kiss her temple. "I'm not going to die, honey, and I'm not going to have the baby now. Even if I did, though, I wouldn't die. It's very, very unusual for that to happen. Something must have been wrong with Caitlin's aunt for that to happen, okay? You don't need to worry about that at all. Not even the tiniest little bit. And if you ever *are* worried about something like that, you need to talk to an adult about it instead of leaving school to try to find me. Promise me that you'll never do that again."

"I promise," she said. "If you promise not to die."

When her contractions began the afternoon of November twenty-first, Eve thought of Genevieve, but her labor was entirely different from that of Cory's mother. The pain was far worse than she'd expected and it seemed to last an eternity before they finally gave her an epidural. She had Jack by her side the whole time, breathing with her, holding her hand, feeding her ice chips, and at times, annoying her with made-up songs that were meant to cheer her on. They called Cory to reassure her that Eve was fine, and as the clock ticked past midnight, to wish her a happy seventh birthday. The new baby would indeed be Cory's biggest birthday present.

One of the nurses said something about this being Eve's first pregnancy, and she shrugged her shoulders at Jack with a nonchalant smile that took some effort.

"Looks like they screwed up my chart," she said, and hoped that he felt no need to set them straight.

Her labor lasted eleven hours and twenty minutes, and by the time she was holding beautiful, black-haired Dru Bailey Elliott in her arms, Genevieve's bloody death was the furthest thing from her mind.

Chapter Thirty-Two

1987

EVE WAS NOT THE LEAST BIT SURPRISED WHEN CORY WOKE up with a stomachache the second Saturday in July. She sat at the breakfast table, her arms hanging limply at her sides as she stared glumly at her untouched cereal. Her Girl Scout troop was going on an overnight trip to Camp Sugar Hollow, and Cory had started getting nervous the night before. Eve knew she'd gotten very little sleep.

"I don't want to go," she said now.

"I know you don't, honey," Eve said as she lifted Dru out of her booster seat. Dru's chubby little legs were already pumping before Eve had even set her on the floor. Then she was off, running into the living room to watch cartoons. At two and a half, Dru was already Cory's opposite. Where Cory was long and lithe, Dru was short and sturdy, much like Eve had been at her age. Dru had the look and nature of a brown-eyed, curly-haired imp, while Cory grew more ethereally beautiful and reserved with each passing year.

"Can you say Sugar Hollow five times fast?" Jack asked her, but Cory didn't bite.

"Please don't make me go," she pleaded, looking from Eve to Jack and back again.

"Look at it as an adventure, Cory," Eve said, then realized how dumb a response that was. Cory went out of her way to avoid adventure.

"You're going to have such a good time." Jack sipped his coffee. "You'll learn silly songs and eat s'mores and the boys from the Boy Scout camp across the lake will sneak over to your camp at night and you can all go tiptoe into the grown-ups' tents and tie their shoelaces together."

"Dad," Cory moaned. "Why can't you come, Mom?"

"You know why." Eve peered around the corner to check on Dru, then sat down at the table again.

"Dad could take care of Dru," Cory said.

"No, Dad cannot," Jack said. "Dad has play rehearsal tonight and his students sorely need it." He was teaching drama at the university now and he was in seventh heaven.

He stood up and carried his cereal bowl to the sink. "Oh, Rocky Raccoon," he sang to the tune of the old Beatles' song, "found Cory baboon, asleep in her tent at the campground. Rocky crept in, and grinning a grin, he nibbled her toes 'til she looked down."

Cory didn't crack a smile. At nine and a half, she was already jaded to her father's corny humor.

"You'll never forget your first time at camp," Eve said, although she'd never been camping in her life. She was nearly as anxious as Cory about her going. Besides the night Dru was born, when she stayed with Marian, Cory had spent only one night away from home, at a well-supervised sleepover she'd somehow managed to get invited to. She had a panic attack in the middle of the night. The mother in charge of the party called Eve and Jack at two in the morning. "She's crying and shaking from head to toe," the woman said. "I'm not sure what got her so scared."

Jack went to pick her up from the sleepover, and Cory was subdued in the car on the drive home. "Maybe a little too young for a sleepover," he'd whispered to Eve when he brought Cory in the house.

And maybe she was too young for Girl Scout camp, Eve thought, but she tried to act as though it was no big deal. She doubted any of the other girls in the scout troop were unable to eat their breakfasts this morning.

Cory eventually gave in, and Eve drove her to the elementary school parking lot. The other girls sat on their rolled-up sleeping bags, talking and giggling, as they waited to get on the bus. Eve kissed Cory goodbye, then watched as she carried her sleeping bag and mess kit across the parking lot, looking as if she were about to walk the plank.

Jack got home from play rehearsal at eleven and flopped onto the bed next to her. Eve lay on top of the covers, reading a book on cognitive therapy. She was back in school, this time working on her master's degree in counseling.

"Any calls?" he asked, and she knew he was wondering how Cory was doing.

"No news is good news," she said.

He kissed her bare shoulder and slipped his hand under the old pink tank top she wore to bed. "Let's never get a place with air-conditioning," he said. His fingers brushed the slope of her breast and she shifted on the bed to give him easier access.

"Why not?" she asked. They had window air conditioners in their room and in the girls' room, but neither of them worked very well.

"Because then you wouldn't lie around in skimpy clothes anymore."

She laughed, reaching for the buttons of his short-sleeved shirt.

"Seriously," he said. "I walked in here and saw you in this thin...rag or whatever it is, with no bra on and your nipples calling my name and it made me forget all my troubles."

Eve set her book on the night table. She would get no more reading done tonight, and that was fine with her.

The call came after they'd made love. *Just* after. She was lying on top of Jack, breathless, her head heavy on his shoulder.

"Oh, no," he said.

She propped herself on one elbow to reach the phone. The clock read midnight.

"Hello?"

"I'm so sorry to wake you, Eve." It was Linda, the assistant troop leader.

"Just tell me she's alive and not bleeding," Eve said.

"She's alive and not bleeding," Linda replied. "But she's having a rough night. She had a rough afternoon, actually."

"What's going on?" She started to roll off Jack, but he held her fast.

"She was fine on the bus and fine until we went to see the horses," Linda said. "A couple of the girls went riding. Just pony rides. You know, being led around a path. And the others hung out on the paddock fence feeding carrots to the horses and that sort of thing. But Cory stayed back. You know the way she does sometimes?"

"Uh-huh."

"I mean, stayed *way* back. We'd walked there, so there was no vehicle she could stay in, and she sort of stood behind a tree so the horses couldn't see her."

"Oh, God," Eve said.

"What is it?" Jack whispered. "Is she all right?"

Eve pressed her fingertip to his mouth and nodded.

"And then she seemed okay at dinner again, but she got scared when it was time to go to bed. She was in a tent with three other girls and she wouldn't turn out her flashlight. She had to go to the bathroom, but was afraid to walk to the latrine at night, and she wet herself. Though I didn't realize that until later. Anyhow, she was afraid of raccoons coming in the tent and—"

Eve smacked Jack lightly on the shoulder.

"Ouch," he said. "What's that for?"

"She was afraid of raccoons coming in the tent," she said to him.

Jack laughed. "Oh, brother," he said. "It was just a song."

"So now she's here sitting in the mess hall with me, but she won't go back in the tent and I'm afraid I can't sit up with her all—"

"No, of course not," Eve said. "I'll come get her."

"Do you know how to get here?"

"I think so."

She listened while Linda went over the directions, then hung up the phone.

"It was just a nice little Beatles ditty," Jack said.

"Oh, I know." She rolled onto the mattress and stared at the ceiling.

"So she's coming home just because she's afraid of raccoons?"

"She also hid from horses that were safely locked in a paddock. She hid behind a tree. And she was afraid to go to the latrine, so she wet herself." Her voice broke on the last word.

"Oh, Evie." Jack pulled her to him and nuzzled her neck. "She'll survive. We all survived the trauma of our childhoods."

"We need to get her counseling, Jack," she said. "I think we've ignored this problem as long as we can." She got out of bed and walked to the dresser. Her feet hurt as she crossed the room. That had been happening a lot lately—her feet hurting when she got out of bed.

"I'll go get her," Jack said.

"No, I want to." She slipped on a bra.

"I don't want you driving those winding roads in the dark."

"I'll be fine." She felt herself tearing up. "I just want to get my little girl in my arms."

Jack propped himself up on his elbows. "You don't worry about Dru the way you do about Cory, do you know that?" he asked.

She'd been about to reach into her dresser drawer for a T-shirt but stopped short, trying to read the tone of his voice.

"What do you mean?"

"Nothing. Just a statement of fact."

She returned to the bed and sat down next to him. She couldn't argue with him about it; she knew he was right.

"I love them both equally," she said. "You know that, don't you?"

"Yes," he said.

"Dru doesn't seem to need me the way Cory did at that age."
Dru's bubbly self-confidence would serve her a lifetime.

"I know," he said.

She thought he regretted starting the conversation and was
easing his way out of it. She would let him. There was no way she
could make him understand what drove her protection of her
oldest daughter. He could never know that, long ago, she and
Cory had saved each other's lives.

Chapter Thirty-Three

CORY WAS QUIET ON THE DARK DRIVE HOME FROM CAMP, unresponsive to Eve's gentle questions about her experience. Eve felt frustrated, as she often did with her oldest daughter these days. Why could she get the most recalcitrant teenagers to open up to her, while her own daughter shut her out? She was learning new counseling skills every day, but when it came to her own family, she might as well be studying carpentry.

Cory went directly to bed when they got home, and she was still quiet the next morning, though contrite enough to help Eve and Jack clean the house after church.

"I don't want to go to school tomorrow," she said to Eve as she ran a sponge over the bathroom sink.

"Why not?" Eve looked up from the tub she was cleaning.

Cory kept her back to her. "My friends are going to tell everybody what happened. They already think I'm a wimp."

"Well." Eve thought about how to respond. "I have an idea how you could handle it."

"How?"

"You call the girls who were in your tent and tell them how embarrassed you—"

"Uh-uh, Mom!"

Maybe Eve could call their mothers, then, and ask them to talk to their daughters about compassion and kindness. Most likely, though, the damage was already done. Fourteen girls in the Scout troop plus fourteen telephones times fourteen different sets of friends would equal a bad day at school for Cory.

"Laugh at yourself tomorrow, Cory," she said.

Cory turned from the sink to stare at her. "*Laugh* at myself?" she asked, as if she must have heard incorrectly.

"Don't you admire people who can just admit their foibles and move on?" Eve asked.

"What's a foible?"

"Their flaws. Their quirks. You just say, 'I was really a chicken at camp, wasn't I?' If you say it first, it doesn't leave them with much ammunition."

Cory rinsed the sponge out under the faucet. "I can't say that, Mom," she muttered. "You must not know me very well if you think I can."

It was seven o'clock that evening before Eve had time to read the Sunday paper. Cory sat at the table in the dining area of the living room, her head bent low over a paper she was writing for school, and Jack was in the girls' room, reading Dru a story. Eve made a cup of tea and sat on the wing chair near the fireplace, her feet on the hassock and the paper in her lap.

The cover of the magazine section caught her eye. Two people were on horseback, one a stiff-spined man, the other a strawberry-blond teenager. The heading read: At Home With Former North Carolina Governor Irving Russell. Eve stared at the words for a full minute before returning her gaze to the picture. All her fantasies that Cory bore a strong resemblance to Genevieve had been accurate. In front of her was the proof—a teenaged girl who reminded her of both Cory and her mother. The long, slender limbs. The small pert nose and fair skin. The hair, though significantly blonder than Cory's, framed her face in waves. She had to be fourteen. Vivian. Vivvie, Genevieve had called her. She opened the magazine and scanned the article.

Russell was now the CEO of a foundation in Northern Virginia and had recently bought property outside Charlottesville. She read that sentence twice; it seemed unreal. A cruel joke. *Please don't let our paths cross,* she thought. She looked at the pictures and realized with relief that the chances of that happening were slim. Russell and his daughter were rolling in money. Their house was huge and white-pillared, with a massive portico above a circular driveway. There were stables on the property, and it was clear the Russells were part of the horse circle. There was one brief mention of Genevieve: His life changed after the 1977 kidnapping of his pregnant wife, Genevieve, who has never been found. Russell has not remarried, but has instead devoted himself to raising the couple's daughter, Vivian, now fourteen.

There was another picture of Vivian with the article. She was hanging upside down by her legs from a tree limb, her long fingers just touching the grass below.

Eve sank low in the wing chair, her body crumpling in on itself. Her chest felt hollow, her muscles slack with an empty sort of sorrow. She looked at the vivacious blonde—Vivian had been a perfect name for her—and then at Cory, sitting at the table on the other side of the room. Cory's bare feet rested on the rungs of one of the ancient, mismatched chairs. She wore hand-me-downs from Shan—a faded blue T-shirt and baggy cotton shorts. One hand was at her mouth as she chewed her stubby nails. Tomorrow she would face her classmates, who would mock her for her fears. Never before had Eve felt this degree of guilt over having stolen Cory from the life she'd been meant to live. Not just a life of riches, but a life filled with the self-confidence that graced her sister's face. She could almost hear Vivian giggling as she hung from the tree branch. It was a sound Cory rarely made.

She'd created a fearful child. The beauty was Genevieve's doing. Maybe they could share the credit for her sharp, incisive brain. But the fears were her responsibility entirely, and she didn't know how to undo whatever she'd done to create them.

Chapter Thirty-Four

1988

"WHAT'S A MILKMAN?" CORY ASKED, WHEN EVE PICKED her up from school.

"Well," Eve said, looking over her shoulder as she pulled away from the curb, "in the old days, even before I was born, they used to deliver milk to people's houses. People had metal boxes on their porches and the milkman would leave bottles of milk in the boxes. Sometimes eggs, too, I think. And cottage cheese."

"Oh," Cory said.

"Why do you ask?"

"Caitlin said my father must have been the milkman, because I don't look like anybody in my family."

Eve silently cursed Caitlin's mother, a woman who spent too much time sticking her nose into other people's business.

"That was a rude thing for her to say," Eve said.

"Was I adopted, Mom?"

Eve glanced at her. Cory's face, her eyes wide and serious, was raised to hers as she waited for her answer.

"Do you remember we talked about this when you were much younger?" Eve asked. "You're my daughter, and when Daddy and I got married, he adopted you."

"So...do I look like my real father?"

"Yes," she said. "You look like your biological father." She thought of telling her he'd had red hair and her fair skin, but couldn't embellish the lie any more than was absolutely necessary.

"What does that mean? Biological?"

"The man whose sperm fertilizes an egg is called a biological father."

"Oh. You said he died, right? In an accident?"

"That's right."

"Were you married to him?"

Ugh. "No, honey, I wasn't. I was very young and I got pregnant." She'd explained the birds and the bees to Cory, but she wasn't certain how much of the explanation she'd understood.

"Did he ever meet me?"

"No, he died before he had a chance to meet you."

"Was he nice?"

"Yes, he was nice. But he was wild. He rode a motorcycle and that's how he was killed. In a motorcycle accident."

"I wish I could've met him," Cory said, deep sorrow in her voice.

Eve reached over to brush Cory's hair away from her cheek. "He would have loved you very much," she said.

Nearly eleven, Cory was not much younger than she'd been when her mother died. She suddenly felt sorry for the little girl she'd been. It was horrible to imagine Cory parentless and alone. Was she doing as good a job with Cory as her own mother had done with her? She didn't think so. With a longing that made her chest ache, she remembered her mother's wonderful letters. What strength she'd had! And poor Ronnie. What had she done with that huge box of letters?

"What was his name?" Cory asked.

"Patrick Smith." Eve had christened Cory's father with the name years earlier. Smith seemed like a smart, untraceable choice for a surname.

"Why did he ride stupid motorcycles?"

"He was young, and young men tend to do things that are risky sometimes."

Cory was quiet for a moment. "So you did sex with him before you were married?" she asked.

"Yes. That was really dumb of me and I hope you never do that. Although if I hadn't, then I wouldn't have you and I just can't imagine that." She smiled at her and Cory smiled back.

"Daddy is Dru's real father, isn't he?" she asked.

"He's *your* real daddy, too, honey. Once someone adopts a person, that makes him or her a real father or mother."

"But he's not my *real* real father."

She decided not to play dense. "That's right. But I hope you know he loves you every bit as much as he would if he was your *real* real father."

Cory fell silent again, and Eve waited for another question.

Instead, though, Cory let out a sigh. "I'm really glad Dru gets to have Daddy for a real father," she said. "Otherwise she might feel very sad."

"Do you feel very sad, honey?"

"No," she said, "but Dru's just little and it would be harder for her than for me."

Eve had to pull the car over to the curb, because she needed to hug her daughter.

"What are you *doing?*" Cory recoiled a bit from the sudden embrace. "What's that for?"

"You're a kind girl," Eve said. "You're a wonderful big sister, and Dru's lucky to have you." She pulled back to look at her with a smile. "And so am I."

Chapter Thirty-Five

1991

IN LATE AUGUST, EVE AND JACK FINALLY WERE ABLE TO buy their first house, a quaint arts-and-crafts-style bungalow not far from the grounds. Although the house was on a busy street, it sat in a veritable cocoon of greenery and had a small, private backyard. Jack laid a curved line of pavers from the back door to a bench beneath the boughs of a magnolia, and the yard became a little haven from the hubbub of the university.

They walked to work every day, since Eve was now a counselor with the Counseling and Psychological Services on the grounds and Jack continued to teach in the Drama Department. It made Eve nervous, though, not having a car at work in case there was an emergency with one of the girls. Still, it was nice to have that time with Jack and the exercise was good for her, though her feet occasionally protested the walk, much as they did when she got out of bed in the middle of the night.

Their first night in the house brought a terrific thunderstorm that kept Eve awake with its unpredictable thunderclaps and flashes of light illuminating the unfamiliar bedroom. She wasn't surprised when Dru came into their room at one in the morning.

"Can I sleep with you and Daddy?" she asked.

Dru was six and fearless, but for the first time, she had her own room. That, along with the storm, was too much for her.

"Sure," Eve said. "Hop in."

Dru scrambled into the bed and lay down between her and Jack, who had not stirred once since coming to bed. In a few minutes, Dru, too was sound asleep.

At three, Eve got up to use the bathroom. Her feet felt as if she were walking on gravel as she crossed the room. The pain had definitely worsened in the past few months and she knew she'd have to break down soon and see a doctor.

She opened the bedroom door and nearly tripped over Cory, who lay on the hardwood floor, her pillow under her head.

"Cory?" Eve whispered. "What are you doing here?"

Cory jerked to a sitting position as if caught doing something wrong. She looked around the hallway as though trying to place her surroundings. "I don't know exactly," she said.

Eve lowered herself to the floor across the hall from her. The hardwood felt cool beneath her aching feet. Summer was coming to an end.

"Some storm," she said.

Cory nodded. She was wearing underpants and a sleeveless pajama top shaped by small, new breasts. She'd gotten a bra in May and her period in June, but Eve had not yet grown accustomed to the changes in her daughter's body. Cory was still a little girl in her eyes.

A flash of lightning cut through the bathroom window into the hall, and Cory winced. She hugged her knees. "Mom?" she asked.

"What, honey?"

"I don't want to go to Darby."

Darby was the private school Eve and Jack had gotten her into for the fall. They'd used the money in Cory's secret bank account to pay her tuition.

"Why not, hon?" The move to Darby was a good one, she felt certain. It would get her away from the kids who had known and taunted her for years and it would put her into a more intellectually challenging environment. She was far ahead of her public school classmates academically, but no one wanted her to skip a grade because she lagged so far behind her peers socially.

"I don't know," she said again, words Eve was hearing regularly from her lips these days.

"It's going to be good for you," Eve said. "You liked it when we visited."

"Yeah, but now it's almost time to go and I'm changing my mind."

"What are you afraid of?"

"I'm not afraid," Cory said. She balked at that question these days, coming up with excuses other than fear when she didn't want to do things.

"Then why don't you want to go?"

"I won't know anyone," she said.

"Think of that as a *good* thing," Eve suggested. "You can be a clean slate there. You can be the person you've always wanted to be. It can be fun to reinvent yourself sometimes."

Cory pondered that. "Maybe," she said.

"Come on." Eve winced at the pain in her feet as she stood to open the bedroom door. "Dru's in the bed, so you'll have to make yourself comfortable on the rug."

* * *

As it turned out, Cory liked Darby from the first day. The kids were nice and very smart, she reported, and the teachers joked with them instead of being "all serious and everything." Eve thought the Darby students were actually a bit nerdy, but then, so was Cory. Her beauty was a front for a hungry, scholarly mind. The classes were rigorous, and that was a challenge Cory could rise to.

"I have four hours of homework!" she announced when Eve picked her up that first afternoon. She sounded sincerely thrilled by the prospect. And Eve was equally thrilled that she'd received no calls during the day from a teacher or a school nurse, asking her to pick up her anxious, frightened daughter.

Chapter Thirty-Six

"GIRLS," JACK SAID AT DINNER SEVERAL DAYS AFTER THE new school year started. "I have a proposition for you."

"Am I one of the girls, too?" Eve asked as she spooned tuna casserole onto Dru's plate.

"No, dear, you're a *woman*." He gave her a lecherous look.

"Ah," she said. "Just checking."

"What's a proposition?" Dru asked.

"Well, I'll tell you," Jack poured iced tea from the pitcher into his glass. "The Children's Theater is auditioning for a play and there are roles for some six-year-old girls and some thirteen-year-old girls in it."

Dru gave a quick intake of breath, her mouth open in a smile. "I could be in a play?" she asked.

"You'd have to audition first," Jack said. "That means we would go to the theater and read a little bit of a part on the stage. Other children will do the same thing, and then the director will pick the children he thinks will work best in the roles."

"I could be on a stage!" Dru bounced up and down.

"It's hard work, being in a play, though," Jack said. "You have to memorize a lot of lines."

"I memorize really well," Cory said.

"You *do*," Jack agreed. "So I think it's worth a shot. It'll be a good experience, whether you get to be in the play or not. So what do you say?"

"I say, *yes!*" Dru pounded her fork on the table, sending a dollop of casserole flying through the air to land somewhere on the floor near the pantry. "Whoops." She giggled, covering her mouth with her hand.

"How about you, Cory-Dory?" Jack asked.

Cory paused. "Okay," she said finally. "What are the lines I have to memorize?"

Two weeks later, Eve and Jack sat in the back of the community theater auditorium to watch the auditions. Jack had worked with both girls on their lines, and they knew them inside out, upside down and backwards. Eve watched Cory take Dru's hand and walk toward the front of the theater where dozens of children were seated. She felt anxious, not about Dru, who was sure to sail through this experience with her ego intact, but about Cory, who probably would not.

And she felt anxious about herself.

She'd expected to get breast cancer some day. With a mother who died of breast cancer at the age of twenty-nine, it seemed almost a given. Yet that had not happened, at least not yet. Instead, her feet seemed to be her biggest problem. She'd finally seen a doctor the week before.

"All your blood work and X-rays are absolutely normal," he reassured her. "There doesn't appear to be anything wrong with your feet."

"Well, that's good," she'd said. "But why do they hurt when I get out of bed?"

"Could you have injured them?" he asked. "Are you exercising in a way that might be causing problems?"

She thought about her activities during the day. "I walk to the university in the morning," she said. "And I walk around the grounds quite a bit. My feet don't bother me much then, though."

He closed her chart. "Well, I think all that walking's just catching up with you while you sleep," he said. "I don't think it's anything to worry about."

It was all in her head. That's what he was really saying, wasn't it? She suddenly felt sorry for Cory, whose anxiety-provoked stomachaches were similarly disregarded by doctors—and, often, by Eve herself.

"Here we go," Jack said, and she pulled her attention back to the theater, where Dru was bounding up the stairs to the stage. The last to audition in her age group, she was a standout. She delivered her lines with punch and passion and with facial expressions and body language that had the adults in the theater laughing. She was so clearly Jack's daughter. People applauded when she bowed and walked off the stage.

Five thirteen-year-old girls were scheduled to audition before Cory, and Eve knew how agonizing the wait had to be for her daughter. Cory's anxiety was palpable when she finally climbed the steps, and Eve was certain everyone in the audience was aware of it as the tall redhead walked to the center of the stage. Cory locked her hands behind her back, then moved them quickly to her sides, as though remembering her father's direction.

She began to speak, her voice so soft and tentative she was almost impossible to understand.

"Louder, honey," Jack whispered into the air.

If anything, her voice grew softer. Eve watched Sherry Wilson, the director, sit forward in her seat as she tried to hear her.

"Oh, Jack, I can't stand this," Eve whispered. She knew the courage it had taken for Cory to get up on that stage at all.

Jack took Eve's hand. "It'll be okay," he said.

As expected, Cory didn't make the cut, while Dru was given the biggest role in her age group. After the parts were assigned, Dru rushed back to Eve and Jack, while Cory walked toward them with a leaden gait.

Eve moved forward to hug her. "I was so proud of you for getting up there, Cory," she said. "That wasn't easy to do."

Cory shrugged her shoulders and looked away. She was quiet as they walked to the car and sullen on the drive home, her head turned toward the window.

"You both showed a lot of guts today, girls," Jack said from behind the steering wheel.

"I wanted Cory to be in the play with me," Dru complained from the back seat.

"It's okay," Cory said. "I don't really care."

The traffic came to a standstill, and ahead of them, blue lights flashed, the color bleeding into their car in rhythmic waves.

"Must be an accident," Jack said.

"I don't want to see!" Cory said. "Can we go a different way?"

"We're stuck on this road, Cory," Eve said. Cory hated driving by an accident, afraid of seeing blood or broken bodies. Eve wondered if it made her think about her fictional father's fictional motorcycle accident.

"Please, Dad," Cory pleaded. "Can't we cut through a parking lot or something?"

"Honey, just relax," Jack said. "Let's sing a—"

"I don't want to sing," Cory said. She lowered her head to her knees, her hands covering her eyes. "Just tell me when we're past it."

Dru craned her neck to look out the window. "It's okay, Cory," she said. "There's no blood or anything."

Cory didn't lift her head from her knees. "I don't belong in this stupid family," she said suddenly.

Her words were a knife in Eve's heart. "Why do you say that, Cory?" she asked.

"Everybody's talented except me."

"That's bull," Jack said. "You're smarter than the three of us put together."

"I don't mean that kind of talent," she said.

"I couldn't act or draw or dance to save my life," Eve said.

"My father's family is probably more like me," Cory said.

Eve glanced at Jack.

"Maybe they are," he conceded. "Maybe that's where your brilliance comes from."

Cory's head rose from her knees. "Stop talking about how smart I am," she said. "That's not what I'm talking about."

"You're one-fourth of this family, Cory," Eve said. "And we love that you're part of it, whether you like it or not."

The next day, Eve did something she would not admit even to Jack. She called Sherry Wilson and pleaded with her to give Cory a small, walk-on role.

"She needs the recognition," Eve said. "She needs to feel better about herself. Please."

Sherry paused. "I understand," she said. "I've got two kids myself, and one of them is a soccer star and the other couldn't find the ball if it were glued to her foot."

Eve laughed.

"I could use her in a group scene," Sherry offered.

"Thank you!" Eve said. "Will you call her, please? And don't let her know I called you?"

"Sure," Sherry said.

Cory heard from Sherry that evening. She came flying into the living room after the phone call.

"Guess what!" she said.

Eve looked up from the book she was reading, and Jack stopped tinkering with his laptop computer to give Cory his attention. "What?" he asked.

"That was the director of the play," Cory said. "She wants me to be in a scene!"

"You're kidding," Jack said before he caught himself. "That's great!"

"Wow," Eve said. "What do you have to do?"

"Just walk on and cheer with a bunch of other kids."

"Fantabulous!" Jack said. "I think you should go wake Dru up and tell her."

"Jack!" Eve complained. "It's a school night." But Cory's face was alight with joy. "Oh, go ahead," she said.

Cory ran upstairs to wake her sister, and Jack looked at Eve.

"Did you have something to do with this?" he asked.

She nodded. "I couldn't help myself," she said.

Jack laughed. "You're one zealous mama," he said. "Though I have to admit, I thought of doing it myself."

The play was a hit, the audience of relatives and family friends proud and enthusiastic. Marian sat with Eve and Jack, and dear Lorraine even made sure Channel 29 had a cameraman there to give the play a little airtime on the late-night news. Dru was superb in her role as the precocious six-year-old, for which she was a natural, and Cory stood out in the crowd of teenagers for her beauty if not her talent. They were both euphoric afterward, and it wasn't until two days later that Cory found the note Eve had scribbled to herself pinned to the bulletin board by the phone. *Call Sherry Wilson*, she'd written, along with the director's phone number.

Cory confronted Eve in the living room when she got home from work. "Did you call Mrs. Wilson and tell her to give me that part?" she asked.

"No, honey." Eve tried to look surprised.

"Then why was her number on the bulletin board?" Cory held up the scrap of paper in her hand.

Eve set her briefcase down on the chair near the door. "I just wanted to have it, since Dru was going to be in the play," she said.

"But you wrote that you should *call* her," Cory said. "Not just her number. You called her about me."

"Cory, I did not."

"You forced her to give me a part. That's so lame. It's so…do you know how embarrassing that is?"

"I know you really wanted to be in the play and that there were parts you could—"

"You *did* do it!" Cory said. She flopped down on the sofa, head in her hands. "I am such a loser," she said.

"Stop it, Cory. You are not and you know it."

"My father was a loser and I got the loser genes."

"He wasn't a loser," Eve said. "He was very smart. He just made some bad choices when he was young."

Cory looked at the piece of paper in her hand. "Do I have grandparents I don't know?" she asked. "Aunts and uncles and cousins?"

Eve sighed as she sat down next to her. "I don't know, honey," she said.

"Well, I *want* to know," Cory said. She looked squarely at Eve, tears in her eyes. "Sometimes I feel like I don't know who I am, Mom," she said.

"Oh, Cory." Eve pulled her into her arms, her own voice thick with emotion. "I'm sorry, sweetie."

"Would you find my relatives for me, Mom?" Cory asked, her head resting on Eve's shoulder. "Please?"

"I think you should do it," Jack said, when she told him about the conversation with Cory. "She has a right to know her relatives."

There are no relatives, she thought. How did you find someone who didn't exist?

"I never met any of them," she said. "How am I going to find Patrick Smith's family in Portland when I don't know anything more than their very common surname?"

"I don't know, Evie," Jack said, "but I think you should try."

The next day, she went to the university library, which had stacks and stacks of phone books for major cities throughout the country. She found the phone book for Portland, Oregon, and copied the two pages of Smiths. That evening, in front of Cory, she began making phone calls as she tried to find the nonexistent relatives of a nonexistent man. She hated the charade, hated that she was setting her daughter up for disappointment after disappointment. There were moments during that week of phone calls that she even hated herself.

"I think I've reached a dead end, honey," she told Cory as she sat on the edge of her bed that Friday night. She was sick of phone numbers, of pushing buttons, of asking questions of kind people named Smith who tried to help her do the impossible. "It could be that he didn't even have a family," she suggested. "Maybe he was an only child and his parents are dead."

In the light from the tiny night-light, Cory's face was hard to read. "Did you call every single one?" she asked.

"Yes," Eve said truthfully. Their phone bill for this month would be horrendous.

Cory's chin trembled. "I had a dream last night that I met a girl who was related to him," she said. "I think she was, like, my cousin or something. She looked just like me and she was so nice. I was so happy to meet her. When I woke up, I…" She started to cry, and Eve took her hand, holding it between hers. "I realized she wasn't real," Cory said. "I just wanted her to be real, Mom."

"It's hard to wake up from a good dream sometimes," Eve said.

"I mean, I love you and Dad and Dru and everything…" Cory let out a sob that shook her whole body. "I just wanted to feel…*whole*."

"I know, honey. And I'm sorry." This week of phone calls had been a mistake, Eve thought. She never should have given Cory hope. She should have said she knew there were no relatives and been done with it.

Cory drew in a long breath, pulling herself together. "Maybe when I'm older, I can go to Portland and look for people who knew him or something," she said.

Eve nodded, brushing a tear from her daughter's cheek with her fingertip. "Maybe," she said, but she hoped Cory would find better things to do by then. Otherwise, she'd be looking for a long, long time.

Chapter Thirty-Seven

1993

AGAIN SHE SAT IN HER DOCTOR'S OFFICE, WAITING TO HEAR that the pain in her feet—and now occasionally in her hands—was her imagination. This time, though, her doctor looked more concerned as he examined her feet. They were swollen now, particularly her right foot, and her ankles were hot and puffy.

"Well," he said, resting his palm on the top of her foot as if checking its temperature. "Your blood work's back and we finally have an answer. Your rheumatoid factor is elevated."

"What does that mean?" she asked.

"You have rheumatoid arthritis," he said. He studied her face.

She was thinking, *I deserve this. It's punishment*. She'd always felt as though, somehow, someday, she would have to pay for what she'd done.

"Do you know what that is?" he asked.

"Well...I know what arthritis is. Joint inflammation." The pain in her feet had gotten much worse over the past two years. Sometimes, after sitting at her desk for a while, she could barely put any weight on them at all, and her fingers and wrists ached when she typed. Plus, she was exhausted. She scheduled her counseling clients so that she could come home midday and just sleep.

"Rheumatoid arthritis is an autoimmune disease," he said. "It can affect your whole body, not just your joints. That's why you're so tired. I'm going to refer you to a rheumatologist."

"Is there a cure?"

He shook his head. "But there's treatment, and the sooner you get started on it, the better."

The first two medications failed her. As the months passed, she began to walk with a limp and her wrists swelled and looked lumpy and misshapened. The worst, though, was her feet, especially her right foot. In bed at night, she cried with the pain. Even when she held her foot perfectly still, it felt as if it was trapped in a vise.

"How can I help?" Jack lay next to her, wiping tears from her cheeks with a tissue.

"You can't," she said.

"What does it feel like?" Even a headache was a rarity for Jack.

"It's like…you know if you step into the ocean in May and it's freezing cold?"

"And your feet go numb."

"Yes, but before they go numb, there's this intense pain?"

"Uh-huh. That's what it feels like?"

"Yes."

"Oh, Evie, let me rub your foot for you," he said. "Let me massage it."

"No." Eve cringed at the thought. "Please don't even touch it."

She knew how helpless Jack felt, but there was nothing he—or anyone—could do.

Her daughters had different reactions to her illness. Dru seemed oblivious to Eve's pain, but Cory was worried.

"Can you die from this disease?" she asked as she sat on the edge of Eve and Jack's bed. Darby had closed early that day, and Cory was surprised to find Eve not only home on her long lunch break, but in bed as well.

"No," Eve said. It was possible, but unlikely, and Cory looked so distressed that Eve saw no need to go into RA's grimmer statistics. She smiled at her daughter and took her hand, holding it next to her on the mattress. "You don't need to worry about that."

Cory looked toward the window, where Eve had pulled the shades for her afternoon nap. She was sixteen now, prettier than ever, and still a loner. Boys asked her out, but she wouldn't even go out in a group with the kids from Darby, much less on a date. Some of them drove, and she was afraid of being in a car with them, terrified of accidents. Although Eve wanted her to have a normal social life, she shared the same fears for her, and didn't push Cory to participate.

"You've changed so much." Cory returned her attention to her mother's face.

"What do you mean?" Eve asked.

"You're really, like, unhappy all the time. You're always frowning."

"I am?" Eve asked, taken aback. "I must be a lot of fun to be around."

"No, I didn't mean it that way, Mom. I just meant…I don't want you to be sick."

"I know, honey. And I thank you. I'm working on getting better."

When Cory left the room, Eve thought about her mother, who

died before her thirtieth birthday. And Genevieve, who died at thirty-two. Here she was, still alive at thirty-three. Every year was a gift, she thought. A gift she didn't appreciate enough. Medical science didn't have answers for her physical pain and the destruction of her joints. She had no control over that, but she *did* have control over how she dealt with it. She vowed to think of her mother and Genevieve every day, to remember what they'd lost and what she still had.

Chapter Thirty-Eight

1995

No one was surprised when Cory balked at the idea of going away to college.

"I want to go to UVA and live at home," she said.

Cory, Jack and Eve were sitting in the counselor's office at Darby discussing Cory's options for college. She had two, and only because her counselor, a clean-cut young man barely out of college himself, had coerced her into applying to a second school back in January so that she'd have options. Eve had been horrified to learn Cory's second choice was the University of North Carolina at Chapel Hill, the memories of her life in that university town coming back to her in a rush. Cory had been accepted by both schools, and now it was time to make a decision.

"My mother's ill and really needs me at home," Cory said to the counselor. Now a stunning seventeen-year-old with long, vibrant red hair, Cory had the young man mesmerized.

"Don't use me as a reason for choosing a college," Eve said. She didn't *need* Cory to stay home. As a matter of fact, it was more tiring for her to have another person around the house to clean up after. But she did *want* Cory to stay home at least another year. She wasn't ready to be out on her own. Plus, the thought of her living in Chapel Hill, a place charged with memories of foolish decisions and one dangerous, seductive man, was impossible to imagine. She was on the losing end of the debate, though. Both Jack and the counselor felt it was time for Cory to move away.

"She's had seventeen years of being afraid to be separated from you," Jack had said in the car on their way to the school. "It's time, Eve. You know that, don't you?"

She did, which was why she was staying out of the debate as much as possible as Jack and the counselor tried to persuade Cory that going away was a good idea.

"All right, I'll go," Cory said, finally giving in. She looked from Eve to Jack and back again. "I never knew how much you wanted to get rid of me."

She sounded as if she were joking. At least Eve hoped she was.

She met Jack at the University Diner for lunch the following afternoon. She arrived first, parking her motorized scooter outside and limping to a booth. She'd started using the scooter a year earlier to get around town, and she had a love/hate relationship with it. It gave her back her freedom, while taking away her hope that she would one day walk pain-free again. She'd gotten used to the stares and the questions and knew she was the envy of some of her colleagues, who struggled to walk around the grounds every day because of their own sore feet or bad hips.

Today in the diner, though, she felt old. The waitresses were so young and energetic. She was only thirty-five and she felt—and worried that she looked—more like seventy-five.

She saw Jack walk in, tanned and slender, and for the first time wondered if he still found her attractive. He seemed so much younger and more alive than she felt.

"Hi, Evie." He gave her a kiss before sitting down across from her. "How's the day going?"

"Good." She tried to smile brightly. "Yours?"

"Crazy, as usual," he said, putting his napkin on his lap. "Did you hear they picked a new president for next year?"

"Is it anyone we've heard of?" she asked. A number of candidates' names had been floating around the grounds during the past couple of months.

"None of the usual suspects," Jack said. "It's a guy named Irving Russell. He used to be the governor of North Carolina."

Eve couldn't speak. Their young waitress, who called them both "honey," appeared, and she managed to order a salad.

"Is it for certain?" she asked once the waitress had left their table.

"Sounds like it, and I don't know enough about him to say whether it's a good choice or not. Do you know who he is?"

She shook her head. "Not really."

"He was in the news a lot in the seventies when he was a governor, but you were probably in Portland or Charleston then. His wife was kidnapped. It was a huge story. These two guys took her to try to get Russell to let their sister out of prison."

How would someone respond who knew nothing of that situation?

"And did he let her out?" she asked.

Jack shook his head. "No, she was executed. They never found Russell's wife."

"I vaguely remember that," she said. "How awful." For the first time, she was relieved that Cory had agreed to go to Carolina. She shouldn't be at the University when Russell was president.

And neither should she.

Chapter Thirty-Nine

"I WAS THINKING WE SHOULD MOVE," EVE SAID TO JACK after Dru and Cory were in bed that night. She was sitting on the sofa, Jack's head in her lap as they listened to the soundtrack from *Les Miserables,* and his eyes flew open at her suggestion.

"What did you say?" he asked. "Did you just say we should *move?*"

She'd felt shivery with anxiety since getting the news about Irving Russell that afternoon and the only thing she could think of doing was to escape. In her early years on the run, she'd expected to have to keep moving. That hadn't happened, and she'd grown complacent. Maybe now, her life of peace and comfort was coming to an end. How did you run, though, when you had the welfare of two children and the professional needs of a spouse to consider?

"Don't you think a change would be nice?" she asked. There was a deep line between Jack's thick eyebrows, and she ran a finger over it, wishing she could erase it. "We've been here so long."

"But you love it here, Evie," he said. "We both do."

"I was thinking of someplace with better medical care," she said. "That's selfish of me, though, I know." She was playing the guilt card and cringed at her own audacity.

"I thought you were happy with the medical care here," he said. "You've got the med school at your back door."

"I know."

"If you feel you could get better treatment someplace else, we can travel to get it for you. Leave the girls with Lorraine and Bobbie and go."

Eve looked across the room toward the living-room windows. They never bothered to pull the blinds. Suddenly she felt exposed, as though Irving Russell himself might be standing out there in the darkness, peering in at her.

"I have *tenure* here, Eve," he said, as if she'd forgotten. "And you love your job. Or at least, I thought you did."

"I still do."

"Oh," he said, as if he finally understood her motivation. He reached his hand up to touch her lips with a fingertip. "You want to move to Chapel Hill so you can be near Cory."

She smiled sheepishly. He was so wrong. Chapel Hill was the last place she wanted to live, but she would let him think that. There was no other way out of a conversation she never should have started.

"You got me," she said. "It's just going to be hard to see her go."

"She'll be back." Jack rolled onto his side, wrapping his arms around her and pressing his head against her stomach. He sounded relieved that the conflict had been so easily resolved. "They always come back."

Eve, Jack and ten-year-old Dru drove Cory to Chapel Hill in late August. For Eve, it was like being in a dream in which everything was the same, only different. The face of Franklin Street had changed; many of the shops and restaurants had been replaced.

The coffee shop where she'd worked with Ronnie was now a clothing store. The students were the same age they'd been when she left them, and she remembered the rush she'd felt at the possibility of being one of them, of belonging on the campus. She found herself looking for Ronnie in the faces of the few thirty-something-year-old women she saw on the street. She was anxious, afraid of running into someone who might remember her. Even in Cory's dormitory, she avoided other parents in the lounge and hallway.

They helped Cory unpack and met her roommate, a girl named Maggie—short for Magnolia—who had jet-black hair and a pierced tongue. Eve wasn't sure whether to hope that Cory and Maggie got along or hope they didn't.

"You're the sorority type, aren't you?" Maggie asked Cory with barely masked disappointment.

"Actually, no," Cory said as she pulled clothes out of her duffel bag. "I'm more the shy, retiring type."

Maggie laughed, and Cory laughed with her, as though she was joking.

The hardest part of the journey was leaving Cory behind when they'd left for the return trip home. It reminded her of Cory's first day in kindergarten. She was that same little girl in the navy blue-and-white sneakers, screaming for her mommy when the door of the classroom closed between them.

Jack insisted they make up songs in the car on the way back to Charlottesville, an attempt, Eve knew, to keep her from crying. She went along with it for Dru's sake.

By the time she got home, there was already an e-mail waiting for her from Cory.

Please call to tell me you got home safely, she'd written. Eve stared at the words. How many new freshmen wrote that sort of message home?

We're home, honey, she wrote back. *Dad made us sing Dad-type songs all the way. I hope you're having fun. Let me know how you and Maggie get along. Love, Mom.*

There was another e-mail, this one from the screen name Barko, with the subject line simply Eve. She opened it.

Dear Eve,
Friend of N and F's needs place to start over. If you can help, reply. If not, peace.

She stared at the message a long time, first in confusion, then in fear, before finally hitting the delete key and wiping it from her screen.

Chapter Forty

EVERY SCHOOL YEAR AT THE UNIVERSITY BEGAN WITH A faculty get-together held in one of the buildings on the grounds, and the very first person Eve met when she arrived was Irving Russell himself.

She literally fell into him in the foyer when she tripped over a book bag someone had left on the floor. He caught her fall, and she looked into his face with a start of recognition.

"Excuse me," she said, flustered. "I'm sorry."

He smiled, and behind the smile she imagined a life filled with loss and fear and sleepless nights.

"And I'm Irving Russell." He held out his hand. She usually offered her less painful left hand for a handshake, but she was so caught off guard by the abrupt meeting that she gave him her right and was instantly sorry. He was a squeezer, his hand clamping down on hers so hard and for so long that it brought tears to her eyes.

"I'm Eve Elliott, President Russell," she said, once she'd rescued her hand from his. "I'm a therapist with Counseling and Psychological Services. Welcome to the university."

"I'm delighted to be—"

Someone pushed in front of her to meet the new president, and she was only too happy for the interruption. She went into the ladies' room and stood in the stall, holding her throbbing hand close to her chest and crying, though from pain or guilt, she couldn't have said.

She heard from Cory several times a day, usually through e-mail and occasionally by phone. The e-mails were easier to bear, because she couldn't hear her crying. Cory begged to come home. She hated Carolina. Everyone was into sports, she said. The kids were wild. They all drank. She hated Maggie and was afraid of Maggie's friends.

"Stick it out," Eve told her. "It's normal to be homesick for a while." But it broke her heart to picture Cory so far away, feeling isolated and scared.

When Cory's situation hadn't improved by November, Eve and Jack agreed it was time to bring her home.

"You've got to see a therapist when you come home, though," Jack told her on the phone, as if it were a condition of her homecoming, and Cory readily agreed. Eve started thinking about family counselors she knew in the area, but caught herself. Cory's issues were all about breaking away. Much as she wanted to be a part of Cory's therapy, this time she would have to let her go alone.

Chapter Forty-One

1998

EVE WOKE UP EARLY THE SECOND SATURDAY IN SEPTEMBER and knew immediately that something was different. She lay in bed and raised her hands in the air above her, making fists, then spreading her fingers wide. *Nothing hurt.* Her wrists and fingers were still disfigured, but not nearly as swollen as usual. Beneath the covers, she moved her feet. A little pain, but barely noticeable.

"Jack?" she said.

He grunted.

She shook his shoulder. "Jack?"

He rolled onto his back. "What's up?" he mumbled.

"I'm not hurting," she said.

He sat up. "What did you say?"

"The drug's working."

Two weeks earlier, she'd started a new drug for RA that had the medical world abuzz. It required Eve to give herself injections, but that was a small price to pay for this result. "I thought I've been getting better a little each day," she said, "but I was afraid to say anything until now."

"Oh, Eve." Jack was truly awake now. "That's the best news!"

For a moment, she thought he would leap to the mattress and do his happy dance, but he was forty-five years old now and, although he was still trim and fit, his leaping days were behind him.

He put his arm around her and she snuggled close.

"I have to tell you," he said, "I was worried that Cory leaving again would make you worse."

They'd taken Cory back to Carolina the day before. After two years living at home while attending UVA and nearly three years in therapy, she was ready to try UNC again and Eve was as ready to let her as she was going to get. She'd gone to see Cory's therapist in April, at Cory's invitation.

"There's a lot of love in your family, Eve," the therapist had said. "But you and Cory have a classic co-dependent relationship and I'm sure you know that. Now, Cory's ready to swim away, and you need to stop trying to reel her in."

Eve taped a note to her bathroom mirror. *Stop reeling,* it read.

"I'm okay," she said now to Jack. "She—and I—have both grown up a lot the past few years."

She got out of bed, wincing as her feet touched the floor. The new drug was no miracle cure. The doctor had warned her that it wouldn't erase the damage already done in her feet and hands, and she had plenty of it. Still, after battling this disease for more than five years, she would settle for any improvement she could get.

Cory was not only swimming away, she was gradually disappearing beyond the horizon. Her e-mails, which came daily at first, quickly fell off to a couple of times a week, and sometimes she was not in her dorm room when Eve called in the evenings. Eve pictured her out with girlfriends. Maybe with men, her beauty always a lure.

In October, Cory asked Eve not to call so often.

"I need to break away from you, Mom," she said. "You know that. Help me out, please?"

Eve felt guilty. Cory sounded like an adult. She could take care of herself now, and that was a good thing.

"Should I let *you* call *me* when you want to talk, then?" She didn't want that! She might have to go weeks without knowing what was happening in Cory's life.

"No, that's okay. Just, not every few days. How about once a week."

"Sure," Eve said. "All right."

"And slow down on the articles."

Eve grimaced. She was always seeing things in the paper about good nutrition and getting enough sleep and the harm loud music could do to one's hearing. Nearly everything she read made her think of Cory, and it took only a minute to tear out an article and pop it in the mail to her. "All right," she said.

Jack communicated with Cory by forwarding jokes sure to make her groan and roll her eyes. Dru e-mailed her regularly, and Cory was faithful about keeping in touch with her. Thirteen-year-old Dru missed her big sister. They were as different as night and day, both in looks and in personality. Outgoing Dru now wore both glasses and braces. She had Eve's wild, dark hair and Jack's thick eyebrows, while introspective Cory had never even suffered a blemish. But there was a sisterly bond between them Eve hoped would always be there.

In early November, Cory e-mailed Eve to say she'd met

"someone very special." Eve stared at those words for a moment. She'd never heard Cory say anything of the sort before. As far as she knew, Cory had never even had a date. She wrote that Ken Carmichael was a TV reporter for a Raleigh news program and that she was falling in love with him.

Eve picked up the phone. She *had* to hear more. How could Cory give her so little information?

"I want to hear all about Ken," she said when she got Cory on the line.

"He's a wonderful guy," Cory said nonchalantly, and Eve could picture her shrugging her shoulders as if to say, *What more do you want to know?*

"Where is he from?"

"Rocky Mount. Which brings me to another subject." Cory hesitated. "I'm going to go to his family's for Thanksgiving this year." She didn't add an "all right?" or "okay?" at the end of that sentence, the way she usually did. She was not asking for permission.

"Oh, okay." Eve swallowed her disappointment. "We'll miss you."

"I know," she said. "I'll miss you, too, but thanks for being so understanding. Dru said you would be. That you're really not tearing your hair out about me being gone this time."

"I'm trying not to." Eve laughed. Her medication was making her hair fall out enough as it was. "When will we get to meet Ken, though?"

"Maybe winter break," Cory said.

Maybe? Eve thought, but she kept her mouth shut.

"I've got to run, Mom. We'll talk later?"

"Sure. I love you."

"Love you, too."

Eve hung up the phone with a bittersweet mixture of happiness and sorrow. Cory was finally behaving like a normal young woman. She'd met someone. A TV reporter! But Eve was losing her daughter in the process. She could feel it.

Cory went to Rocky Mount for winter break as well, and her calls and e-mails grew further and further apart. She sounded cooler, more distant, each time Eve spoke to her, sharing less of herself and her feelings. Eve missed her, but when she had her on the phone, it was like talking to an imposter, someone with Cory's voice but without her warmth and caring. At times, Eve teared up as she spoke to her, struggling to find the words that would bridge the chasm growing between them. She'd enjoyed twenty-one years with Cory, she reminded herself, every one of them stolen. Maybe that was all she would get.

"He's divorced," Dru announced at dinner one night.

"Who is?" Eve asked.

"Ken. Cory's boyfriend."

Eve and Jack looked at each other. "Did she tell you that?" Jack asked.

"Uh-huh," Dru said. Her unruly hair rested on her shoulders in a puff of dark, wiry curls. "Not only that, but he's twelve years older than her," she added.

"Oh, no," Eve said. "No wonder she hasn't wanted to tell us much."

"Or have us meet him." Jack's lips were white. They always turned white when he was angry but trying to hold it in.

"Well, we're going to meet him at spring break," Dru said, "because I told her if she didn't come home then, I was going to have sex."

"What?" Eve asked.

Dru laughed, her braces glinting in the overhead light. "Just seeing if you're listening," she said. "Anyhow, she said they'd come. But they want to sleep in the same room."

"Forget that," Eve said. "He can have her room and she can have the sofa."

"You're fightin' a losin' battle there, Evie," Jack said.

She couldn't stand Ken Carmichael. Her dislike of him was instantaneous—and probably unfair. He walked into the house carrying Cory's suitcase, reaching his hand out to shake Jack's. He had a sweet, almost pretty, face, too tan for March, with thick dark blond hair neatly cut and sprayed into place. He had eyes every bit as green as Tim Gleason's and the slick charm to match.

She didn't give them a hard time about sharing Cory's old room. Jack was right: it would only lead to an argument and that was not how she wanted to spend her precious time with Cory.

Ken complimented her and Jack on the house and the yard, which made her distrust him more than his green eyes did. This time of year, the garden was a mass of naked trees and vines and shrubs that looked as though they would never come back to life. In a few months, it would look fabulous, but for now, Ken was merely kissing up to his girlfriend's parents.

"We're making dinner in the kitchen," Eve said to them. "Come on in and chat."

"You go ahead, hon," Cory said to Ken. "I have to go upstairs and I'll be down in a minute."

Ken walked with Eve and Jack into the kitchen, which was filled with the aroma of the pork tenderloin roasting in the oven. Dru was cutting peeled potatoes into chunks and she dropped the last piece into a pot of water as they came into the room.

"You must be Dru," Ken said. He looked appropriately awkward, as though he wasn't sure what to do with his hands. He rested them on the back of one of the chairs.

"That's me," Dru said. She picked up a can of Pepsi from the table and leaned against the counter, her eyes boring into his from behind her glasses. "So, what are your intentions regarding my sister?" she asked.

"Dru," Eve laughed as she started snapping the ends off the green beans in the sink. "Give him a chance to relax before the inquisition."

Ken looked unflustered. "My intentions are to treat her as she deserves to be treated," he said.

"That could mean a lot of different things," Dru said. She took a sip of her soda.

"What would you like to drink, Ken?" Jack opened the refrigerator to peer inside. "We have soda and wine and beer and..." He leaned over to peer behind the gallon container of milk. "Apple juice," he said, straightening up.

"Do you have bottled water?" Ken asked.

"No, sorry," Eve said. "But the tap water's filtered."

"That's okay, I'll do without," Ken said. "I've been drinking special water lately. I'll pick some up tomorrow."

Dru was studying him intently. "So, are you, like, one of those reporters you see on TV at a car crash?" she asked.

"That would be me." Ken flashed a smile at her.

"What's the worst thing you ever had to report about?"

"Dru," Eve said again. "Let Ken relax, okay?"

"That's all right," Ken said. "The worst was a school bus accident."

"Were people killed?" Dru asked.

"Uh-huh."

"Kids?"

He nodded. "Elementary-school kids," he said. "It tore my heart out."

Eve snapped the end off a bean. Why didn't she believe him? Was it that no man was good enough for her daughter? Had she truly become that type of mother? Or was it that he reminded her of Tim, the most dishonest person she'd ever known?

Cory walked into the room, her face lighting up when she saw Ken. He put his arm around her shoulders and she put hers around his waist. They both wore navy-blue sweaters and khaki pants. They looked like one person with two very beautiful heads.

"You have an inquisitive little sister," Ken said to Cory.

"I know," Cory said. "She's always badgering me for the dirt on you."

"Help yourself to something to drink, Cory," Eve said.

"There's no bottled water," Ken informed her.

"There never is," Cory said. "We should have brought some."

Facing away from them at the sink, Eve rolled her eyes. She thought of the pork tenderloin.

"Are you a vegetarian, Ken?" she asked.

"No, I eat meat. I just try to balance what I eat. You know, a certain percentage of protein, carbs and fat. And I try to make the fat olive or hazelnut oil, of course."

Oh, of course, Eve thought to herself. *How about some friggin' pork fat?*

"I used olive oil in the salad dressing," Jack said, as he turned the knob on the salad spinner.

"Corinne told me you have rheumatoid arthritis," Ken said to Eve.

"Yes, I do," she said.

"I know a lot of people who've been able to get rid of their arthritis by eliminating sugar and wheat from their diets."

She saw Jack's smile of sympathy as he opened the spinner. He knew how irritating she found it when people offered their simple solutions to a complex medical problem, and she particularly loathed it coming from Ken. It took her a moment to come up with a response that would not be harsh or sarcastic.

"Well," she said finally, "there are many different kinds of arthritis and I doubt anyone's cured themselves of RA through changing what they eat."

"What would it hurt to try, Mother?" Corinne asked. Since when did she call her "mother"?

"I follow my doctor's treatment plan," she said. "And I'm having good success with it."

"But the drugs you take are so toxic," Cory said.

Eve was losing her patience. "So is this disease, Cory," she said.

"Mom is doing really well on her drugs and they really don't have bad side effects," Dru said.

"Since when did you become a pharmacology expert?" Cory asked her.

"Since when did you become an asshole?" Dru responded. She whipped past Cory and out of the room before Eve or Jack had a chance to reprimand her.

"That's unacceptable, Dru," Jack called after her, but there wasn't much volume in his voice.

No one said a word for a minute. "Can we help with anything?" Cory asked.

"Just go sit in the living room," Eve said. "It'll be ready soon."

She shook her head at Jack as they left the room. Their special welcome-home evening with Cory was off to a rocky start.

Ken went out in search of bottled water after dinner, and Dru went upstairs to do her homework. Cory helped Eve and Jack clean up the kitchen in silence. Eve figured they were worn-out from trying to be polite throughout the meal. Even Ken had refrained from saying anything provocative.

Cory closed the dishwasher and pushed the start button, then turned around and leaned against the counter, arms folded across her chest. "I need to talk to you," she said to them.

"Sure." Jack put his arm around her and kissed her cheek. "We miss talking to you, Cor."

Cory gave him a weak smile, then broke away and sat down at the small kitchen table.

"Ken and I are going to move in together after I graduate next year," she announced.

Eve sat down across the table from her and pressed her hands together in her lap. She would choose her words very carefully. "Ken seems very intelligent," she said, "and I can see that he cares about you. But he's so much older than you. Have you thought about—"

"Mom, listen to me," Cory interrupted her. "You need to butt out of my life. Please. Let me make my own decisions for once."

Eve fell silent.

"I still have fears, Mom. I'm afraid of…so many things. Even driving here. We left an hour early because I insisted we take the back roads. Ken is so tolerant and patient with me and I love him for it. And—" She looked down at the table, tears welling in her eyes. Eve reached over and rested her hand on Cory's, but Cory drew hers away. She looked at Eve. "What I was going to say is that Ken's helped me understand that *you're* the reason I have so many fears," she said.

"Cory." Jack was pouring himself a cup of decaf, but he looked up to sound a warning.

"It's true, Dad." She looked at Eve again. "You never let me *do* anything when I was growing up. You smothered me. You made me feel like I couldn't be trusted to figure out how to do things on my own. Ken's...for the first time I'm doing something physical. We work out together." She held up her arm, bending it to display the small bulge of biceps beneath the sleeve of her sweater.

"How did I hold you back from working out?" Eve felt defensive.

"By making me feel as though everything was dangerous." Cory was not yelling. Not even impassioned or unkind. She was stating facts as she saw them—or as Ken saw them—by rote, much the way she'd read her lines in the audition years earlier. "You controlled so much of my life. One thing I'm *not* going to let you control is who I pick as a boyfriend. And *please* stop sending me articles, Mom. I don't read them. I'm figuring things out for myself now. Finally. I need to build my own life...and that includes Ken."

"Does it also include your family?" Eve asked. She felt wounded and raw from Cory's words.

"You'll always be a part of my life, but I need to focus on my future now," Cory said. "And there's one other thing that's been bothering me."

"Spill it." Jack sat down at the table next to Eve. "That's what this is all about, right? Dumping on Mom and Dad?"

"No, Dad, that's not what this is all about." Cory sounded annoyed. "I've just done a lot of thinking while I've been at school and so much has become clear to me."

"What's the other thing that's been bothering you?" Eve asked.

Cory looked at her squarely. "I think you kept information from me about my biological father because you wanted to keep me close to you," she said. "You wanted me to think of Dad as my father, and you didn't want to allow me to have other relatives because you'd have to share me with them. I have a right to know who they are, Mom, in case I might have inherited health problems, if for no other reason. I don't believe you've done everything you could to try to find them."

"Did Ken tell you that, too?" Eve said, biting down both anger and guilt.

"You know, Cory, that's really enough." Jack looked tired. "Mom's telling you the truth. Your father's name was Smith. How's she supposed to find your relatives with a last name like Smith? If she could help you, she would."

"And you always stick up for her, Dad," Cory said. "She's got you under her thumb, too."

Jack stared at Cory, who stood her ground, returning his steady gaze. Finally he spoke.

"I think you still have a lot of growing up to do, Cory," he said.

It was the best insult he could have handed her.

"You just don't get it," she said, standing up. "I'm going to my room."

Eve waited until she heard the door close at the top of the stairs. She looked at Jack. "Am I overreacting, or is she being brainwashed?"

"No, you're not overreacting," he said. "But it's normal, I guess. You're always telling me how rebellion is a developmental stage and if people don't go through it when they're teenagers, they have to go through it later. Maybe that's all that's happening."

Eve offered that explanation whenever Jack complained about one of his students. Somehow, she couldn't make it fit her daughter.

"I don't like him," she whispered.

"He's hard to take," Jack whispered back. "But our baby girl's obsessed with him, so I guess we have to make the best of it."

Eve nodded. She remembered her obsession with Tim. She could at least console herself that Cory had picked a newsman rather than a felon.

Chapter Forty-Two

2004

EVE CAME HOME FROM WORK AT NOON TO FIND A LETTER she'd sent to Cory back in her own mailbox. *Refused: Return to Sender* was written across the front of it in what she was sure was Ken's handwriting. Had Cory even gotten to look at the letter inviting her and Ken to the play at the Helms Theater? Dru was following in her father's footsteps as a drama major, and the two of them had lead roles in a summer production of *Wait Until Dark*. Eve had welcomed a legitimate reason to write to Cory, who hadn't been home in two years. She rarely answered her phone anymore, at least not when Eve called. Cory had caller ID, and Eve pictured her looking at the display, seeing that she was the caller, and going back to whatever she was doing without a second thought.

Cory and Ken had been living together and engaged for several years, with no wedding date in sight, at least as far as Eve knew. Cory didn't let her or Jack in on their lives. "I turn to Ken with my problems now," Cory had told her the year before, when Eve said she missed the relationship they used to have. Cory communicated with Dru, though, so at least they knew she was still alive, still teaching the fourth grade, and still afraid of far too much.

Eve turned on the TV to watch the news as she ate a turkey sandwich in the living room. The words *Breaking News* were across the bottom of the screen in red letters, and one of the familiar Channel 29 reporters faced the camera. "The remains were identified through dental records," she said. "Irving Russell could not be reached for comment. Back to you, Stan."

The news anchor returned to the screen. "Amazing," he said. "Some of us have been in the news business long enough to remember when Genevieve Russell disappeared. Thanks for that story—"

Eve grabbed the remote and switched the channel.

"And this just in from our affiliate station in Raleigh," a news anchor said. "While breaking ground for a new development along the Neuse River near New Bern, North Carolina, yesterday, a construction crew came across the remains of a woman. Dental records later showed the remains belonged to Genevieve Russell, wife of former North Carolina Governor Irving Russell, who was kidnapped twenty-eight years ago. Russell is now President of UVA. Let's go to New Bern."

"John," a young male reporter said, "this cabin you can see behind me is the only building for miles around in this isolated area on the Neuse River."

The camera showed the small deteriorating cabin, its windows boarded up. Eve's heart pounded in her ears. That cabin still haunted her dreams.

"A construction crew was leveling the forest surrounding the cabin when they discovered the remains," the reporter continued, "reopening the investigation into the 1977 kidnapping of the governor's wife. This is the foreman of the crew, Bill Smart," he said, as the camera panned to the man next to him. "Can you tell us what happened here?"

Bill Smart wore a baseball cap and a full, muddy-colored beard. "We cut down this here patch of woods." He pointed off camera. "And we were digging up the earth where the development's community center's supposed to go, and one of my fellas called out he saw something in the pile of dirt. Turns out it was the skeletal remains of Mrs. Russell."

"As you can see," the reporter said, "the area is cordoned off while the authorities sift through the soil looking for more clues in the long-ago disappearance of Genevieve Russell. That's all we have now. We'll report again as soon as we get more information."

The anchor was back on camera. "She was pregnant when she disappeared, wasn't she, Chuck?" he asked.

"Yes, John, she was. I'm sure this is both a sad time as well as a relief for the Russell family."

Eve sat stiffly in front of the TV, the bite of sandwich she'd eaten stuck in her throat. She flipped the channels again. Most stations had moved on to other news.

She hesitated only a moment before calling Lorraine at Channel 29. She wasn't sure what she would ask her old friend, but she had to know more, and if anyone knew all there was to know at this point, it would be the producer of Channel 29 news.

"Hey, girlfriend," Lorraine said when she picked up the phone. "How are you doing?"

"Fine," Eve said. "But I just heard about President Russell's wife being found. Her remains, I mean."

"Yeah, isn't that something? Juicy news day. I love it."

If Lorraine thought it strange for Eve to call her about a news item, she didn't let on.

"Has Russell said anything?" Eve asked. "And what about the baby his wife was carrying? Was she...was she still pregnant?"

"Still pregnant? Well, yeah. I guess. Why wouldn't she be?"

Eve cringed at the slip. "They just didn't mention anything about it, so I was wondering."

"Well, I don't know for sure," Lorraine said. "And Russell's not talking to anybody yet. Believe me, we're trying, but not a peep out of him so far. I just heard a rumor that they found a gun buried with her, though. We're trying to get confirmation on it."

Eve remembered the feeling of the gun handle between her gloved hands. She'd worn the gloves the whole time, hadn't she? The memories were blurred now, as if they belonged to someone else. She recalled holding that gun on Genevieve, telling her to shut up. And she remembered pulling the trigger, splintering the bathroom door.

She didn't know what else to say to Lorraine. What would someone say who had no guilt?

"It's sad," she said. "The trail to whoever took her is probably ice-cold by now, too."

"Oh, you never know," Lorraine said. "The remains were found near a cabin, so that might provide some clues. I hope they get a bead on something. It'll make for better news."

It might have been the first time that she and Lorraine were on opposing teams.

"I wanted to make sure you know about Jack and Dru's play on the—"

"*Wait Until Dark,* right?" Lorraine asked. "We'll be there."

"Great. Tell Bobbie I said hi."

"Good to talk to you," Lorraine said. "Let's do lunch soon."

"For sure," Eve said.

She returned to the grounds and struggled through the afternoon with her clients, wishing she could get to a TV instead of being stuck in her office. By the time she got home, Jack was already making grilled-cheese sandwiches for dinner.

"Did you hear?" he asked, after greeting her with a kiss.

"About President Russell's wife?" Eve asked.

"Uh-huh." Jack pulled two plates down from the cabinet above the sink.

"I'm going to turn the TV on," she said. "Is there anything new since this afternoon?"

"They can't find the baby," Jack called after her.

Oh, Lord. "Do you mind if we eat in here?" She hit the remote button and sat down on the sofa. "The news should be on in about five minutes."

"That's fine," Jack said. "It's almost ready."

She put on Channel 29 and watched commercials as she waited for the news to start.

"Good evening," the anchor said. "The story out of New Bern, North Carolina, is getting more disturbing by the minute. According to sources in the New Bern sheriff's office, although the skeletal remains of Genevieve Russell were found, the remains of the infant with whom she was eight months' pregnant were *not* found with her. That's left authorities scratching their heads. A search of the area is underway—"

"I've got grilled cheese." Jack walked into the room, singing to the tune of "I've Got Rhythm." "I've got—"

"Shh!" Eve held up a hand to hush him. She looked at him quickly. "Sorry," she said. "I just want to hear this." She'd missed whatever the anchor had said about a search.

Jack set the tray on the coffee table and sat next to her. The smell of the grilled cheese turned her stomach.

"Police have cordoned off the entire area until that's completed," the anchor said.

"Hmm, charming place," Jack said, alluding to the run-down cabin on the screen.

She remembered the front door, the way it was set back from the wall of the house. She remembered the rushing sound of the river, the spray of water on her face when she and Tim stood on the overlook. Before everything happened. Before everything changed.

The reporter in the field held her microphone toward a police officer.

"Do you think this is where Genevieve Russell's kidnappers held her hostage?" she asked.

"Well, that's just speculation at this time," the officer said, "and we're not playing any guessing games until we've finished our investigation."

"Have you found anything in the house?"

"We're not at liberty to talk about that at this time."

What? What clues could they possibly find in the house after all these years? How many people had stayed in the cabin since then? She'd left nothing of herself behind. Not even a fingerprint. She was sure of it. She thought of the mask. Had Forrest buried it with Genevieve? Would they find it as they sifted through the soil?

Would her skin cells be on it? And if they were, could that somehow lead them to Eve Elliott?

Irving Russell suddenly appeared on the screen. He stood next to his daughter, Vivian, in front of the Rotunda on the grounds.

"I saw the Channel 29 van on campus today," Jack said. "I figured they were looking for—"

She rested her hand on his arm to shut him up. "Please," she said.

"This is a difficult time for me and for my family," Russell said. He looked weary, and she remembered seeing him on TV shortly after Genevieve's disappearance. He'd been almost gaunt then. His build was stockier now. More robust. Yet the hollow look in his eyes was the same now as it had been then.

Two children, about five and eight, came into view as Vivian drew them close to her. Russell's grandchildren, most likely. Vivian looked so much like Cory. Couldn't Jack see the resemblance? She held her breath, waiting for him to mention it.

"I feel both deep sorrow and profound relief that Genevieve has at last been found," Russell said. "Words can't express, though, my...my horror at the fact that the baby she was carrying is missing. I don't understand it and I'm afraid to think of what that might mean."

Was his lower lip trembling? Eve watched while Vivian slipped her hand around her father's arm and held it tight, as if trying to prevent him from falling.

"I only hope that Genevieve didn't suffer too much," he said. "And I'll never rest until I find out what happened to that baby. To my son or daughter."

"That poor guy," Jack said, when the news team moved on to another story. "Can't even imagine what this must be like for him."

Eve struggled to find her voice. "I'm sorry I snapped at you to be quiet before," she said. "I've just been…you know…I've heard rumors all day and wanted to find out what was really happening."

"That's okay. Eat your grilled cheese. Dru'll be here soon."

She'd forgotten that Dru was coming over to run through her lines with Jack. She looked down at the sandwich. Jack was great at grilled cheese. The bread was a rich brown, not too greasy. Melted white cheddar spilled onto the plate. She could see a sliver of red, the sliced tomato he'd put inside.

"I'm not very hungry," she said, studying the sandwich, her stomach churning.

Jack looked concerned. "Are you in a lot of pain today or something?"

She shook her head. "No, it's…stomach stuff, I think. Maybe Dru would like this when she comes."

"Want me to wrap it up?"

"I'll do it." She got to her feet and carried the sandwich into the kitchen. She was wrapping it in plastic wrap when the nausea hit for real, and she just made it to the powder room off the hallway before throwing up. Her heart raced as she sank to the floor and leaned against the wall, eyes shut. She could see Russell's trembling lip. Vivian's pale and fragile face, so much like her sister's.

"Evie?" Jack knocked on the door. "Are you sick?"

"Yes," she said in a whisper.

"Evie?"

"Yes," she said, louder this time.

"Can I come in?"

"No, honey. Thank you. I feel better. I just need to…to sit here for a while."

"I'll call Dru and cancel."

"Don't do that," she said.

"I want to take care of you."

"I'm all right," she said. "I think I just ate something funky." She didn't want him to take care of her tonight. She needed to be alone with the only person who knew the cause of her distress: herself.

She rinsed out her mouth and left the bathroom.

"You can't be pregnant, can you?" Jack asked.

"Lord, I hope not." She laughed. "Wouldn't that be something?"

"Fun, maybe."

"Oh, Jack, you're crazy. I'm going to take a bath and go to bed," she said. "Give Dru a hug for me."

"Can I get you anything?"

"Thanks, no." She walked past him toward the bedroom, closing the door behind her. In the bathroom, she turned on the water in the tub and sat on the edge, fighting the nausea that rose up inside her again. She undressed, dropping her clothes to the floor, then stepped into the tub, holding tight to the grab bars as she sank into the water. She pulled her knees to her chest, hugging them, her eyes squeezed tightly shut.

"I'm scared," she whispered into the air. "I'm so scared."

She woke up later that night around ten, her entire body aching. She'd always discounted the idea that stress could exacerbate her arthritis. In the decade she'd been struggling with RA, she could find no correlation between the pain and the events going on in her life. Some of her most painful and crippling times had been during the most placid periods in her marriage, and some of her best times had been during the stressful period when they were taking care of Jack's ailing mother.

But right now, she couldn't deny the mind-body connection. Her hands and feet had the viselike pain she remembered from the days before the new drug had come on the market. Was she going to have to dust off the scooter again? she wondered. She hadn't needed it in a couple of years; it would be like going backwards, admitting defeat. *You've lived fifteen years longer than your mother did,* she told herself as she got out of bed. *Count your blessings.*

Dru was still here—she heard her voice in the living room. Swallowing an anti-inflammatory, she pulled on a robe and walked out to greet her.

Jack and Dru sat on opposite ends of the sofa, scripts open on their laps.

"Hi, honey," she said to her daughter. Dru looked great. She'd finally found the right hairstyle. Her dark hair was cropped very short, the curls and waves tight to her head. With the focus off her thick hair, her large brown eyes took center stage.

"Are you feeling any better?" Jack asked.

"I'm having a little pain tonight," she said.

Dru got up to give her a hug. "You're limping, Mom," she said. "And Dad said you got sick earlier."

"Maybe I've got a bug." Eve sat down in the chair near the fireplace. "I forgot to tell you, Jack. The letter I wrote to Cory and Ken inviting them to the play was returned unopened. Someone—I'm guessing it was Ken—wrote 'return to sender' on the envelope."

"Their loss," Jack said.

"I got an e-mail from Cory this afternoon," Dru said. "She didn't mention the invitation, so I bet she never even got to see it. She said that Ken's been assigned to the Russell thing, so she's all excited. It's really the first big assignment he's had and apparently it's a big deal that they gave it to him."

"What does that mean, he's assigned to it?" Eve asked.

"I don't know. Just, like he's the reporter who covers it for his station, I guess."

"How else is she?" Jack asked.

"Enigmatic, as usual," Dru said with a laugh. "She told me she's being considered for a big promotion. Then in the next sentence, she says she can't take the kids on a field trip because it involves going more than a couple of miles outside Raleigh."

"Tell her about the play," Eve said. "Maybe she'll come if the invitation is from you."

"I doubt it," Dru said, "but I'll tell her."

Eve made herself a cup of tea, while Jack and Dru continued rehearsing. She said good-night to them, carrying the tea to the bedroom, where she turned on the eleven-o'clock news. There was nothing new in the Russell case on 29, and she flipped through the channels. Larry King was interviewing a guy who suggested that Genevieve Russell had been kidnapped for her baby. "The baby was cut out of her," he said. "That crime is far more common than anyone knows."

King seemed skeptical. "But she was taken by the Gleason brothers to try to force then-Governor Russell to get their sister off death row, right?"

"That's what was understood at the time. But why then is the baby missing?"

"Good question," King said, then he looked into the camera. "We'll be back after this message."

Eve clicked off the television.

So, Ken was reporting on the Gleason case, she thought. His plum assignment. What was he learning? What did he know? She looked at the clock. It was too late to call Cory now, but she'd try her early in the morning. It was a Saturday; Cory wouldn't have to rush off to work. With any luck, she might even answer her phone.

Chapter Forty-Three

Cory *did* answer her phone when Eve called her the next morning.

"Oh, hi, Mom," she said. She sounded disappointed, and Eve guessed she'd picked up the receiver without looking at the caller ID display. Still, she felt the way she always did when she had a connection with Cory, no matter how fragile that connection might be. She wanted to reach through the phone line and hug her. Tell her how much she missed her. She'd learned not to even try.

"Hi, honey. How are you?" Eve sat on the sofa in the living room, not wanting to disturb Jack, who was still asleep. She'd awakened in pain, hobbling to the bathroom and then out here to make this call.

"I don't have much time," Cory said. "I'm going to the gym in a few minutes."

"I just…" Eve closed her eyes. Oh, she missed Cory! She missed the girl Cory used to be. The girl she'd loved and kept close to her. *Too* close, Cory would say. But she didn't dare tell Cory what she was thinking.

"Dru told me that Ken got a plum assignment on the Russell

news story," she said, "and I just wanted to call to say congratulations."

Cory was silent, probably thinking that this was a very weird communication from a mother she hadn't spoken to in months. A mother who had never hidden her disdain for Ken. It *was* very weird.

"Yes," Cory said finally. "He's pretty happy about it. I guess it's big news up there, too, huh?"

"Very. Though it doesn't seem as though they're getting very far with their investigation. The last I heard was that they couldn't find the…the baby."

"Right. Which is bizarre. Ken's actually down in New Bern now."

"I guess they're still searching the grounds?"

"Ken said they're tearing the place up. Did you hear about the gun and knife?"

"Lorraine thought they'd found a gun."

"And a bloody knife," Cory said. "They haven't said that in the papers yet. They told Ken to keep it quiet, but I think they'll be going public with it really soon. It's a major scoop for him."

"So…" She remembered cutting the cord. Gloves on. Had her gloves been on? How long would fingerprints last on a knife buried in the dirt for nearly three decades? "I'm surprised blood would last all these years on a knife."

"Yeah, well, it did," Cory said. "So they've got both a gun and a bloody knife and they don't know yet which killed her."

Eve was quiet for a moment. It hadn't occurred to her that they would see the knife as a murder weapon. It had been used to bring Cory into the world.

"Hmm," she said, just to acknowledge that she was still on the line.

"Now some people are wondering if they cut the baby out of her and then shot her. Or vice versa."

"I heard that on Larry King last night."

"If that's what happened, I sure hope she was dead first."

These were the most words she'd heard from her daughter in ages. Maybe the key with Cory was to talk to her about something other than their relationship. Maybe that had been her mistake all along.

"Well, I'm very glad for Ken that he's gotten this."

"Why?" Cory asked. "You don't like him."

"I never said I didn't like him, Cory."

"Oh, come on, Mother."

"It doesn't matter if I do or don't," Eve said. "I love you and you love him, so what's good for him is good for you."

"That's true," Cory agreed. "Thanks. And I'm sorry, Mom, but I've got to run."

"One more thing." Eve hurried. "I sent you a letter telling you that Dru and Dad are going to be in a play together at the Helms Theater next week. Did you get it?"

"A letter? Uh-uh."

"Well, you—and Ken—are invited as my guests if you'd like to come."

"I don't think we can, but thanks for letting me know."

"I miss you, honey." The words slipped out of Eve's mouth.

"Don't start, Mom. Please."

"I can't talk to you and pretend…" She shook her head. "Never mind. Thank you for picking up the phone."

"You're welcome," Cory said. "And tell Dad I said hi."

Chapter Forty-Four

"I THINK YOU'RE OBSESSED," JACK SAID WHEN HE WALKED into the living room an hour later. She was eating breakfast—a bowl of Cheerios, which was all she could manage—in front of the TV.

"I'm just fascinated by it, that's all," she said. She *was* obsessed. She was certain other people were following the Russell story almost as intently as she was, but they were hoping for some new intriguing tidbit. Eve, on the other hand, wanted as few new tidbits as possible. She was waiting to hear something she didn't want to hear. She was waiting for the name CeeCee Wilkes to pop up in connection with Genevieve Russell.

"They're going to have a press conference in a minute," she said.

Jack sat next to her. "How are you feeling?" he asked, brushing her hair over her shoulder.

"Okay. Better." She forced a smile as he put his arm around her.

"You kind of scared me last night," he said. "I haven't seen you in that much pain in so long."

"Scared me, too," she said. "I'm still a little stiff." That was an understatement. "But I'll be okay."

"You're better because Cory talked to you."

"Maybe."

She'd told him a little of her conversation with Cory, but not that she'd picked her daughter's brain about the Russell case. She felt an emptiness inside her chest that she could not open up to Jack. She hadn't felt this way since Russell first came to UVA, when she'd been unable to let Jack know why she suddenly wanted to leave Charlottesville. She hated the wall between them, the wall he didn't even know was there. Or maybe he did. Maybe that was part of the concern she saw in his face this morning.

"Here they are," he said, nodding toward the TV as a uniformed officer stepped up to a bank of microphones.

The officer chatted with another man quietly for a moment, their words silent on the television. Then it was the officer alone on the screen. He cleared his throat as he checked his notes.

"We've found both a gun and a chef's-type knife in the shallow grave where Genevieve Russell's remains were discovered," he said. "Fingerprints could not be recovered from either the gun or the knife, but the gun was registered to Timothy Gleason, who along with his brother, Martin, is suspected of kidnapping Mrs. Russell. The blood on the knife, we know, was Mrs. Russell's."

"No surprise there," Jack said. "Whose else would it be?"

A picture of the brothers was on the screen. Tim was on the left, Marty on the right. Even after all this time and in spite of all she knew about him, young Tim's sexy grin tugged at her belly. How could that be? How could she not be repulsed by him?

"Of course," the officer said, "these pictures were taken twenty-eight years ago. The Gleasons are now in their late forties and early

fifties, and are almost certainly living under assumed identities."
The officer looked to his left. "Yes?" he asked.

A male reporter out of camera range addressed the officer. "Is the gun the only evidence that Timothy Gleason was at this cabin?" he asked.

"Does that sound like Ken?" Jack asked her.

"Don't know," she said quickly, wanting to hear the police chief's answer.

"The people who owned the cabin at the time of the abduction were relatives of the Gleason brothers," he said.

She'd forgotten that. Tim and Marty used to stay there with their cousins.

"Were the relatives involved in the abduction?" a female voice asked.

"We don't know that right now," the officer said. "We have reason to believe there were others involved, but that's something I can't get into at this juncture."

Eve tensed, wishing she knew what he was talking about. What others was he referring to?

"What does 'juncture' actually mean?" Jack asked. "It's a great word, don't you think? Juncture." He repeated it to himself, because he knew she was not listening to him. "Junc-ture," he said again. Then he tousled her hair. "Hope they find those guys and hang them by their earlobes."

"Mmm," she agreed, but she was really hoping that Tim and Marty were underground so deep they would never be heard from again.

"Could the baby have been born while Mrs. Russell was in captivity," a voice asked, "and then thrown over the cliff into the river, and that's why you haven't found it despite tearing up every square inch of this property?"

"*Oh,*" Eve said. The thought of beautiful baby Cory being tossed alive into the river was unbearable. Her eyes filled with tears.

"Eve?" Jack was looking at her.

She tried to listen to the officer's answer, but her mind felt thick and foggy.

"Eve? Honey, what's wrong?"

She looked at him. "I was just thinking of how cruel that would be," she said. "Throwing the baby…" She shook her head, unable to even say the words.

Jack had deep frown lines between his eyebrows. "You're not yourself, Eve," he said. "Is it the RA? Are you trying to cover it up so you don't upset me? Because I don't want you to do that."

"I'm just feeling a little emotional these days," she said with a shrug, but his words echoed inside her head. *Not yourself.* She felt CeeCee slipping back inside her, full of the insecurities and craziness that led her to do things Eve never would have done.

Chapter Forty-Five

SHE WAS GETTING READY TO GO TO THE PLAY THE following Friday night, smoothing the wildness out of her hair with her curling iron, when Jack walked into the bathroom.

He picked up his toothbrush. "They found one of those guys," he said.

No. She lowered the curling iron to the counter. "One of what guys?" she asked.

"You know, those kidnappers." Jack spread toothpaste on the bristles of his brush.

"You're kidding," she said. "Where? How did you hear?"

"It was just on the news."

She walked into the bedroom and turned on the TV, changing the channel to CNN.

"Did they show pictures or anything?" she called to Jack. Maybe they had the wrong guy. *Please let them have the wrong guy.*

Jack stood in the doorway, toothbrush in hand. "I just caught the tail end of it. They said they found him in California." He looked at his watch. "Honey, we only have about twenty minutes."

"I know," she said. "I'm ready. I just..."

A picture of a man flashed on the screen. He was handcuffed and being led by a guard or a police officer, someone in uniform. Eve sat on the bed, leaning close to the screen. The prisoner was fiftyish, wiry and bald. For an instant, the camera caught his eyes, translucent as green glass. Tim.

You pig, she thought. *You lying, cheating pig.*

"Timothy Gleason, suspect in the kidnapping and murder of Genevieve Russell, has been arrested in California," a male voice said. "Gleason was living in Modesto under the name Roger Krauss and was working as a bartender." A police officer, the same man who had given the press conference the week before, appeared on the screen, again in front of a bank of microphones. "Gleason accompanied the arresting officer without resistance," he said. "We expect him to be extradited to North Carolina immediately, where he'll be charged with the kidnapping and murder of Genevieve Russell and her baby."

The camera returned to Sophia Choi at the news desk. "Police reported that Gleason was turned in by a cousin, David Gleason, whose family owned the cabin near where Russell's body was found two weeks ago," Choi said. "David Gleason said he knew that his cousins had gone underground, but hadn't realized the seriousness of the charges against them until Russell's body was discovered. He said that the other suspect, Martin Gleason, died of a heart attack in 1998."

"Okay." Jack laughed from the doorway of the bathroom. "You got your news fix. Now let's get going."

She nodded, getting to her feet. The room spun and she nearly lost her balance. Was she going to get sick again?

She walked woodenly into the bathroom and leaned against the counter as she waited for the dizziness to pass. Then she switched off the curling iron and turned away from her reflection in the mirror. Right now, her hair was the last thing on her mind.

During her break the next day, she went to the faculty lounge to watch CNN. She was glad she was the only person in the lounge, because she probably looked as crazed as she felt when the footage of Tim aired. He was being led quickly toward a car in preparation for extradition to North Carolina, but a reporter managed to dive in front of him to ask if he killed Genevieve Russell and her baby.

"I kidnapped her," he said, a bit breathless as he was rushed past the camera, "but I didn't kill her or her baby."

A man walking next to him—his lawyer, most likely—whisked the reporter away with a wave of his hand. "We have no further comment," he said, grasping Tim's elbow and pushing him forward.

Eve sat still when the footage ended. She stared into space, wondering if Tim had already told his attorney about the girl who knew he'd murdered no one. The girl who knew what really happened in the cabin on the Neuse River.

She looked at her watch. Nearly one. Time for her weekly appointment with a first-year student, Nancy Watts, whose obsessive-compulsive disorder was getting in the way of her studies. Eve walked back to her office thinking that she was the last therapist who should be working with a student who had OCD. At least now, she could have some real empathy for the demons Nancy had to deal with much of the time.

Nancy was waiting for her, and Eve ushered her into her office. She was a likable young woman who was highly motivated to conquer the hand washing and repetitive thoughts that were dogging her. She started to tell Eve about the improvement she'd made during the week, but Eve barely heard a word she said. She felt tense and jumpy and kept shifting her gaze from Nancy's face to the window, through which she could see the entrance to her building. At any moment, she expected to see a police officer walk through that entrance with a warrant for her arrest.

Okay, she thought to herself. *Stay calm.* So Tim tells his lawyer about CeeCee Wilkes. How would they be able to find out that CeeCee became Eve Bailey, who became Eve Bailey Elliott? Maybe it would be impossible. Maybe her tracks were so well covered that no one could ever learn the truth.

If, though, they somehow found Naomi and Forrest and could get them talking, she was doomed. Did they still live on that run-down piece of property outside New Bern? Were they still together? God. She remembered the box of disguises, the magically appearing documents and the general insanity in that household. *Ugh.* She'd been such a fool. If only she could turn back the years and make different choices. Take herself back to the coffee shop where she'd worked with Ronnie and ignore the overtures of the sexy guy in the corner. If only she had kept her mind focused on her goal: getting into school. If only.

Then of course, she would never have had Cory, and that thought, despite her daughter's antipathy toward her, was so painful it made her jerk in her seat.

"Eve?" Nancy asked. "Are you all right?"

"What? Oh, yes." She smiled. "Just had a sudden chill." What had Nancy been talking about? She tried to rewind the young woman's dialogue in her memory, but it was gone. She hadn't registered a word of it.

"Nancy," she said. "I'm sorry. Could you repeat what you just told me? My mind slipped away for a moment."

Thank God, Nancy was the easygoing sort. "Sure," she said, and she proceeded to tell her about the ritual she went through before bed every night and how it was driving her roommate crazy. Eve managed to pay attention, nodding and empathizing, for only another minute or two before her mind returned to her own travails. So the cops would somehow find Naomi and Forrest, who would tell them they'd sent CeeCee Wilkes to live with Marian Kazan in Charlottesville. Marian would be easy to find; just stop anyone on the street and ask if they knew her.

"Marian?" they'd say. "Of course! Everyone knows Marian. She lives in the retirement home on Sycamore Street."

At eighty-nine, Marian was still sharp as a tack, if not particularly agile. Eve visited her a couple of times a month, taking her books or magazines or movies for her VCR. Marian would do her best to protect her if the cops questioned her, but she might realize the jig was up. Even if she denied that Eve had ever lived with her, there were a hundred people who knew the truth. The connection would be made. The path to Eve's door suddenly looked easy to follow. *I'm trapped,* she thought. She would be caught, but it was Cory who would suffer most when the truth came out. She couldn't let that happen.

"I think your mind is slipping again," Nancy said.

She was looking straight at Nancy without hearing her.

"Eve?" Nancy asked again.

Eve brought her attention back to the young woman in front of her. "Yes," she said.

"I don't think you've heard a word I said today."

"I'm so sorry, Nancy." Eve let out a long breath. "You're right. I've got some things on my mind, and I probably shouldn't even have tried to work today. Listen, can you come in tomorrow?" She reached for her Day-Timer. "I promise I'll have my head back together by then."

Nancy looked concerned. "Are you sure you're okay? You're really pale."

Would Nancy know the truth in a week? In two weeks? Eve would be the talk of the university. People would speculate as to whether or not Jack had known what she'd done. If he did, then he was a criminal himself, they'd think. If not, his marriage had been a lie.

"I have class all morning," Nancy said. "Do you have anything in the afternoon?"

Eve's hands shook as she opened the Day-Timer, and it took her a moment to find the right page. "Three o'clock is free," she said.

"Okay." Nancy handed her a pen. "Write it in. Do you want me to write it in for you?"

Eve laughed, the sound false and jarring. "I'll do it," she said, writing *Nancy,* unable to remember the girl's last name. She got to her feet. "And again, I apologize," she said. "Tomorrow will be better."

Then again, she thought, *tomorrow I might be in jail.*

Chapter Forty-Six

As she walked through the entrance of the independent-living residence, Eve spotted Marian feeding the fish in the lobby's huge aquarium. Even with her back to Eve, Marian was instantly recognizable. That straight spine. The white hair that she still wore in a pageboy. It was hard to believe she was nearly ninety.

Eve came up behind her. "How's my favorite octogenarian?" she asked, slipping an arm around Marian's shoulders.

"Well, hello, Eve!" Marian said as she bussed her cheek.

"I thought I'd stop by to invite you to a play," Eve said. "Jack and Dru are both in it and it runs for a couple more weekends."

"I'd love that," Marian said. She used a key to open a cupboard near the aquarium and put the box of food inside. "Let's have a seat and catch up." She motioned toward the large area off the lobby where residents played cards or read or people-watched. There were a lot of those—the people watchers—and Eve felt exposed as she walked across the room. Several residents looked up from their card games. A couple of women, recognizing her from previous visits, waved.

Marian guided her toward the alcove near the window, and Eve wondered if she'd intentionally selected the spot for privacy. Did she know what was going on and want to talk to her about it?

"How are you doing?" Eve asked Marian, as she took a seat in the corner. "You look terrific, as always."

"Fantastic," Marian said. "And how about you?"

"I'm fine."

"Jack and the girls? Is Cory talking to you these days?"

"Not much," she said.

"She's still engaged to that fool?"

Eve laughed. "I'm trying to be more kindhearted about him."

"Well, you're welcome to think of him however you like," Marian said. "But I don't like a man who comes between a woman and her family."

"Cory loves him, though."

"I'm hoping she'll outgrow it."

A moment of silence stretched between them as Eve readied herself to dance around the issue she'd come to discuss. Did Marian remember her long-ago reaction to the news about Genevieve's kidnapping? *Are you aware of the situation with the wife of UVA's president?* she could ask. She'd planned to question her carefully. Instead, she blurted out in a whisper, "Have the police come here to see you?"

"The police?"

"Shh," Eve said. "Have they?"

"No. Why would they?"

Eve hesitated. Maybe Marian didn't remember any of it. Maybe she didn't remember that she'd taken her in under an assumed name or that she'd supplied her with a high-school transcript. She'd only known her as Eve Bailey, and she'd known her that way for a very long time.

"I just——"

"Are you in trouble, Eve?"

Eve hesitated. "I hope not," she said.

"The past catching up to you?"

"I hope not," she repeated. "I——"

"Hush," Marian said quickly. "Don't tell me anything. Don't remind me of anything. All I remember is that you came to my house to help me with my day care. In return, I gave you room and board. Then I took care of Cory while you went to school. I introduced you to Jack. You married him, and we're the best of friends. I don't remember more than that." She looked hard at Eve.

"You really don't?" Eve asked, not sure if she believed her.

"That's right. But I *would* remember if the cops had come to see me. That you can be sure of."

"And they haven't."

"No, dear. They haven't." She cocked her head, narrowed her eyes. "You're really scared, aren't you?"

Eve nodded.

"How realistic is it that they could be looking for you?"

"Very realistic. Frighteningly so."

"Then you'll be in my prayers," Marian said. "I never knew what brought you to me. I didn't know what had happened to you or what you'd done. But whatever it was, you are not that person—that little girl—anymore. If the police come, that's what I'll tell them. That you're a marvelous woman. A marvelous mother."

"I haven't been that marvelous when it comes to Cory," Eve said. "I smothered her. I made her fearful."

"A mother never loved her daughter more," Marian said. "Every mother I know screwed up somehow with her kids and only with the best of intentions. If I'd had kids, I'm sure I would have screwed up, too." She leaned forward to pat Eve's hand. "Now, tell me what night we're going to this play."

Chapter Forty-Seven

TIM'S TRIAL WAS SCHEDULED FOR LATE AUGUST, BUT HIS attorney, Len Edison, asked for and received a two-week delay.

They can't find me, Eve thought. *They need more time to track me down.*

She waited for someone to arrive with a subpoena. From her office, she watched the entrance to the building, waiting for a stranger who would change her life and the lives of her family. It was like waiting to die and take everyone she loved—and had lied to—with her.

Both *Dateline* and *20/20* featured the case, *Dateline* even using some of Ken's coverage of the story. Eve would have been impressed by his confident presentation if she could have been at all objective about the subject matter.

Tim's attorney asked for yet another delay when the first expired, but this one was not granted. They hadn't found her, but certainly they would continue their search. Her hypervigilance was taking a serious toll on her health. Her heart rate never slowed from a gallop, and her eyes were always wide-open, searching for the person who would slap the handcuffs on her wrists. By the day of the trial, she'd lost fifteen pounds and her clothes hung from her frame. She needed to use the scooter more and more, riding it around the grounds, dealing with the concern of her friends and co-workers, who'd thought she was getting better. The joints in her feet and ankles, her hands and wrists, were so swollen that her doctor increased the dosage of one of her medications and told her if that didn't make a difference, he would take her off her current regimen and try something else. He took vast quantities of blood from her for testing, worried about her weight loss, her pallor, her poor concentration. She knew that no blood test could tell him what was ailing her.

Court TV televised gavel-to-gavel coverage of the trial. She longed to stay home and watch, but that would be both impossible and irresponsible. She had to work, whether she could concentrate on her clients or not. In the evenings, though, she sat in front of the TV to watch the recap of the day's events in the courtroom. Jack was no longer surprised by her interest in the case; he thought it made her feel closer to Cory because of Ken's involvement with the coverage in North Carolina. He watched the recap with her, as if determined to share in what interested her. She'd shut him out of her interior life the past couple of months, unable to tell him what she was thinking and feeling, and she guessed this was his attempt to breach the wall she'd erected between them.

The prosecutor's name was Sal Schreiner, a surprisingly small, ineffectual-looking man—until he opened his mouth and began moving around the courtroom. He had a strong voice, a jumpy, darting way of walking and gesticulating, and a slick style of questioning that instantly grated on Eve's nerves.

He started with Irving Russell himself. On the stand, Russell was not the imposing figure he was on the grounds. For the most part, he was stoic, but his voice quavered as he described the night of the kidnapping. He'd been working in his downstairs office in the mansion as he waited for his wife to come home, he said. The first indication he'd had that something was wrong was when the day-care supervisor called to tell him that his five-year-old daughter, Vivian, had not been picked up at the usual time. Worried, he'd been about to leave the mansion to try to find Genevieve, when he received the first phone call from Timothy Gleason.

"He said he had her," Russell recalled. "He said she was safe and would be returned to me unharmed if I commuted Andrea Gleason's sentence."

The camera lingered occasionally on Vivian, where she sat in the courtroom, a tissue pressed to her eyes. It was hard for Eve to watch either of the Russells. She tried to separate herself from the case, to pretend she had nothing to do with it, but that was impossible. Tears filled her eyes as Russell's testimony came to a close. She wondered if the jury members were similarly affected, or if it was her closeness to the case that made his testimony hit her so hard.

During the recap on the following evening, Tim's cousin, David Gleason, took the stand. Long-haired and brown-eyed, he looked more like Marty than Tim, and he spoke with a slow drawl so thick he was hard to understand at times. He testified that Tim had asked if he and Marty could use the cabin "for a few days of R and R" and that he'd given them a key.

"Did it seem odd to you for them to want some 'R and R?'" Schreiner asked.

"No," David Gleason said. "Marty had some problems and Tim was kind of his caretaker, so I figured it had to do with that. Tim jes' wanted to get Marty out of town for a while, someplace peaceful." He ran a hand over his beard. "'Course, I figured out what was goin' on when the news came out about them kidnappin' the governor's wife and all, but I was confused."

Schreiner raised his eyebrows. "Confused about what?" he asked.

"'Cause the news said they were talkin' to the governor on the phone, and the cabin didn't have no phone."

"Did it occur to you to call the police when you realized what your cousins were doing?"

Gleason looked down at his hands, then shook his head. "No," he said. "I mean…I was young."

"Great excuse," Jack said sarcastically. He and Eve were watching the TV from beneath the covers of their bed. "'I was young,'" Jack mimicked him. "This guy should go down with his cousin."

"I was different than I am now," Gleason continued, "and I cared about Andie…Andrea…too. I was actually sort of rooting Tim and Marty on when I figured out what they were up to. 'Course, I had no idea the…uh…Mrs. Russell was dead."

Eve was tense as she waited to hear him say the name "CeeCee Wilkes." She didn't like watching the trial secondhand this way. She found it increasingly hard to sit in her office during the day, wondering if CeeCee's role in the kidnapping was being exposed while she counseled her student clients. Who would bring her up first? Maybe no one would mention her until Tim took the stand. It certainly seemed as though David Gleason knew nothing about her.

"When did you next go to your family cabin?" Schreiner asked him.

"The next spring, most likely. I'm not sure."

"Was there any evidence of the brothers having been there?"

Gleason shifted his weight in the chair. "The one thing I do remember was that the bathroom door was busted," he said. "The jamb was splintered near the knob."

At that point, Schreiner started his energetic dance around the courtroom as he presented two large photographs of the cabin bathroom and one of the hallway. He paraded them before the jury, then set them on easels at the front of the courtroom. With a pointer, he showed where a bullet had been found in the wall of the bathroom. He then produced the bullet itself, bagged in plastic, and laid it on the table near the easels.

"What was your next contact with the Gleason brothers?" Schreiner asked the cousin once he'd finished his display.

"Tim called…I don't know when, exactly," David Gleason said. "Maybe a week after they used the cabin. He told me that the cops were after them and they were going on the run." David Gleason looked apologetically at Tim, who sat calmly next to his attorney. "He told me he'd get in touch when he could."

"And did he?"

"Yes. 'Bout a year later I got a call from him. He said he didn't want to lose touch with me—we'd been great friends all our lives, you know—but I should never…" He looked down at his lap again, his jaw muscles working. When he lifted his head, there were tears in his eyes. "He said I should never let anyone know what his new name was."

"Why didn't you call the police when you realized Mrs. Russell was still missing?"

Gleason shrugged. "I didn't want to get Tim and Marty in trouble."

"Nice guy," Jack said.

"Marty was...schizo, you know?" Gleason said. He shrugged. "I figured he'd killed her, most likely without meaning to or somethin', and Tim was trying to protect him."

Jack stretched his arms over his head and yawned. "Have you had enough of this yet?" he asked.

"I'd like to watch a little longer," she said. "I'll go into the living room."

"Well——" Jack leaned over to kiss her "——don't stay up too late, all right?" He looked worried.

She smiled as she got out of bed. "I won't," she promised.

In the living room, she turned on the TV to see the next witness for the prosecution take the stand. Terry Newhouse, Tim's friend in Jacksonville who had owned the house from which the calls were made to the governor, was clean-cut and clean shaven. He gave his profession as "semi-professional accountant."

"Did you know what the brothers were up to?" Schreiner asked, once Newhouse had been sworn in.

Newhouse nodded. "Pretty much. Yeah."

"Where did they tell you they'd left the governor's wife?"

"In a cabin with a friend watching her."

Eve knotted her hands together in her lap.

"Did they identify the friend?" Schreiner asked.

"No, sir."

"Do you know the gender of the friend?"

"In my mind, I think it was a female. I thought maybe it was Tim's girlfriend, but I can't remember why I thought that. I mean, I don't know if they said that or not."

"Do you remember the girlfriend's name?"

Eve held her breath, but Newhouse shook his head. "I just told you, I'm not even sure it was a girl." He was getting a little testy.

Eve suddenly remembered Bets. Maybe they would think it was Bets who'd kept watch over Genevieve, then later killed herself out of guilt for having participated in the kidnapping! She felt relief, but it was short-lived as she realized that once Tim had his turn to tell the story, Bets would no longer be a suspect in anyone's mind.

The following evening, she watched the trial alone, since Jack was holding auditions at the university. She sat on the sofa as the woman who had been Bets's roommate took the witness stand. Jeannie Rose was a pretty fifty-one-year-old registered nurse with short blond hair and wide, believable blue eyes. Did she know about CeeCee? Eve was glad Jack wasn't home, because she didn't think she'd be able to mask her anxiety as she watched Jeannie Rose swear to tell the truth.

"Bets and Tim were together for two years," Jeannie said when Schreiner started questioning her. "I thought she knew something about the situation when Tim kidnapped Governor Russell's wife, because she didn't really act surprised, but I don't think she was actively involved. She and I worked together at that time, so I saw her all day and night while Tim was…doing whatever he was doing." She kept her eyes glued to Schreiner, and Eve wondered if it was to avoid looking at Tim.

"Where was she at the time Genevieve Russell was kidnapped?" he asked.

"She was working with me. I know she couldn't have been the

person that witness…Mr. Newhouse…was talking about guarding Mrs. Russell, because that whole week she was barely out of my sight. She was upset, though. She just told me it was because Tim was out of town and she missed him. When I thought about it later, I realized she must have known what was going on."

Schreiner questioned her a while longer, then Tim's lawyer cross-examined her, but Jeannie Rose offered little ammunition to either side of the case. After her testimony, court was recessed for the day. *A good day,* Eve thought with relief. Any day that the name CeeCee Wilkes was not mentioned was a good day in her eyes.

Chapter Forty-Eight

TIM WAS SCHEDULED TO TESTIFY IN HIS OWN DEFENSE ON the fifth day of the trial. Eve waited until Jack left the house before calling the Counseling Service to say she was sick and wouldn't be coming in. She would be useless at work today. She had to know what Tim was going to say.

She sat on the sofa, rubbing her aching wrists while he was sworn in. He took his oath in a soft, serious voice, then sat down. He looked calm, but she could see the tension in him as he drew in a breath and let it out again. He looked so little like the young man who had been her lover. He may even have had plastic surgery. His face was more gaunt, his lips thinner, but it was the shaved head that made him look like a different person. His eyes were the same, though. He would have those recognizable green eyes until the day he died.

"Did you kidnap Genevieve Russell?" Sal Schreiner asked.

"Yes," Tim said. "With my brother."

"How did you do it?"

Tim described the kidnapping. It was just as he'd planned it, though not quite as Eve had pictured it, since she hadn't realized that Genevieve knew Tim from her class.

"I asked her if I could talk to her for a minute, and she said sure, so we sat in my van. She didn't know Marty was in the back. I started driving and Marty blindfolded her. We eventually put handcuffs on her because she kept trying to grab the steering wheel."

The camera found the Russells in the courtroom. President Russell put his arm around Vivian, whose head was lowered, her fist pressed against her lips.

"Did you drive directly to the cabin?"

"Yes."

"And what happened when you arrived at the cabin?"

This is it, Eve thought. *This is it.*

"We tied her up inside and then Marty and I drove to Jackson-ville, where we stayed with Terry Newhouse."

Tied her up? Eve leaned forward, the pain in her wrists forgotten.

"You left her *alone* in the cabin?" Schreiner looked as though he didn't believe him.

"Yes," Tim said.

"My God," Eve said out loud.

"Where did you tie her up?"

"On the sofa. We tied her hands and feet."

"Lying down?"

"Yes."

"Was she still blindfolded at that time?"

"No."

"Not blindfolded at that time," Schreiner said, as though that had some significance. "And the gun found buried with Mrs. Russell," he continued. "That was yours?"

"Yes."

"Did you use it?"

"No."

"Yet there was a bullet from that gun—*your* gun—found in the wall of the bathroom."

"I don't know how it got there," Tim said. "Maybe my brother fired it."

"Wouldn't you have known that?"

"Maybe I'd stepped out of the cabin for a minute."

"Liar!" The voice came from the courtroom and a camera swung toward it. Vivian Russell was standing, hands gripping the back of the bench in front of her and her face red with rage. "Stop lying!" she shouted at Tim.

Irving Russell stood up and put his arm around his daughter as he tried to get her to sit down again.

"He's making things up, can't you tell?" Vivian glared at the judge.

"Sit down, Ms. Russell," the judge said.

Vivian bit her lip, going limp as her father drew her into her seat again.

"Please continue," the judge said to Schreiner.

"Isn't it true that you killed Mrs. Russell in or near the cabin?"

"I didn't kill her," Tim said.

"Did your brother kill her?"

"Neither of us killed her," Tim said.

"Did you tell Mr. Newhouse you had left Genevieve Russell with someone guarding her?"

"Yes," Tim said. "We told him that because he would have thought we were foolish to leave her alone. Which we were."

"Why didn't one of you...you or your brother...stay with her?"

"We thought it would be okay. There was no place she could go even if she managed to get herself untied."

Eve was so absorbed in the testimony that it was a moment before she realized Jack was standing in the doorway between the living room and kitchen. She gasped in surprise, hand to her throat.

"Hi," he said.

"You scared me," she said. "How long have you been standing there?"

"Just got home." He walked through the room and sat down next to her on the sofa. "I called your office and they told me you were home sick, so I thought I'd better check on you between classes." He studied her face, and she felt her cheeks go hot under his scrutiny. "What's wrong?" he asked.

"I'm okay. Just felt a little iffy when I got up this morning." She tried to listen to the television as she spoke.

Jack looked at the TV. "So, what's happening?" he asked.

"They've got Tim...Timothy Gleason on the stand," she said. Schreiner was speaking again, his voice powerful and insistent.

"...and you expect us to believe that someone else stumbled across this cabin in the middle of nowhere, unbound and killed her and somehow got a baby out of her and—"

"I don't know what happened," Tim said. "I've told you that. All I know is that when Marty and I went back to the cabin, it was empty. We figured that she'd gotten out somehow and taken the gun with her. We were shocked when we heard that she never went home. I always wondered what happened to her."

"You left her with the gun?" Schreiner wore a look of mock surprise. "Why didn't you take the gun with you?"

"We had another one and didn't need it."

Wow. As good as he'd been at lying to her, he was doing a lousy job of it now. But now he wasn't lying to hurt her; he was lying to protect her. That was clear. Eve was stunned. He could so easily free himself of the tangled web he was weaving if he said: *There was someone else involved. A girl I knew. A girl I could make do anything.* But he didn't. Instead, he let the sticky web of lies draw him in. *He's changed,* she thought. *He's softened.* No matter how hard his interrogator pushed and prodded, he was not going to tell them about CeeCee. He would hang himself to keep her out of it.

She filled with both gratitude and guilt, willing the jury to find him innocent of Genevieve's murder. How could she let him be convicted of a crime she knew he didn't commit when she could exonerate him? His lies were so ludicrous that, while they might save her, they were never going to save him.

"Did you know she was pregnant?" Schreiner asked.

"I didn't know she was as pregnant as she was," Tim said. "I thought maybe she had the baby while we were gone and died."

"And the baby did what? Walked out of there on its own?"

People snickered in the courtroom and the judge called for order.

"This idiot's a bad liar," Jack said. "Can you imagine how President Russell must feel, sitting there looking at this guy? I'd want to get up and strangle him."

"He should have said Marty did it," Eve said.

"What?"

"His brother. Marty. Martin. Even if it was a lie, he should have just said his brother killed her and that would have been enough to give the jury reasonable doubt."

"Why do you care?" Jack asked. "This guy should hang."

"I thought you were against the death penalty?"

"I'm speaking metaphorically," Jack said. "Even if his brother had been the one to pull the trigger or stab her or whatever, this guy— Gleason—put her in the position to get killed. He's scum, Eve."

She needed to shut up. "I know," she said. "I'm just…it's fascinating."

They watched the trial in silence for a few minutes. Then she heard Jack draw in a breath. She knew what he would say even before he said it.

"Eve, did you call in sick so you could watch this?" he asked.

She rested her head against his shoulder so he couldn't see her cringe at the question. "Don't be silly," she said, but she wondered if the uncertainty in her voice gave her away. Her life had not felt so out of her control since she was sixteen and Tim's partner in crime.

Chapter Forty-Nine

"CORY SAID SHE'S NEVER SEEN KEN SO CHARGED UP AS HE'S been covering the trial," Dru said as she munched her salad at the kitchen table. It was Sunday night and she was over for lasagna, which had been a team effort, Jack cooking the noodles and Eve assembling the casserole at the table, where she could sit down. Eve loved it when Dru came over, and not only because she enjoyed the company of her younger daughter. Dru was her lifeline to Cory. She would never know what was going on with Cory if Dru didn't keep her and Jack informed.

"Cory said he's got some unique angles on the story," Dru said, "so it's different from the way the other stations are covering it. She said he's definitely going to be nominated for that Rosedale Award."

Oh, Eve thought, *what a unique angle I could give my daughter's fiancé!*

"And I have one more important piece of Cory news," Dru announced.

"Did they set a date?" Eve asked, hoping they had not.

"She's pregnant," Dru said.

"Oh, no." Jack made a face as though the lasagna tasted bad, and Eve couldn't find her voice. She'd hoped the relationship between

Cory and Ken would eventually wear itself out and that Cory would, at least metaphorically, come back to the fold. A baby would tie her to Ken forever. She couldn't even feel joy about a potential grandchild—a child who would never know its biological grandfather.

"Happily pregnant?" she asked.

"Yes, and I probably wasn't supposed to tell you but she didn't say not to, so…" Dru shrugged. She couldn't keep a secret if her life depended on it.

"Are they going to get married?" Jack asked.

"I think so," Dru said. "I mean, *she* thinks so. She only told Ken last night."

Jack leaned forward, resting his elbows on the table. "Who's dragging his or her feet there, Dru, do you know?" he asked. "When it comes to marriage, I mean. Is it Ken or Cory?"

Dru hesitated, as though she knew she'd already said too much. "It's just inertia, I think," she said. "They've been together so long, they're afraid to rock the boat. But this will probably propel them to take the big step. Anyway, the cool thing is that I'm going to be an aunt! And you two are going to be Grammy and Grampa."

Eve barely heard her. Her mind was somewhere in the past, and all she could picture was Genevieve Russell, lying still and lifeless on a blood-soaked bed.

She sat at her computer late that night, staring at the screen for a long time before starting to type.

Dru told us about your pregnancy, Cory. Congratulations! I'm excited for you. She hesitated, then continued typing. *I know you don't like it when I try to tell you what to do, but this is important: red-haired women can have a problem with he-morrhaging after they give birth. That's something you should ask your doctor about. Okay? I love you.*

She clicked on Send and instantly wished she could pull the e-mail back. What was she thinking? No wonder Cory never wanted to hear from her. Sending the e-mail had been stupid and impulsive—maybe even cruel. Cory didn't need to hear this particular concern for months, if ever.

She was between clients the following morning when Dru showed up in her office.

"What did you *do,* Mother?" she asked, plunking down in one of the upholstered chairs. "Cory said you sent her this ridiculous e-mail about redheads hemorrhaging after childbirth."

"It's true," Eve said from her desk. "I thought she should know, although I realized after I sent it that she didn't need to know right this minute."

"God, Mom, I have to agree with Cory on this one," Dru said. "It's like you were trying to scare her or something. Just being pregnant for the first time with an imbecile for a fiancé is bad enough without you adding to it."

"You're right," Eve said. "I shouldn't have. I just…I want her to be healthy and happy and have a healthy baby."

Dru hesitated, staring at Eve as though uncertain if she should say what was on her mind. "You're…Mom, you're not thinking real well these days," she said. "I know you're in a lot of pain and every-thing and maybe the medicine you're taking is screwing up your head or something. I know you can't help it. But please, if you get the itch to call Cory or e-mail her or write to her, promise you'll check with me first, okay? Let me be your brain for a while."

It was humiliating to have her nineteen-year-old daughter treat her like a child, especially here in her office, where she was usually the one doing the counseling. Worse, though, was the knowledge that Dru was right: she needed guidance. She could barely trust herself to find her way from her bed to the bathroom in the morning.

"All right," she said with a nod. "I will."

Chapter Fifty

ON FRIDAY AFTERNOON, TIM WAS CONVICTED OF THE kidnapping and murder of both Genevieve Russell and her infant, even though the baby's body had not been found. The jury deliberated less than an hour. They didn't believe a word out of his mouth. The sentencing was set for the following Tuesday and would determine if he'd receive life in prison or the death penalty.

The talking heads on CNN and *Court TV* and *Larry King* had a field day debating the merits of the case, trying to predict the outcome. Vivian Russell herself appeared on the *Larry King* show. Eve barely heard a thing she said because she was too absorbed in searching every delicate facet of her face for traces of Cory.

Vivian was furious. "He took my mother from me," she said, thick tears lining her lower lashes. "My children's grandmother from them. My father's wife from him. It was calculated and cruel, and what makes it hardest is not knowing how…how she died." Her chin quivered. "How he killed her," she said. "If she suffered. It's unbearable to think about, and yet I can't stop thinking about it."

People calling into the show were angry and impassioned. One man whose own wife had been abducted and murdered said, "He should fry, and I want to be there to cheer when he does." That seemed to be the majority opinion of the callers. They were out for blood.

The night before Tim's sentencing, Eve couldn't still her mind. She lay awake listening to Jack's light, even snoring, wondering if she should stay home the following day to watch the sentencing or go to work. Just forget she knew him. Forget she had anything to do with the charges against him. Forget that he was innocent of murder and that she was the only other person alive who knew that. She'd waited for someone to come forward who could clear him of that charge. She'd waited for Tim's attorney to say something that would put reasonable doubt into the minds of the jurors. Neither had happened, and now she couldn't sleep.

It was very warm for October. She got out of bed, pulled on her robe and limped outside in her slippers. She followed the stone pavers through the small backyard to the garden bench, where she sat down. The moonlight gave the trees and shrubs and vines an unearthly, ghostly look befitting her dark thoughts.

Leaning against the back of the wooden bench, she looked at the night sky fringed by the leafy greenery of her yard. *I don't want to lose this,* she thought. *I want to be able to sit here in my tiny yard and feel the air on my skin and see the sky above me filled with stars.*

And what about Cory? What would the truth do to her? Tears welled up in Eve's eyes, and a sudden, unexpected sob escaped her throat. Her physical pain, her day-to-day worries, paled next to the thought of hurting Cory. Cory would be torn apart. And Eve would lose the little bit of relationship she had left with her.

Then she thought of all Genevieve had lost. All the Russell family had lost. And what Tim, guilty though he was of many things, was about to lose over a crime he should not have to pay for.

What were *her* crimes? She ticked them off in her mind: Aiding and abetting in the kidnapping of Genevieve Russell; kidnapping Genevieve's infant and crossing state lines with her; changing her identity solely to flee the law. Surely there were any number of smaller laws she'd broken as well. In her mind, though, one of the worst things she'd done was what she was doing right now—letting a man pay for a crime she knew he had not committed.

"Eve?"

She turned to see Jack standing on the small deck. He was wearing the white T-shirt he slept in and he'd pulled on his jeans.

He walked down the path and reached his hand toward her. "Come back to the house, Eve," he said, the way someone might speak to a person about to jump from a ledge.

"I'm all right." She smiled at him to prove it, to try to erase the lines of worry across his forehead. "I couldn't sleep and it's such a beautiful night I thought I'd sit out here a little."

"Please come into the house, honey," he said again. "I want to talk to you."

His tone told her not to argue. She stood up and let him guide her into the house, where he pulled out a chair at the kitchen table and motioned for her to take a seat.

She sat down. "I'm sorry if I woke you when I got up," she said.

"You didn't. I woke up on my own and saw you weren't there, so I went looking for you." He sat down himself. "I'm worried about you, Evie," he said. "I'd like you to see a therapist."

"I don't need—"

"Hear me out," he said. "Dru and I both agree on this."

She squirmed at the thought of Jack and Dru having a discussion about her mental health.

"We both feel that this flare…this relapse of your RA…has taken a huge toll on you," he said.

Oh, no. She felt guilty for allowing his sympathy to be so misplaced. Her tears started again.

"It's all right." He moved his chair up against hers so he could put his arms around her. "It makes sense, honey. You were doing so well healthwise for so long. It was almost as though you were in remission. Then this flare came along and you suddenly had to admit that you still have the disease. I know going back to the scooter was terrible for you. Like admitting defeat. I know you didn't want to be seen riding it around the grounds and have everyone ask you what was wrong. I know the questions get to you."

Leaning forward, she rested her head against his shoulder, glad to be able to hide her face from his eyes.

"I kept waiting for you to suggest a therapist on your own." Jack rubbed her back. "You usually go when you have a problem. Then I remembered that the woman you used to go to—Janet? Was that her name?"

"Yes," Eve whispered.

"I remembered she moved away and that you might not know who to go to. It's hard when you're a therapist yourself and have to find someone who…you know…who you won't cross paths with professionally. But you really need to, Eve. I've never seen you like this. You've lost so much weight. You're depressed, watching TV all the time. I don't know what to do. How to help you. And Cory's made it harder for you, cutting you out the way she has. She'll come around. When she has a baby, she's going to want her mommy."

"I'm sorry I've worried you so much," she said into his shoulder.

"It's going to be okay," he said. "I'm here for you."

She loved how he was rubbing her back, but she didn't deserve his comfort and she sat up straight again.

"Can we talk about this tomorrow?" she asked.

He ran his hands down her arms, his love-filled eyes worried as they searched her face. Lying to him, keeping secrets from the man who had loved her for so many years, suddenly seemed like the greatest crime of all.

Chapter Fifty-One

SHE WENT BACK TO BED WITH HIM, BUT DIDN'T EVEN TRY to sleep. Instead, she stared at the dark ceiling, thinking. Jack was right that she needed help. She felt crazy, driven part by impulse, part by emotion. By five in the morning, when the birds started chirping in the yard outside their bedroom window, she'd made up her mind. The cost of doing something would be terrific; the cost of doing nothing even greater.

She got out of bed at six. Her body ached, but the pain in her heart was worse—prickly and sharp. In the kitchen, she made coffee and heard the sound of Jack's alarm clock. She poured the coffee into two mugs and carried them into the bedroom.

He'd turned on the shower and was starting to take off his T-shirt when she walked into the bathroom.

"I need to talk to you," she said.

He looked at her, his gaze falling to the mugs in her hands. "Can it wait until after my shower?"

She shook her head slowly, and he hesitated only a moment before turning off the water.

"Okay," he said, taking one of the mugs from her. He followed her to the armchairs by the bay window.

She sat down, resting her mug on the small table near her chair, afraid the tremor in her hands might cause her to spill it.

"Is this about our conversation last night?" he asked.

Oh, how she wished it were that simple! She shook her head. She didn't want to hurt him, but there was no way to do this without pain all around.

"There's something I've never told you," she said. "Something terrible. And I'm so, so sorry."

He tilted his head to the side as if trying to guess her secret. She imagined the naïveté in his thoughts: She'd been molested as a child. She'd been married before she ever met him. Nothing he could imagine would prepare him for what she was about to say.

"I thought I knew all there was to know about you." He was steeling himself; she could tell by the way he held his coffee cup with both hands.

"Eve Bailey is not my real name," she said. "Not the name I was born with."

He frowned, waiting for more.

"My name was CeeCee Wilkes."

"What? Are you…are you kidding me?"

She shook her head. "The things you know about me growing up are basically true," she said. "My father disappeared when I was little. My mother died when I was twelve. I lived in foster homes after that. But I never did live in Oregon."

"You lived in Portland," he said, as if reminding her.

"I didn't. I've never even been to Oregon."

"Why did you tell me you grew up there?"

"I'll get to that," she said. She was taking the long way around the barn, but could think of no other way to tell him. "When I was sixteen, I worked in a little coffee shop in Chapel Hill and…" She looked out the window, where the early-morning sun filled the yard with a lemony light.

"Eve," Jack said. "Please don't drift off. What are you trying to tell me?"

She shifted her focus to her husband's eyes. "I know Timothy Gleason," she said. "I mean, I *knew* him. He was my boyfriend when I was sixteen."

Jack sat back in the chair. "Are you…tell me you're making this up. Please."

"I wish I were," she said. "He was a customer at the coffee shop. I fell in love with him. I…" She pressed her hands together in her lap. "It's so hard to explain how I could have done something like this." Her mind raced ahead to all she knew, all Jack didn't know and was going to have to hear. It was overwhelming, but she'd started and now she needed to finish.

"Tim was a member of an underground organization called SCAPE," she said. "He mentioned it during his testimony. Do you remember?"

"I wasn't hanging on every word of the testimony," Jack nearly snapped. "Now I understand why you were." He narrowed his eyes at her. "Do you still have feelings for him? Is that what this is about?"

"Oh, no, honey." She was stunned he'd jumped to that conclusion. "It's nothing like that."

"What is SCAPE?" he asked.

"An organization against the death penalty. I don't even

remember what the letters stand for. He was against it because of his sister being on death row."

"The sister he was trying to get out of prison."

"Right. See, he lied to me. He told me she'd killed a photographer after he raped her, and——"

"I thought the photographer she killed was a woman," Jack said.

"Exactly," Eve said. "That's what I mean about him lying. He tried to win my sympathy for his sister by saying she'd been raped."

Jack looked frustrated. "What the hell does this have to do with you having a different name?"

"I'm getting there," she said. "He wanted me to be sympathetic to his sister because he needed to...to *use* me. I had no idea, though. I thought he was in love with me. He was much older than I was and I was so...God, I was so seduced by his attention. After a while, he told me about his plan to kidnap Genevieve Russell."

"I'm afraid of where this is going." Jack wore the expression he usually saved for their daughters when one of them did something seriously wrong. It didn't fit the lines of his face. When he looked like that, she sometimes didn't recognize him.

"It's unimaginable now," she said, "but I got swept up in the whole thing. I thought his sister had been treated unjustly, and I was——" she shook her head "——I was actually *touched* that he loved her so much he was willing to turn his life upside down to help her. He persuaded me to watch...to guard...Genevieve Russell in that cabin. The one on the Neuse River."

"Where her body was found?"

She nodded.

"Did you kill her?" he whispered.

She started to cry, her hand over her mouth. Unable to speak, she shook her head so he didn't have to wait any longer for her answer. She wanted him to touch her, to put his arms around her in comfort the way he usually did, but he sat like a rock in the armchair, his untouched coffee still clenched between his hands.

She wiped a tear from her cheek with her fingers, then cleared her throat. "She went into labor while I was alone with her," she said. "I was so scared. I was sixteen and knew next to nothing about pregnancy and labor. At first I thought she was faking, but when I realized she wasn't, I...I just panicked." She was speaking quickly now. She felt manic, anxious to get it all out. "I didn't know where there was a hospital and it was night and we were out in the middle of nowhere," she said. "I wanted to get her in the car but it was too late. The baby was on its way. She delivered it on a bed in the cabin and I used a knife to cut the cord. That was the bloody knife they found in the grave with her. It wasn't used to kill her. No one killed her. When the baby was born, Genevieve started hemorrhaging. She had red hair and she told me redheads had a tendency to hemorrhage after childbirth, and—"

"That's why you told Cory about—"

She watched the light dawn in Jack's eyes. They flew open wide, and he stood up abruptly, his full mug falling to the carpet. "*No,*" he said. "Please tell me Cory isn't..." His voice trailed off.

She nodded, looking up at him. "I wrapped her in a blanket and drove to the house of some other SCAPE members," she said. "I was hysterical. A mess. I stayed there a few days and—"

Jack turned away from her and walked out of the room. In a moment, she heard the back door slam shut. She sat still, but it was as though her muscles were shaking inside her skin. She felt a little as she had that night in the cabin: she knew she had to do something quickly, but she wasn't sure what it was. Should she go to Jack? He wouldn't welcome her now, but she had so much to do and time was critical. It was nearly seven-thirty. What time would the jury meet to deliberate Tim's sentence?

She stood up, then went into the backyard to find Jack sitting on the bench in the garden, head lowered to his hands.

He looked up when she neared him. "I don't know you," he said. "I've never known you."

"Yes, you do." She sat down next to him on the bench. "You know me better than anyone. You know the person I've been for nearly thirty years. Eve Bailey. The person I grew up to be."

"How could you…" His voice trailed off as he shook his head. "How could you keep her? Why didn't you make sure Russell got his daughter?"

"I tried. The people who were helping me gave me new identification as well as identification for Cory. They gave me Marian's name and told me to—"

"Marian?" He looked stunned.

"She was involved…peripherally involved with SCAPE because of her husband's execution."

"I can't picture Marian allowing you to—"

"Marian didn't know anything except that I needed a safe place to live," Eve said. "She didn't want to know anything else. When I was driving to her house—to Charlottesville—I tried to drop the baby off at the governor's mansion in Raleigh, but there were guards everywhere. I tried to put her in a police car, but the alarm went off when I opened the door and I ran. I didn't know what to do. Jack, please understand! I was a kid. I barely knew how to drive the car I was in, much less how to get the baby to Irving Russell.

When I got to Marian's, she assumed Cory was mine. By that time, I was in love with her. With Cory. I felt it was my duty to keep her safe. To be worthy of having her. To take care of her the way Genevieve would."

Jack shook his head slowly. "This is so sick," he said.

"I know it sounds that way and I know this is too much to lay on you at once," she said. "It must sound horrible to you. Beyond horrible. I did those things, though, and I can't undo them." She looked at her watch and saw that her hand, her entire arm was shaking.

"I don't know you," Jack repeated. "The woman I know would never have kept someone else's baby."

"I wasn't a *woman*." She began crying again, or maybe she hadn't stopped. "I was a girl. But I'm not telling you all this to make excuses for myself."

"So, why *are* you telling me all of this?"

"Because…because Tim hasn't given me away. Do you see that?" She grabbed Jack's hand. It felt like a cool, hard stone beneath her palm. "Tim wasn't even there when Genevieve died." She wanted him to understand. "I was the only one there. I'm the only person who knows he didn't kill her. He knows I was there, but he's *protecting* me. Protecting *CeeCee*."

"Stop saying that name!" Jack pulled his hand away from hers. "I don't know who that person is."

"It's *me*. It's who I was then. And Tim knows that if he says his old girlfriend, CeeCee Wilkes, was there, they'll start a manhunt for CeeCee and it would lead them right here." She shuddered. "*Right here*. I've been waiting for that," she said. "Waiting for the subpoena. The cops at the door." She looked through the grape arbor toward the front of the house as though she might see a police car on the street. "That's why I've been so crazy lately. I'm not…depressed, Jack. I'm *terrified* and guilty and ashamed of myself. That's why I've been glued to the TV. I was waiting for Tim to say I was there, but he didn't say a word. He's taking the bullet for me. For CeeCee. And today they'll probably give him the death sentence for a murder I know he didn't commit."

"What are you saying?"

"I have to go public. I have to—"

"Oh, no, you certainly do not." Jack shook his head again.

"I've thought it through," she said. "I can't let him pay for something he didn't do."

"Why the fuck not?"

She had never—*never*—heard Jack use that word.

"*He's* the criminal." Jack waved his arms through the air. "If he'd been there instead of you, he probably *would* have ended up murdering her."

"I don't think so," she said. "And he *wasn't* there. *I* was. I know what happened. He's guilty of a lot of things, but he's not guilty of murder."

"So let me get this straight," Jack said. "You're willing to destroy your life—because that's what this will do, Eve. Have no doubt about it. Your career will be over. Maybe mine, too. You're willing to do that and to drag me through the mud with you. Drag Dru through the mud with you. And worst of all, turn Cory's world upside down and…oh, God." He pressed his fingers to his temples. "I can't even imagine what this will do to Cory," he said.

"I know," she whispered. "That scares me."

"This will be the end of your relationship with her," he warned. "Maybe with all the people you've betrayed."

"With you?" she asked tentatively.

He ignored the question. "All to save this scummy son of a bitch from a fate he deserves?"

She fell silent, letting his words sink in. He wanted there to be a pat solution to this problem. If he could give her one, she would grab it, but she knew better.

"There's no way you can prove you didn't...cut the baby out of Genevieve Russell and murder her yourself," he said.

She hadn't thought of that. "I'll have to take that chance."

"You'll go to *prison,* Eve!"

"I know." She remembered sitting on this bench the night before, looking at the night sky. She was going to lose the stars and the moon. She was going to lose *Cory.* She had to call her before she did anything else. She looked at her watch again. Nearly nine. Cory would be in the classroom by now.

Jack seemed to read her mind. "This Russell thing is in the tabloids," he said. "Do you want Cory in the tabloids, too? Do you want everyone in the grocery store to know her life story?"

"Maybe I can protect her some—"

"Dream on! You've got to think this through, Eve."

"That's all I've been doing for weeks," she said quietly.

"You're already flaring. Can you imagine how much sicker you could get in prison?" He suddenly got to his feet, raising his arms in the air as he spun around to look at her. "I can't believe I'm talking about my wife going to *prison!*" he said. "This is insane."

"If I don't come forward, I'm going to get sicker anyway," she said. "*This* is why I've been flaring, Jack. I can't carry the guilt around with me any longer. I'm sorry to put you and the girls in such a terrible position, but please, try to imagine yourself in my place."

"Very, very difficult," Jack said.

"You don't know what you might have done if you'd been in my shoes when you were sixteen," she said.

"I never would have gotten myself mixed up with a scheme like that, and that I *do* know."

"I made stupid choices," she said. "I admit it. But imagine you did do what I did and now you're watching someone take the fall for you. Does it matter what sort of person he is? Does that *matter,* Jack?"

He said nothing, and she knew she'd hit a nerve in him. Jack was a good man, and she'd struck him in the heart of that goodness with her question.

He looked away from her, running his hand over his chin. "I need time to digest this," he said.

"That's the thing," she said. "I don't have time. I've taken too much time being afraid to say anything. And today he's going to be sentenced. I need to do it *today.*"

"No," he said firmly. "This is not just your life you're talking about, Eve. Or whoever the hell you are. This is *my* life, too. And your daughters'. You may think you need to come to the aid of that scumbag in prison, but I think you've forgotten who really matters. You're putting him ahead of your family."

Was she? Oh, God. Should she swallow her integrity for the sake of her family? It would be so much easier, but she was certain it wouldn't be right.

"None of us is going to die if I tell what I know," she said. "But Tim is almost certainly going to die if I don't."

"Ask me if I care," Jack said.

"I just...I have to do it, Jack. I'm sorry."

"This is unreal." He looked at her and she was afraid she saw hatred in his eyes. "*You're* unreal." He looked toward the house. "I've got to get out of here," he said.

"What do you mean?"

"Just what I said. I'm going to get dressed and go to my office, and I hope by the time I get home tonight, this whole...this mess will turn out to be a bad dream."

She stood up, grabbing his arm. "Don't go," she said. "Please. I have to figure out what to do *now*, and I need you to help me think through how to do it."

"That's asking a lot, Eve." He shrugged his arm out of her grasp. "You seem bent on doing something that's going to hurt everybody you supposedly care about. Where do you get off asking for my blessing?" He turned away from her and walked toward the house.

Knees shaking, Eve lowered herself to the bench as Jack slammed the back door shut behind him. She could lose him. She could truly lose him. He loved her—loved *Eve*—unconditionally and with all his heart; she knew that. But it must seem as though Eve had suddenly died, as surely as if she'd been run over by a bus. What had she expected? She'd had decades to adjust to the bizarre truth about her life; he'd had only minutes. Was it his blessing she wanted? His forgiveness? She couldn't say. All she knew was that he was right: she'd already decided what to do.

Chapter Fifty-Two

INSIDE THE HOUSE, SHE LEFT A MESSAGE ON CORY'S CELL phone.

"It's Mom, Cory, and it's urgent," she said. "Please call me as soon as you get this message." She worried that Cory would think something had happened to Jack or Dru. "Everyone's safe," she added, "but I need to talk with you right away. Please call me on your break."

She stared at the phone after hanging up. Should she try Jack's cell number? Ask him to come home? He'd never walked out in the middle of an argument before. But then, arguments had been rare in their marriage. Certainly there'd been no arguments of this magnitude. He needed space and time from her, she thought, as she walked away from the phone. She would have to give it to him.

So, now what? She could call the police and tell them what she knew. Would they instantly arrest her? Would they let her talk to Tim's lawyer? Or would they extradite her to North Carolina without letting her say her piece? Maybe she should try to reach Tim's lawyer directly. She bit her lip, uncertain what to do. She didn't trust herself to make the right decision.

She dialed Cory's number again and left another message,

then turned on the TV in the living room, wishing Jack were with her as she pressed the buttons on the remote. CNN showed video of the exterior of the Wake County courthouse, where a few reporters interviewed people who had sat through every day of the trial, getting their opinions of Tim and the depth of his guilt.

She'd be able to get out on bail after her arrest, wouldn't she? What if they saw her as too great a flight risk, though? She'd run before, she might run again. She swallowed the fear building inside her.

She picked up the phone again and dialed Information to get the number of the courthouse, letting the phone company connect her. A mechanical voice came on the line, offering her a maze of choices and she couldn't seem to grasp what any of them meant. Court costs? Wills and estates? Civil division? Criminal division? That was it, wasn't it—the criminal division? She pressed the appropriate number and was offered another set of choices. Frustrated, she pressed zero, and was relieved when a live human being, a woman with an accent thick as honey, answered.

"Um," Eve began, "I'm not sure what number to call to reach Len Edison. Timothy Gleason's attorney," she added, as if anyone on the planet did not know the name of Tim's lawyer by now.

"I can't put you through to him, ma'am," the woman said. "I suspect he's here, but you have to call his office to reach him."

"Do you have the number?" Eve asked.

"No, ma'am," she said. "Sorry."

She called Cory again after hanging up. She was leaving too many messages for her; Cory would only be annoyed, but maybe she would realize how urgent it was that she call. Then she dialed information for Len Edison's office number.

"He's at the courthouse," the receptionist said after Eve had asked if he was in.

"It's urgent that I speak to him," Eve said. "I have information that can exonerate Timothy Gleason of Genevieve Russell's murder."

The receptionist didn't respond right away. Then she sighed. "A little late with that, aren't you?" she asked.

"Please tell me how to reach him."

"Give me your name and number and I'll let him know you called."

Eve hesitated. She had the feeling Edison would never get the information. "I need to talk to him this morning," she said.

"Do you have any idea how many calls we get from people wanting to talk to him about this case?" The receptionist was definitely burned-out.

"This is important!" Eve said.

"Give me your name and—"

"All right." She told the woman her name and number and made her promise to contact Edison right away. Hanging up, she pictured the receptionist tossing the information into a trash can beneath her desk.

She tried Cory's home number. Maybe she hadn't gone in to work today. Maybe she had morning sickness. She even tried calling Ken at the WIGH office, but was told he was "in the field." At the courthouse in Raleigh, no doubt, waiting to hear the jury's decision on Tim Gleason's future.

"Could I have his cell phone number, please?" she asked the receptionist. "This is his...his future mother-in-law, and it's urgent."

"We can't give that out," the woman said.

Eve thought of arguing with her, but hung up instead. She stared at the phone, wishing Jack would call, fighting the urge to call him. Instead, she dialed the number for Dru's cell phone. She knew her schedule; she could catch her between classes.

"I need to talk to you," she said when Dru answered.

"What's wrong?"

Eve imagined she'd been walking across the grounds and now stopped short at the urgency in her voice.

"It really should be in person, honey," Eve said, "but there's no time, so please forgive me for telling you this over the phone."

"What is it?" Dru sounded frightened.

For the second time that day, Eve upended the world of someone she loved.

"I can't believe this," Dru said, over and over again as Eve told her the story she'd kept inside for so many years. "It's just… Cory's not…she's President Russell's daughter?"

Eve thought she'd explained it all thoroughly and carefully, but there was still confusion in Dru's voice.

"Yes," she said.

Dru started to cry. Even when she was a little girl, Dru's tears had been so rare that Eve had always been surprised by them.

"Honey, I'm sorry," she said. She heard one of Dru's friends ask if everything was all right, but she couldn't hear her daughter's response.

"Did Dad know any of this?" Dru asked.

"No," Eve said. "Not until this morning."

"Is he there?" Dru asked, as though needing to verify Eve's story with Jack.

Eve hesitated. "He's upset," she said. "He's at work."

"He went to *work*?" Dru asked. "He left you alone? How could he go to work?"

"I think he needed some time to process what I'd told him," Eve said. "I don't blame him."

Dru read between the lines. "Is he angry?"

"Yes," Eve admitted. "It's a lot to take in. And he doesn't think I should tell Tim Gleason's lawyer what I know."

"You *have* to, though," Dru said, and for the first time in days, Eve felt the weight on her heart lift, if only a little. Dru, not even out of her teens yet, felt like Eve's lifeline to sanity, and she was touched by her support.

"You understand?" she asked.

"Oh, totally, Mom." Dru's voice was thick with tears. "I totally get it. I just…it's still awful, though. But Cory…I'm scared how she'll take it. She already has such a hard time with…" Dru started crying again, and Eve wished she had a magic wand to take away her daughter's pain. "You have to talk to her before you do anything," Dru managed to say.

"I'm trying, but she won't return my calls."

"She keeps her cell phone off during the school day," Dru said.

"Maybe I could reach her through the school office?"

"Maybe." Dru sounded doubtful. "Or I can try to reach her at school and tell her she has to call you, okay?" she offered. "She'll take a call from me."

"Thanks, honey," she said. "And thanks for…being so accepting."

She hung up the phone, then stared at it for a moment, willing Tim's lawyer to call. She looked at her watch; time was passing too quickly. Had the lawyer even received her message? On the television, reporters jabbered, filling time with opinion and speculation as they waited for something concrete to report. When the cameras panned the area outside the courthouse, she was surprised to see a Channel 29 van parked on the street. That made sense, though. The Charlottesville station had been covering the story all along. As Lorraine had said, it was juicy news.

The phone rang and she grabbed it. "Hello?"

"It's Dru. They told me Cory's at a museum with her class and they can't reach her."

For the briefest of moments, Eve forgot her own plight. "Wow," she said. "That's good she could go on a trip with them, isn't it?" Cory was taking one step forward; her news could sent her back a hundred.

"Yeah, I was surprised," Dru said.

"Will you leave a message on her cell phone to call me the second she can?" she asked. "I've left half a dozen, but she'll be more likely to answer one from you."

"I plan to," Dru said. "And I'm coming over there. You sound fried, Mom. Please don't do anything crazy."

"I already did the crazy thing, Dru. A long, long time ago."

She hung up the phone and turned back to the TV, trying to find Ken in the crowd of people and reporters. She spotted the Channel 29 van again.

Lorraine. Her mind suddenly raced with possibilities, and she picked up the phone and dialed Lorraine's direct line at Channel 29.

"Lorraine Baker," Lorraine said.

"It's Eve, Lorraine." She felt a huge sense of relief at reaching her friend. "You're going to think I'm nuts," she said, "but I have information that can clear Timothy Gleason of Genevieve Russell's murder, and I need to go public with it before I lose my nerve."

Chapter Fifty-Three

THE NEWS CREW ARRIVED IN TWO VANS, AND WITHIN minutes, she felt as though her house was not her own. People swarmed her living room, trying to decide whether it would be better to televise her interview inside or outside. Lorraine arrived, and the sea of people parted for her as she rushed toward Eve, who stood uncertainly in the middle of the room.

"I'm sorry." Lorraine rested her hands on Eve's shoulders. She looked at the mass of people around them. "This must be over-whelming, having them take over your living room like this." She suddenly clapped her hands together. "Outside!" she called. "Set up on the lawn. We'll put Mrs. Elliott on the front porch."

Lorraine put her hands on Eve's shoulders again and looked hard into her eyes as the crew began funneling out of the living room. "You feel wobbly to me," she said. "Sit down."

Eve took a few steps toward the sofa and sank onto it.

"Where's Jack?" Lorraine asked.

"At work." She'd called Jack to tell him her plan, not wanting him to be broadsided by the news that was sure to spread like wildfire through the university.

He'd been as furious as she'd ever heard him.

"You're going to destroy our family, and for what?" he shouted into the phone.

"I'm sorry," she said, but the words sounded as empty to her as they must to him. She had to seem like a stranger to him, a stranger bent on harming him and their daughters for the sake of someone he cared nothing about.

"Do you want him here?" Lorraine looked confused. "Should we wait for him to get here?"

Eve shook her head. "I don't know if he'd come, even if I begged him," she said.

Lorraine tipped her head to the side. "What's going on, Eve?" she asked.

"I don't have time to explain it," Eve said.

Dru sat down next to her on the sofa, putting an arm protectively around her. Her eyes were red-rimmed, her nose stuffy from crying. Wordlessly she rested her head on Eve's shoulder.

"All right," Lorraine said. "I'm going outside to get things organized. I'll come get you when we're ready."

Eve nodded, lacing her hand with her daughter's.

Once the room had cleared out, Eve sat alone with Dru.

"You're really brave, Mom," Dru said.

Eve tried to smile. "Brave or stupid, I'm not sure which," she said. "The only thing I'm afraid of right now is that the police will come the second this airs. And I'm afraid they're going to...to take me away." She teared up, tightening her hand around Dru's. The moment she'd been dreading for nearly thirty years was finally upon her and she was bringing it on herself. "I can't let them do that until after I've spoken to Cory. So somehow, as soon as this is over, I need to drive to Raleigh."

Dru nodded, her head still on Eve's shoulder. "They'll be looking for your car, though," she said.

"I'll have to take that chance."

"Take my car," Dru offered. "I can drive you."

Eve's throat tightened up. It was Jack she longed to have at her side when she spoke to Cory. Remembering his angry words stung her. "I should go alone," she said. She wouldn't put Dru through any more of this than she had to.

"Maybe they'll still figure out where you've gone," Dru said, "but in my car, it will at least take them a little while longer to find you."

Eve looked through the window at the crowded street. Neighbors stood on the sidewalk now, wondering what was going on. There would be no way to get to Dru's car in the driveway without being seen by dozens of people.

Dru read her mind. "I'm going to move my car right now," she said quietly, as if used to such clandestine dealings. "I'll put it on the other side of the block. You just have to go through the Samsons' driveway." It was the route Dru had taken as a child to get to her friend's house on the street behind them. She lifted her head from Eve's shoulder. "Can you walk that far okay?" she asked.

Right now, she wasn't sure she could make it to the front porch, but she nodded.

Dru stood up. "I'll go move it," she said. She bent over to kiss Eve's cheek. "Keep to the speed limit when you drive to Cory's," she warned.

Eve nodded. Dru left the house, and through the window, Eve

watched the crowd turn in her daughter's direction as she walked toward her car.

Lorraine pushed the front door open. "Let me pin this on you, Eve," she said. She crossed the room, holding up a tiny microphone and receiver. Sitting down on the sofa, she clipped the receiver to the pocket of Eve's jeans and the mike to the crew-neck collar of her sweater. "When you're ready," she said, "just come onto the porch. I'll be the person asking you questions, all right?"

Eve nodded and got to her feet. She walked through the front door onto the porch, her mouth suddenly dry as paper. She saw neighbors she knew and passersby she didn't, all crowding the sidewalk to see what was going on. Two huge cameras were on the lawn, along with blinding lights. She hadn't expected that, and she blinked against their glare.

Her gaze was drawn to the street, where she spotted Jack's car jerk to a stop in the middle of the road. She watched him leap from the car, run across the street and push through the throng, and she guessed he intended to prevent her from making her statement. She braced herself to stand firm, but it was unnecessary. He stopped short at the bottom of the porch stairs.

Looking up at her, breathing hard from his sprint across the lawn, he mouthed the words, *I'm here.*

Tears filled her eyes, and she nodded at him. In front of her, Lorraine stood on the porch step, opening her mouth to ask a question, but Eve didn't wait for it.

"Timothy Gleason is not guilty of murdering Genevieve Russell," she said. "And I can prove it because I was there."

Corinne

Chapter Fifty-Four

HER MOTHER LOOKED SMALL AND FRAGILE ON THE TV screen. She'd lost weight, and perhaps she'd also lost her mind. She'd been there? *Where?* What did she mean?

"What the hell is she talking about?" Ken asked. "This is *my* story! She has nothing to do with it."

Corinne thought of the string of phone messages. Was this the reason for all those calls?

"Have you told her anything about what I've uncovered?" Ken sounded accusatory.

"I haven't even spoken to her," Corinne said. They were standing in front of the TV in the bedroom, and her arm was around him, her hand clutching the fabric of his T-shirt. "And you certainly haven't uncovered anything that exonerates Timothy Gleason, have you?"

"Hell, no."

"Maybe someone told her something confidentially," Corinne suggested. "You know, as a counselor. And now she feels she has to go public with it."

"Well, it would have been nice if—"

"Shh," she said, as Lorraine Baker suddenly appeared on camera.

"I'm here at the home of UVA student counselor Eve Elliott in Charlottesville, where Eve is speaking publicly for the first time about information she has regarding the Timothy Gleason case. Eve? What do you mean, you were there?"

Her mother cleared her throat. "I was there when Genevieve Russell died," she said.

"She has so totally lost it," Ken said.

"Shh!" Corinne said.

"Where was that?" Lorraine asked.

"In the cabin on the Neuse River near New Bern."

"Where Mrs. Russell's remains were found?"

"Yes."

"How did you come to be there?"

Her mother's face suddenly went blank as she looked into the camera, and Corinne recognized her expression: panic. She'd seen that look in the mirror any number of times.

"How did you know the Gleason brothers?" Lorraine tried a different question.

Her mother glanced at Lorraine, then seemed to pull herself together. "I met Tim when I..." She stopped, then shook her head. "My name's not really Eve Elliott," she said abruptly. "I was born CeeCee Wilkes, and I met Tim Gleason when I was sixteen years old and...we dated."

"Oh, my God, Ken, she *has* lost her mind," Corinne said in disbelief.

"I helped him and his brother with their plan to kidnap Genevieve Russell," she said.

For a moment, it appeared that even Lorraine was at a loss for words.

"Why?" Lorraine asked. "What made you help them?"

"I…" Her mother licked her lips. "Tim lied to me about why his sister was in prison…he said she'd been wrongly convicted. I stupidly…naively…believed him, and said I would help them."

"How did you help them?"

"I was supposed to guard her in the cabin. Tim testified that he and Marty left her there alone and that she was gone when he returned, but he was saying that to protect me…or rather, to protect CeeCee Wilkes." She rubbed the back of her neck. "He has no idea who I am. Who Eve Elliott is."

"This is bananas," Corinne whispered. "She's the last person who would…" Her voice trailed off as her mother continued speaking.

"She went into labor while I was alone with her," her mother said. "She was early by about a month, and she told me that she'd had problems with hemorrhaging after the birth of her first child. Something to do with having red hair."

"That's where she got the redhead thing from," Ken said.

"Did *you* deliver the baby?" Lorraine asked, and Corinne could still hear the disbelief in her voice.

Her mother nodded. "Yes, and Genevieve hemorrhaged after the baby was born. *No one* killed her." She spoke that sentence forcefully, directly into the camera. "She died of natural causes."

"What did you do with the baby?" Lorraine asked.

Her mother hesitated. "I panicked," she said after a moment. "I left Genevieve there, but I grabbed the baby before I ran out of the cabin. I drove to the house of some people the Gleason brothers knew. They got—"

Corinne didn't hear whatever her mother said next. She was

running dates through her mind. Genevieve Russell had been kidnapped in 1977. The year Corinne was born.

"Oh…my…God," she said quietly, then to the TV. "You incredible bitch!"

"Shh." Ken sat down on the edge of the bed, leaning toward the television.

"So they made new IDs for me and for…the baby. I tried to drop her off at the governor's mansion on my way to Charlottesville, but there was too much security around."

"Are you saying you kept the baby?" Lorraine asked.

Her mother swallowed, her eyes wide and vacant like a deer blinded by headlights. "Yes," she said, regaining her composure. "She's my daughter, Cory."

"No!" Corinne wailed, raising her hands to her mouth. "Oh my God, Ken. Tell me I'm not hearing this."

The phone rang.

"Don't pick it up!" she said.

Ken checked the caller identification display. "It's work," he said, lifting the receiver to his ear. "Hello?"

"You stole me from my life!" Corinne shouted at the TV while Ken carried the phone into the other room.

Corinne sank to the floor, leaning back against the bed while the room spun around her. Her mother was still speaking, answering Lorraine's questions, but it was as though their conversation had been muted. She didn't hear them. Her heart filled with hatred, like a poison entering her bloodstream. *Your mother ruined you,* Ken had said to her more than once. She pictured Irving Russell. The president of the University of Virginia was her father! She thought of the photo of him they always used in the paper and on the news, and of the smiling picture of Genevieve Russell shown in the media. Her mother. Her real mother. The mother who wouldn't have sucked the breath out of her with a pathological need to keep her safe. Who wouldn't have made her afraid of the world. They'd had another daughter, too. Corinne had seen her interviewed on *Larry King*. Ken had even mentioned a resemblance between Corinne and the beautiful Vivian.

Ken returned to the bedroom holding the phone limply at his side. His face was bleached of color.

"That was Darren," he said. "They're giving me what they call 'a break.' 'Too bad about the Rosedale,' he said, like it's no big deal." He looked at the television, where the footage of her mother's interview was being repeated. Ken laughed bitterly. "Now we've both been screwed by your mother," he said. He looked at her sitting on the floor, as if only now noticing her. He crouched next to her, his hand on the back of her neck. "Are you all right, Cor?" he asked. "I'm sorry. You must feel——"

The phone rang again and he stood to pick up the receiver from the bed. "It just says *Virginia*," he said.

She reached for the phone. "That's Dru's cell." She hesitated a moment, then pressed the button as she lifted the receiver to her ear.

"Dru," she said.

"Oh, Cory." Dru sounded breathless. "Do you know what's going on?"

Corinne's eyes filled at the sound of her sister's voice. Her treasured baby sister. "It would have been nice if she'd told me before she told the rest of the world," she said. She watched as Ken, lost in his own disappointment, left the room. "How could she do this to me?"

"She tried to reach you a million times today," Dru said. "She felt like she had to do it before he was sentenced."

"I *knew* I didn't fit in," Corinne said. "I knew it from the time I was little. I just never realized how much I didn't fit in. I can't believe she did everything she said she did. And I can't believe she had the gall to tell the world about it."

"I think it's been so hard for her the past couple of months," Dru said. "Keeping the secret while the trial's been going on and everything. Her RA is much worse lately."

"Don't defend her to me, Dru," Corinne said. She heard Ken turn on the TV in the living room. "*You're* still her daughter. You've always known right where you belonged."

Dru fell silent, and Corinne regretted her words.

"I'm sorry," she said. "None of this is your fault."

"Please stay my sister." Dru's voice was thick with tears.

"Forever," Corinne said. "You're the only good thing about being raised an Elliott. Did Dad…did Jack know all this time?"

"She only told him today. He was as shocked as you are." Dru paused. "He actually left for a while, but he came back when Lorraine started interviewing her. He's really upset and angry."

It was hard to picture Dad angry. "They practically canned Ken," she said. "They're giving him a so-called break."

"Oh, no. Does that mean the award—"

"No award," Corinne said.

Dru paused. "Mom and Dad are on their way down to see you," she said. "They left as soon as the press conference was over."

"I don't want to see them," Corinne said. "Call them and tell them to turn around and go home. Why didn't the cops arrest her?"

"That's why she got out of here so fast," Dru said. "She wants a chance to see you first, Cory. I let them take my car."

"I don't want to see her," she repeated.

Dru was quiet again. "You need to talk to her," she said finally.

"I hate her." Corinne pounded her fist onto the floor. "I really, truly *hate* her."

"Please don't," Dru pleaded. "She was a good mother. She—"

"To you, maybe," Corinne said. "You're her flesh and blood."

"She's coming here?" Ken asked as he walked back into the room, and Corinne nodded. He grabbed the phone from her hand. "Dru, you call her and tell her to stay home. She comes here, I'll have the police here to greet her."

"*No.*" Corinne got to her feet. She wasn't sure what she wanted, but that wasn't it. The police would catch up with her mother soon enough. She took the phone back from Ken.

"Just tell her not to come here, Dru. Please," she said. "I'm afraid of what I might do if I see her."

Chapter Fifty-Five

WHEN SHE GOT OFF THE PHONE, SHE WENT INTO THE DEN, sat down at the computer and pulled up images of her biological family on the Internet. Ken stood behind her, kneading her shoulders as he studied the monitor over the top of her head.

"I don't look much like...like President Russell, do I?" She couldn't say the words *my father*. She wondered if she'd ever be able to. The image of Irving Russell on the computer screen was a professional shot, above the caption, A Greeting From The President Of The University Of Virginia. He was handsome, yet she saw the evidence of a difficult life in his face. She reached out and touched the slight bags beneath his eyes, the crevices at the corners of his mouth as he smiled for the camera.

"A little around the eyes, maybe," Ken said. He bent over to kiss the side of her throat. "I'll tell you one good thing that can come of this," he added.

"What?"

"You're going to be rich. That family's worth a fortune."

She craned her neck to look up at him. "Do you think I care about that?"

"I think you should," he said. "It's nice not to have to worry about money."

"Money's the last thing on my mind right now." She clicked to another picture, this one the familiar shot of Genevieve Russell used in the media. "I wish I could find more of her," she said. "This is the one you see everywhere."

"That's definitely your mother," Ken said. "Same nose. Same gorgeous hair." Ken lifted her long red hair, then let it fall back to her shoulders.

Corinne found a picture of Vivian. "We're like twins, except for the hair color," she said.

"You're prettier," Ken said, as if it mattered.

Corinne suddenly had an image of Dru, her true sister, so bubbly and full of life. "Oh, Dru." She buried her head in her hands. "I'm so confused." She looked up at Ken. "I don't know who I am," she said. "I mean, will these people accept me?" She nodded toward the image of Vivian on her computer screen. "No wonder Dru always thought Mom was so normal and I thought she was wacky. She treated us differently from the start."

"She overcompensated with you," Ken said. "It was like she was trying to make it up to you for what she'd done and she went overboard. Way overboard."

"I'm so…" She could barely give words to her emotions. The blood in her veins suddenly felt different. Her arms itched and her legs felt cold. "I don't know which way is up." She swiveled her chair around to look at him. "Marry me," she said. "Please, Ken. Let's get married and have this baby. Let's create a real family. We'll be three people who absolutely belong together. We'll do everything right with our son or daughter." She put her hand on her stomach.

Ken nodded slowly. "Okay," he said.

She got to her feet, joy and relief coursing through her, and put her arms around his neck. "Can we do it soon?" she asked. "Before I start to show? I don't care if it's a little wedding. I don't care if it's just the two of us with the justice of the peace. I just want to be your wife."

"Okay," he said again. His voice was flat. "We'll work it out."

It was not the reaction she'd hoped for. "What is there to work out?" she asked. "I know you don't think the time is right, but we need to be a *family*."

He nodded. "I know, and I want that. But there's something I haven't told you." He let go of her and lowered himself to the chair near her desk. "I've been…cowardly," he said. "Too chicken to tell you."

"What?" She sat down again, and he leaned forward to roll her chair close to his.

He took her hands. "You and I have been together for a long time," he said.

"Almost six years," Corinne said.

"And you know I love you more than anything, don't you?"

She nodded. She was certain of it. He told her all the time that he loved her.

"I've kept something from you," he said. "Only one thing, but it's a…it's a big thing."

She wasn't certain she could handle another surprise today. "What?" she asked.

"My divorce from Felicia," he said. "It was never really final."

Corinne recoiled, letting go of his hands. "What do you mean by 'never really'?"

"I mean…we're not divorced. When we separated…that's when she got sick and I couldn't just…she begged me not to divorce her then, so…" He shrugged. "We had the property settlement drawn up and everything. I just never did the final paper-work."

Corinne felt anger rise up in her, boiling hot as lava. "Why didn't you ever tell me this?" she asked.

"At the time I met you—"

"You said you were divorced."

"No, I didn't," he said hurriedly. "I said I was separated and filing for divorce. That my marriage was over. You jumped to the conclusion that I was divorced and—"

"And you never bothered to set me straight."

"I felt divorced in my heart."

She stood up, furious. "You told me you felt married to *me* in your heart."

"I do," he said.

"Your heart has nothing to do with what's legal and what's not," she said.

"Corinne…" His eyes pleaded with her to understand. "Felicia knows our marriage is completely over. She knows I'm committed to you. She's just one of those insecure women who needs to be able to say 'my husband this and my husband that.'"

"You've been sending her money all these years," Corinne said. "I thought it was alimony."

"It is, in a way. Just not court-ordered alimony. I send it to her because I care about her. You always said it was so great that she and I still got along. That we communicated."

"I wouldn't have said that if I'd known she was still your wife!" Corinne said.

He stood up and tried to put his arms around her, but she brushed them away.

"I know it's hard for you to understand," he said, "but the circle she's in…the social circle…she would have felt humiliated if she had to tell them she was divorced."

"What about humiliating *me?*" Corinne asked. She felt like hitting him. She'd never wanted to hit anyone in her life.

"You're stronger than she is," Ken said.

"Well, that's a first," she said. "You're always telling me I'm weak and how lucky I am to have big strong *you* to lean on."

Ken sat on the edge of the computer desk. "Look, I admit I've been wrong," he said. "And I'm going to make it right. I'll divorce Felicia. I don't know how long it will take for the divorce to go through, but the second it does, you and I can get married."

"I want you to leave," she said. The words sounded so foreign in her ears she could hardly believe she'd said them. Neither could Ken.

"What?" he asked, as if he'd misunderstood her.

"You heard me."

"You can't kick me out," he said. "This is my house, too."

"I don't care. You can't stay here right now, because there's a really good chance I'll kill you if you do." She knew the fire behind the words showed in her face, because he backed away from her.

"I love you," he said. "Please marry me. I want to marry you."

"That's just the kind of proposal I've yearned for all these years we've been together." She threw her pen at him. "Marry me, darling, as soon as I divorce my wife. You son of a bitch." She looked for something larger and more lethal to throw.

"You're angry at your mother, not me," he said. "Don't take it out on me."

"Oh, shut up," she said.

"You can't function without me." Ken picked up her pen from the floor. "You can't even go to the mall without me. You need me, Cor."

She walked out of the den, pressing her hands to her ears. "Get out of this house!" she yelled. It felt so good to yell! She wanted to scream.

"Don't you want me to be here when your mother shows up?" He followed her into the living room.

"No!"

"You've forgotten all I've done for you," he said. "You wouldn't be able to walk out of this house if it weren't for me. You were afraid of your own shadow before I came along."

"Oh, it was all you, is that what you think?" she shouted. "I'm the one who had to do the walking out the door. I'm the one who drove on 540 today. I'm the one who'll have to get on the elevator, who has to do the hard stuff. You can't even tell Felicia you want a divorce."

She sat down on the sofa, suddenly too drained to stand any longer, and looked up at him. "Do you still love her?" she asked.

He ran his hands through his hair. "Not at all," he said. "It's more like I hate her. She tied a noose around my neck and—"

"You are so pathetic," Corinne said with a groan. "Don't blame her. You're the one making the choices. Now get out of here."

He hesitated, and she thought he was going to continue arguing with her, but instead, he gave in. "All right," he said. "I'll be on my cell if you need me. I know you're furious right now and I don't blame you. But don't throw the baby out with the bathwater."

She gave him a long, hard look, and felt very brave. "I'm not throwing the baby out, no matter what," she said.

He turned to leave the room. She listened to him pack in the bedroom as she idly surfed the Internet, not really caring about anything on the screen. He was right: she couldn't function without him. She was terrified to have him leave. The dead-bolt lock on the back door was broken, she remembered. And it had rained earlier, causing the sump pump to produce an occasional *thud* in the basement. She sat frozen at the computer, not typing, barely breathing as she waited for him to go.

Chapter Fifty-Six

FOR OVER AN HOUR, SHE DIDN'T MOVE FROM HER SEAT AT the computer except to lock the doors and check the windows.

What had happened to her world? She was dazed by changes she could not yet grasp. In the space of a couple of hours, she'd lost the family she'd always known and the man she'd long planned to marry. She stared at the picture of Genevieve Russell, who looked so alive and happy. How could her mother have let this beautiful woman die the way she did? It was tantamount to murder. Why didn't she get her help?

She felt sick as she waited for the doorbell to ring, when she would come face-to-face with the woman responsible for her real mother's death. The woman who had raised her in suffocating protection and who had lied to her over and over again.

She heard the slamming of car doors in her driveway. In the living room, she unlocked the door and pulled it open. Turning her back on her parents, she walked over to the love seat and sat down, arms folded across her chest like armor, firmly in place.

Her mother limped into the room, her father's hand on her back. Her eyes were puffy and red, her dark hair pulled back from her face in a scrunchie. She seemed to know better than to try to hug Corinne. Instead, she stood in the middle of the room, holding her arms at her sides with an air of defeat. "Cory," she said, "I'm so sorry, honey."

Corinne shut her eyes.

"Sit down, Eve." Her father guided her mother to the sofa. He was being so protective of her. He didn't sit next to her, though, choosing instead to take a seat near the fireplace.

"What exactly are you sorry for, Mother?" Corinne glared at her. "For lying to me all these years? Lying to me my whole life? Are you sorry for destroying the family I was born into? For killing my mother? Are you sorry for stealing me from my father and sister? Are you sorry for—"

"That's enough, Cory," her father said. "That doesn't help."

Her mother was crying, tears flowing freely. She leaned forward as if she wanted to get as close to Corinne as she could. "I'm sorry for hurting you in any way," her mother said. "I loved you from the start. I've always loved you."

"You loved me, so you stole me, you selfish bitch." She choked on the word.

"Cory, stop it," her father said.

"It wasn't that simple," her mother said. "But I'm not here to make excuses for my behavior. It was inexcusable. I'm just here to tell you how much I love you and how sorry I am for hurting you."

Corinne couldn't look at her. If she looked at her, she might see her paleness, the circles around her eyes, the swollen wrists. She didn't want to feel any sympathy for her, so she rested her head on the back of the chair and stared at the ceiling instead.

"So explain," she said. "You said you waited at that cabin while those guys kidnapped my mother. What was she like when she got there?" She braced herself for the answer. How horrible to have to learn about Genevieve from the woman responsible for her death!

Her mother hesitated. "She was more angry than afraid," she said. "Maybe if she'd been the one to raise you, you wouldn't have had the fears you do, because she was a very strong and feisty woman. And beautiful, Cory. The kind of beauty that could sweep you away. Like your beauty. You look so much like her."

She wouldn't cry. She wouldn't give her mother the satisfaction of her tears. "More," she said as she lowered her head to look at her. "Tell me more."

Her mother told her everything about that terrible night in the cabin—how Genevieve directed her to prepare for the birth and how, as Corinne came to life, Genevieve faded away. She told her about wrapping her in a blanket and running away with her.

"I was so afraid," her mother said. "I fell in love with you, but I knew I needed to get you to your father. I tried to do that. I was going to put you inside a police car in front of the governor's mansion, but when I started to open the car door, an alarm went off. So I took off with you. I was terrified the police would come after—"

"It makes me sick." Corinne looked her in the eye.

"What does?" Eve asked.

"You keep talking about what was happening to *you*. What *you* felt like. It was all about *you*, wasn't it? All about you."

"Actually, no," her mother said. "I was very concerned about *you*. About what I'd done to you. I didn't know what else to do other than keep you and love you and take care of you."

"You told me my father was killed in a motorcycle accident."

"I didn't know what else to—"

"You didn't know. You didn't know. If you say that one more time, I'm going to scream." She sat forward. "You did *too* know what you should do. You should have gone to the police and told them the truth so they could take me to my father. My real father." She kept her eyes on her mother, not daring to look at Jack at that moment. He was an innocent bystander in all of this. She didn't want to hurt him, but she was too angry to censor her words. "That's what you should have done," she said, "and even at the tender age of sixteen, you knew that, didn't you?"

"Yes," her mother whispered. "I knew that."

"How could you let my mother die like that?"

Her father sat forward. "Cory, what do you want her to say?"

"How do you feel, Dad, knowing she's lied to you all these years?" She asked the question of her father, yet she felt the betrayal in her own heart. Ken's lies rang in her ears. Had anyone ever been honest with her?

"It feels like crap," her father said. "I'm still struggling to understand all of this myself. But I love…your mother. We've both worked hard to give you and Dru a loving family. She's not the girl she was back then, Cor—"

He suddenly turned his head at the sound of car doors slamming outside. Leaning back, he peered out the window, then closed his eyes. "Damn," he said quietly.

"Who is it?" Corinne got to her feet and looked through the window into the darkness. A police car was in the driveway behind Dru's car. Another stood in the street. Three uniformed officers were walking to her front door.

"The police are here." She looked at her mother, who only nodded, unsurprised.

Corinne pulled open the door before the three men had a chance to ring the bell.

"Are you Corinne Elliott?" one of them asked.

She nodded.

"Is Eve Elliott here?"

"Yes." She stood away from the door to let them enter.

They walked in, as her mother rose unsteadily to her feet, leaning on her father's arm once again.

"Eve Elliott?" one of the officers queried.

"Yes," her mother whispered.

"You're under arrest for the kidnapping of Genevieve Russell and baby girl Russell, false identification, conspiracy, tampering with public records…"

Corinne listened as the officer read a laundry list of her mother's many crimes, all the while thinking, *Who is baby girl Russell?* It took her a moment to realize he was talking about her. Her skin prickled. She was two people. Who would baby girl Russell have grown up to be? She felt the room blacking out from the edges and gripped the arm of the sofa to keep herself upright.

"Don't handcuff her." Her father grabbed one of the officer's wrists as he started to put handcuffs on her mother, but he quickly let go. "Please," he said. "Her wrists are painful."

"It's all right, Jack," her mother said. She submitted easily, barely seeming to notice the cuffs on her wrists. Her eyes were on Corinne, who liked seeing her treated like the criminal she was. She wanted her mother to share some of the pain she felt.

"I'll follow you in Dru's car," her father said to her mother. He was so solicitous of her. So understanding. He'd always been such a wimp.

She watched them head down the sidewalk toward the police car. From the rear, her mother's faltering gait was pronounced. It was always worse when she was walking with someone else, as she was with the officers, trying her best to keep up with them. For just a moment, Corinne wanted to call out to the police, *Don't make her walk so fast!* The muscles in her chest contracted as she watched the only mother she'd ever known limp down the front walk and away from her.

Chapter Fifty-Seven

WHEN THE CALLS STARTED FROM THE REPORTERS THE following day, and they gathered outside the house in a feeding frenzy, Corinne pulled the blinds in the bedroom and sat on the bed to watch the news. J. B. MacIntyre, Ken's rival at WIGH, reported from the Wake County Courthouse that Timothy Gleason had been sentenced to life in prison. An hour later, she watched him report from in front of her house.

"Ironically," he said, "the latest development in the Timothy Gleason case led authorities to the home of WIGH reporter Ken Carmichael."

Corinne hated J.B.'s voice. He dramatized everything. He could turn a pimple into a life-threatening event.

"Eve Bailey Elliott, aka CeeCee Wilkes, was arrested last night at the home Carmichael shares with his fiancée, Corinne Elliott," J.B. said. "Eve Elliott admitted that she kidnapped Russell's newborn infant in 1977 and raised her as her own daughter."

A picture of Corinne, taken from a WIGH award dinner she and Ken had attended and which Ken kept on his desk at work, appeared on the screen, followed by a picture of Genevieve

Russell, the same one the media had been flashing for days. "Elliott had publicly announced her role in the kidnapping shortly before taking refuge at the Carmichael residence with her husband and daughter."

Refuge? Corinne thought. Hardly.

"No comment yet from Irving Russell, nor from his other daughter, Vivian," J.B. said. "And Corinne Elliott—aka, baby girl Russell—has so far refused to speak with us."

Would Irving Russell call her? she wondered. She had more parents than ever before, and yet she felt as though she had none. Eve and Jack seemed like strangers to her. Here she was, barricaded in her bedroom, listening to van doors slide open and closed on the street, while reporters and camera crews chattered outside her front door. She felt trapped. She missed Ken. He was right: she needed him. He was a buffer between herself and the world.

She didn't leave the house for two days. She didn't have to call in to work. They called *her* to ask if she needed time off, and she supposed they were glad to give it to her. She was the object of gossip. She didn't want to face people who would be wondering about her parentage when she felt so uncertain of it herself.

She was sitting at her computer in the den when the phone rang for what must have been the thousandth time in the past couple of days. She checked the caller ID display and felt overjoyed to see Ken's number illuminated on the screen. She clicked the talk button.

"Please come home," she said, instead of hello. "I'm sorry I blew up."

He hesitated. "I'm the one who's sorry. I can't believe everything that was dumped on you the past few days and I just made things worse."

"By telling me the truth."

"That I should have told you years ago."

"I don't know what to do, Ken," she said. "The reporters are hounding me."

"Don't answer the phone or the door and keep the blinds closed."

"I am."

"I'm coming home," he said. "I don't want you there alone."

"Okay." She was relieved. She would let him take care of her.

He paused. "Your mother hurt you even worse than I thought," he said finally.

"I'm so angry at her," Corinne said. "I can't stand how angry I feel. I want to throw something through the window."

"I don't blame you," he said. "She kept you from your real family. Has Russell tried to get in touch with you?"

"No. Unless he's been one of the zillion calls I've ignored this afternoon."

"You know what I did when I left the other day?" Ken asked.

"What?"

"I went to my lawyer and reactivated the divorce proceedings. And I called Felicia to let her know."

She smiled. "Good," she said.

He hesitated only a moment. "Corinne," he said. "Will you marry me?"

Ken screened every phone call that came into the house. She didn't want to talk to her father—to Jack. She'd started out calling him Jack as a child; now she reverted to it. She didn't want to hear him plead with her to visit her mother in jail. She wasn't even ready to picture her mother there. Was she behind bars? In a tiny, cold cell? She didn't want to think about it.

The call Corinne was truly waiting for—with both dread and longing—came in an unexpected form.

As usual, Ken answered the phone, but this time he handed it over to her. "It's Irving Russell's attorney," he said.

She took the phone from him, her hand suddenly damp with perspiration.

"This is Corinne Elliott," she said.

"My name is Brian Charles." He spoke with a quick, sharp force. "I represent Irving Russell. President Russell would like to know if you'd agree to a DNA test to determine if you're his daughter or not."

She felt an instant of betrayal, a feeling that was becoming all too familiar. Was Russell hoping she was not his? Maybe he didn't want to deal with the messiness she'd bring into his life.

"Of course he's very much hoping that you do prove to be his kidnapped daughter," Brian Charles said when she didn't respond. "But I'm sure you understand his need to be certain about this. It's best for you to be certain as well."

"Yes," she said. "I understand. What do I have to do?"

"We can arrange for the test to be done through your family physician, if that's agreeable to you."

Was it? Could there be a problem with doing it through her doctor? Could they have gotten to her doctor in some way? Maybe paid him off to do…what? She felt like a child who no longer knew what was good for her and what was not.

She covered the receiver with her hand and spoke to Ken.

"They want me to take a DNA test with my regular doctor," she said. "Is that okay?"

Ken nodded. "It's a good idea," he said. "You need to be sure. Who knows what the truth is when it comes to your mother?"

She lifted the receiver again. "Yes, that's fine," she said.

"All right. If you give me his number, I'll get in touch with him and tell him to expect your call. We'll handle any cost involved, of course."

Ken drove her to the doctor that afternoon. She wore her sunglasses in the car as they passed the reporters lining their driveway. She suddenly understood why people wore dark glasses in situations like this. Her eyes were no longer bloodshot from crying, but she didn't want to be seen. She didn't want to risk eye contact with any of the hungry reporters. Ken was usually one of them, she realized. He'd get a scoop, then come home and boast about it. He'd boasted about this very case.

"I'm sorry you…" She couldn't think of a way to give words to her thoughts. "You lost out on this story."

He laughed. "Big-time," he said. "I've become *part* of the story." He smiled at her; he'd been so kind since coming home. "Don't give it a thought, okay?" he said. "What's going on with you is more important than whether I win the Rosedale or not."

They were at a stoplight, cars tight on either side of them, and she felt panic setting in. Her heart beat fast and hard enough that she could feel it in her throat. She gulped air, trying to keep her breathing even.

"We're almost there." Ken glanced at her. He knew she was struggling. "It's just a couple of blocks away."

She was relieved when they started moving again. Ken drove into the parking lot of the medical building and groaned when he spotted a woman standing near the entrance.

"There's a snitch in your doctor's office," he said grimly as he took the keys out of the ignition. "Don't get out."

He came around to her side of the car, his eye on the woman standing at the office door.

"Come on." He opened the car door, taking her arm as she stepped out. "Stay close."

The woman approached them. She was older than Corinne had first thought. Her blond hair was brassy, and thick makeup covered acne scars.

"Back off, Liz," Ken said. Apparently she was a colleague. She ignored his direction.

"Corinne," she said, walking toward her, notepad at the ready, "what are you here for? Is it for a DNA test?"

"Don't answer her," Ken said. He walked so quickly that her own legs, wooden and suddenly too long for her body, nearly tripped her. "We have no comment," Ken said. He pushed open the door and guided Corinne into the foyer. "Don't even think about it," he said to the reporter as she started to follow them in. This time she listened, and Corinne was relieved when the door closed safely behind her.

No one mentioned why she was there. She didn't even see the doctor, only a nurse who had the good sense to pretend taking a sample of cells from the inside of Corinne's cheek was an everyday event. Corinne was grateful for her matter-of-fact demeanor.

"How long 'til we get the results?" Ken asked, when the nurse had finished.

"About a week," she said.

And then what? Corinne wondered as the nurse wrote her name on the plastic container. Who would she be then?

Chapter Fifty-Eight

THE CALLER ID DISPLAY SHOWED A *VIRGINIA* NUMBER, which usually meant that Dru was calling from her cell, so Corinne didn't hesitate to answer the phone.

"Hi, Dru," she said.

Silence greeted her.

"Dru?"

"I'm trying to reach Corinne Elliott." The voice was deep. Masculine. Mature.

She held her breath. Something told her this wasn't a reporter on the line. "This is Corinne," she said.

"Corinne, this is Irving Russell."

"*Oh,*" she said. "Hello."

"I received the report from the DNA test this afternoon. It shows that you're definitely my daughter."

Had his voice caught on that word?

"I'm so…thrilled," he said. "I'm overjoyed that you're alive, Corinne. I'd given up all hope."

She closed her eyes. She'd been waiting for this call and now was unsure what to say. She opened her mouth to speak, but nothing came out.

"Are you there?" he asked.

"I'm here," she said. "I'm sorry. I guess I'm in shock. It suddenly makes everything my mother said so real."

"The woman you *thought* was your mother," he corrected.

"Yes." *I hate her,* she wanted to add. She felt the hatred well up in her again.

"I'm sorry you never got to know your real mother," Irving Russell said.

"Me, too." She felt like crying. Finally, here was someone who had known her mother well. "I want to know everything about her," she said.

"Of course." There was a smile in his voice. "Vivian—that's your sister—and I want to invite you up to Charlottesville for the weekend. We have more room than you could imagine. You can bring your fiancé, of course." She wondered how he knew about Ken, but she guessed the world knew everything about her by now.

Even with Ken at her side, though, she didn't think she could make the drive to Charlottesville. She felt fragile these days. She was to return to work the following week and had the feeling she'd be taking the back roads once again. "I um…I don't travel very well," she said.

"Are you ill?"

"No. I just…it's a silly phobia."

He was silent and she had the feeling he was a man who had never been afraid of anything in his life.

"We'll come to you, then," he said. "I don't mean we'll stay with you," he added quickly. "But we'll drive to Raleigh Saturday and spend the day with you, if that's all right. Then drive back in the evening. How's that?"

"That would be good," she said. "If you give me your e-mail address, I'll send you directions."

He gave her the information, and she wrote it down with trembling fingers, knowing that once again, her life was about to change. This time, it would be for the better.

Chapter Fifty-Nine

A LEXUS PULLED INTO THE DRIVEWAY AT NOON ON Saturday, and Corinne was glad that the reporters were no longer staking out her neighborhood. She'd prepared chicken salad—the fancy chicken salad her mother had long ago taught her to make for company—along with croissants and fruit. She wouldn't be able to eat any of it, though; her stomach filled with knots as she watched Irving Russell and his daughter get out of the car and head toward the front door.

"Are you all right, Cor?" Ken asked, his hand on her back. "Do you want me to get the door?"

She shook her head, waiting for the bell to ring. She suddenly wished Ken were not with her. This moment felt too private to share, even with him. Despite how kind he had been recently, her feelings for him had shifted since the revelation about his divorce, or rather, his lack of divorce. She couldn't help it; he was not the person she'd thought he was.

The Russells knocked instead of ringing the bell. She opened the door and faced a woman who looked so much like herself that she felt light-headed at the sight of her.

"Oh, my God," Vivian said. She stepped inside and pulled Corinne into an embrace, holding her close, her shoulders heaving slightly. Corinne felt love pour into her from the woman, a love so real and pure that it could be mistaken for nothing else. Her own eyes filled with tears.

"It's okay," she said, patting Vivian's back, but she didn't want to let go, either.

"I'm Ken Carmichael, President Russell," she heard Ken say.

"Call me Russ," Irving Russell said.

She and Vivian drew apart as the two men shook hands. Then she looked into the face of the man who was her father. His eyes were dry, but reddened from days of uncertainty and hope and disbelief.

"You are so much like her," he said softly. Resting his hand on her shoulder, he leaned over to kiss her cheek, an awkward gesture. For a moment, no one said a word. Then he smiled. "I'm overwhelmed," he said, as he had on the phone.

"He is," Vivian agreed. "Dad's never at a loss for words."

"Well, it's understandable," Ken said. "Come in and have a seat. We've got iced tea or soda or wine."

They moved into the living room, and Vivian sat close to Corinne on the sofa and took her hand. It was a gesture both odd and welcome, and Corinne felt as though her heart was beating in sync with her sister's. Their palms were pressed together, and she couldn't tell if it was her pulse she felt beneath her fingers or Vivian's.

Russ smiled, tears welling in his eyes as he studied his two daughters. "Where do we begin?" he asked.

"We want to know all about you," Vivian said. "What your life's been like. Though," she glanced at her father, "I think we're a little afraid to hear about it. To hear everything you've been through when you should have been with us."

Everything she'd been through? She shrugged. "It was actually a pretty normal life," she said.

Ken shook his head. "I wouldn't call it that," he said. "Her parents are…they're nice people. Her father—at least the man she's always thought of as her father—"

"Jack Elliott," Russ said. "He's a fine professor, from all reports. I don't think he knew."

"He was deceived by her mother," Ken said. "Just like the rest of us."

"It…distresses me beyond words that you had to spend your life with a kidnapper," Russ said. "And she says she didn't kill Genevieve, but I don't think we'll ever know that for sure. She kept you, so it looks to me like she wanted a baby. I've been reading about women who long for a baby. They find a pregnant woman and cut the baby out of them."

Corinne was horrified by the thought. "Oh, I really don't think so," she said. "My mother isn't that sort of person. And she was only sixteen."

"How do you know what sort of person she was, Cor?" Ken asked. "Would you ever have guessed she could be involved in a mess like this to begin with? I think she was mentally ill back then. Who knows what she was capable of?"

"If she hadn't wanted you desperately, she could have found a way to get you to us," Vivian said. "Where you belonged. Where you still belong."

Vivian's eyes filled with tears again, and Corinne wondered if it could be true. Eve had stolen her, that much was known. Could she have intentionally killed her mother in order to take her? It was unthinkable.

"Well, I'll make sure she'll pay, one way or another," Russ said. "I can't believe the university's had her on staff—as a counselor, no less—for all these years."

I think she was good at it, Corinne wanted to say, but she had the feeling Ken would disagree with her again and she didn't want to hear it. You could be lousy at raising your own kids and still be great at helping others find their way.

"Listen, Corinne." Russ nodded to the briefcase at his side. "Do you want to see pictures?"

"Pictures?"

"Of Mom," Vivian said. "You won't believe how much you look like her. We both do."

"Yes," she said. "I tried to find pictures on the Internet, but could only find the one that's been on the news."

"You poor girl," Russ said, lifting the briefcase to his lap. "Reduced to finding pictures of your mother on the Internet. We should have gotten in touch sooner," he said, looking at Vivian, who nodded. "We needed to be sure, though. If Eve Elliott could lie about one thing, she could lie about a lot of things. I hope you understand why we didn't get in touch right away."

She opened her mouth to say she understood, but Ken beat her to it.

"Of course she does," he said.

Russell pulled a large, fat envelope from the briefcase and walked across the room to give it to her, his hand trembling. He touched her arm before pulling away, and she had the feeling he wanted to embrace her, to hold on to her forever. She smiled at him.

Vivian took the envelope from Corinne's hand. "Don't overwhelm her, Dad," she said. She pulled the messy stack of photographs out of the envelope and handed one to Corinne, leaning over to look at it with her. "This is a picture of Mom and Dad on their honeymoon," she said.

The picture had a yellow cast to it, but the redheaded woman was a combination of Vivian and herself. "You definitely got her hair," Vivian said. "Mine's more like Dad's."

"Like Dad's used to be." Russell offered a weak smile as he ran his hand over his thinning, graying hair.

"I never looked like anyone in my family," Corinne said in a near whisper. "Not even a little."

"And that was a good thing," Ken said with a laugh.

"*Ken,*" she said. "That's mean."

"You don't sound like a fan of the Elliotts," Russ said.

"Well, Jack is a nice guy," Ken said. "He can be kind of a buffoon. The perennial actor. And Dru is nice. Dru's really nice."

"Dru is your...sister?" Vivian asked.

Corinne nodded. "I thought she was my half sister, but now I realize we're not related at all," she said with some sadness. "She's great, though."

"Eve, on the other hand..." Ken looked at Corinne. "I don't know how much to say."

"Ken's never really liked my mother," she admitted.

"I had an instinct about her," Ken said. "And...well, you know how Corinne said she couldn't drive up to Charlottesville?"

Russ nodded.

"She's got a whole slew of fears. Some she's overcome and she's working on the rest of them. But I blame her mother for them."

"She was overprotective," Corinne said. "Pathologically over-protective. She made me afraid of the world. I'm much better than I used to be, though." She was worried she was sounding pathetic.

"At least she didn't neglect you," Vivian said. "That's what we were afraid of—that she was an incompetent mother."

"There are all kinds of incompetence," Ken said.

"You're a teacher, right?" Russ asked.

She nodded.

"Isn't that amazing?" he asked. "Your mother was a teacher all her adult life. She didn't need to work, but she loved teaching and wouldn't give it up."

"I love it, too," Corinne said.

"And next year she'll have a special position training other teachers in a reading program," Ken boasted. "As long as she can get the travel phobia under control."

"I can," she said. She wished he'd stop trotting out her fears in front of her brand-new father and sister. She was more than her phobias. They had always been Ken's focus, she realized. He liked to think of himself as her savior.

"She had to separate herself from her mother to grow up," Ken added.

"What does that mean, you separated yourself from her?" Russ asked.

"We're...basically estranged," she said. "We've hardly spoken for the past few years. She came here with my father...with Jack...right before she was arrested to tell me everything, and that was the first time we'd really talked in a long time." She winced, remembering that night. "If anything, she was *too* good a parent to me. Too protective. She was suffocating and even my therapist told me to break ties with her for a while."

The Russells were quiet, and Corinne wondered if the word *therapist,* used so easily in the Elliott household, might be taboo in theirs.

"Well." Russ shifted in his chair and let out a long sigh. She thought there were tears in his eyes again. "I'm so sorry, Corinne. I feel like I failed somehow. Like there was something I should have been able to do to save you."

"Dad, what could you have done?" Vivian looked at Corinne. "He's always asking himself the 'what-ifs'," she said. "What if he'd picked Mom up from the university that night? What if he—"

"I hated her walking in the parking lot at night," Russ said, "but she always insisted I was being silly. I was making too much out of it, she'd say. And then if I'd agreed to commute that girl's sentence right off the bat, maybe they would have freed Gen—"

"You couldn't do that, Dad," Vivian argued. "You couldn't give in to that kind of terrorism or you'd have people kidnapping other people left and right to get what they wanted."

"I just wish I could have spared you." Russell leaned forward in his chair, elbows on his knees, his gaze on Corinne. "I could have raised you the way you should have been raised."

"I think she turned out fine," Vivian said, as though she knew her well.

Corinne wondered how she and Vivian looked, sitting there like near-twins. They sat so close together, she was certain her hair was tangled with her sister's.

"I..." Russ reached into his briefcase again and pulled out a slim white envelope. "I want you to have this," he said, taking a few steps across the room to hand it to her. "I know this doesn't make up for all the lost years, but I would have sent you to the best private schools, like I did with Vivian. You would have had your pick of universities. So I want you to have this. And I'm giving it to you with Viv's blessing."

Vivian nodded. "Absolutely," she said.

Corinne opened the envelope and peered at a check made out in her name for three hundred thousand dollars.

She felt the color drain out of her face. "Oh, no," she said. "I can't possibly take this."

"You have to," Russ said. "Please don't be insulted by it. I know you're a teacher and your…Ken here is a reporter, and you're well able to support yourselves. That's not it. It's—"

"I went to all private schools," Vivian said. "And then to Sarah Lawrence and grad school. Dad would have done the same for you."

"I'm just not…comfortable with this," Corinne said.

"I'm sorry," Russ said. "I should have held off on giving it to you. I just…I want to give you everything I can." He smiled at her with such kindness. "Think about the money," he said. "You don't need to take it now. Just know it's yours whenever you want it."

"Thank you," she said. "That's so generous of you."

The men stayed in the living room, while Vivian helped her set the table.

"I've missed you," Vivian said, smiling. "I know you were raised with a sister and got to do all these simple sisterly things, like setting a table together." She nodded at the basket of croissants.

"But I never had that and I knew what I was missing. Even though I was so young when Mom was pregnant with you, I fantasized about all the things we'd do together. They even let me help decide what to name you."

"What was I going to be named?"

"Lara," she said.

Corinne tried to imagine living her whole life with that name. "Pretty," she said. She started back to the kitchen, but Vivian caught her arm. "You have to understand something about Dad." She smiled. "He's like a lot of guys. He doesn't really know how to express his emotions, so he does it with money. With gifts. We thought you were dead, and we're so glad you're not, so now he wants to give you the world. It's the only way he knows to show that he loves you."

"He doesn't even *know* me yet," she said.

"That doesn't matter. You're his daughter. That's enough for him."

They'd given her several pictures of Genevieve to keep, and she carried them to the table and spread them out around her plate, unable to stop looking at her. Russ talked about the first time he saw her. He'd been the escort of another young woman at a country club dance, but he couldn't take his eyes off Genevieve. She wore a royal-blue dress, and between that and her red hair, he could find her anyplace in the room. His own date grew annoyed at him for his in-attention to her. The next day, he called Genevieve and asked her out. Their first date was to the movies, where they saw *Midnight Cowboy,* and she'd cried inconsolably. He'd held her hand to comfort her and knew he wanted to be with a woman so free with her emotions.

"The opposite of me," Russ said, "as Viv will tell you. I needed someone different from me to express that part of myself. When she was gone…" He ran a finger around the rim of his glass. "I withdrew for a long time. Just focused on work and on Vivvie. It was like I didn't know how to operate in the world without Genevieve. I was only half a person."

Vivian was wrong about her father. He did, too, know how to express his emotions. He was doing so right now in a way that brought tears to Corinne's eyes.

"And you didn't know what had happened to her," she said. "Or if she was dead or alive. That must have made it so much harder for you."

"Exactly," he said. No one said it, but everyone knew who was to blame for his grief. "When a year had passed, I assumed she had…that she was dead. That they'd killed her. Along with our unborn baby. With you." He tried to smile at her, but the sadness in his face was too deep and too old. She wanted to wrap her arms around him. Her real father. In a stubborn corner of her heart, though, she felt the pinch of guilt, as if she were cheating on a lover, enamored by the newness of the affair. She remembered Jack's face when he left the house with Eve and the police. She pictured her mother carefully clipping newspaper articles for her, designed to protect and advise. She saw her vivacious sister, short and sturdy in comparison to the lithe Vivian. Her heart twisted in her chest. Their love for her was based on years of living together and had remained unchanged, despite her belligerent withdrawal from them. Could she live long enough to have that kind of love with Russ and Vivian? Why didn't she feel the instantaneous sort of love they seemed so capable of?

"It destroyed me, the kidnapping," Russ continued. "It destroyed my life. If it hadn't been that Vivvie needed me, I'm not sure if I would have gone on, despite my responsibilities to the state. This is between us, of course." He looked from her to Ken, and they both nodded.

"But you did go on, Dad," Vivian said. "You were a great governor."

"I'm good at losing myself in my work," he said.

Vivian laughed. "For sure."

"My sadness turned to a righteous anger over time," he said. "I wanted to kill those guys. I'm not the killing type. I—"

"He carries ants outside instead of killing them," Vivian said, and Corinne laughed.

"Right. But if I'd seen one of those men and had a gun in my hand, I would have done it. When they caught Timothy Gleason…" He shook his head. "I would love to have a chance to strangle the life out of him. Then your…so-called mother shows up with her version of what happened." He balled his hands into fists and growled, a sound that seemed to rise up from his toes. "I think about your life and how different it was from the way it should have been."

"Dad, you just have to be thankful that she's—that Corinne is alive and well," Vivian said, and Corinne had the feeling this was an ongoing conversation between father and daughter.

"I am," he said, "but that doesn't stop me from wanting to see Eve Elliott pay for what she did. Plus, she had the gall to work at the university while I've been president!" He shook his head. "Just unbelievable."

"Yes," Ken agreed, "like she was playing a game of cat and mouse."

"And *winning*," Russ agreed. "But she's not winning now." He looked at Corinne. "You were raised by the woman who was responsible for your mother's death," he said, "but don't worry. My lawyer is going to make sure she pays for this for the rest of her life. The only job she'll ever hold from this day forward is making license plates."

Chapter Sixty

JACK CALLED HER ON THE DAY SHE RETURNED TO WORK. Ken was at the store and Corinne stared at the caller ID display on the bedroom phone for a moment before deciding to answer it.

"Finally!" Jack said when she picked up the phone. "I was afraid Ken was never going to let me speak to you again."

"Have you been calling?" she asked as she sat down on the bed. She hadn't realized Ken had been censoring all of her calls, not just those from the media.

"About a half-dozen times," he said. "I've been down to Raleigh twice to visit Mom and I asked if I could stay with you and Ken. He said no, but I wasn't sure if he'd even checked with you or not."

She was glad Ken hadn't told her. She would have had a hard time telling Jack he couldn't stay with them. "He didn't," she said.

"Well, how are you?" he asked. "Have you gone back to work?"

"I'm okay." She thought of telling him about her visit with Russ and Vivian, but that could only hurt him. "And I went back today."

"Was it all right?"

Define "all right," she wanted to say. A couple of reporters stood across the street from the school that morning, filming her as she got out of her car and walked to the entrance. Students and faculty alike talked about her behind her back. She caught them staring. Whispering. Her strange life no longer belonged to her alone.

"It was fine," she said.

He paused. "Mom really wants to see you, Cory," he said finally. "She *needs* to see you."

"She's not my mother," Corinne said.

Jack was quiet. "She loves you as much as any mother could love a daughter."

"Dad, do you realize that she might have killed my real mother and cut me out of her?"

"*What?* Who the hell put that idea in your head?"

"Maybe it's true," she said. "How can we believe anything she says at this point?"

"She's telling the truth," he said. "Did Ken suggest she might have killed—"

"No," she interrupted him. "Why do you always blame Ken for everything?"

"He's your keeper, isn't he?" Jack asked. "Your defender and protector?"

"Ken protects me, just like you're trying to protect Mom. The big difference is I'm not a felon."

"No," Jack said, "you're a selfish little girl."

His words stung, and she was suddenly afraid of losing him. "You've stopped loving me," she said.

"I love you with all my heart, Cory," he said. "But it's time you took responsibility for who you are, all right? Yes, your mother was overprotective. You got dealt some crappy cards. But you're the one who has to decide how to play them."

"So what am I supposed to do? Just forgive her for killing my mother and stealing me from my family?"

"She didn't kill your mother. She made some extremely poor decisions. Are you the same person you were when you were sixteen?"

"I would never have made the choices she made."

"Well, maybe that has something to do with the upbringing you had in our terrible substitute for your real family."

Touché, she thought.

"Dad, I'm pregnant, have you forgotten that? When I think about my baby, and I imagine what it would be like to be kidnapped and pregnant…" She *couldn't* imagine it. It was too awful.

"I know this must be terribly hard for you, Cory, but you need to think for yourself for once," he said. "You believe Ken saved you from your mother's overprotectiveness, but he just substituted his set of rules for hers. Not only that, but he doesn't have one one-hundredth of the love for you that your mother does. He's self-serving. He cut you off from us so he could control you himself. Can't you see that? You complained that Eve didn't let you grow up. Well, you still haven't grown up, and it's about time you do."

She hung up on him, then slammed the phone down on the bed. What was with her father? *Terribly hard for her?* An understatement. He had no idea how it felt to suddenly discover you were not who you thought you were. He was so busy defending Eve that he'd forgotten who had paid the dearest price for her crimes.

The phone rang again after a few minutes, and this time the caller ID display read *Virginia.* It had to be either Dru or Russ. She lifted the receiver to her ear.

"Why did you hang up on Dad?" Dru asked.

"He made me angry," Corinne said. "That's why."

"Well, that's a good way to resolve a conflict," Dru said.

"This is a conflict with no possible resolution, Dru," she said. "Are you at the house?"

"No. Dad called to say you hung up on him."

"And he said you should call me to tell me Eve Elliott needs to see me, right?"

Dru paused. "Do you always call her Eve Elliott now?" she asked. "That's so cold."

"It helps me keep some emotional distance."

"I wish you'd go see her," Dru said. "She wants to see you. I'll come down there and go with you if you're afraid. Is it a bad drive from where you live?"

Corinne hesitated. All drives were "bad drives" these days, but it was not that far and she didn't want to admit to Dru that she couldn't make it by herself. But walk into a jail? She shuddered. Unimaginable. "It's bad enough," she said.

"She hasn't gotten her meds yet," Dru said.

Corinne was surprised by her own indignation. "Why not?" she said. "They have to provide medication to a prisoner who needs it, don't they?"

"Yes, but she needs some kind of approval that's taking too long, so she's flaring really badly," Dru said. "You're *right there*, Cory. Please go see her."

"No, and if you keep asking me, I'll hang up on you, too."

"All right, all right," Dru said tiredly. "I won't ask you any more. It's just that…" Dru fell suddenly silent.

"Dru?" Corinne prompted her.

"They're…" Dru was crying, unable to get the words out.

Corinne knew how her little sister looked when she cried—her eyes scrunched up, her mouth open in an little inverted U-shape. It always broke her heart.

"Oh, Dru, honey, what?" It didn't matter what Dru was crying about; her own tears started in sympathy for her.

"I'm so scared, Cory," Dru managed to say. "They're building a huge case against Mom. I miss her so much, and she's going to be in prison forever. Maybe the rest of her life." Her voice caught on a sob.

Dru was right. The case against their mother was strong and getting stronger by the day. While Vivian's e-mails contained family trees bearing the names of relatives anxious to meet her, Russ's were serious and angry, filled with vitriol toward Eve and descriptions of evidence his attorney planned to use against her.

"I'm sorry," Dru said. "I know you probably feel she *should* be there forever. I might feel the same way if I were you. But she's such a good person. CeeCee Wilkes deserves to be in jail, but Eve Elliott doesn't."

Corinne swallowed her tears. "They're one and the same person, Dru," she said. "That's the problem."

The night of Dru's call, the WIGH news showed a tape of Eve limping from a police car into a building. There was resignation in her face, as though she knew she deserved whatever suffering she had to endure. Corinne was mesmerized by the footage, but Ken picked up the remote.

"We don't need to see this," he said.

She grabbed his hand. "No," she said. "I want to."

Her mother's wrists looked as swollen as Corinne had ever seen them. Thank God, the guards no longer had handcuffs on her. Eve held her hands close to her body, the way she did when she needed to protect them from bumping into anything. A guard grabbed her arm to either help or hasten her up the steps into the building, and Corinne saw her mother flinch with pain. Someone else might not have noticed it, but Corinne had seen that quick alteration of her features too often to miss it.

The image played over and over again in her mind as she lay in bed that night. She would never sleep. Finally, at two in the morning, she shook Ken's shoulder.

He rolled over to look at her. "What's the matter?" He sat up quickly. "The baby?"

She had the sudden, horrible feeling that he would welcome a miscarriage. "No," she said. "I've decided I want to see my mother."

Ken groaned. "Your mother is dead," he said.

"Stop that," she said, annoyed. "You know who I'm talking about."

"Why in God's name do you want to see her? It's just going to make you feel more...conflicted about this whole mess."

"I guess I'm hoping it will make me feel *less* conflicted."

"It's a bad idea."

"I need to understand why she did what she did," she said. "I want to see her, Ken."

He sighed. "Be my guest."

"Will you take me tomorrow? It's Saturday. I don't have to work."

"I told you I think it's a bad idea. How can you expect me to take you if I think it's wrong for you?"

"Because you love me," she said. "Because I want to go and you know I can't drive there alone."

Ken stared at the ceiling. "What do you plan to say to her?"

"I don't know. All I know is that I can't stand seeing those pictures of her on TV."

"Even felons can look like vulnerable human beings," Ken said. "Ted Bundy looked like the boy next door."

"She isn't Ted Bundy," she said, and to her own surprise, started to cry.

Ken reached over to pull her into his arms. He stroked her hair for a moment, then sighed. "Okay," he relented. "I'll take you tomorrow."

Chapter Sixty-One

NEITHER SHE NOR KEN SAID A WORD DURING THE DRIVE TO the jail. He might have been angry with her or disappointed or simply tired. She didn't care. Her mind was on the visit that lay ahead of her. It had been four weeks since she'd seen her mother. The image of her limping from the police car into the building, flinching as the guard grabbed her arm, played repeatedly in her mind. She felt like crying, but she didn't want to cry. She didn't want to give her mother the gift of caring that much. She'd spent years hardening her heart to Eve Elliott. She needed to be tough with her today. All she wanted was information that would help her understand why everything had happened the way it did.

The guard at the jail wouldn't let her take her purse into the visiting area with her, so she left it in the car with Ken. He hadn't offered to go in with her, and that was just as well. She didn't want him there, even though she could feel her heart speeding up as she sat behind the Plexiglas partition, waiting, hands tightly folded in her lap.

Then she saw her. She was in a wheelchair, being pushed by a guard. She'd aged in the last month. She was only forty-three, but she looked a decade older. When she spotted Corinne, she tipped her head back to say something to the guard, who stopped pushing her. Then she stood up and limped over to the booth.

Mommy. The word rose in her throat and she choked it back. Eve smiled at her as she sat down, and Corinne saw some of the mother she'd always known in that smile. Eve nodded toward the phone as she picked up the receiver on her side.

"I'm so happy to see you, Cory," she said.

"You look like you're in a lot of pain," Corinne said.

Her mother shrugged. "It's not too bad. I'll get my medication soon."

"I don't understand how they can keep it from you," Corinne said. "Isn't that cruel and unusual punishment?"

"Something with the paperwork." Her mother tucked a lock of her dark hair behind one ear. "I'm sure I'll be better once I get it. There's a little too much stress in my life at the moment. And I know there's been way too much in yours, too," she added. "Dru told me you've met Irving Russell and his daughter."

"I need to understand why you did what you did." Corinne didn't want to get caught up in a conversation about the Russells.

Her mother looked confused. "You mean why I turned myself in?"

"No, Mother. I mean why you kidnapped a woman and stole her baby. Stole *me.*"

Her mother flexed her free hand, open, closed, open again. "From my adult perspective, it's even hard for me to understand," she said. "And I doubt I can make you understand. All I can do is tell you."

"Then tell me."

Her mother licked her lips, which looked dry and chapped. "I've thought a lot about it over the years," she said. "About why I let myself get involved in the whole mess." She studied her swollen knuckles. "I think the bottom line is that I wanted to be loved." She looked through the glass at Corinne. "You know I lost my mother when I was twelve and then spent time in foster homes, right?"

Corinne nodded. She'd known that once but had forgotten.

"My own mother was very loving and…just a wonderful mom," her mother said. "When she died, I felt lonely for someone who would love me the way she did. The one person who treasured me unconditionally was gone." She looked past Corinne's head as though she could see into the past. "When I graduated from high school at sixteen, I went to work as a waitress in a little coffee shop in Chapel Hill."

"In Chapel Hill?" Corinne asked. "When you brought me to school at Carolina, you said you'd never been there before."

"One of many lies I told to cover my tracks," her mother said. "So, I worked as a waitress. I'd never had a boyfriend and I was very…needy. I don't think I could have put it into words at the time, but I was desperate to have someone love me. Validate me."

Corinne tried to imagine what it would be like to move from twelve to sixteen feeling love from no one. That was one thing she'd been sure of: love. Sure enough of it that she could, at times, abuse it and know it would still be there for her.

"One day, Tim Gleason came into the coffee shop," her mother said. "He was twenty-two to my sixteen. He was attentive to me. He took me out and bought me things and was fun to be with. He told me he loved me. No one had said those three words to me since my mother." Her mother frowned. "I'm not making excuses for anything I did, Cory. I'm just trying to explain why I did it."

Corinne nodded. "Go on," she said.

"He made me feel beautiful and smart and…happy. I felt so happy. Shortly after I met him, I received a package containing five thousand dollars in cash."

"From him?" Corinne was confused.

"I'm sure it was, because his family was wealthy, but he would never tell me. Anyhow, that would have been plenty for me to go to Carolina and not have to work. He'd encouraged me to go and knew I was trying to save enough money to do that. So you can see that he was manipulating me in many different ways."

Corinne nodded.

"Then he started talking to me about his sister, Andie," her mother said. She told Corinne how Tim Gleason had lied to her about Andie's murder of the photographer. "He asked me if I could do a favor for him and his brother and warned me it would be dangerous. They wanted to save their sister the only way they could think of. First I said no, but I was so—"

"No to what?" Corinne cut her off. "What did he ask you to do, exactly? I don't understand."

"He asked me to help with the kidnapping of Governor Russell's wife. Not the actual kidnapping, but guarding her in that little cabin outside New Bern while he and Marty negotiated with Governor Russell."

"And you said yes?" Corinne couldn't picture anyone in her right mind agreeing to the scheme. But then, she wasn't sixteen years old and desperate for love, smitten by someone who seemed to adore her.

"I did. He made it sound neat and simple. I was weak then. I needed him and would do anything I could to please him. To keep him, I guess. I don't think I knew what I was getting into until they actually brought...Genevieve to the cabin and I realized she was not a character in a play but a real, live human being. And she was pregnant." Her mother looked into her eyes. "I'm so sorry, Cory," she said.

Corinne turned her head away from her, afraid she was going to cry. What more was there for either of them to say? She already knew the rest of the story. She wanted it to end differently. She wanted to change the unchangeable.

"Did you keep me to have someone to love you?" she asked after a moment.

Her mother bit her lip and looked down at the counter in front of her. "Not consciously," she said. "All I know is that I was desperate to keep you safe. Your mother said to me, 'Don't let her die,' and I—"

"She did?" Corinne asked. She felt soft inside, hearing the only words her biological mother may ever have spoken about her.

"Yes," her mother said. "When she knew she was dying...and I believe she knew it...she asked me not to let you die. I fell in love with you very quickly. I'd helped bring you into the world and survive your first few days of life. It gave me a huge emotional attachment to you. I was barely past the age of needing a teddy bear to cuddle with, and you were so much better than that." She smiled. "It's hard to describe how desperately I needed to keep you safe. I wanted to be with you every single moment to make sure you were still breathing. I stayed awake all night sometimes to make sure you were. You were so many things to me. You were the most important and most priceless thing in my world. And you were my responsibility. I owed it to your mother to keep you safe. I know I went overboard, honey. I know I created fears in you and I'm so sorry for that. Maybe you needed to cut yourself off from me to make your own path. Maybe that was the right thing for you to do, no matter how hard it's been for me."

"Why didn't the guy—Timothy Gleason—tell the police about you? Why did he protect you?"

"I don't know. Maybe he developed a conscience somewhere along the line and knew he'd been wrong for involving me in the first place. I just don't know."

"You could have stayed quiet," Corinne said. "You didn't need to admit to anything."

"I had to," her mother said simply.

"But, Mom," Corinne said, "how will you survive this? You can't go to prison. You're sick. They won't give you your medication."

"I'm all right, honey. I'll get my meds and I'll be okay." Her mother paused for a moment. "Tell me what's going on with *you*," she asked.

Corinne couldn't shift gears that quickly. She looked down at the counter, uncertain what to say.

"You mean besides learning I'm not who I thought I was?" she asked.

Her mother gave her a rueful smile. "I guess there isn't much room for anything else, is there," she acknowledged.

"Well, actually, there is," Corinne said suddenly. "I pressed Ken to let us set a date. And guess what? He told me he never got divorced from Felicia. His wife." The words spilled out of her, and she was surprised to be taking her mother into her confidence.

"What?" Her mother's mouth fell open in disbelief. "Oh, honey. Do you mean he's been lying to you all this time?"

"Lying through the omission of some crucial information," she said. "He said she was sick and it would have been too hard on her if he divorced her."

"How about too hard on you if he didn't?" Her mother looked angry. "Oh, Cory, I'm sorry. I know how it feels to be betrayed by the man you love."

"I want to have this baby, Mom."

"Will you still marry him?"

Corinne hesitated. Did she even love him anymore? She wasn't sure she could ever live alone, with no one to turn to when she needed to drive more than a few blocks from her house. She started to say that she needed him, but wasn't it need that had pulled her mother to Timothy Gleason? She thought of Ken waiting outside in the car and was filled with resentment.

"I'm so afraid of being alone," she said.

"Cory," her mother said, "as long as I'm alive, you'll never be alone."

Her mother pressed her palm against the Plexiglas, and almost without thinking, Corinne lifted her own hand and pressed it to the glass as well. Her hand looked smooth and youthful against the misshapened knuckles and swollen wrist of her mother's. Aside from that, though, their hands were a perfect fit.

Chapter Sixty-Two

"SO, ARE YOU GOING TO TELL ME HOW SHE'S DOING?" KEN said. They'd driven a mile from the jail and neither of them had said a word.

Corinne hesitated. "It was hard to see her there," she said. "Locked up like that."

"Did you have to talk to her through Plexiglas?"

She nodded. "That was hard, too." She thought of telling him about the wheelchair, the swollen knuckles, but didn't bother. She didn't feel like telling him anything at all.

"She's where she belongs. You know that, don't you?"

"Ken." She looked at him. "I want some...time apart."

"From your mother?"

"No. From you."

He stared straight ahead at the road, the muscles tight in his jaw. "I swear," he said. "You spend two minutes with her and she's got you back in her clutches."

"It doesn't have anything to do with her," she said, although she knew it did. She'd just witnessed courage. Maybe she didn't have Eve Elliott's blood in her, but surely she'd picked up some of that courage along the way.

"I'm going to get a divorce," he said. "I told you that. It will only be a matter of weeks. Then we can get married whenever you want."

"That's not it."

"What is it then?"

"You weren't honest with me."

"I've been extremely good for you, Corinne. How many other men would have put up with your fears?"

"I won't stay with you out of need," she said.

"What are you going to do about the baby?"

"My mother raised me alone in the beginning."

"Oh, right, and look how great you turned out."

"Fuck you."

"Well, that's a first. The f-word coming out of Corinne Elliott's mouth."

She wished she could tell him to let her out of the car right there, but she couldn't. They were too far from home.

"I'm done talking about this," she said.

"Do you expect me to move out?" he asked.

"Yes."

"The house is in both our names."

"I'll buy you out," she said. She would find a way. Russ would certainly give her the money, but she wanted to do it on her own.

"I'm not leaving," he said. "You'll make me move all my stuff out and then the next thing I know, you'll call me in the middle of the night to say you hear a noise. And I'll have to drag myself back over there to rescue you."

"Well, if I've been that hard to live with, you should be happy to go."

"Corinne." He sounded frustrated. "I love you," he said. "This is silly. Let's get married and have this baby and—"

"No."

"Come on, Cor. You're not thinking straight. Your mother did some number on—"

"Let me out."

"What?" He laughed, but there was no mirth in the sound.

They were less than two miles from their house. Two measly miles. She could manage. "Stop the car and let me out," she said. "I don't want to be with you anymore."

He pulled over to the curb and she got out of the car. She watched him drive away, amazed he would actually leave her there. She looked at the street stretching ahead of her into the distance and felt nauseous. It was hard to swallow around the knot in her throat.

One foot in front of the other, she told herself as she started to walk. *Just keep going.*

She thought of her mother getting out of the wheelchair to walk to the little cubby in the jail. She hadn't wanted Corinne to see her infirmity or her pain. She'd always been that way; it was another way she protected her family.

Corinne crossed the street, one hand on her belly, vowing never to protect her own children from life's hard truths. She'd help her children cope with reality rather than hide it from them.

What was it like, she wondered, to spend your adolescence in foster homes, never knowing how long you'd be in any one place? If you felt love at all, you knew it was transitory. You could count on no one for the long haul. No one to stick with you when you were sick or grumpy or mean. You'd just get kicked out. Move on to another place where the only thing you could count on was change.

Her mother had been on her own at sixteen, trying to carve out her place in the world with no one to guide her. For the first time in her life, Corinne felt spoiled. Images raced through her mind. Christmases with everything she'd asked for under the tree. What had her parents gone without so that, for one day each year, she and Dru could have anything they wanted? She saw her mother tucking her into bed at night. Reading to her, holding her on her lap when she was very small, turning the pages with her. She remembered how the paper felt, the musky smell of her mother's shampoo. The scent filled her nostrils even now as she walked down the street, bringing with it the surprise of tears. She brushed them away with her fingers, but they kept flowing. If Ken pulled up next to her in his car, she wouldn't even notice him.

She'd been overprotected, yes. Smothered, yes. There were worse things than being smothered with love.

She looked up to see that her house was less than a hundred yards in front of her, and she broke into a run. She raced up the front steps and turned her key in the lock, and knew she was home now, in more ways than one.

Chapter Sixty-Three

"I'LL TAKE TIME OFF FROM WORK AND COME STAY WITH you," Dru said over the phone. Corinne had called her the minute she walked in the house, breathless and a bit euphoric from her walk home alone. She'd told Dru that she'd asked Ken to leave, but had not yet mentioned her visit with their mother.

"Thanks," she said, "but I'll be all right." She hoped she wasn't kidding herself. The house felt so empty it echoed. Although she'd been alone in the house plenty of times in the late afternoon, this felt different. She knew he wasn't coming back tonight. He might be waiting for her to call and beg him to come home, but she wouldn't do that. She would ask a friend to stay with her before she'd ask Ken to return.

"I suddenly feel…" Corinne hesitated, searching for the word. "Well, *scared,* to begin with." She laughed. "But safe, in a way. I feel like the baby and I are safe. I don't have to fight to have this baby anymore. It's my decision and I don't have to justify it to anyone."

"That's so good, Cory," Dru said.

"I'm going to call a security company tomorrow and have them install an alarm," Corinne said. "I just have to get through tonight."

"Well, we can talk on the phone all night then," Dru said. "It will be like I'm there with you."

"You're the best sister."

"You should have the locks changed, too," Dru said.

"I don't think Ken would try to get in or anything."

"It's not that. I was just thinking that if he *did* come in, it would scare you if you weren't expecting him."

"You're right," Corinne said. She pulled the shade on the kitchen window. "I want to have this baby, Dru, so Ken's going to be in my life one way or another. Maybe he can change. Maybe we should go to counseling. But I don't want him back if he's going to smother me again. Why couldn't I see that he was doing the same thing to me that Mom did?"

"You were too close to see it," Dru said.

"Could you?"

Dru hesitated. "I could see that he needed you to need him," she said. "Think about it. His ex-wife—his wife, actually, I guess—still needs him, according to Ken. So he stayed married to her."

"He told me I was trying to deal with too many of my fears too quickly," Corinne said, angry with him all over again.

"I know you've been doing it on your own, Cor," Dru said. "But maybe it's time to get some help."

"I know." Ken had talked her out of seeing a therapist and she'd agreed with him. Her mother being a therapist had colored her confidence in any other therapist's ability to help her. "I don't want to have a child and screw her up. I don't want to pass my fears along to her. Or him."

"You won't," Dru said. "You're going to be the best mother."

For a moment, neither of them spoke.

"So," Dru broke the silence. "You told me all about Ken letting you out of the car and you walking home and everything, and nothing about seeing Mom. How was it?"

Corinne pictured the guard pushing her mother into the visiting area in the wheelchair.

"She doesn't belong there," she said.

"Whew." Dru let out her breath. "I'm glad to hear you say that."

"She doesn't," Corinne repeated. "She did some terrible things, Dru, and I guess she needs to pay in some way, but not this way. This is brutal. What's her lawyer doing to get her out of there?"

Dru sighed. "It's not going to be easy," she said. "President Russell has a whole legal firm working on it. Dad and I met with her attorney yesterday. We're going to have a bunch of character witnesses, including me."

"That's good."

"Mom committed so many crimes," Dru said, "I lost track of them while her attorney was going through them, and she's totally guilty of every one of them. She confessed to everything, which I guess was a mistake."

"Maybe a mistake in terms of her defense, but not a mistake for her conscience," Corinne said.

Dru hesitated again. "You sound like the sister I knew years ago," she said finally. "I wish you'd dumped Ken long before now."

"It's not Ken," Corinne said. "It was seeing Mom. Seeing how…I don't know, Dru. She looks bad and she's obviously in a lot of pain. She feels terrible for hurting everyone but…I think this has freed her somehow. It's given her a kind of peace. I just felt it from her." She thought of her hand pressed against the Plexiglas. "I realized how much I love her," she said. "I know she raised me the best way she knew how."

"Oh my God!" Dru said. "Do you mean that, Cory?"

"I do." Corinne couldn't help but smile at her sister's enthusiasm.

"I'm so relieved to hear you say that!" Dru said. "Would you… this might not be fair to ask."

"What?"

"Would you be a character witness for her?"

"Oh, Dru, I can't," she said. Just the thought of sitting trapped on the witness stand was enough to make her heart gallop.

"Mental-healthwise?" Dru asked.

"Yes." She paused. "But also…no matter how I feel about her, she's still responsible for my biological mother's death and for taking me from my family."

"I know," Dru said. "Can you talk to President Russell, though?" she asked. "Mom's attorney said that he can influence the case. He has a lot of clout and he's the one pushing to keep her in prison for a long, long time. Can you talk to him about it?"

Corinne cringed at the thought. She was embarrassed to realize that she was intimidated by him.

"I could talk to Vivian about it," she said.

"Well, maybe she could talk to her father, then?" Dru asked.

"Maybe," she said. "They really think Mom is scum, though."

"You can't blame them," Dru said. "But I think it's worth a try, don't you?"

A siren sounded in the distance and somewhere nearby, a dog barked. It was growing dark outside, and she felt the anxiety creeping in. She wished she *could* keep Dru on the phone all night long.

"I'll call her tonight," she said in a fit of courage. "Let me get off and I'll do it right now."

She locked every window and pushed a chair in front of the back door with the broken dead-bolt lock. Then she picked up the phone to call Vivian, but cowardice overcame her. How could she word her request? And she'd be putting Vivian on the spot. She would e-mail her instead. It would be easier on both of them.

Chapter Sixty-Four

Dear Vivian,
I visited my mother—Eve Elliott—today. She's in pain from rheumatoid arthritis and hasn't yet received her medication. It's awkward to describe to you how I felt. She's the only mother I've ever known. I certainly don't condone what she did, but she was a good mother to me. I know I didn't make her sound that way when you and your father were here. I was caught up in the horror of learning what she'd done and in the realization that I'd been kidnapped and kept from my biological family. But she did her best to raise me well. She was a good therapist at the university and helped a lot of young people over the years. She's been a good citizen—maybe even a model citizen. I'm writing to ask you and your father to take it easy on her. Remember she was a juvenile when your mother died.
Corinne

Dear Corinne,
I've thought about your e-mail and how to respond to it all day. I've reread what you wrote several times, trying to

imagine how you must feel. I'm sorry to say, I can't get past my own emotions to really put myself in your shoes. I know you didn't know our mother, so you can't get in touch with what it was like to lose her, but try to imagine losing someone else you love—your sister, perhaps?—in a terrible way.

I guess you can see that I can't let go of my anger toward Timothy Gleason or your mother. They were in it together. Your mother has said as much. She may have been "only" sixteen, but she was old enough to know right from wrong, and she made the wrong—and very illegal—decision at every turn. (By the way, sixteen is NOT considered a minor in the North Carolina legal system, so that argument is moot.) People have to pay for the choices they make. It doesn't matter whether they're someone's mother. It doesn't matter if they have a terrible illness. That doesn't exempt them from paying their debt to society. I could never share your e-mail with Dad. It would hurt him to know you feel this way. He adored my mother. He never remarried or seriously dated anyone after her death. He devoted himself to taking care of me and grieving for her. Even though I can somewhat understand your feelings, he would never be able to and I don't want to say anything to him to make him dislike you. He thinks you're beautiful and perfect.

So, sisters can disagree and still love each other, right? I feel lucky to finally have a sister with whom I can disagree!
Love, Vivian

Chapter Sixty-Five

"DRU TOLD ME YOU ASKED KEN TO LEAVE." HER MOTHER sat on the other side of the Plexiglas, the phone to her ear. She'd had her first injection of her medication and already looked a little better.

"I did," Corinne said.

"How are you managing alone?"

"So far, so good. I now have the most intricate alarm system on the block. And I changed all my locks."

Ken had come back the night before, ostensibly to pick up more of his things, but really to beg her to take him back. The divorce from Felicia would be final in a couple of weeks, he said. They could be married the next day if she wanted. But although she'd had to have a friend do her grocery shopping for her, and she'd had to take a taxi to the jail rather than drive, she wasn't going to budge.

"I'm proud of you, Cory," her mother said.

"I think I'm ready to see a therapist," Corinne said. "I'm starting a new position in September and it involves travel around Wake County and I want to do it, but I don't see how I can if I can't even drive to the grocery store."

Her mother nodded with a smile. "Good for you," she said. "What's the new position? And how will the baby fit into taking a new job?"

Corinne described the job and the child-care arrangements she was looking into for the baby. "I'm scared I can't pull this off," she said.

"Talk about stress," her mother agreed. "But I think it's great you're giving it a try and great that you're planning to find a therapist. You want someone who—" She stopped herself. "Do you want me to tell you what I think you need or let you figure it out on your own?" she asked.

Corinne smiled. "Good catch, Mom," she said. "But please tell me. All I know is that I don't want to have to go back through my childhood and pick apart every little incident, like I did with the woman I saw when I was in college. Especially now that the whole world knows how my childhood started."

"You're right," her mother said. "You don't need that. You need someone who'll work fast and focus on your fears. You're very strong right now and you need someone who will make good use of your strength."

Corinne recognized her mother's "therapist voice," and for the first time in years, she didn't recoil from it.

"So how do I find someone?" she asked.

"Call Valerie," she said, referring to a family friend who was also a student counselor at the university. "Ask her to do a little research to find someone for you in Raleigh."

"Can I get well enough by next September?" she asked. "I've been so screwed up for so long."

"You're not screwed up, honey," her mother said. "Not in the least. You have something to work out. Everybody has some issue to work out. Yours just gets in the way more than most. And look at all you've accomplished in spite of it. You'll need to work hard. The therapist won't be a magician, but if you get the right one and you put your mind to the task, you can do it." Her mother looked delighted to be giving her guidance. She switched the phone from one hand to the other. Corinne knew that her hands ached when she held the phone too long. "Here's my two cents' worth of advice for now," she said. "Can you think of a time you felt really brave?"

"No." She laughed.

"A time when you felt self-confident and in control?" Her mother wasn't taking no for an answer.

Corinne leaned her head back and studied the ceiling, thinking. "In the classroom," she said. "I know what I'm doing in front of twenty kids."

Her mother smiled. "That would have most people shaking in their boots," she said.

"I love it," Corinne said, and she meant it.

"The next time you're afraid of something, remember how you feel in front of a class of kids. Remember everything about it. How the classroom smells and sounds and especially that calm feeling you have inside."

"It's more like an excitement," Corinne corrected her. "A good excitement."

"Even better. Remember that positive excitement you feel and try to carry that feeling with you into the new situation. Think of this as a mantra—'Carry the confidence.' Say that to yourself when you're afraid of something, and let it remind you of how you feel in front of a class of kids."

"Hmm," Corinne said. "Is this advice from Counseling One-O-One?"

Her mother shook her head. "It's something I learned way before I was in college," she said. She grew quiet, her smile fading.

"Mom?" Corinne didn't like the sudden change in her.

"Oh, Cory," her mother said.

"What's the matter?"

Her mother let out a sigh. "Of all the skills and techniques I learned as a counselor, that one…" She hesitated again.

"What's wrong?" Corinne asked.

"I've used this technique for so long, I'd forgotten where I learned it," her mother said finally. "Before I helped kidnap Genevieve…your mother…Tim and Marty Gleason and I spent the night with some friends of theirs who were living underground, for a reason I never did know. The woman—her name was Naomi—talked to me about guarding your mother. I said I was afraid and she told me to think about a time I felt brave and take that feeling into the situation with me. It worked. It helped."

Corinne leaned away from the Plexiglas, horrified.

"Of course, since that time, I've learned much more about the technique," her mother said. "I've learned to make it much more elegant, but the basics are still the same. Take that old calm, confident feeling with you into the new situation. I used it or a variant of it with clients all the time." She knit her eyebrows, looking hard at Corinne. "I used it for evil during the kidnapping," she said. "Now you can use it for good."

The idea sounded more palatable when put that way. "I'll try," she said. "When you used it for…the kidnapping, what did you choose as the time you felt brave?"

"Staying with my mother while she died."

"Oh, Mom. You were only…twelve?"

Her mother nodded. "I was brave then," she said. "And that's the feeling I'm using to get me through every day in here."

Corinne stared at her small, courageous mother. There was so much about her she didn't know. So much she'd never taken the time to know. What if her mother was locked up forever and she never got the chance?

Chapter Sixty-Six

A FEDEX DELIVERY WOMAN WAS ON THE FRONT STEPS OF the house when Corinne got out of the taxi after visiting her mother.

"Glad I caught you," the woman said as Corinne walked toward her. "You need to sign for this." She held out a package about the size of a shoe box. Corinne noticed the Charlottesville return address as she signed the form.

"Thanks," she said, handing the clipboard back to the woman.

She carried the package into the house and opened it in the kitchen. Inside were three small boxes and an envelope. In the envelope was a short note from Irving Russell and a check for three thousand dollars.

If you won't take your money in one lump sum, I hope you'll take it in bits and pieces, he'd written. *The contents of the boxes belonged to your mother.*

For a brief, surreal moment, she felt perplexed over how he had gotten hold of anything belonging to her mother. Then she realized he was referring to Genevieve.

She opened the first box to find an emerald-and-diamond ring.

The second held a sapphire necklace. The third, a strand of seed pearls. The jewelry was exquisite, and she spread it out on the ceramic tile top of the kitchen table. She studied it for a while, wondering if she could ever wear it. She wanted to. She wanted to feel the jewelry that had touched her birth mother's skin against her own.

The check lay in the center of the table, and she pulled it toward her, studying Russ's illegible signature. Would he forgive her if he knew what she was about to do with his money? Would Genevieve?

It was growing dark out, so she checked all the doors and windows in what had quickly become her evening ritual. Then she sat down on her bed and dialed her parents' number.

"Hi, Dad," she said, when Jack answered.

"Hi, sweetheart," he said. "I hear you saw Mom today. She's thrilled that you're visiting her, you know."

"She looked a little better."

"Finally got her meds," her father said.

Corinne hesitated a moment, then plowed ahead before she changed her mind.

"I have three thousand dollars I want to contribute to Mom's legal expenses, Dad," she said. "And, also…" She tried not to think about the confines of the witness stand, the tension of a courtroom. "I want to testify in her defense."

Chapter Sixty-Seven

TALKING TO JACK WAS ONE THING. TALKING TO HER biological father would be another. It took her until nine o'clock that night to get up the nerve. She sat at the kitchen table, the jewelry still displayed in front of her, and dialed his number.

He answered the phone himself.

"Hello, Russ," she said, "this is Corinne."

"Corinne! Hi!" He sounded excited to hear from her. "Did you get the package?"

"Yes, and thank you very much. The jewelry is beautiful."

"I thought you'd like to have something that belonged to your mother."

"Did she wear these pieces a lot?" She fingered the emerald ring. She felt anxious. She should have tried that carry-the-confidence technique in this conversation.

"The sapphire necklace most of all," he said.

"I love them," she said. "And I'm very grateful for the money. But I need to ask you something."

"What's that?" he asked. "I hope you know you can ask me for anything."

She doubted he'd still feel that way when he heard the purpose of her call.

"I know." She drew in a breath. "I've been talking to my…" She wasn't sure how to refer to Eve. Adoptive mother wasn't accurate. "To Eve," she said. "And I've realized that she was very young when everything happened, and I really don't want her to suffer." She cringed, worried that her words sounded hollow and somehow insulting.

Russ didn't respond right away, and she guessed she was right.

"Have you forgotten what she did?" he asked finally.

"No, of course not," she said. "But I also can't forget all the years she's been my mother."

"You yourself said she'd been a bad mother."

"I don't think I said that," she said. Had she? "I think I said that her overprotectiveness caused me problems, but that's not the same as being—"

"Has someone gotten to you?" Russ interrupted her. His voice was sharper now. "Has her attorney called you? Or your adoptive father?"

"No." She felt as if she were shrinking. Her voice grew smaller as his grew louder. "No one's gotten to me," she said. "I'm just calling to ask you not to be too hard on her. I know you're furious at her and I understand that," she added quickly, "but I—"

"I'm disappointed, Corinne," he said, and she shut her eyes.

"I'm sorry," she said. "I don't think I'm expressing myself very well."

"I'd like you to think about what it was like for me to lose my wife the way I did," he said. "What it was like for Vivian to lose her mother that way. How it was for us to live with uncertainty for twenty-eight years. And most of all, I'd like you to think about what it was like for your mother——your real mother——to die that way and that young. Imagine being eight months' pregnant and being kidnapped and going into labor with a teenaged kidnapper the only person there to help you. And you know you're at high risk for dying, as is your baby. You imagine all that, all right? Then call me back and tell me how you think I should treat your so-called mother."

The line went dead. *Ouch.* She was no match for him, and her mother's attorney would probably be no match for his.

She lay in bed that night, her hand on her belly and did what he'd asked her to. She imagined herself five months from now, when she'd be eight months' pregnant. She imagined being stolen from the parking lot at Carolina by two strange young men, driven in the dark hours to a cabin in the woods and left in the care of a sixteen-year-old girl. She imagined herself going into labor, but found it very hard to get in touch with what that would be like. It didn't matter, because the person she found herself feeling sorriest for was the teenage girl, in so far over her head that she had no idea what to do.

Chapter Sixty-Eight

Dear Corinne,
Dad and I are hurt and confused. We understand that you still
care about Eve Elliott, but how can you testify for her when we
are trying so hard to have justice served in the wrongful death
of my mother? Your mother. I don't understand this. I'm asking
you to refrain from testifying for her so that justice can be served.
Vivian

SHE DIDN'T BOTHER TO RESPOND TO THE E-MAIL VIVIAN
sent her late that night. She and Vivian would have bickered
nonstop as kids, she decided. And she would have rebelled against
Irving Russell. She might not have had panic attacks if she'd grown
up in that family, but she doubted the three of them would be on
speaking terms by now.

She turned on the television in the bedroom while getting
dressed the next morning. The *Today Show* was on and Matt Lauer
was interviewing an attorney she'd never seen before.

"You know, there's the issue that Eve Elliott was only sixteen
at the time of the kidnapping," the attorney said, "and that she's

been a model citizen as an adult, but the prosecution is mounting a massive offense. You've got to feel for the Russell family. They just went through this with Timothy Gleason and they thought everything was wrapped up tight. Then Eve Elliott shows up with her own part of the story."

"She didn't have to confess, though," Matt Lauer said. "Does she get points for that?"

"Oh, sure. She won't get the death penalty. Her attorneys can make the case that she was under the control of Timothy Gleason. But her real blunder, if you want to use that word, was that she stole the baby. She knew what she was doing and she had twenty-seven years to correct the mistake. The prosecution's going to use that to their advantage."

"So what do you think?" Lauer asked. "Life in prison?"

"That's a good bet," the attorney replied.

So, her mother's life had become something to bet on. Corinne imagined office workers standing around the water coolers, wagering on the outcome of tomorrow's preliminary hearing.

She walked into the kitchen, started the coffee brewing, poured cereal into a bowl and sat down at the table. She had a plan, and she thought briefly of calling Ken to help her with it, but that would be a cop-out. This was something she had to do alone.

Closing her eyes, she imagined standing in front of a classroom of twenty kids at the start of a new reading lesson. She could smell the crisp-air scent of the squirmy fourth-grade bodies and see their rosy skin. She imagined looking down at the stack of new textbooks resting on her desk. Her breathing was even, her heart rate a little elevated with the excitement of teaching a new lesson. She knew exactly what she needed to do and how to do it.

Standing up, she left her cereal on the table and turned off the coffeemaker without pouring herself a cup. "Carry the confidence," she said as she picked up her car keys from the counter. "Carry the confidence."

It was one hundred and fifty highway miles from Raleigh to Charlottesville. She hadn't driven on the highway since that day she'd managed to take the 540 expressway to work. Cars whizzed past her as she pulled gingerly into the traffic, stealing her breath away. She was going far too slowly, and she felt the wind from the other cars smacking into the side of her little Honda. The trucks were worse. She felt as if she were choking. How often had she felt that way? Yet had she ever actually choked? No. Never.

"Carry the confidence." She repeated the mantra to herself. It helped, but even so, she had to pull off four times in the first thirty miles to gather her courage around her again. At the side of the road, she'd tell herself that her staccato heartbeat was the same as she felt when about to teach a new lesson. She'd imagined being in front of the class again. She was getting good at picturing the scene, feeling herself a part of it. It became easier each time she did it.

For the last twenty miles, she didn't need to pull off the road at all, and soon she was in the familiar territory of Charlottesville. She thought of stopping home to see if her father was there. He'd be stunned to know she'd driven a hundred and fifty miles alone! She could hardly believe it herself. There was no time to stop anywhere, though, and frankly, she didn't want to let anyone in on her plan. She couldn't risk being told it was foolhardy. She didn't care if it was. It was what she had to do.

She knew the grounds well, and she parked in the lot closest to

Madison Hall. She felt so much older than the students as she walked toward the building. Older and wiser. Once in Madison Hall, she quickly found the president's office, and she walked inside.

The receptionist was on the phone, but she looked up when Corinne entered.

"Oh my God," she said into the phone. "I'll call you back."

She set down the phone, then stood up and grasped Corinne's hand.

"You're Corinne," she said, smiling. "I've seen your pictures, but I didn't realize how much you looked like Vivian until now."

"Is President Russell in?" she asked.

The receptionist glanced at the blinking buttons on her phone. "He's on a call. You have a seat and I'll let him know you're here."

Was there a chance he would refuse to see her? She saw the door to the receptionist's left, the name Irving Russell on a plaque next to it.

"I need to see him right away," she said, moving toward the door.

"Wait!" The woman put out an arm to stop her, but Corinne dodged it. "Let me call him and——"

Corinne pushed the door open. Russell was indeed on the phone and he looked up in surprise.

"I'll have to get back to you," he said into the receiver. "Right. Goodbye." Setting the phone on its cradle, he stood up. "Corinne," he said.

"I need to talk with you."

"Good." He motioned toward a chair. "I think we do need to talk in person. E-mail and phone calls don't do the job sometimes, and I apologize for hanging up on you last night. You touched a raw nerve in me."

She sat down across the desk from him, knowing she'd be touching the same nerve again today. She had to take control of this meeting. If she didn't, he would run right over her. She folded her hands in her lap. Her palms were damp.

"You and Vivian talk about love like it's automatic," she began. "As though one day I know you as the president of UVA, the next day I know you're my father and I'm supposed to automatically love you."

"I would never ask or expect that of you," he said, "but for me, it *is* automatic. You're my flesh and blood. That's enough for me. That's why I want to give you…" He held his hands out to his sides. "I want to give you the world," he said. "I want to give you more of the jewelry that belonged to your mother. Vivian has most of it, and some of it went to Genevieve's sisters—your aunts. But I saved some pieces because…I guess I hadn't given up on Genevieve still being alive. I hoped that someday she'd be able to wear it again. It never occurred to me that I would have the opportunity to give it to my daughter." He smiled, and she felt deeply sorry for him. He'd been through so much, but she couldn't be deterred from her reason for this visit.

"I apologize that love isn't so automatic for me," she said. "I need more time for that."

"That's fine, Corinne," he said kindly. "I understand. Vivian does, too."

"I think you see me as someone I'm not," she said. "You see me as your daughter. Not as Corinne."

He cocked his head at her. "True," he said. "You *are* my daughter."

"But I'm not going to be your fantasy daughter."

He laughed. "Few children turn out to be our fantasy children," he said.

"I want you to try to understand who I *am*." She leaned forward in the chair. "I'm a good person. I'm a really great teacher. I appreciate the money you sent, because I know that you want me to have it because you care about me. About your daughter. And I would love to own and wear my mother's jewelry. I appreciate all of that. But if you really want to do something for me, it would be to help me free my...free Eve."

He lost his curious smile.

"I *love* her," she said. "I need her in my life. She did a terrible thing. She—"

"Things," he said. "Plural."

She wouldn't argue with him. "She did terrible things," she agreed. "She knows that and she's lived an exemplary life to try to make up for it. What purpose does it serve to keep her locked up?"

"It's payment, Corinne," he said calmly. "You commit a crime, you have to pay."

Crying had not been part of her plan, but she felt the tears well up in her eyes. Her throat tightened around her vocal cords, so that her words came out in a whisper.

"She *is* paying," she said. "If you could see her right now, you'd know that. She can hardly walk." She took a tissue from the leather tissue holder on his desk and pressed it to her eyes. She thought of the long trip here, of having to turn around and make it again to get home. A sliver of panic ran through her and she pushed it away. She'd gotten here; she could get home again. "My mother...Eve Elliott's in pain, but she doesn't complain. I think she's paid for this her whole adult life."

Was something shifting in him? She saw a new softness in his eyes.

"Please don't cry, dear," he said.

"If you love me…if you have this automatic love you say you do, then please don't hurt her anymore. I don't want your money or jewelry. *This* is the gift I really want."

He frowned, deep lines visible across his forehead. "You don't seem to understand what you're asking of me," he said. "And of Vivian."

"I think I do," she said. "I know I'm asking a lot. I'm asking you to love not only the daughter…the child…you longed for all those years ago. I'm asking you to love *me*. Corinne Elliott."

He stared at her, then shook his head, and as if finished with the discussion, he changed the subject.

"I thought you didn't drive long distances," he said.

She sat back in the chair, thrown off guard temporarily by the abrupt change of topic.

"I don't," she admitted. "I'm terrified of driving on the highway. I was scared the whole way here and pulled off the road a dozen times." She looked squarely into his eyes. "But some things are just too important to let fear stand in the way."

Eve

Chapter Sixty-Nine

Dear CeeCee,
When I first found out I had cancer, I felt trapped. It was the
worst feeling I've ever had in my life. It didn't have much to
do with death or pain or being sick or anything like that. It
had to do with knowing I had no control over my life. It was
like being in prison. Then one morning, I woke up with a
completely new thought in my mind. I realized that only my
body was trapped. My spirit was still free. What an amaz-
ing feeling that was! So I couldn't go to Europe or climb a
mountain or even take you to the boardwalk at Wildwood.
My spirit could still soar. It's a cliché to say that having an
illness can be a gift. Sometimes, though, it's also the truth.
Love, Mom

A WOMAN CAME TO VISIT EVE DURING HER THIRD WEEK AS
a prisoner in the North Carolina Correctional Institution for
Women. Eve sat down behind the sheet of Plexiglas, wondering
if she was supposed to recognize her visitor. The woman was her
own age, with salt-and-pepper hair, and she did not look at all

familiar. Eve *did* recognize the box the woman held on the counter in front of her, though, and her hand flew to her mouth.

She looked at her visitor. "Ronnie?" she asked.

Ronnie smiled, almost shyly. "I wasn't sure you'd remember me," she said.

"Of course I do," Eve said, then offered a white lie. "You still look like Olivia Newton-John."

"The hair's a little different." Ronnie laughed. "Not to mention the rest of the body."

Eve pointed to the box. "Is that…?"

Ronnie nodded. "I saved them," she said. "I knew how important they were to you and I've just carried them around with me from move to move, hoping someday I'd find you to give them to you. I have to admit, I never expected I'd find you here, though." She waved her hand through the air to encompass the prison.

Eve smiled. "Unreal, isn't it? I guess you know the whole story?"

"Is there anyone breathing who doesn't?" Ronnie asked. "I'm sorry, though. You were so young and Tim was so good at sucking you in."

"I'm very lucky it's only a year," Eve said. She knew she would have received a far worse sentence if Irving Russell hadn't intervened on her behalf. Why he and his daughter had had a change of heart, she would never understand, but she would be forever grateful to them for their help.

She looked at the box with longing. "I don't know if they'll let me have that in here," she said.

"They will," Ronnie nodded. "I called ahead and spoke to a woman who said they'd have to search them, which they did this morning while I was waiting. So now you can have them in your room…your cell."

"Oh, Ronnie," she said. "I can't tell you how much this means to me." She managed to ask her old friend about herself, and learned that Ronnie worked with computers, was divorced and had three children. Eve listened with as much interest and caring as she could muster, but all she wanted to do was sort through the box to find whatever words of wisdom her mother might have to offer a forty-four-year-old woman in prison.

Chapter Seventy

One year later

FOR ONCE, EVE WAS SITTING ON THE OTHER SIDE OF THE Plexiglas, a question in her mind that she'd been waiting decades to ask. She'd made this detour to the men's prison in Raleigh on her way to visit Cory. The men's prison felt different than the women's correctional institution. It smelled staler, the air thicker, fouler. Women sat in the cubicles on either side of her, talking to men on the phones as Eve waited. She couldn't make out what the women were saying, but one of them was crying.

She'd been out of prison for four glorious months. She and Jack were in counseling, but she knew things would work out between the two of them. The bond was strong, and she'd married a man who was not only forgiving but committed to her, no matter what. He'd proved that during the past year and a half. Best of all, his sense of humor and playfulness were back. She had been afraid she'd killed the joy in him for all time.

Dru was home again, living with them while she taught drama at the same high school Jack had taught at so long ago. Jack had needed her there while Eve was in prison, and Eve was in no rush to push her out of the nest. Dru had a boyfriend—a terrific guy with an animated personality that matched her own. She'd be out of the nest soon enough.

The only truly dark moment Eve had experienced while in prison was during Cory's labor and delivery, when she could not be with her daughter. The memories of Genevieve were so strong during those hours when Cory was in labor, that she could see the bloody bed in the cabin whether her eyes were open or closed. Dru was with her sister in the delivery room, where Cory gave birth to a long, slender redheaded boy she named Sam, who was now nine months old and the most gorgeous grandchild in the universe. Cory'd had to give up on her dream job with the school district, though. Not because of her phobias but because of the demands of motherhood. Irving Russell was helping her out financially while she stayed at home with Sam. In a year or two, she'd go back to work, but for now, she was grateful for the help from her biological father. So far, his path and Eve's had not crossed, and she thought that was best. They would live out their lives loving the same daughter, the same grandson, in their separate spheres.

Eve's attention was suddenly drawn to the door at the back of the visiting area. Tim walked in dressed in his orange prison uniform, led by a guard who followed him right up to the cubicle. Tim smiled at her as he took his seat and lifted the phone to his ear.

"You never, ever should have admitted your part in the kidnapping," he said, instead of hello.

He was still handsome, bald head and all. In another setting at another time, she might still have been taken in by his eyes.

"I had to," she said. "I couldn't let you—or anyone—pay for a crime I knew you didn't commit. I appreciated that you tried to protect me, though."

"And I appreciate that you saved my life. I'd be on death row if it hadn't been for you."

She shifted in her seat. "I have to ask you something," she said. "Are you the person who sent money for Cory for all those years?"

He nodded. "Yes," he said. He studied her face for so long she began to feel uncomfortable. "I need to tell you something, CeeCee," he said. "First, I'm ashamed of the guy I was back then. I had one thing on my mind, and that was helping my sister. I didn't care how I did it or who I hurt in the process. I used you and I used Genevieve Russell. You were so young and…" He hesitated.

"Gullible," she said.

"Naive." He smiled. "It made you very easy to seduce. But Genevieve had been even easier."

She was confused. "You mean…when you kidnapped her?"

"She was my Spanish professor," he said.

"Yes, I know."

Tim shrugged. "I thought I might be able to get to Russell through her, so I…started a relationship with her."

Eve gasped. "You mean…you had an affair with her?" She suddenly recalled Genevieve telling her that Tim had had an affair with a married woman.

"Her husband was so busy that it was easy," Tim said. "She needed the attention, and I think she fell in love with me. At least she said she did. But it turned out she didn't have much influence over Russell's political decisions anyway, so I ended the relationship. A few months later, I started working on the plan to kidnap her. Bets, who was my girlfriend at the time, didn't want to be in on it. And that's where you came in."

Eve shook her head. "You really were a user, weren't you," she said.

"Of everyone," he admitted. He tilted his head to look at her. "Do you understand now why I sent you money for your daughter?"

"Out of guilt?" she asked, but then the reality dawned on her. "Oh my God," she said, shaking her head in disbelief. "You thought she was yours!"

He nodded. "Genevieve was never sure, but in case she *was* mine, I wanted to support her in whatever small way I could. Of course, I know now that she wasn't mine." He looked a little wistful. "That's best, really. Better that she has the security and status of being Russell's daughter instead of having a convict for a dad."

She nodded. "And she had my husband, Jack, for a dad. She couldn't have gotten any luckier than that." She looked down at her hands, then up at him again. "Did you...you were on the run for so long," she said. "Just like I was. What was it like for you? Did you have a good life before they caught up with you?"

He shrugged again. "A good life, maybe," he said. "A peaceful life, no. You can never have peace if you're living a lie."

She nodded, remembering how he'd seduced her with words like those. She was no longer vulnerable to his powers of seduction, but she still knew a good truism when she heard one.

"Right," she said. "I know all about that."

She left the prison after her visit, savoring the sunshine and the open road as she continued her drive to Cory's. She felt freer than she had since Tim's capture nearly two years earlier. Freer than she had since her mother's death so long ago. There were no questions left to answer and nothing to get in the way of the future.

And in another few minutes, she could hold her daughter and grandson in her arms.

Chapter Seventy-One

Dear CeeCee,
I hope you can read my handwriting. I'm having trouble holding the pen now, and I can't sit up in bed very well today.

It's so strange to write letters for you to open when you will be so much older than I will ever be. What advice can I possibly give someone with so much more life experience than I have? Maybe I'll just tell you that I will miss not getting to know you as an adult. I'll miss not getting to watch you grow up and to keep you out of trouble as you pass through your inevitable rebellious stage, to listen to you as you become more introspective and thoughtful, to help you pick out your wedding gown, to hold your babies in my arms, and to be there for you at those moments when life hurts. Just know, darling girl, that if I could, I would call you every day of your life just to say "I love you," with nothing else attached to those words. No criticism. No advice. No requests. Just to say I love you.

I think this is the last letter I'll be able to write to you.

Maybe I'm wrong, but today is so hard. I can barely breathe, and I think I'm just tired of living. I feel my mind moving from this world to the next. It's not a bad feeling.

Let these letters be my legacy to you, CeeCee. I have no money to leave you, just all the loving thoughts in the world. And I know the legacy you leave your children will be ten times richer.

I love you with all my heart,
Mom

The marvelous sequel to
the evocative *Silent in the Grave*

DEANNA RAYBOURN

Fresh from a six-month sojourn in Italy, Lady Julia
returns home to Sussex to find her father's estate
crowded with family and friends—but dark deeds
are afoot at the deconsecrated abbey, and a
murderer roams the ancient cloisters.

When one of the guests is found brutally murdered
in the chapel and a member of Lady Julia's own family
confesses to the crime, Lady Julia resumes her unlikely
and deliciously intriguing partnership with
Nicholas Brisbane, setting out to unravel a tangle
of deceit before the killer can strike again....

SILENT *in the* SANCTUARY

"Fans of British historical thrillers will welcome
Raybourn's perfectly executed debut."
—*Publishers Weekly* on *Silent in the Grave*

Available wherever trade paperback books are sold!

www.MIRABooks.com

MDR2492TR

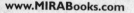

The first book in the Dakota trilogy
by New York Times *bestselling author*

DEBBIE MACOMBER

Buffalo Valley, North Dakota. Like so many small Midwest towns, it's dying. Stores are boarded up, sidewalks cracked, houses need a coat of paint. But despite all that, there's a spirit of hope here, of defiance. The people still living in Buffalo Valley are fighting for their town.

Lyndsay Snyder is an outsider, even though she spent childhood vacations here. Now she returns to see the family house again, to explore family secrets and to reevaluate her life.

Her decision to stay marks a new beginning for Buffalo Valley and for Lyndsay, who discovers in this broken little town the love and purpose she's been seeking.

Dakota BORN

Readers are "certain to take to the Dakota series as they would to cotton candy at a state fair."—*Publishers Weekly*

Available the first week of August 2007 wherever paperbacks are sold!

The compelling sequel
to *Poison Study*

Maria V. Snyder

Yelena is a survivor. Kidnapped as a
child, held prisoner as a teen, then
released to serve as a poison taster, she
is now a student of magic. But these
magic skills place her in imminent
danger, and with an execution order
on her head, she has no choice but to
escape to Sitia, the land of her birth.

But nothing in Sitia is familiar. As
she struggles to understand where
she belongs and how to control her
powers, a rogue magician emerges—
and Yelena catches his eye. Suddenly,
she is embroiled in a situation not
of her making. And once again, her
magical abilities will either save her
life…or be her downfall.

MAGIC STUDY

"Snyder's lively, charming mix
of romance and fantasy is sure
to gain her new fans."
—*Publishers Weekly* starred review
on *Magic Study*

*Available wherever
trade paperbacks are sold!*